ACQUA MORTA

Adam Bane

George made me write this.

ONE

Martelli stared out of the passenger side window at the houses of Toirano. No dogs, he thought. Normally the neighbourhood mongrels would be prowling the boundaries, poking their snouts through garden gates, barking furiously at every passing car, but not today, today was too hot for even the most cursory patrol. The beasts had sought out patches of delicious shade and would pretend to sleep until the sun drifted behind the hills. The digital sign at the pharmacy in Loano had said forty-four degrees, making it the hottest day of the hottest summer in years. Those houses without air conditioning - and in this village that was most of them - had every window open. The rest were sealed tight shut, their occupants, if they had any sense, lying naked and spread-eagled on the counterpane.

"So, Commissario," said Bracco, "have you thought about what you might do in your retirement?"

"I think we can lose the siren now," said Martelli gruffly.

"Anyone with their faculties intact is indoors with the air conditioning running."

As though on cue, a little three-wheeler, a Piaggio Ape, ubiquitous on the narrow roads of the Ligurian hills, trundled out of a side road causing Bracco to swerve violently. The tyres screeched on the hot, sticky asphalt and the two men exchanged glances. The colour had drained from Bracco's face.

"Slow down," said Martelli. "He's already dead. Five minutes won't make a difference."

And so Martelli avoided Bracco's question.

The young detective eased off the accelerator and cut the siren, and for a while they continued in silence, leaving behind the glittering Ligurian Sea and climbing higher on the narrow, winding mountain roads. Martelli reached out and adjusted the vents so that cold air blew directly into his face, then he leaned back in his seat, closed his eyes and counted slowly, silently towards twenty. He'd reached thirteen before the garrulous Bracco could hold his tongue no longer.

"Amazing sunrise this morning, Commissario. I woke everybody up to see it: the wife, the kids, even the mother-in-law. She wasn't happy, I tell you, but the kids loved it, sitting out on the terrace in their pyjamas. They watched a dragonfly wake up as the sun warmed its wings. Even the baby enjoyed it. It's like you say, Chief, sunrise is the best part of the day. Full of hope."

Martelli stifled a grimace at Bracco's use of the word 'Chief'; he didn't want to be ungracious with him today of all days. Bracco was a kind and thoughtful young man who'd been part of Martelli's squad for just ten months. He was a good detective who put in long hours despite having a young family. Martelli thought him an asset, an exemplary member of the team.

"So this has got to be organised crime, don't you think?" continued Bracco. "Who else would do such a thing? It sounds like a punishment killing."

"Well, until we get there we don't really know what we're dealing with. It may turn out to have been a bizarre accident. Unlikely I know but still a possibility. As for who did it, it really is pointless speculating." Martelli paused, aware that he was being a little unkind. Bracco was merely making conversation. "Have you ever read Hannah Arendt?" he said, speaking in gentler tones.

Bracco shook his head. Martelli knew this without opening his eyes.

"She writes about the 'banality of evil'. It's in a very different context of course but nonetheless the principals apply. Don't be surprised if the killer turns out to be just a normal person. Evil hides in ordinary places, behind unremarkable faces: the quiet teenager who mows your lawn, the smartly dressed woman who helped you fill out your mortgage application. Let's wait and see."

Bracco looked disappointed. Martelli knew this too. They fell silent again.

* * *

Bar Reale sat on vertiginous crags high above the village of Carpe, on the outside of a tight hairpin bend. The whole complex had been thrown together in a haphazard fashion during the nineteen eighties with little regard for aesthetics or indeed building regulations. It had never been beautiful, far from it, but now it was an eyesore; in Martelli's opinion a disgrace, though he rarely passed that way. The builders, perhaps wary of those speeding drivers who occasionally overshot such corners, had constructed a substantial concrete plinth for the low building to sit on. Its kerb and narrow pavement were high enough to fend off even the largest of out of control vehicles. But the single storey glass and white stucco box visible from the road was merely the reception area; the majority of the establishment, hidden from the view of passersby, lay beyond and below it and consisted of three large open terraces, tonnes of concrete anchored to the ground rock, stepping down the hillside. In the bar's heyday people had come from miles around to sip cocktails and marvel at the spectacular views of the Italian Riviera, but now it sat in ruins, the windows smashed, the blue and white striped awnings filthy and hanging in tatters, the neon tubes grey and lifeless. Its elegant terrazzo floors were littered with fragments of broken tiles and evidence of numerous ransackings by bored teenagers out for a midnight drive.

Bracco brought the car to a standstill and turned off the ignition and both men immediately felt the loss of the air conditioning. A dozen other vehicles were parked at the roadside, including a fire engine, an ambulance, five police patrol cars and three vehicles in the dark blue and thin red stripe of the Carabinieri. Of the latter, two were ordinary saloons but the third, Martelli was pleased to see, was the tatty Land Rover belonging to Gianpiero Nardi, his friend for more than five decades.

Either side of the road the vegetation was parched and desiccated, leaving mostly barren earth punctuated with pale clumps of jagged stalks. The succulents continued to thrive but, at this altitude, on this rocky outcrop so exposed to the elements, very little other greenery remained. Piles of fly-tipped rubbish, much of it from building sites, sat festering on the verge in ragged black plastic sacks. The road itself shimmered as it baked, its surface appearing liquid in places.

Martelli took a deep breath as though to inhale the last remaining cool air then opened the car door and stepped out into the sunshine. Bracco followed close behind.

The main entrance to the bar was just twenty metres away but by the time they got there Martelli could already feel sweat running down his temples and onto his cheeks. He crossed the threshold, hoping for a little respite in the shade, but instead was hit by a wall of stifling heat, like stepping off an airliner in the tropics. The smell of stale urine stung his nostrils. He took out a handkerchief and mopped his face then crunched across the detritus strewn floor and out onto the huge rear terrace.

Leaning against the parapet, he took a few moments to admire the view, which was even better than he remembered. Below and to his right lay the ancient village of Carpe, its houses nestled in a steep valley. Opposite the village, a small quarrying operation had cut a pale, marble scar in the hillside. To his left rose the mountains around which he and Bracco had just wound their way, and directly in front of him, in the distant notch of the valley, almost lost in the shimmering heat haze and the dazzling golden sunshine sparkling on the surface of the sea, sat Loano, town of his birth and, but for a short stint in the army, his home for nearly sixty years.

He looked down onto the two large terraces below and sighed with dismay. Around twenty people, most of them in uniform, were tramping around the crime scene, rendering the collection of physical evidence almost impossible. One of the uniformed officers was smoking a cigarette and would doubtless simply grind the butt under his heel. Not one person was wearing gloves. Two blue plastic barrels appeared to be at the centre of all the activity. The first lay on its side with its lid pressed firmly against the guardrail of the middle terrace. Directly below it, the second barrel sat upright in the centre of the lowest terrace. Around the base of this second, upright barrel, a brown-tinged continent of dried fluids had formed a stain on the paving. A few feet away was what appeared to be a small mound of vomit, its surface alive with black flies.

"Ah, there you are, Commissario. We were wondering when you would get here."

Martelli closed his eyes and took a deep breath before turning to face the man who would replace him as head of Squadra Mobile, Sezione III, otherwise known as Murder Squad. Commissario Fabrizio Rubini was a political appointee and, in his friend Nardi's words, 'an enthusiastic sniffer of the arses of other ambitious poodles'. There had been a handover period of six weeks during which Martelli was supposed to have shown the new man the ropes, but Rubini had been absent for most of it, spending his time wining and dining the region's politicians and business leaders rather than getting to know the officers on his team. On more than one occasion Martelli and Rubini had had a 'frank exchange of views' – Nardi's words again - and relations between them were frosty at best. Rubini thought Martelli a plodder; Martelli thought Rubini an oily swine with little regard for anyone but himself. He had no doubt that representatives from the local and national media had been alerted to the situation in Carpe and would soon arrive in force.

"Why isn't this crime scene taped off, Rubini?"

"This is my crime scene, Commissario." Rubini stared intently at Martelli. "And I will decide how best to deploy my men."

He took from his pocket a toscano cigar: a short, shiny, dark, turdlike thing, and twisted it between thin lips.

"And I was just about to have someone do that very thing." There was an infuriating hint of amusement in his nasal voice. He glanced from Martelli to Bracco then gestured towards the lower terraces. "Come on."

Rubini turned and headed down a set of wide concrete steps to their right. Martelli followed; Bracco, hesitant, brought up the rear.

"Who found the body?"

"An old biddy down in the valley heard howling and moaning during the night. She thought an animal was trapped in the building." Rubini snorted. "She called her son and he came up here at lunchtime to have a look around. He prised the lid off the bottom barrel. That's his puke down there."

"What time did the old lady hear the noises?"

"Early hours of the morning. Went on for quite some time, she says."

"Did she see anything else?"

"She's ninety years old, she lives half a kilometre away and it was dark. What exactly do you think she might have seen?"

"Headlights perhaps; maybe she heard other noises too. We don't know until we -"

"An officer is with her now, taking a full statement," cut in Rubini with undisguised impatience.

They arrived at the bottom of the steps. Rubini pointed at the first barrel, the one lying on its side, and said, "This is the . . . cistern I suppose you could call it. Better not go near it, it's still half full, apparently."

They continued down the next flight of steps to the lowest of the three terraces, where around a dozen uniformed officers were standing around. Martelli stopped and momentarily hung his head in exasperation before addressing Rubini in a voice loud enough to be heard by everyone present.

"Commissario Rubini, you need to clear this area immediately. Dio santo! We'll have the press in here next."

"My crime scene, Commissario," said Rubini firmly, turning to face Martelli. He extracted his cigar and smiled before continuing in softer, smarmier tones, "But do feel free to look around." He was about to walk away but stopped and scowled, as Martelli spoke sharply.

"Twice you've said that, Commissario Rubini, and twice you were wrong. You are not the senior officer on duty here. I am. And I will remain on duty until this crime scene has been processed to my satisfaction. Now, get everyone off this terrace and out of this building. I don't want anything disturbed until forensics have had a chance to do their work. Establish a hundred-metre perimeter and have men in marked cars set up road blocks down in Carpe and also all the way back in the other direction, at Bardineto. Tell them they are not to let anyone through without first getting my permission; not your permission and not anyone else's. I don't care if the minister himself turns up

- nobody enters unless I say it's okay. Call Leggiero in Savona and tell him we need more officers up here to help with knocking on doors. I want every householder within two kilometres questioned about where they've been and what they've seen since sunset last night. The killer didn't walk up here and he must have needed a sizeable vehicle to transport those barrels. Somebody might have spotted him arriving or leaving. And post a man at the entrance immediately. Bracco and I just wandered in here unchallenged, like we were turning up at a cocktail party. And do not forget, Commissario Rubini, that, until I tell you otherwise, this is my crime scene. Got that?"

He glared at Rubini, who held his gaze for a moment before turning abruptly and stomping away, the bright red flush of his anger showing through his even tan. The terrace had already begun to clear.

"Well, that told the little stronzo," said a familiar voice behind him.

"He'll hear you," said Martelli, turning to greet his old friend.

Gianpiero Nardi stomped down the steps, huffing and wheezing but with a look of delight on his face. He wore a peaked cap and a smart, dark tunic with the epaulettes of a Carabinieri Colonnello on the shoulders. An overweight man in his sixties, his twinkling eyes had remained in their twenties.

"Let him," he said breathlessly, reaching the bottom step and dismissing Rubini with a wave of his hand. "What do I care? He's a despicable little shit." He took out a handkerchief and began mopping his face.

"Piero, today is my last day. That's it - the end. So you

probably should care because, like it or not, you're going to have to work with him." Martelli reached out and shook Nardi's hand. "Thanks for the call, by the way. I don't suppose he was going to contact me."

"I doubt it." Nardi shrugged and continued resignedly, "One of these days, Mimmo, Commissario Rubini and I are going to come to blows."

Bracco, still standing next to his boss, raised his eyebrows and slowly turned his back.

"I would like to see that," said Martelli quietly.

Nardi flashed a sliver of grin then gave a theatrical sigh and began to unbutton his tunic, revealing a broad triangle of white shirt so saturated with sweat it had become translucent. Even his tie was damp. He gestured towards the blue plastic barrel.

"Come on," he said. "The Frenchman is here. Let's do this before we poach in our own juices."

TWO

Thunder clouds invaded the valley like a fleet of warships. Slab-like and anvil-shaped, grey as graphite, they sailed low over the hills and obscured the mountains, hanging above the landscape like a threat. Parched dryness gave way to stifling humidity and soon the air was pregnant with static electricity. A strong wind picked up, sending fragments of dried grass and leaves swishing around the terraces and tugging hard at the nylon canopies as uniformed officers struggled to erect tents over the key areas of the crime scene. The Frenchman wanted everything covered before the downpour erased precious evidence, assuming any had survived the earlier stampede. The fire crew, brought in for their specialist knowledge of dangerous chemicals, had drained the barrels, neutralised the remaining contents and carried them up to the road. They were now hurrying to load them into a truck for transportation to the forensics lab.

Martelli stood and watched from the highest parapet as the dark shadow swept across the valley and down to the shore, doubtless a source of great consternation for the thousands of sunbathers lying in neat rows on Loano's beaches. As the clouds rolled out across the sea, he turned around and watched through the myriad cracks in the glass of the main building as Rubini addressed the journalists gathered beyond the flickering police tape. He sighed. It was, he conceded, quite right that Rubini should be the man in the spotlight. His was the face people would see over the coming weeks as the investigation progressed. He just hoped the glare of publicity would not lead the ruthless young Commissario to make any hasty arrests.

"Chief?"

"Hmmm?" said Martelli.

"Everything's loaded and ready to go."

"Okay," said Martelli. "Did you speak to the son?"

"Si, Guido Laghi . . ." Bracco consulted his notebook. "Thirty-four, married with two kids, lives in Finalborgo; runs a bicycle shop in Finale. It's exactly as Commissario Rubini said - Signora Laghi called her son this morning, just after seven o'clock. He was at work and promised her that he would come up here at lunchtime to have a look. He came alone, found the main door wide open, wandered out onto the terrace, and saw the sludge oozing out of the holes in the barrel."

"Sludge?"

"That's how he described it: 'reddish brown sludge'."

"And he decided to open the barrel."

Bracco nodded. "He prised the lid off with a tyre iron from the back of his car."

Martelli pondered this, biting the inside flesh of his cheek as he did so. "Come on then," he said eventually. "Let's see what the Frenchman has to say."

Together he and Bracco walked back to the car.

* * *

Philippe Lelord had begun his career as a physician in Paris but moved to Savona to pursue a love affair with a serious Italian girl called Allegra, whom he had met in the Louvre one crisp winter's afternoon. Allegra had long since moved on but the Frenchman had stayed, first as a pathologist at the Santa Corona Hospital in Pietra Ligure, the next town along the coast from Loano, and later as a forensic scientist for the local police, where he had now been head of department for more than a decade. His erudition and somewhat brusque manner had led many to keep their distance but Martelli and Nardi had liked him from the start; Martelli because they shared a love of old movies and classic literature, and Nardi because he was a fellow gourmand. The three had formed a strong friendship and the two Italians had even come to call Lelord Pippo, though at work he remained 'the Frenchman'. He had small, dark eyes, placed too close together, and a nose like the prow of an upturned boat. In the laboratory, he controlled his unruly cloud of curly, grey hair with an elasticated net and he insisted that his staff and visitors did the same.

"Adult male, Caucasian, around forty years of age; hands bound behind his back with what looks to be gardener's wire. In a squatting position, inside a plastic barrel, he was immersed to a depth of sixty-five centimetres in a highly corrosive liquid – a concentrated solution of sulphuric acid."

Instinctively Martelli reached for his left hand and fingered the shiny scar tissue extending from his wrist to his knuckles. Nardi and Lelord noted this but said nothing. Bracco remained unaware.

After a barely perceptible pause, the Frenchman continued. "The acid was fed into the barrel from a second barrel, or reservoir, at a slow but steady trickle. Barring any obstructions, my guess is that it would have taken at least four hours for the acid to reach its maximum depth, possibly five or more. As you can see, his hands, feet, buttocks and pelvic region, the first parts of his body to be fully submerged, have been almost completely stripped of flesh. The softer tissues, such as the genitals, are gone altogether. His lower organs have come adrift and have also been mostly liquefied. If you look over there," The Frenchman pointed at the barrels, which sat on a large ceramic tray in the corner of the laboratory, "you will see that air holes have been punched in the lid, doubtless to rob this man of a quicker death by asphyxiation."

"What?" said Nardi, horrified. "Do you mean he was alive when he went into the barrel?"

"Oh yes. As you can see, the acid hasn't simply followed the same trail over his skull and onto his chest. This man was conscious and moving around, and there are signs that he struggled for a considerable length of time before he finally died. He appears to have dislocated his shoulder while exerting pressure against the broad inner ridge, two thirds of the way up the barrel." The Frenchman paused and took a deep breath. "The most significant indication that he was alive, however, is the fact he slipped his bonds. If you look at his right wrist, you'll see it's no longer circled with wire."

Martelli frowned and opened his mouth but the

Frenchman answered his question before he had a chance to ask it.

"The heel of his hand was eaten away by the acid. It became smaller. That's how he was able to slip it through the loop of wire."

The four of them stood in silence for a moment, pondering the horrific significance of this. Nardi held his hands together in front of him, kneading the fleshy heels of his palms.

"A further series of holes have been punched through the body of the barrel at a height of sixty-five centimetres. These acted as a sort of overflow, preventing the liquid from rising any higher and, I suppose, robbing the victim of relief by drowning had he survived that long." He paused and looked at each of their faces. "No doubt he passed out intermittently because of the intense pain and it's possible his heart gave up altogether quite early on." He shook his head. "I certainly hope so. I will attempt an examination of the heart to try to determine whether that is the case but it's unlikely I'll be able to say for sure as all the major organs, with the exception of the brain, have been severely damaged by the acid. Like I said, this man suffered greatly, more than any victim I have dealt with." He shook his head again and fell silent.

For a minute or two, nobody spoke. The Frenchman continued his work while Martelli, Nardi and Bracco stood and stared at the grotesque remains, all three lost in their own thoughts. What lay before them constituted about half of a human being. The rest, along with the contents of the intestines and gut, had combined with the acid to form a rust-coloured porridge at the bottom of the second barrel. The victim's face had been damaged beyond recognition by the constant trickle of acid through the hole in the lid. The eyeballs, eyelids, lips and nose had gone altogether, as had all of the flesh from the forehead and most from the cheeks and jaw. The teeth had survived as a monstrous grin. There remained fragments of clothing, including the knees of the victim's jeans and the upper portion of his shirt; around a quarter of his scalp had survived and with it a patch of dark brown hair. On the right shoulder were the remnants of a tattoo, now blurred and bloodied. It looked like the letter 'F' in curly script but Martelli couldn't be sure.

"So the killer might have stayed to witness the entire spectacle or he might have been long gone before this poor soul died," said the Frenchman, walking to the next examination table. "As for identification, I found this in the breast pocket of his shirt, above the level of the acid." With plastic tongs, he held up a small wallet, the type used just for bank and credit cards. "It's remarkably well preserved given the environment in which it was found. The heavy leather is quite corrosion resistant although the stitching has been dissolved."

The cards sat separately in a shallow bowl of clear liquid. The Frenchman fished one out with long tweezers and held it up for Martelli, Nardi and Bracco to get a closer look.

"If these do indeed belong to him," he said, "then our mystery man has an account with Banca Carige."

"And his name is Steven Fink," said Bracco, squinting at the card.

The Frenchman raised an eyebrow. "Actually it is Finch," he said, drawing out the soft sound. "An English name, I think, and also a little bird. In Italian it is 'un fringuello'."

Martelli and Nardi exchanged glances but neither showed

recognition.

"What about the acid?" said Bracco hoarsely. "Is it exotic in any way? Is it easy to get hold of? Where do you buy it?"

"All good questions but I'm afraid it's ordinary sulphuric acid. As far as we can tell there's nothing special about it. It's used in industrial processes, of course, such as the production of fertilisers, but also by smaller concerns for etching, paint stripping and cleaning. Interestingly, it is also used in the production of heroin and cocaine." The Frenchman shrugged. "But, as I said, there are many legitimate uses and it is widely available. Also, depending on the concentration, you don't always need a licence to buy it or to use it."

"What about the containers?" said Nardi.

The Frenchman shook his head. "Sorry but they're not much help either, I'm afraid. They're standard acid-resistant chemical containers. You see them all over Italy, all over the world. Barrels of this particular type are normally used for the transportation of dry chemicals – powders and pellets, food additives perhaps - but they're nonetheless made of acid resistant plastic. And unsurprisingly there are no fingerprints to be found on the outside of either of them, or on the hose that linked the two."

"The hose is special, I take it?"

"It's not a garden hose, if that's what you mean. It's acid resistant; pricey but easy to get hold of. I have a reel of it myself for cleaning the pool."

"So what do we have to go on?" said Martelli.

"Well the bank cards and the tattoo are a pretty good start I would have thought."

"And the bank cards were found in the breast pocket of his shirt?"

"Exactly."

"So someone else - the killer perhaps - could simply have slipped them in there after the poor devil was already in the barrel?"

"I suppose so, yes." He shrugged again.

Martelli stood silent for a long time, long enough for the Frenchman to turn away and busy himself with a closer examination of the grotesque residue of human flesh and faecal matter in the bottom of the second barrel, and long enough for Nardi to leave the room and return with four espressos in tiny paper cups. Martelli looked up as his friend re-entered the lab with a loud clatter, pushing the door open with his foot.

"You want coffee?" croaked Nardi, offering one to Martelli.

Martelli took one and knocked back the bitter, black liquid in a single, swift gulp. Bracco took another but couldn't overcome his queasiness for long enough to drink it. The Frenchman shook his head so Nardi downed two in quick succession.

"Has it stopped raining?" asked Martelli.

"Si," said Nardi, nodding. "The skies are clear again."

"Then I'm heading back up to the crime scene." Martelli crumpled his paper cup and dropped it into a waste bin.

"Mimmo, it is past midnight. Can't it wait until morning?"

The Frenchman turned around suddenly and Nardi blanched as he realised what he had said. No, it could not wait until morning. Morning, for Martelli, was another life. As soon as he clocked off and went home, his career would be over.

"Look . . ." Nardi faltered.

Martelli smiled wistfully and nodded his head gently. "It's okay, my friend," he said.

"Are you really going up there, Chief?" said Bracco.

"Yes. I want to see the place as the killer saw it."

"I'll drive you."

Martelli smiled and nodded his thanks. He looked over at Nardi, who gave a half shrug of resignation.

"Don't worry, Piero. I'm not going to stay up there all night, brooding. I'll see you tomorrow for coffee."

THREE

Six hundred miles away, in south east London, Ted Logan lay in bed listening to rain lash the windows and wondering where the summer had gone. After more than a week of storms the day had actually started quite brightly but by the time he was ready to head home again the weather had deteriorated and he had only just made it through his front door before the heavens opened once more. In the several hours since then there had been no let up in the downpour and he couldn't help but think that autumn must have come early. Outside, a neighbour's fence was slowly being dismantled by the gale, emitting a tortured squeal every time the wind changed direction. Ted found himself lying there waiting for the next groan, unable to switch off. When Chester started nudging him, he knew he might as well give up so he slid out of bed, taking care not to wake Caroline, unhooked his dressing gown from the back of the door, then tiptoed to the kitchen and switched the kettle on.

He sat at the table with a cup of tea and pondered the events

of the day while the ginger tom nuzzled his hand with great
enthusiasm, purring loudly, evidently delighted.

It had actually all started a couple of months ago when, in
advance of his fortieth birthday, and in an effort to stave off the
effects of irregular mealtimes and an over-reliance on the
neighbourhood curry house, he had joined his local gym, more a
boxing club really; a tatty place above a hardware store five
minutes' walk from his house. The clientele were mostly drawn
from the neighbouring council tenements, a notorious sink estate
crackling with racial tension, whose residents ranged from
frightened pensioners living alone and lonely to large families of
asylum seekers, six to a room in long term emergency housing.
They shared the estate with a few dozen teenage mums and their
undernourished kids, ten or so cadaverous alcoholics and a large
shifting population of jobless young men. The majority lived on
government handouts supplemented with unskilled shift work and
petty crime. Every flat had a rusting satellite dish staining the
brickwork; many of the windows framed a sagging cross of St.
George. The lifts were broken and the stairwells blighted with
graffiti. In between the buildings the bleak open spaces were
littered with amputated cupboard doors, battered kitchen
appliances and rotting mattresses. The few cars were untaxed and
many had been cannibalised for parts. It was a dismal place, a
cauldron of squalor and hopelessness.

Ted attended the club two or three times per week. He hadn't
advertised that he was a police officer but it hadn't take long
before conversations started to end abruptly when he arrived. His
suspicions had been further aroused when he'd walked out of the
showers one evening to find three familiar young men huddled

together and gazing wide-eyed into a plastic box held by a fourth man whose face he didn't recognise. When he appeared, their grins had vanished immediately. The younger men had practically elbowed one another in their haste to get through the door, leaving the fourth man, older and more assured, to calmly reseal the box and place it in one of the lockers. Clearly illegal business was being transacted and Ted couldn't ignore it.

A quiet word with the proprietor, the perpetually cheerful Harry Jay, confirmed that while membership records were indeed kept up to date, including addresses and mobile phone numbers, nobody was obliged to show proof of identity. Also, crucially, members were expected to provide their own padlocks for the changing room lockers. It was a common enough system in London but it meant that many of the lockers were simply out of circulation, always fastened shut, and Harry had absolutely no idea who owned which padlock. So, periodically, he was forced to put up a notice warning members to remove their padlocks and take away their belongings. He would then leave it a few days before borrowing a set of bolt croppers from the hardware store downstairs, cutting off the unclaimed padlocks and throwing the haul of stained vests, collapsed trainers, ragged shorts, jockstraps, gloves and assorted drinks containers into a paint-splattered dustbin kept next to the reception desk. The dustbin was emptied every now and again, usually when his wife, who sat behind the reception desk ten hours a day, watching a portable television, complained about the smell. It was, in Harry's own words, 'not a perfect system'.

That morning an officer from the Met's Dog Support Unit had led a gleaming, bright-eyed Springer spaniel on two complete circuits of the club, after which Ted, with Harry's reluctant consent, had instructed his subordinate, DC Burns, to cut the padlock off every locker in the place.

When Ted eventually left the gym at nine thirty that evening, Burns and a forensics team, aided by uniformed officers from nearby Woolwich Police Station, were still cataloguing the contents. By that time, among the fetid sweatshirts and threadbare undergarments, they had found a loaded Mac-10 machine pistol, a break-open sawn-off shotgun, a pair of dusty but serviceable Makarov semi-automatic pistols, dozens of rounds of ammunition, assorted knives, around a thousand ecstasy tablets, three kilos or thereabouts of vacuum-packed marijuana, several cardboard trays containing dozens of vials of an as yet unidentified clear and colourless liquid, and anabolic steroids in both tablet and liquid form. However, in Ted's opinion the most interesting find was a tatty vinyl holdall containing the best part of two hundred thousand euros along with a change of clothes, a bag of toiletries and three British passports. The toiletries included two packets of hair dye and a tube of fake tan, the money was in used notes of all available denominations and the passports, although in three different names, carried photos which were all quite clearly of the same man. Unsurprisingly, Harry had pleaded ignorance and none of the membership records matched any of the three names.

* * *

Ted yawned, pressing the palms of his hands to his cheeks and squeezing his face; thinking about his increasing workload. He already had two cases on the go: a burglary at an Indian food wholesalers in Plumstead, during which a night watchman had been violently assaulted and the building severely damaged by fire, and a break-in at an old people's home opposite the Common, which had ended with one of the care assistants being punched in the face and an elderly resident pushed to the ground. Now he'd been asked to coordinate all the investigations arising from the raid at Harry Jay's, working on the reasonable assumption that some would be connected, and in addition had been set the task of tracing the owner of the euros and fake passports. But Ted wasn't sure if that meant his other cases were to be reassigned. He scrunched his eyes until his face ached. He had to speak to his boss to clarify the situation, and he also had to remember to call the hospital to find out when the night watchman would be able to answer questions. He'd been laid up for a fortnight now, spending the latter ten days of that in a coma, so Ted wasn't hopeful. He yawned again, wondering gloomily, and somewhat resignedly, how long it would take for Caroline to notice that he no longer went to the gym.

After twenty minutes, he knocked back the cold dregs of his tea and addressed the blissful cat.

"Well, boyo, I'd better try to get some sleep. Hopefully tomorrow we'll find our mystery man."

FOUR

"No address yet for the dead guy," said Bracco as he slipped his mobile phone back into his jacket pocket. "That was Valli. Apparently he has to wait until tomorrow to speak to Banca Carige. The owner of the bar finally got back to him though. He lives in Milano; should be here first thing tomorrow. Jesus Christ, he'll have to set off soon."

"You know," said Martelli quietly. "I've a feeling the poor soul was left up here, overlooking the entire town, as a warning to others."

"But who, Chief?"

"Who indeed."

The storm was long gone, leaving a starry night so vivid that their view of The Milky Way arching overhead was breathtaking in its clarity. Martelli leaned back and stared and, for a little while, was lost. There lingered in the air that comforting smell of rain on hot paving stones, an aroma somehow reminiscent of childhood. Martelli took a deep breath, filling his lungs with its freshness.

Bracco stood silently nearby. The night was so peaceful and still that Martelli could hear him breathing.

Down in the valley a dog barked, yanking him back to reality. He looked at his watch. It was two o'clock; time to go home, time to call it a day, time to bring his career to a close.

"Come on," he said. "Let's go."

"No need to hurry on my account, Chief."

Martelli smiled faintly.

"Thank you. But it's time."

* * *

The descent into Loano on the twisting roads evoked fond memories of summers spent entirely barefoot, of fishing boats hauled onto the beach, of pastel shades and pipe tobacco, of freshly baked biscotti and his grandmother singing as she hung out the washing on their little balcony. He wound down the window and closed his eyes as the smell of the sea grew stronger.

He had Bracco drop him by the railway crossing at the north end of Piazza Italia, then he strolled, hands in pockets, through the caruggi, the maze of cool, narrow streets in which the buildings appeared to stand on tiptoe, shoulder to shoulder - frozen in the act of jostling one another. At his house in Via Richeri, he stopped and peered through the window of the shop on the ground floor – a habit he'd developed since finding Eduardo, the wine merchant who rented the tiny cantina, fast asleep one morning, curled up among his cases and bottles. He then unlocked his front door, stepped inside, and stood at the bottom of the stairs, in almost complete darkness, hesitating before switching on the light, as though his career hadn't already ended, as though flicking the switch would mark his passage from one stage of his life to the next.

He pressed the switch gently, blinked in the sudden brightness, and found himself staring directly into the face of a severed head lying on its side on the ninth of the fifteen stone steps. Carved from solid granite, the head weighed the best part of forty kilos. He'd put it there more than a decade previously, unable to carry it any further without taking a breather. He had then wandered through the house looking for a permanent place for it, and had quickly come to the conclusion that he liked it just where it was.

He climbed the stairs to the first floor, an open plan space divided into living and kitchen areas by a tall counter. He emptied his trouser pockets onto a low, hexagonal table at the top of the stairs then, suddenly famished, headed straight to the fridge and assessed his options.

He ate standing at the counter, rolling thin slices of dark red ham between his fingers and popping little tomatoes into his mouth two at a time. He attacked a hunk of Parmigiano using a short knife with a stubby, triangular blade, breaking off large, irregular nuggets and shoving them greedily into his face. He relished the sting of the intense flavour and the pleasing granularity of the hard cheese. It contrasted beautifully with the buttery ham and the fresh, juicy tomatoes.

In the twenty years since he had bought the house, he had not changed the decor, so it remained suspended in time, trapped in the nineteen fifties - the last time the building had undergone any significant changes. Perhaps that should be his retirement project, he thought, a full refurbishment. He surveyed the room with its morose oil paintings, dusty rows of books and dark, heavy furniture. Yes, maybe it was time to spruce the place up.

Hunger satisfied, he approached the low, square table which dominated the living area. At its centre, among the newspapers and candle holders, stood a large, shabby-looking brass buffalo with a moulded blanket and saddle bags over its back. Removing a decorative pin from one of the saddle bags, he lifted a hinged hasp, allowing the entire back of the animal to open and revealing a hidden compartment within. Inside was a battered old tobacco tin containing a handful of dried marijuana flowers. Alongside it were a few packets of cigarette papers and a box of matches.

The house was in a prime location within the fifteenth century streets of the old town and yet still only sixty metres from the sea. Renting out the cantina to Eduardo brought in enough money to cover his small mortgage and a good portion of his quarterly bills. On the second floor there were two large bedrooms - the smaller one a repository for a lifetime's worth of clutter - and a roomy, if outdated and a tad bleak, bathroom. The space was more than ample for a single man and, but for the gloomy decor, the house could quite reasonably be described as a fairly luxurious bachelor pad. But what had really attracted Martelli to the place, what had convinced him to buy it, was the roof. A rickety spiral staircase, pierced iron kites hanging precariously over the edge of the second floor landing, led to a trap door which gave access to a wide terrace encompassing the entire top of the building. By day it was sun-drenched from dawn until dusk; at night he had the stars.

Shortly after he first moved in, he and Nardi had rigged up

a block and tackle and hauled a heavy wooden garden bench up the outside of the building. They had placed it in the middle of the roof and there it still sat, nearly two decades later, its varnish all but gone, its golden surface now mostly grey. In front of it stood a deteriorating waxed teak table, its joints expanding from the regular drenchings and fierce scorchings it had received over the years. Beneath the table an old metal travelling trunk contained flowery cushions sewn by a girlfriend who had long since grown tired of his working hours.

And so Martelli spread his cushions and settled on his hefty bench among the rarely seen protruberances of the old town: the humming and spluttering air conditioning units, the rusting and drooping television aerials, the washing lines and chimney pots, the pigeon lofts and rabbit hutches, the sky lights and tiny dormer windows, the flaking paintwork and the soft warmth of the beautifully patinated terracotta tiles on the shallow pitched rooftops all around him. He dragged gently at a long, thin joint, savouring the resinous blue smoke as it filled his lungs and hissed out slowly through his nostrils. He sipped from a small bottle of dark La Rossa beer. He contemplated life without commitments.

Six months previously, his annual check-up, at which he always expected to be told there were 'shadows' on the ghostly images of his internal organs, had grown into a week-long medical circus, at the end of which he was told he was no longer fit for active duty. His heart, they said, was not up to it. And yet he had felt no different. He had suffered no seismic event of the chest, no drop in pressure, no loss of equilibrium; he wasn't breathless or red-faced or lopsided; he had taken no funny turns.

He had protested. He had shouted and pointed and

thumped desks and slammed doors so hard that fragments of plaster had come adrift. But all to no avail. The decision, he was repeatedly told, was irreversible.

He'd had six months to ready himself for retirement and he had failed to do so. Here he was, he thought to himself sleepily, sitting on his roof a retired person, and yet he still wasn't ready. He wasn't ready to give it all up and spend each day . . . What? Bumbling about? Killing time? He didn't know. That was the problem. There remained a restlessness inside him and it wasn't about to subside. On the contrary it seemed to grow in intensity as he grew older, to require more from him.

He had tried to explain this to Doctor Bassi but had struggled to find the right words and his faltering attempts had been misinterpreted as fear; fear that this condition would kill him, he supposed. But this thing, this murmur, wasn't merely killing him. It was uprooting him and plunging him into limbo, into emptiness. It was damning him. He was being exiled from his own life.

He took another hit off the joint, and then another, followed by a good swig of the plummy beer; and before long his head began to swim. He imagined himself swaying from side to side, and perhaps he was.

In time the rattle of keys from the street below marked the beginning of the working day at the bakery on the corner. It was followed shortly by the muffled clatter of metal trays and the gentle hum of the extractor fans as the ovens were fired up. Soon the mouth-watering aroma of hot, fresh foccacia, with strong overtones of rosemary and sweet onion, was drifting on the night air. Exhausted and anaesthetised, he watched from behind sagging eyelids as the rising sun tinted the sky pink in the east. He was still awake for the rattle and buzz of the baker's tiny delivery van, come to collect the first batch of the day. He heard too the rhythmic clunk, squeak, clunk, squeak of a badly maintained bicycle as the florist, Marco, pedalled past on his way to work. The distant crowing of Signora Miconi's cockerel didn't disturb him at all; nor did the rumble of a freight train heading southwest towards Albenga. By the time the dawn had begun to set the huge dome and cupola of the Church of San Giovanni Battista aglow and the early risers were out in number, keen to tackle their day's work before the summer heat forced them off the streets, he had already floated into the arena of dreams.

And his last thought before he crossed over into sleep? They were noisy and narrow and smelly and stifling, and in some places there were unmistakable signs of squalor, but after nearly sixty years he was still in love with these old streets, these caruggi.

FIVE

Martelli shivered and opened one eye. The warm night had given
way to a period of coolness before the rising sun sent temperatures
soaring again. He didn't know how long he'd been asleep but it
couldn't have been more than an hour or two. His skin felt slimy,
as though coated in a day's worth of congealed bodily grease,
which he supposed it was. Directly in front of him lay his empty
bottle of beer.

His light linen suit had felt loose and airy the day before
but now it was twisted, tight and uncomfortable, bound around his
thighs and biceps like coils of rope. He had kicked off one of his
shoes while he slept and his shirt had come untucked and risen
above his navel. I must look like un vagabondo, he thought, a
tramp. A movement caught his eye and he raised his gaze to find
himself looking directly into the faces of two small boys, the
mischievous fratelli Trigiani, staring at him from the dormer
window of the house across the narrow street. One of them
pointed and said something. They both grinned. Martelli blinked,

made a feeble, lopsided gesture, scarcely a wave, and hauled himself into a sitting position.

A clock began to chime. He counted seven. In six minutes a competing clock would also chime seven times. The two mechanisms had been out of synchronisation for many years and would likely remain so, unchecked, for many more years to come, a fact which usually made him smile whenever he thought about it - but not today. He stood up, a little unsteadily, walked to the parapet wall and looked down into the street below. At the far end, the queue for the bakery, by now into an intense period of croissant and pain au chocolat production, mingled with the fledgling queue for the fresh pasta produced by hand in the pokey shop opposite. Parents led their children to the local schools; elderly ladies with baskets headed out in search of the day's supplies; scooters and bikes and the little three wheeler vans competed for space with pedestrians. Dogs barked, bells rang and people shouted greetings at one another. Well, it sounded to Martelli as though they were shouting. The hubbub, the clamour, the cacophony of daily life in the caruggi was getting well and truly underway.

Directly below him, Eduardo was unloading cases of wine from a sack truck while chatting animatedly to Signora Bartolotti, Martelli's nextdoor neighbour, she of the brown-stained poodles and thuggish, over-muscular son whose eyes roved like an addict's. He'd lost count of the number of times he'd heard the boy, actually the young man, cursing and swearing at his mother, berating her in the early hours of the morning. The whole street knew their business and some people had openly criticised Martelli for his failure to intervene. But what, he had asked those people on more than one occasion, would you have me do? Eduardo's dense mop of dark, curly hair flopped around on his head as he stooped to pick up another case of wine. Hopefully his infectious cheerfulness would have an uplifting effect on the perpetually downcast woman.

Having retrieved his shoe, Martelli wearily clanged down the iron spiral and headed into the bathroom, where he gazed resignedly into the mirror. Not too many years ago, I used to look into this mirror and see a young man, he thought. Now I see my father. How soon before it's my grandfather staring back at me? He shaved and showered and spent more time than usual brushing his teeth. Then he put on clean clothes and headed out into the bright morning.

* * *

Nardi sat reading La Repubblica at their usual table beneath the trees outside the cafe in Piazza Italia, directly opposite the magnificent dome. The moment he spotted his friend approaching, he waved to the proprietor, their old friend Giacomo Orso, who, by the time Martelli was taking his chair, had brought over two espressos, two glasses of water and two pastries: for Martelli a plain croissant; for Nardi a bulging bombolone - a fried doughnut filled with custard and a spoonful of apricot jam. Nardi raised one hand in greeting while pushing the bombolone into his mouth with the other. A dollop of custard rolled down his chin and splattered onto his plate.

"So, Mimmo," he said, reaching for a napkin, his mouth still full. "Did you sleep well?"

"Not really. Any news this morning?"

"About our unidentified murder victim, you mean?" Martelli nodded. "Nothing yet but it's barely eight o'clock. What were you expecting?"

Martelli shrugged and toyed with his croissant.

"You know I . . ." began Nardi.

"I know," said Martelli, nodding, heading off another apology about what had been said at the lab the night before.

Nardi grinned. "So have you thought any more about buying a boat?" he said.

"What is it about you and boats?" said Martelli, chuckling.

"I just think we could spend a few of these hot days out on the water. We could explore up and down the coast, do a bit of fishing, drink a few beers, enjoy the cool breeze . . ." Nardi tailed off, shrugging. "It would be a healthy thing to do together, I think."

Martelli nodded and reached for his coffee. "You're right, it would. But I know nothing about boats. Why don't you buy the boat? And you," he pointed, "could take me fishing?" He knocked back the espresso.

"Alas, Mimmo, I am not blessed with your generous pension."

Martelli snorted.

Nardi rummaged in the side pocket of his tunic and retrieved two red and white capsules. He blew on them to remove the fluff, popped them into his mouth and sank them with his grainy espresso, throwing back his head, swallowing, and then jerking forward with a mildly startled expression on his face. His phone buzzed under his newspaper and he rolled his eyes as he reached for it. Martelli took a bite of his croissant, watching

Nardi's face as he read the text message.

"I've got to go, Mimmo. The bar owner has arrived from Milano. He must have driven through the night. Your man Bracco wants me to speak to him. How about you? What are your plans today?"

"Shopping and cooking." Nardi looked at him askance. "Valentina is coming over for lunch. She needs my help with something; some family thing." He gave a half shrug. "But before that I think I'm going to go for a swim."

"A swim?" said Nardi, making an expansive gesture with both hands. "Well, that sounds terrific. I wish I could join you."

Martelli raised his eyebrows and glanced at Nardi's ample belly as his friend rose a little shakily. It had been a long time since Nardi had got even his feet wet.

"Ciao, Giacomo," he said a minute later as the jovial proprietor popped outside for a quick half a cigarette.

"He gets bigger," said Giacomo, grinning and pointing at Nardi's retreating back.

"Yes, but he still has short arms," said Martelli, laughing and waving the unpaid bill with his free hand as he took another bite of his croissant.

Giacomo laughed, nodding repeatedly as he did so.

SIX

The young woman with the ponytail smiled wearily as she opened the door.

"Hi," she said.

"Hello," said Ted. "I'm sorry to bother you. I'm with the police. We're investigating a break-in at one of the flats across the road. Do you mind if I come in and ask you a few questions?"

Somewhere in the house a baby started to cry. The young woman glanced briefly behind her.

"As long as you don't mind me changing him," she said, stepping back to let Ted past.

The front door, actually at the side of the house, opened directly into a spacious living room with French windows onto a pink-flagged patio. The room was clean and tidy despite a great deal of baby paraphernalia. In one corner a television burbled away quietly; in another an electronic keyboard stood on one end, leaning against the wall. She directed him to the sofa.

"Would you like tea?" she said, stifling a yawn.

"No, thanks," said Ted, sitting down. "I won't be staying long. I just have a few questions I'd like to ask you."

She strode out of the room and returned a few seconds later with a struggling baby in a pink sleep suit nestled in the crook of her arm.

"He's a boy," she said. "But my mum was hoping for a girl." She gestured oddly at the baby and it took Ted a moment or two to realise what she meant.

"Ah," he nodded. "She bought pink."

"Everything," said the woman. "Pink clothes, pink shoes, pink bedding, even a pink pushchair - it's ridiculous. I'm Jen, by the way."

"Ted," he said. "Ted Logan."

"So which flat was it?" she said, placing the baby at the centre of a changing mat on the dining table near the French windows.

"The lower ground floor at number twenty-three. It's directly opposite."

"And it happened last night? I didn't hear anything."

"We don't know exactly when it happened. It could have been more than a fortnight ago."

She looked up, frowning deeply. "And you've only just got round to it? When did he ring you?"

"Well, that's part of the problem. You see, he hasn't reported it yet."

"So how do you know about it then?"

How indeed, thought Ted.

* * *

First thing that morning, armed with copies of the three passport photos and a list of members' names and addresses reluctantly provided by Harry Jay, a pair of uniformed officers from the Plumstead Safer Neighbourhoods Team had begun what Ted had fully expected to be fruitless door-to-door enquiries. There were more than three hundred names on the alphabetical list.

Warren Devlin was number four.

The door to Devlin's lower ground floor flat was hidden from the street by the coal cellar and the steps to the flat above. The officers had found it ajar, kicked open, a footprint clearly visible next to the doorknob. A scattering of mail had collected on the floor in the hallway, the oldest dated two weeks previously. It seemed the postman had simply neglected to report the break-in.

The bedroom, living room, kitchen and bathroom had all been turned upside down. The sofa, armchair and beds had been upended and slashed, the contents of the cupboards and wardrobes had been strewn across the floors; a small, reddish brown patch in the middle of the kitchen floor was probably blood, and the panel on the side of the bath had been kicked in and wrenched aside. In the garden, the door to the shed banged in the wind, left wide open by whoever had trashed the place. Even Devlin's bicycle, or someone's bicycle, had been pulled out from under its plastic cover and cast onto the small patch of grass beneath the kitchen window.

All of this interested Ted and the two questions to which he really wanted answers were these: Where was Warren Devlin, whose photo, pinned to a cork notice board in the kitchen, was a perfect match for the pictures in the bogus passports? And was that his blood spilled on the patterned vinyl floor halfway between the oven and the sink?

* * *

"So, do you know Mister Devlin?"

"Who, Warren?" said Jennifer.

"Yes."

"Not really. I bump into him in the street sometimes, you know. We chat a bit, but I wouldn't say I know him, no." She lifted the baby's feet, slipped the dirty nappy out from under him and reached for a pack of wet wipes.

"Is this him?" He held up a grainy copy of one of the passport photos, blown up to the size of a paperback book. She paused to take a closer look at it.

"Yes, that's him." She smiled and arched an eyebrow.

"What's funny?"

"He looks weird with a 'tache, that's all."

"So he doesn't have the moustache now?"

She shook her head. "Not as long as I've known him," she said, turning back to the baby.

"What do you talk about when you see him in the street?"

"Oh, you know - this and that: sometimes the weather, sometimes the litter in the street, that sort of thing. We get a lot of litter because kids from the local school go to the corner shop to get crisps and stuff at lunchtime. They drop all the wrappers and they blow all over the place." She looked at Ted hopefully. "Maybe you could do something about that?"

"Do you know where Warren works?" he said, ignoring her question.

42

She looked disappointed. "He works for himself, I think. He's always coming home late; early hours of the morning sometimes. I see him from the front bedroom window, you know, when I'm up feeding Josh."

"So two, three o'clock in the morning?" said Ted, wincing slightly as the smell drifted over to his end of the room.

She nodded.

"And does he come home by car, on his bicycle, on foot?"

She chuckled, wiping the bottom of the now smiling little boy as she did so. "He drives a Porsche Boxster. A little silver thing. Very flash. My David says it's a girl's car."

"David?"

"My husband."

"Ah," Ted nodded. "And does your husband speak to Warren as well?"

"No, I don't think so. I don't know that he's ever spoken to him, to be honest." She folded the nappy into a little plastic bag and stuffed the used wipes in after it. The baby made gurgling noises and spread his arms wide.

"Can you remember when you last saw him?"

"Sorry. No idea. It was more than a fortnight ago though. He's away a lot – two, three, four weeks at a time; always going on holiday. Italy mostly, he says. I think he has friends out there."

"So he might be away on holiday now?"

"Probably. How would I know?" She turned to look at Ted, irritable, probably through tiredness, he thought. "I'm not the local busy body, you know."

"No no." Ted held his hands up. "I didn't mean to suggest you were. You're being very helpful. I just have a couple more questions."

"Okay." She sighed.

"Have you any idea what line of work is he in?"

"Something to do with boats."

"Boats?"

"Boats. He has a boat down in Kent; near Margate somewhere, I think. Or Herne Bay. He rents it out, you know, for sailing trips. I think he's an instructor."

Ted raised an eyebrow. "He teaches sailing?"

She finished fastening a clean nappy onto the baby and turned to look at him. "I think so. Why's that a surprise? If you don't believe me, ask Paul."

"Paul?"

She furrowed her brow. "Paul," she repeated slowly, as though he'd said something particularly foolish. "Warren's flatmate."

SEVEN

The crystal water of the Ligurian Sea brought Martelli to life in a way his earlier shower and the cup of muddy espresso in Piazza Italia had not. Instead of merely jolting him, it invigorated and calmed him too. He floated on his back, drifting, arms wide, legs akimbo, luxuriating in the contrast between the hot sun on his stomach and the coolness of the water as the waves washed over him. He'd swum out to the furthest buoy, fully intending to loop around it and head immediately back to shore, but the lure of this gentle Mediterranean massage had proved too much and he'd allowed himself to pause, eyes closed, for several minutes, letting the soothing waves relax him, accompanied by their own mesmerising soundtrack.

Satisfied, he rolled onto his stomach and resumed his lazy front crawl. After just three strokes he felt his hand touch something in the water and lifted his head to find himself staring into brilliant white teeth under tight goggles and a faded, blue swimming cap.

"Buongiorno," she said, grinning broadly and sweeping past in an elegantly executed breast stroke.

"Buongiorno," he tried to say but got a mouthful of water and managed only a strangled attempt at the first syllable.

He spun around but she was already heading away from him. He coughed and frowned as he watched her bobbing up and down, powering smoothly through the water. She had sounded . . . He wasn't sure. English, perhaps?

The beach was already very warm. Soon the sand would be too hot for bare feet. He retrieved his towel from where he'd hung it under a large parasol and rubbed himself briskly for a full minute before lying on a dark green lounger, closing his eyes and letting the sun finish the job. Bagni Perelli, the nearest of the beach clubs to his house, was just starting to see the first holidaymakers arrive for another day in the sun. A few of the youngest kids were already at the water's edge, festooned with inflatable swimming aids in garish colours, shrieking at each wave. Eyes still closed, he smiled and listened to one little girl as she urged her father to lower her into the water, then screamed for him to lift her out again, then pleaded to be lowered, then howled again as she found herself unable to touch the sandy bottom with her toes. He chuckled to himself.

"I hope you're not laughing at me," said a voice directly overhead.

He sprung into a sitting position, squinting.

"Sorry," said the voice. "I didn't mean to creep up on you."

Martelli twisted around and found he was looking at those brilliant white teeth again. The faded blue swimming cap had been lifted to reveal long hair the colour of hazelnut shells, the tight goggles removed to uncover grey-green eyes bright with optimism and curiosity.

"Ciao," said Martelli.

She raised her eyebrows in anticipation but that was all he managed. He frowned a little and, for a moment, her smile faltered.

"Cristina," she said, extending a slim hand.

Tentatively Martelli reached out and took it.

"Domenico," he said, examining her smooth, pale, freckled face.

She tried a smile again and this time, to his own great relief, he smiled back.

"Are you here on holiday?" she asked.

"No," he said, finally releasing her hand. "I live just through there." He gestured vaguely towards the nearest buildings of the old town.

"Really? I haven't seen you here before."

"Usually I'm at work, I'm afraid."

"Ah." She nodded. "I suppose you're skiving. Don't blame you when the weather's like this. It's fantastic." She smiled again and his eyes were drawn once more to those teeth.

"Actually I . . ." He gave a half shrug. "Something like that," he finished, rather feebly he later thought.

She scanned his eyes as though expecting him to elaborate or to ask her a question in return but Martelli, caught off guard, distracted, uncharacteristically unsure of himself and unsure quite what he was doing, said nothing.

"Well, nice to meet you, Domenico. Perhaps I'll see you here tomorrow if you decide to skip work again."

Still smiling, she turned and walked away. He watched her until she'd climbed the steps to the promenade and disappeared from view.

Not English, he thought. German perhaps, or Danish.

* * *

"Pronto."

"Chief, where are you?"

"I'm shopping. Where are you?"

"I'm at Steven Finch's apartment on Via Monte Pasubio. It's opposite the old Radiological Institute."

"And?" Martelli tried not to sound eager.

"Nothing," said Bracco, the disappointment evident in his voice. "There's no sign of a break-in and nothing unusual. The place is just . . . ordinary. Finch is English. The neighbours say he's been living here on and off for about two years and the landlord confirmed that. He pays his rent on time and he keeps to himself. One of the neighbours didn't even recognise the name. She thought the apartment was empty. The others say he's polite and . . . well . . . not unfriendly but he doesn't go out of his way to talk to them. He keeps late hours – that's all they could really say about him."

"What, he works late or he socialises late?"

"They didn't know but apparently he often doesn't get home until the early hours. Or else he leaves early – like three or four in the morning."

Martelli stood pondering this information for a moment, idly rotating a peach on the fruit stall.

"Chief?"

"I'm still here."

"How's your first day of freedom? Done anything interesting?"

Martelli thought of his encounter at the beach and started to smile, but his focus quickly flickered back to the brutalised body on the Frenchman's examination table and his brow knitted instead.

"I've been for a swim," he said stiffly.

He could hear Bracco breathing, waiting for him to say more. And he wanted to say more. He wanted to ask about the investigation. He wanted to find out what the bar owner had to say for himself and whether anything had come of the door to door enquiries in Carpe. He wanted to know if the dead man's family had been contacted or if any progress had been made in the search for friends and associates here in Loano. But he was no longer the head of Murder Squad, no longer Bracco's boss, and it was inappropriate for him to demand details of a confidential police investigation, so he gritted his teeth and tried to think of something else to say.

In the end they both started to speak at the same time.

Bracco laughed. "Go ahead, Chief."

"No," said Martelli. "What were you going to say?"

For a moment Bracco fell silent, then: "Well, Chief, Catarina . . . er, my wife, has told me to invite you for dinner."

Martelli closed his eyes. He shook his head, and then he smiled, and then he started laughing quietly to himself. At the other end of the line, Bracco began to laugh too. A spell had been broken.

"What should I tell her, Chief?"

"Tell her . . . Tell her that I thank her for her kind invitation and that I would love to come to dinner."

EIGHT

"F, I, N, C, H," said Lelord, mouthing the sounds as he completed the form. To the man sitting across from him, he said solemnly in English, "I'm sorry to say there was considerable trauma, a great deal of . . . injury to the person. Identification is not always so . . ." He paused, choosing the next word carefully. "Straightforward."

His visitor blinked once but said nothing. He sat upright, hands on his thighs, the look on his face impassive. He wore a thin, white, short-sleeved shirt with a pair of sunglasses hooked in the neck, a pair of khaki trousers and slip-on sandals. The clothes were expensive though not exactly formal attire, thought the Frenchman, but then what should one wear on such an occasion?

"There is a tattoo," he continued. "Perhaps if you were to examine a photograph, you could confirm . . . and, well, there would be no need to -"

"È un cavalluccio marino blu," said the visitor. "Ah, scuse . . ." He shook his head and started again in English. "It's a blue seahorse. It's on his right shoulder. He got it when he was in the navy." The man paused, took a deep breath. "But I would like to see him, please." He spoke in measured tones. The determination in his eyes was unmistakable.

"Of course," said Lelord, nodding slowly. He put down his pen and pushed back his chair. "Please follow me."

* * *

Ted peered through the jagged hole in the side of the yacht, careful not to touch anything. Inside was a jumbled mess of ripped fibreglass, shattered plywood fixtures, smashed electronic equipment, chunks of foam, stained cushions, twisted cables, tangled ropes and detached fenders, along with assorted, mostly broken items of kitchen equipment and a mess of sand and gravel. The outside of the hull was gouged and scraped all down one side, as though it had been dragged for many miles over harsh terrain. The hole was roughly four feet square. Ted shook his head then stepped back to take in the whole vessel once again. It was forty feet long, he guessed, perhaps a little more. The decks and cabin were white but the hull sides were dark blue above the water line. The interior was all mahogany veneer in a style that appeared terribly dated to Ted, who knew little about boats, but he supposed it must be practical. It seemed rather sad really, defeated, hauled from its intended environment onto this patch of hardstanding, keel severed, belly propped upright with mismatched offcuts of timber and paint-spattered scaffolding poles, surrounded by numerous other boats in various states of disrepair. It brought to mind images of dead elephants; victims of poachers he'd seen on the television news.

"So," he said, "can you tell me exactly what happened?"

The young man nodded, took his hands out of his pockets and folded his arms.

"Well, the coastguard station at Dover picked up the DSC shortly after five in the morning," he said.

"DSC?"

"It's a distress call. It automatically gives the boat's position."

"So someone spoke to whoever was on board?"

"No, the crew didn't put out a voice call, a Mayday, just the DSC. It's electronic, like a beacon."

"Okay. Sorry, go on."

"So the coastguard called the Margate all-weather lifeboat. They also relayed the vessel's position to RAF Kinloss in Scotland, which is where all aerial searches are coordinated from."

"Kinloss? That's a bit far from here, isn't it?"

"It's not ideal," said the young man, blinking repeatedly, momentarily losing his train of thought.

"Sorry," said Ted. "I'll keep quiet."

"Er . . . So the boat had run aground on the Hook Sands, about two miles off Reculver between Margate and Herne Bay. You know the towers?" Ted shook his head. "Well, there's a narrow channel between the sands. At low water it's down to six feet deep. This boat draws more like seven. They were mad to even try it. God knows what they were thinking. When the lifeboat got there, she was listing badly, like forty-five degrees, and taking a real beating in the storm - it was blowing force six or seven that morning; we've had hellish weather this past few weeks. Anyway, the lifeboat hailed her repeatedly but there was no response and they couldn't see anyone in the water. Mind you, it was dark and they were in rough seas, so . . ." He tailed off, shrugged. "Anyway, the crew tried to get a line onto her but it was far too dangerous. Like I said, the weather was pretty bad and she was under full canvas so she would have been thrashing about something hellish. Then the Belgian Sea King arrived -"

Ted raised his eyebrows. "Belgian?"

"Belgian Air Force; it was the nearest one." He shrugged again. "That's normal." Ted gestured for him to continue. "So the helicopter arrived and searched the area but *they* couldn't find anyone in the water either. The captain of the lifeboat decided there was nothing his crew could do, not without putting their own lives at risk, so she was left to fend for herself. She lifted off the sandbank on the rising tide and came ashore on the beach at Herne Bay a few hours later. She was already swamped when she made land because she'd lost her keel on the sandbank but it was the groyne that did all this damage." He nodded towards the gaping hole.

"What do you mean?" said Ted.

"Well, there're groynes along the beach there, y'know, rows of ironwood posts driven into the sand with boards between. They're all along the north Kent coast. You've probably seen them. She lodged on one of those posts on her port side and the waves smashed her against it for a few hours. That's what made the hole."

"And what time did she wash up?"

"About half ten, they said. They called us in the afternoon: me and my dad, and Brian the crane operator. We had her off the beach by about five thirty and we brought her straight here."

Ted pursed his lips. "So nobody has any record of who was on board?"

The young man shook his head.

"And you've no idea if any lifejackets are missing, or a dinghy, or anything like that?"

The young man unfolded his arms and made a gesture of helplessness. "There's probably lots of stuff missing but look at the state of her."

"So what happens now?" said Ted, resignedly.

"You'll have to ask my dad. He's the official Receiver of the Wreck. I imagine she just sits here until the financial side of things is sorted out. The insurance company hasn't been in touch but I guess that's because the bodies haven't turned up and nobody's called them."

"So has no one contacted you?" said Ted, surprised.

The young man shook his head. "No, but that's not unusual. She's only been here a couple of weeks."

"And you haven't tried to contact Mister Devlin, the registered owner?"

The young man frowned. For a moment he looked confused. "My dad's left loads of voicemail messages for him," he said, indignant. "In fact, according to the diary, he even popped round to his place."

"Your dad's been to Devlin's flat?"

"Flat?" He smiled. "It's a caravan."

It was Ted's turn to look puzzled. "What?"

"The address of the registered owner is a caravan."

"Where?"

"Just up the road, in Monkton. There's a holiday park there.

Wait, I'll get you the address." The young man disappeared into the office, a converted shipping container, dark blue with white lettering stencilled on the sides. It stood right next to Warren Devlin's ruined yacht. Ted shook his head and touched his hand to his forehead. He had visions of the investigation turning into a wild goose chase, and of struggling to explain to his boss why he'd gone off gallivanting around north Kent, seventy miles from his jurisdiction, instead of simply contacting Kent Constabulary. The young man reappeared and handed him a piece of paper.

"Thanks," said Ted. "So she just sits here?"

"Once the money side of things is sorted out she'll be scrapped. I don't suppose there's anything can be salvaged."

"And how much does a boat like this cost?"

The young man waggled his head. "Probably three hundred grand - something like that."

"Bloody Hell," said Ted.

"Boats are not cheap, especially boats like this one."

"And how do I get in touch with your dad?"

"Well, he's in hospital at the moment."

"I'm sorry to hear that. What's the matter with him?"

"They don't know yet. He collapsed a couple of days ago, right here in the office. I was away on holiday. I only got back late last night. Came home a few days early. I saw him for a half hour this morning. He looks terrible. The doctors don't know what's wrong with him."

A telephone rang; the ringer an old-fashioned bell mounted high on the outside of the shipping container. At some point someone had made a very bad job of spray-painting it red.

"And you're certain Mister Devlin or his family haven't

called?"

The young man nodded and turned towards the office door, distracted by the ringing phone.

"And his flatmate?" persisted Ted, raising his voice as the young man dashed inside. "Have you heard from a Paul Finch?"

* * *

"This way, please, Mister Finch."

"Please, call me Paul."

Lelord nodded and smiled faintly. "Of course," he said, his voice barely more than a whisper. "As you wish."

He led Paul Finch down two flights of stairs and along a chilly corridor, its walls scraped and cratered from the careless passage of gurneys over the dozen or more years since it was last painted. Overhead, the white paintwork on the curved brick ceiling was discoloured by overlapping water stains, which blossomed and faded through the decades, like clouds drifting in infinitesimally slow motion. Bare bulbs hung from pendants thick with dust and cobwebs. The air smelt damp and earthy. They passed a dozen heavy oak doors adorned with metal studs and oversized ironmongery. It was, Lelord always thought, like descending into the bowels of an ancient fortress. He invariably felt a little ashamed on those all too frequent occasions when he brought grieving relatives into these catacombs. But, despite his position as head of department, the management of the building, its upkeep, was beyond the scope of his remit, so there was little he could do about the shabbiness. Of course, he reminded himself, the decor was probably the last thing on their minds.

They reached door number thirteen and Lelord stopped.

"We are here," he said, trying to maintain a reassuring air of formality.

Finch met his gaze but said nothing.

"I always ask, at this point, if you are sure you wish to proceed."

Finch nodded without hesitation. "Of course, of course," he said, with an unmistakeable hint of impatience.

Finch took a deep breath and pulled himself to his full height, steeling himself, thought Lelord. He was an athletic man; broad chested, narrow at the waist and half a head taller than the Frenchman, with short curly dark hair and a mahogany tan. He slipped his right hand into his trouser pocket then changed his mind and took it out again, leaving his arms hanging awkwardly at his sides. A gesture of nervousness, thought Lelord, and yet his manner was not quite as the Frenchman would have expected. He seemed too . . . composed, perhaps? Was this the famed British stiff upper lip? Lelord dismissed this thought as unfair. After all, how was one supposed to behave in such appalling circumstances? There were no rules.

The Frenchman pushed open the door and reached inside to turn on the lights. There was a fragmented buzzing accompanied by an intermittent pinging noise as fluorescent tubes strobed into life. He stepped inside and held the door for the visitor.

The body lay on a metal table under an opaque, white plastic sheet in the centre of the room. Lelord breathed a sigh of relief when he saw that the laboratory assistants had followed his instructions to the letter. Towels had been rolled up and fashioned into the shape of human legs to bulk out the profile under the sheet. Paul Finch need never know the extent of the damage to the deceased; would not see that the lower regions of the body were all but missing.

Lelord walked to the far side of the table and stood to attention at the head of the corpse, hands clasped together in front of him. He waited until his visitor had done the same on the opposite side of the table then he gave him a searching look.

Finch nodded.

Slowly, and in what he hoped was a respectful and dignified manner, Lelord folded back the upper portion of the plastic sheet.

Finch stared as though transfixed by the horror on the table - the livid scalp, the melted facial flesh, the gaping wet cavities of the eye sockets, the jaw hanging slack, the grotesque silent cackle of the stripped rows of teeth, the glistening scorched upper torso. Lelord watched discreetly as his visitor took in every detail. He felt his heart pounding. He let go of the plastic sheet and allowed his arms to swing to his sides. He took a deep breath. Several seconds passed during which he bowed his head and all but closed his eyes.

Suddenly, without warning, Finch grabbed the plastic sheet and whipped it upwards and away from the body. Lelord staggered back in surprise. A strong smell, a gust of antiseptic vapours assaulted their noses as the sheet ballooned and drifted and settled on the floor in the corner of the little room.

Finch gestured at the rolled towels, his palms raised upwards in query. He shook his head and gave Lelord an accusatory look.

Lelord floundered. He pressed a hand to his throat; a peculiarly feminine gesture. "Signor . . . I . . . To spare you . . ."

"I didn't come down here to be spared anything," said Finch, his deep voice a mesmeric rumble in the confined space. "Does anyone?"

"Well . . ." Lelord faltered again. His shoulders, still tense from the shock of Finch's actions, sagged forwards. He sighed and shook his head. He put a hand to his temple. "No . . . No they don't. I . . . Forgive me. Perhaps it was ill-judged."

But, as he said this, the Frenchman thought that actually most people did wish to be spared any horrific details of their loved one's death. They did not wish to see evidence of suffering. And suffering on this scale . . . Well, it was unheard of.

He watched with increasing interest as Finch surveyed every aspect of the remains, taking his time, ducking down, leaning his head this way and that, peering at the ruined hands and the unrecognisable mess of partially dissolved abdominal organs. And when the Englishman was done, when at last he stood upright and took a step back, he seemed . . . Lelord struggled to find the right word to describe his visitor's demeanour. They gazed at one another awhile, the Frenchman blinking nervously, still not having fully recovered from the shock of Finch flinging aside the plastic sheet.

"How long did he suffer?" said Finch eventually.

Lelord hesitated. Should I claim that the end came quickly? he wondered. No - this man would see through such obvious falsehood. He shook his head slowly, on his face a look of profound sadness. "It is impossible to tell. Perhaps . . ." He lowered his eyes before adding, "Hours."

Finch inhaled slowly, returning his gaze to the horror lying between them. "And what finally killed him?"

Lelord felt relief at being able to answer immediately and with confidence. "Almost certainly his heart gave out."

Finch pursed his lips but didn't respond.

"So . . . my apologies . . . but can I confirm that this is . . ?" The Frenchman tailed off.

"Yes," said Finch, nodding once, firmly. "This is my brother. This is Steven."

NINE

Ted sat staring through the windscreen at the brownish grey waves rolling onto the greyish brown sands of Minnis Bay. Somewhere out there, he thought, not too far from where I'm sitting, Warren Devlin's yacht foundered and was wrecked. He took a bite of the cheese and pickle sandwich he'd bought at the deli in Birchington and munched away, his brow puckered. A huge seagull with a wingspan close to five feet swooped down onto the pavement in front of his car and padded mechanically around looking for food, looking angry, thought Ted. The landscape had been shrouded in dense cloud when he left the house that morning, but the grey had gradually grown patchier and suddenly, as he took a second bite of his sandwich, the sun broke through. In the distance a kite surfer leapt into the air as though energised by this dramatic improvement in the weather. Ahead and to his right the Kentish Flats Offshore Wind Farm stood out on the horizon, the bright white turbines hanging lifeless. To his left, beyond a gaudy pub, a long row of beach huts stretched away into the distance. A mile or two further along the coast, looking more like a factory building or a military installation than a twelfth century church were the Reculver Towers to which the young man at the marina had referred. In front of him, down on the beach, a dog walker threw a tennis ball for a pair of graceful lurchers, which went bounding joyfully after it, delighted by this simple pleasure. Ted sighed and wished, not for the first time, that he had a dog.

His mobile phone began to vibrate. It was DC Burns. Carefully he placed his sandwich on top of the road atlas on the passenger seat. He swallowed hurriedly and answered.

"Hey. Any progress?"

"Warren Devlin has a girlfriend. Her name is Rebecca King. She lives in a canal boat just off Kingsland Road in Dalston. I've just texted you her address and phone number."

"Thanks. Have you spoken to her?"

"No. I thought I'd leave that to you."

Ted glanced at the clock on the dashboard. "I'll call her in a minute and arrange to meet in the morning."

"What about Devlin's yacht?"

"Smashed to smithereens. Wrecked two weeks ago; washed up in Herne Bay. We need to get an expert to look at it - I know nothing about boats. No sign of any bodies though." He sighed.

"I suppose that explains why no one's seen him for a couple of weeks . . ." Burns tailed off.

Ted paused before answering. "Possibly," he said. "It doesn't explain the break-in at his flat though. And it certainly doesn't explain why he has three fake passports. We just don't know. What about the flatmate?"

"According to the letting agency, there is no flatmate, not

officially anyway. But the neighbours all seem to think he had someone staying with him and there were a few letters addressed to a Paul Finch among all the junk. Another letter arrived for him this morning actually."

"What was it?"

"Just more junk mail."

A faint bleeping told Ted the text had arrived with Rebecca King's address and number.

"You live round here, right?" said Burns.

"Ye-e-e-es," said Logan cautiously.

"Is there anywhere I can get a decent bite to eat?"

Ted smiled. "Head up to the top of Shooters Hill and turn right just before you get to the water tower. I think the road's called Kenilworth Gardens. Follow the sign to Oxleas Wood Cafe. It's nice in there. And the view is terrific."

He smiled again as he heard the rustling of paper from the other end of the line. Burns was writing it down.

"Okay," the young officer said eventually. "Thanks. I'll give it a try. I'm starved."

"Have you plenty to be getting on with this afternoon?"

"I'll head back to the boxing club, I think. Try to find out if anyone knew Devlin or the flatmate."

"Who's going over the flat?"

"Simpson's in charge."

"Good. He knows what he's doing."

"Are you heading back to London?"

Ted tutted. "No," he said. "That's the other thing. It turns out Devlin has a caravan down here in Kent. I'm on my way there now."

"A caravan?" said Burns. "What, a big thing? A static?"

"That I don't know," said Ted. "But it's the address he gave the marina where he keeps his boat . . . or kept it until he smashed it. Or someone smashed it."

"Right."

"I'll call Devlin's girlfriend now and arrange a time for us to meet her tomorrow. I'll try to make it first thing in the morning."

He heard a noise like the wind blowing on the other end of the line.

"Hello?"

"I'm still here," said Burns. He hesitated before continuing. "Erm, tomorrow's Saturday. I've the day off and I'm supposed to be -"

"Ah!" said Ted, cutting Burns off. "Damn!" He sighed, pressing the heel of his hand to his forehead and scrunching his eyes tight shut. "Okay," he said, sounding pained.

"Is everything all right?" said Burns.

"Yeah. Listen, I'd better go. There's something I've forgotten to do. I'll see you when? Monday?"

"Yeah. Okay, have -"

But Ted had already hung up.

What he had forgotten was that he was supposed to buy wine. Caroline was due back from Bristol and had arranged for her sister and brother-in-law to come over for dinner. He was supposed to pick up the booze and . . . something else maybe? He couldn't remember what and really didn't want to risk trying her limited patience by calling to find out. He flicked through the text messages on his phone but found, to his dismay, that he had already deleted Caroline's request. Damn! he thought to himself.

Perhaps it would come to him later. He started the car and reversed quickly out of the parking space, spinning the steering wheel abruptly as he did so. The road atlas shot off the passenger seat and fell into the foot well, taking with it his cheese and pickle sandwich.

Where the Hell was Warren Devlin? he wondered for the umpteenth time that day. Perhaps Rebecca King would be able to answer that question. Perhaps she had a simple explanation for the blood in Warren's kitchen. Perhaps she and Warren were sitting in Warren's caravan right now, lamenting the loss of their boat. No, no – surely they would have made an insurance claim. He would speak to her first thing in the morning. And if she couldn't answer his questions then he would just have to find the flatmate, Paul Finch. He stamped down hard on the accelerator.

TEN

"Commissario Martelli? Hello-o-o-o-o! Commissario?"

Martelli leaned over the parapet and stared down at the visitor three floors below. The man removed his sunglasses and blinked several times. He was taller than average, with dark brown hair, deeply tanned skin and an athletic physique. He wore a thin, white, short-sleeved shirt, khaki trousers and sandals. His voice was deep. It boomed and reverberated in the narrow street. He spoke in English.

"Commissario Martelli?"

"Si," said Martelli.

"Sorry to bother you, dottore. I rang the bell and there was no answer. But the windows were all open so I thought . . ." He shrugged. "Monsieur Lelord sent me . . . the Frenchman."

"How can I help you?" said Martelli. He was intrigued but also acutely aware that his neighbours were listening. Money and goods changed hands in these streets, naturally, but the real currency was gossip. He strove to keep any urgency from his voice, all the while wondering if Signora Bartolotti or the Trigiani's, or for that matter his unexpected visitor, would understand his rusty English.

The stranger answered his question. "My name's Finch, Commissario, Paul Finch. I'm Steven's brother."

* * *

"You know, Mister Finch -"

"Paul."

"Paul, I am no longer involved in the investigation. I'm . . . I do not work for the police anymore."

"Yes, Monsieur Lelord explained."

"So how exactly do you think I might be of help to you?" Martelli emerged from behind the kitchen counter carrying two bottles of beer. He handed one to Finch.

"Thank you. I'd like to hire you."

Martelli froze, unable to hide his astonishment.

Finch nodded, perched on the edge of the sofa, holding his beer away from his body as though it might explode.

"Hire me to do what exactly?" Martelli sat down heavily and took a swig from his own bottle.

"I want you to find my brother's killer."

Martelli stared. Finch held his gaze. They sat like that for several seconds, stock still but for the rhythmic flexing of Finch's jaw muscles.

The doorbell rang.

Martelli sprang to his feet, spilling beer on the rug. "I'm afraid that's my lunch guest. I'd invite you to join us but we've a private matter to discuss."

Finch remained seated. "You will consider my proposal," he said. To Martelli it didn't sound like a question but he supposed that could be down to his unfamiliarity with the language. He paused on his way to the top of the stairs and tilted his head, looking at his guest sideways.

"Your brother's death is a police matter, Mister Finch."

Finch replied assuredly. "There's no law against a private individual making enquiries as long as he doesn't interfere with the official investigation."

"True, but . . ."

"Commissario Rubini will not solve this case. My brother's killer, or killers, will go unpunished." Finch stood up, leaving his beer on the table. "Please say you will at least consider it. I'm happy to pay you a decent daily rate and, of course, I'll cover your expenses."

Martelli looked down at the floor. Finch was right. It was unlikely Rubini would bring anyone to justice. He'd blame foreigners, illegal immigrants, whatever suited the public mood. He wasn't a cop, he was a politician.

The doorbell rang again.

Martelli nodded. "Okay. I'll . . . I'll think about it."

Finch sighed and smiled wanly. "Thank you," he said, fishing in the breast pocket of his shirt. "This is my number." He handed Martelli a piece of paper with his mobile number already written on it. "I'm staying at my brother's apartment. It's opposite -"

"I know where it is," said Martelli.

He followed Paul Finch down the stairs to the front door.

* * *

"You know, Valentina, beneath the choppy waters of our lives there are many submerged rocks," said Martelli as he swirled the spaghetti around the pan, trying to remember how long it had been in there. "And, I'm afraid," he added pointedly, "the occasional sea monster." He chuckled at this metaphor then stopped himself, unsure quite where he was going with it. "I . . ." But he had lost the thread.

Beneath his politeness, Finch had been tense, he thought. But wasn't that understandable given the circumstances? The man had suffered a terrible loss and may well have been in shock. And he had presumably arrived at Via Richeri having just identified his brother's body. Not an experience one would wish on one's worst enemy, especially given the dreadful condition of the deceased. He may have been close to his brother in a way that Martelli was not with his own siblings. He shook his head. Yes, it was no wonder the man was edgy.

He frowned and tried to regain his momentum. "You know, Val-"

"Uncle Mimmo, my father is in trouble. He owes a lot of money. I'm afraid he'll lose everything." Valentina spoke so quickly and with such anguish that Martelli spun round, flicking starchy water onto the kitchen floor. "People have been round to the house," she continued. "I'm terrified he'll do something stupid."

"What? He owes money to the bank, you mean?"

Aldo, Valentina's father, was an old school friend and later army buddy, someone Martelli had known since they were toddlers. He had always been such a reliable, sensible man. It was almost inconceivable that he could have got himself into financial difficulties.

"No," said Valentina, tears welling up in her eyes. "Much worse. He owes Aricò. He owes two hundred thousand at least."

Aricò? thought Martelli, hardly able to believe what he was hearing. A notoriously crooked landlord and developer, and the owner of a shady import export operation, Aricò had somehow always managed to outmanoeuvre the Guardia di Finanza, Italy's customs officers - like the Carabinieri a branch of the military. Best known for swindling the local authority out of millions during protracted negotiations over a failed marina project further along the coast, Aricò was a menace, a pariah, a sugar-coated gangster. How had Aldo become involved with such a person? Martelli shook his head again.

"They're threatening to take the house," said Valentina. "Aricò's *people*." She put her head in her hands and began to weep and Martelli felt his heart, his dicky heart, lurch in his chest. He crossed the room and dragged a chair close to hers then sat down and put an arm around her.

"Tell me everything," he said gently. "Start at the beginning. Leave nothing out."

ELEVEN

Martelli dawdled on the lungomare, the seafront promenade,
absently following a trail of blobs of melted ice cream dropped by a
chubby little boy toddling alongside his mother a couple of metres
ahead. The ice cream looked huge in the little boy's hands – two
large scoops of stracciatella teetering precariously atop a sugar
cone. Martelli smiled absently and breathed deeply of the
mother's perfume. She was pushing a buggy in which the boy's
baby sister lay fast asleep. Her phone rang and she answered it,
launching immediately into a barrage of loud chatter, a kind of
white noise which rendered clear thought impossible. Martelli
stopped and leaned against the railings, gripping them firmly with
both hands and looking out to sea, listening to the prattle dwindle
as the woman and her children moved slowly on.

He had promised Valentina, rather rashly he now realised,
that he would talk to her father, his old friend Aldo, he of the
neatly pressed trousers and public sector pension. It seemed that
Aldo, perpetually prudent Aldo, disciplined and, some might say

ascetic, Aldo, someone he had always thought of as the most shrewd and judicious of his friends, faced penury, having been persuaded by his brother Antonio - a chain-smoking freeloader with a conspicuous sports car but never any money to put petrol in it - to invest in a development which, it turned out, was entirely spurious. And now Antonio was nowhere to be found and Aricò's errand boys — because of course Aricò was behind the whole scheme - were putting increasing pressure on Aldo to hand over the keys to his house. What Martelli was supposed to say to Aldo he did not know.

And then there was Mister Finch and his unexpected proposition; a chance to continue the investigation independent of Rubini, a chance to bring his final case to a satisfactory conclusion. In all likelihood it was also a chance to tread on the toes of every last one of his former colleagues, to alienate them and to squander the good name it had taken most of his lifetime to foster.

And yet clearly the Frenchman did not disapprove.

Would Piero?

He puffed out his cheeks and released the air in a long burst. It was another glorious day on the Riviera delle Palme - the sky was cloudless and the sea flat, calm and clear. Yachts made slow progress along the horizon, dinghies and pedalos wallowed in the shallows; he counted twelve games of bat and ball on the shoreline.

Mind wandering again, he wondered, were he to take a dip the following morning, would he be able to orchestrate another chance encounter with Cristina? And would she give him an opportunity to redeem himself or simply smile and breeze past? He scanned the water for her faded blue swimming cap, examining every bather, looking for her powerful, efficient stroke.

The bagnino brought him back to reality with a sharp blast on his whistle followed swiftly by a barely intelligible announcement made through a loud hailer. Martelli shook his head and smiled at his own foolishness.

Finch, Aldo and the tantalising possibility of Cristina, he thought. This retirement business was not nearly as empty and purposeless as he'd feared.

Aldo he could postpone for a day or two as his old friend was in Napoli visiting an ancient aunt; Cristina had been a dream, a fantasy, nothing more; and that left Finch. He took out his mobile phone and dialled. The Frenchman answered after just one ring.

"Pronto."

"Pippo? It's Mimmo."

"Hey."

"Hey."

For a moment, neither man spoke.

"So," said the Frenchman, "did you get a visit from Mister Paul Finch?"

"Have you finished your report?" said Martelli.

"Si."

"Can I have a copy?"

The broad smile was evident in the Frenchman's voice as he said, "I'll have Di Mateo bring it round first thing in the morning."

TWELVE

"Commissario Rubini seems to think that to be murdered in this town my brother must have been involved in something illegal."

Martelli nodded. "Well, that's simply not true. The overwhelming majority of murders here are crimes of passion. Not that we have many murders, you understand. In fact we have very few, and . . . well . . ."

Finch raised an eyebrow, his expression grave. "And nothing quite like this one. Is that what you were going to say?"

Martelli met Finch's gaze, then he closed his eyes and nodded regretfully, squeezing his lips together until they felt a little numb. When he opened his eyes again, Finch was sipping iced water, staring at him.

"Commissario Rubini seems . . ." Finch searched for the right word. "Distracted," he said finally.

"Mister Finch -"

"Please, call me Paul."

"Paul, the team investigating your brother's death is a good one. I should know - I trained them. I'm confident they will find your brother's killer."

"I wish I shared your conviction," said Finch gloomily.

Both men fell silent.

They were sitting at a table outside Il Bagatto, Martelli's favourite restaurant, and only a few dozen metres from his front door. It was nine o'clock, still early for dinner, so they had the place to themselves. Overhead a whirling galaxy of moths hurled itself relentlessly around the nearby streetlight; at their feet a cat, little more than a kitten, snaked her tail around their ankles and purred unashamedly. Il Bagatto was famous for its fish dishes and she was clearly eager for tidbits. What she didn't know was that they had yet to order any food. Martelli sipped his Campari and soda and felt his stomach rumble.

Il Bagatto opened onto Via Antonio Ricciardo, a street almost as narrow as nearby Via Richeri in which Martelli's house stood. Looking up, the buildings seemed to lean inwards, as though they were closing overhead, swallowing up the diners. Their table was overlooked by more than a dozen windows but this time Martelli wasn't worried about being overheard. He was sure the Italians in this street did not speak any English.

Finch was dressed in the same clothes he'd been wearing that afternoon: sandals, loose fitting khaki trousers and a thin, white, short-sleeved shirt. He still had his sunglasses hooked over his top button and Martelli wondered if he'd managed to get back to his brother's apartment or if he'd been too busy in the town, perhaps enquiring about the repatriation of the body. For his own part, Martelli had spent the hours since calling Lelord faffing about, doing anything to take his mind off what he would say to

Aldo when his old friend returned from Napoli. He'd tried opening *Moby Dick*, which he'd been struggling with for a fortnight, but after finding himself repeatedly reading the same line, he'd headed back out of the house in search of distractions. In the end he had found himself willingly roped into a comprehensive, and in all likelihood pointless, rearrangement of Eduardo's tiny shop. One by one they'd carted just a few cases and bottles shy of Eduardo's entire stock out into the street and then they'd dusted them all and returned them to the cool depths of the cantina in a different order. Eduardo seemed pleased with the results. Martelli had struggled to see the purpose of the exercise but he had been glad of the diversion. In fact he'd enjoyed it, had found it a pleasure to spend time with Eduardo, whose unyielding optimism always raised his spirits. The one sour note of the day had come at around six o'clock when Signora Bartolotti's shameless son, having presumably only just dragged himself out of his pit, had started shouting at his poor mother with particular ferocity. The prolonged outburst had prompted several of the neighbours to close their shutters noisily and pointedly, which seemed only to anger him further. He had briefly aimed his curses outward, once even spitting into the street. Eduardo and Martelli had stood and listened, Eduardo red-faced with embarrassment, Martelli grim-faced with frustration. The thug got worse.

Afterwards he'd ventured out to buy groceries - coming home an hour later with an interesting variety of produce but little that would constitute a meal. He'd tutted at each item, tutted really at his own preoccupation, as he loaded the fridge. Now though, as his stomach rumbled again, he would happily have picked at those mismatched ingredients.

"Let's order some food," he said, shuffling in his seat and luxuriating in the warmth from the centuries old walls.

Finch surprised him with a smile. "Yes, let's do that," he said, almost brightly. "What do you recommend?"

With Martelli's guidance, Finch eventually ordered l'insalata di polpo e patate calda - the warm octopus and potato salad - followed by tagliolini con la bottarga - pasta with mullet roe. For their main courses they both plumped for the filetto di pesce alla ligure, the local speciality, served with pine nuts. Martelli asked for a glass of white wine, which the waitress refilled three times during the course of the meal, pouring generously every time.

The food seemed to perk Finch up even more than merely the prospect of it. He pronounced the octopus delicious, polishing it off in short order.

"You speak English very well," he said as he finished, wiping his mouth with his napkin. "Did you learn in school?"

Martelli shook his head. "In the army."

Finch gave him a quizzical look.

"We joined the army straight from school," said Martelli, smiling faintly at the memory. "Aldo, Piero, Giacomo and me - there was nothing for us here. I ended up an MP in Napoli, at the NATO base, collecting drunks from the local bars on a Friday and Saturday night. This was in the sixties and seventies. Italy was very different then. Many people still didn't even speak Italian. The Italian language came later, from television. I had to learn English so I could communicate with the Americans and British at the base but also to communicate with some of my own countrymen." He laughed. "At first we lived at the barracks but after a while Aldo and I lodged with his aunt near Pompeii." He stared at his wine glass, rotating it in the tiny puddle of condensation on the tabletop. "I remember she grew tomatoes in soil mixed with ash from the slopes of Mount Vesuvius. The sweetest tomatoes I have ever tasted." Smiling wistfully, he added, "I fell in love with her daughter."

For a moment neither man spoke.

"How long were you there?"

Martelli glanced up at Finch. "Oh, I left soon after that. I came home to Loano and joined the police."

"What made you leave the army?"

"The army made me leave the army." He snorted and took a sip of wine. "I was thrown out."

"What for?"

Martelli thought for a moment then replied hesitantly. "I got into . . . an altercation I think is the right English word."

"Don't tell me you punched a superior officer?"

"Actually," said Martelli, leaning forward conspiratorially, "he was an *inferior* officer. And that's why I punched him."

Finch laughed. Martelli laughed too and decided to take the case.

* * *

Later, as Finch reached down to feed a morsel of fish to the cat, Martelli watched surreptitiously, examining the geometry of the man's face, looking for points of fraternal resemblance to the corpse on the Frenchman's examination table. At first he saw none. Then, just as the little cat was tucking in, a dog sprinted past, a Jack Russell, its claws clicking on the paving like a typist at a hundred words a minute. The cat leapt as though electrocuted, spinning in the air and landing with its tail high and its feet splayed. And Finch laughed again, heartily, a deep grunting noise full of warmth. He raised his face, grinning broadly, teeth shining brightly in the light from the streetlamp, and that's when Martelli fancied he saw what he was looking for, in that grin. He shuddered; thought of his own brother, Gennaro, to whom he rarely spoke, and made a mental note to call him. Finch turned away and craned his neck to stare down the street, but no one came after the dog.

"So, said Martelli, after the waitress had brought him a diminutive glass of limoncello as a digestivo. He slid down in his seat a little. "Tell me about your brother. If not something illegal, what did bring him to Loano?"

"Boats. He ran a small boat charter company with an Italian guy called Mario. They took people fishing, taught sailing, did a few daytrips along the coast. They have a boat down at the marina: a motor fisher." He gave a half shrug and leaned back in his seat.

"And where is this Mario now? Have you spoken to him?"

"No. He's away and I've no idea where he's gone."

Martelli sat upright. "Have you tried to contact him?"

"Yes, but a recorded message says his phone is switched off."

"And when did you last hear from him?"

"Oh, months ago, when I last visited my brother." He shrugged, his brow creased. "April, I think."

"And how was your brother's relationship with this Mario?

Were there any problems . . . with money or a woman perhaps?"

"Yes."

Martelli hadn't expected such a direct answer. He leaned forward, eyes narrowed. "And which was it - money or a woman?"

"Money. Business wasn't bad but my brother never seemed to have any cash, whereas Mario always had plenty. He thought Mario was ripping him off, stashing money somewhere."

Martelli nodded. "And what's this Mario's surname?"

"Rossetti."

"And do you have his address?"

"He lives up in the hills, in a place called Castelvecchio something or other. I've been to his house but I don't know the actual address."

Martelli nodded. "It's okay, I'll find it."

* * *

Martelli sat on his rooftop bench and rolled a long, thin joint by the light of a waxing moon. The stars shone brightly despite the glow of the town. He dragged greedily at the joint, pulling the fragrant smoke deep into his lungs and feeling a tingling in his extremities as he did so. In between drags he drank gulps of fruity beer. Combined with the wine and the sweet limoncello, the weed quickly took effect and he was soon pleasantly insensible.

When he eventually made it to bed, he was unable to sleep and lay listening to pigeons cooing as they scratched around on the Trigianis' shabby copper guttering. He made another brief foray into *Moby Dick* but again, this time unsurprisingly, he found himself unable to concentrate. His thoughts kept drifting back to

Piero and their arrangement to meet for coffee the following morning. He was afraid of what his old friend would say. Because he would surely say that to take the case, to compete directly with Rubini, was the act of an egotist and a fool.

THIRTEEN

"Eggs," said Caroline. "I asked you to get eggs."

Ted sighed and let his shoulders sag. Behind Caroline, her brother-in-law gave him a grin and mimed a slap on the wrist. Caroline's sister, Gemma, scowled at him openly. He and Gemma had never really got on; a reflection, he supposed, of her cynicism about the police rather than her disapproval of him personally.

"I'll pop out and get some now. The shop'll still be open won't it?"

"I don't know," said Caroline moodily.

* * *

He'd told Caroline that he was late because of bad traffic through the roadworks on the A2, but the truth was that he'd spent too much time poking around in Warren Devlin's caravan. Actually, he'd done less poking around and more just sitting around, staring out of the window and indulging in pointless speculation about

Devlin's disappearance. The inescapable truth was that he hadn't really wanted to go home.

At first Ted had been asked for a warrant, something the manager of the holiday park had doubtless picked up from detective dramas on television, but he was a harried man with a vortex of shrieking children scurrying around him so he'd relented without much persuasion. Thus, with the manager otherwise engaged, Ted had entered 11 Meadow View alone.

He wasn't sure quite what he'd been expecting but it certainly wasn't a spotlessly clean, two bedroom park home surrounded on all sides by neatly tended shrubs and flowers. One of the bedrooms even had an en suite bathroom. It was a far cry from the caravan holidays of his childhood, of which he remembered very little other than a general dampness and a lack of sufficient cupboard space in which to cram the car load of equipment his mother had always insisted on bringing with them. As well as two bedrooms, Devlin's caravan had a proper living room with a pair of comfy sofas and a big television. It also had central heating, broadband, a fully equipped kitchen and an abundance of peace and quiet. Ted was impressed.

What the caravan did not have, however, was any sign that it was occupied. The beds – a double in the main bedroom and two singles in the spare – were made up ready for use, but there were no clothes in the wardrobes and no food in the fridge, only a few bottles of beer, to which Ted was momentarily tempted to help himself. He opened every one of the many cupboards and found only a vacuum cleaner, an unopened first aid kit, a few spare light bulbs and a bucket filled with cleaning products under the sink. There was a bar of soap in the bathroom but no toothbrushes, razors or deodorant. In the kitchen there were no tea bags, coffee granules or sugar. Indeed everything in the place had a thin coating of dust, even the shower tray, as though it was a neglected exhibit rather than a holiday home.

After two complete circuits, he sat down on one of the sofas, dialled the number Burns had texted to him and went straight through to Rebecca King's voicemail. He left a message in which he introduced himself and suggested he would visit her the following morning at nine o'clock. Then he leaned back and told himself he wouldn't return to his car until he'd remembered what it was that he was supposed to buy along with the wine. It could have been bread or milk, but then it could just as easily have been apples. He sighed. He really had no idea. He closed his eyes to better concentrate but found himself unable to steer his thoughts away from Warren Devlin. Hopefully Burns would have turned up something interesting at Harry Jay's club. Listening to the breeze hissing through the trees, he tipped his head back and stared at the ceiling. He yawned.

He opened his eyes and was immediately disoriented, unsure where he was. He lay perfectly still. A lone bluebottle circled the room, its buzzing loud and insistent in the stillness. A young boy flashed past the window on a rattling micro scooter. The sun had drifted behind a stand of very tall trees, giving the impression of twilight. He didn't know how long he'd been asleep but he knew without even looking at his mobile phone that he was going to be late home.

As he was returning the key, he asked the harassed manager how long Devlin had been renting the place.

"Oh, he doesn't rent it, he owns it."

"Oh," said Ted, raising his eyebrows. "And when did he buy it?"

The manager made much of having to look this fact up. "Two months ago," he said eventually. "Just over, in fact."

"And how much did he pay for it, do you know?"

"Twenty-five thousand, near enough."

"And there are fees on top of that, I suppose."

"Yes, it's three thousand per year plus utilities."

Ted was taken aback.

"And are you still receiving those fees?"

"What do you mean?" said the manager.

"I mean, when is Mister Devlin's next payment due?"

The manager frowned. "Oh no," he said. "There's no need to worry about that. He paid for the whole year; paid in cash."

"And do you have any idea how often he stays here?"

"I don't think he has yet." He shrugged. "I haven't seen him anyway."

* * *

Adrian and Gemma annoyed Ted at dinner by wittering on about a couple they'd met while on their honeymoon in the Seychelles and with whom they had recently enjoyed a weekend in Dorset. Gemma, the younger of the two sisters, never missed an opportunity to mention weddings, honeymoons, children or the joys of marriage in general. It made Ted squirm. And he felt sure she knew that.

After the meal, Ted wearily rinsed the plates and arranged them in the dishwasher, while Caroline got out her laptop and showed Gemma and Adrian pictures of properties she was interested in. She was putting Ted under increasing pressure to move, to buy a house, to get married and to start a family. He swore under his breath as he tried in vain to balance the wine glasses on the metal prongs in the upper basket.

Chester purred at him and got under his feet as he wiped the kitchen surface. He loved Caroline but was he in love with her? It was a question he'd asked himself on more than one occasion, and perhaps the truth was that if he had to ask the question then she was probably not the woman for him. But to end things required a cataclysm, not mere vagueness, and so they trundled on, neither of them able to put their finger on quite what it was that was wrong.

He felt something underfoot, something squashy, and looked down to find that Chester had brought him a dead mouse. He smiled. He was a cat person and Caroline was not. Was it as straightforward as that? Could they have saved themselves a lot of time and trouble by simply establishing that on the day they met?

"You'd better watch out, boyo." He reached down and scratched the top of Chester's head. "Don't let her catch you doing that."

It was as though their love, their enthusiasm for one another, their whole relationship had dwindled over time, and had finally shrunk to a lifeless husk.

He folded a piece of kitchen paper, picked up the tiny corpse and nipped quickly to the bathroom where he flushed it down the loo.

FOURTEEN

Martelli woke with an aching jaw, as though he'd been grinding his teeth in the night. Was it a result of anxiety, he wondered sadly, or perhaps a bad dream? He opened his eyes and lay staring at a discoloured patch on the ceiling. On the bedside table his mobile phone began to vibrate, setting a handful of coins buzzing on the glass surface and rotating his spare house keys. He pulled the duvet up over his head and counted to twenty, then waited for the chirping noise signalling a voicemail message. To his relief it was Piero calling to cancel breakfast at Giacomo's. Martelli smiled. Piero always referred to their morning rendezvous as breakfast – colazione - despite his having already had breakfast before he left his house, usually eggs cooked by his German wife, Lena. Martelli listened to the rest of the message. There was to be a team briefing, chaired by the Vice Questore himself and Piero had chosen to be there to represent the interests of the Carabinieri. He breathed deeply and gave his head a good hard scratch, wincing as he did so. While he would have appreciated hearing his old friend's opinion on Aldo's situation, he was thankful he didn't have to face censure just yet over his having taken on Steven Finch's brother as a client.

The doorbell rang. He wrapped himself in a dressing gown, padded downstairs, accepted an envelope and then rang Lelord to thank him.

"A blushing schoolboy just turned up with your report," he said, chuckling. "When you said you were sending Di Mateo, I thought you meant the old boy. I guess that was his son."

"Gesù Bambino, Mimmo - that was his grandson. Di Mateo's seventy years old. Didn't you speak to the lad?"

"Ah. No, no, I didn't."

Lelord sighed, his breath roaring in Martelli's earpiece. "Listen, Mimmo, there's all sorts of pressure being applied to this case, from every quarter. If you *are* going to start poking around, make sure you steer clear of Rubini until you've reached a solid conclusion."

Martelli snorted. Standing at the kitchen counter, he opened the envelope and started leafing through the photographs.

"And, Mimmo, please don't let on that you have a copy of my report. Things are difficult enough here as it is." Lelord paused, waiting for a response. He received none. "Mimmo?"

Martelli was staring at a snapshot of the human remains lying on the metal table in the Frenchman's examination room. He shook his head. During nearly four decades as a policeman, he'd seen much that would unsettle the average citizen: crushed skulls, bludgeoned faces, violent dismemberment; people destroyed beneath the wheels of speeding trains, bodies burned beyond recognition, corpses quite literally shredded by machinery. But something about this, this deliberately drawn out immersion of a living human being in acid, the painstaking preparation, the calculation, the cold bloodedness of it all sent a little shiver dancing between his shoulder blades.

"Mimmo?"

"Yes, sorry, I was thinking."

"Okay, well I'll leave you to it. Be sure to watch the news this evening. Rubini's organising a press conference. He's probably off choosing an outfit as we speak."

Martelli grunted. "What do you make of Finch?" he said.

Lelord described the incident at the mortuary, his shock at the sheet being whipped aside, and though he didn't say so explicitly, it was clear from his voice that he was still a little troubled by it.

"After that," he said, "he was absolutely charming. Perhaps . . . Perhaps he was simply unwilling to accept that his brother was dead. I have seen it many times before, that reluctance. And . . . well, he came in simply to report Steven missing and ended up identifying his body. It must have been a terrible shock."

"Presumably he spent most of the day with Rubini."

"An hour or so, yes, but he came to see me afterwards and asked about you."

"Really? How odd," said Martelli, frowning.

"Not so strange. Your name is well known in this town."

"I suppose so."

"He would easily have found your address, so I thought I might as well send him along to see you and let you make your own decision. People make a good living in private investigations, you know."

"What?" said Martelli with derision. "Spying on cheating

husbands? Catching people at it?"

"Or tracing missing persons," countered Lelord. "Tracking down unsuspecting heirs even - it doesn't have to be grubby."

Both men fell silent for a moment.

"I would need a licence."

"Yes," said Lelord. "Otherwise you can't take payment."

"So," said Martelli slowly, "Now we have due fringuelli."

"Si," said Lelord. "Two finches. But only one still singing."

FIFTEEN

Rebecca King kept a very untidy boat. The place was such a mess that she was unable to find a matching pair of flip flops and ended up leading Ted to The Towpath Café wearing one pink and one black one.

She had replied to his voicemail with a text message, sent late at night, long after he and Caroline had gone to bed. He'd noticed it when he popped to the bathroom in the early hours. It said '9ish fine', as though she was slurring her words, and now it made him smile to imagine that she had been drunk when she sent it.

In the absence of a doorbell or knocker, Ted had gently rapped his knuckles on the roof of the little boat at five minutes to nine. After a polite interval he'd rapped again, and then called out her name, and eventually, having decided she was not at home, he'd re-dialled her number only to hear her mobile phone ring just a metre or so from where he was standing. In a little window at knee level, a mildewed curtain had been yanked back to reveal a face blurred with sleep and possibly tears. It was a face much older and heavier than he'd been expecting and at first he'd thought it must be Rebecca King's mother. She appeared to have slept in her clothes. Certainly there was not enough of an interval between her appearance at the window and her arrival at the door for her to have dressed herself.

The interior of the boat was shambolic, with far too many things crammed into far too inadequate a space. She too was a shambles: her long, flowery dress was moth-eaten and wrinkled, her hair had been bleached almost to the point of extinction and had begun to go thin on top, and her breath, he noticed immediately, reeked of cigarettes. He found it difficult to picture her on the arm of the kind of man who drove a Porsche and owned a three-hundred thousand pound yacht. But the really surprising thing about Rebecca King, Ted reflected, was that she had bothered to get up at all.

As they walked the hundred metres to the café, Ted noticed that the murky waters of the Regent's Canal were peppered with patches of vivid green algae, like a gently undulating map, its regions drifting; slow motion schisms forming newly independent nations, subsequent collisions creating superpowers and federations. A party of ducks kept pace with them, quacking a constant commentary, hopeful of bread.

"I'm afraid I don't have any money", said King when they'd covered about half the distance, and Ted was not at all surprised. They walked the rest of the way in silence.

He found London's canals a fascinating netherworld, an alternative view of the city, like looking at it from the inside. There were rubbish tips and redundant industrial buildings, car breakers and scrap yards, and the neglected backside of some of the city's great thoroughfares, but there were wonders too: magical waterside gardens; terrific pubs, bars and cafes; and the boats themselves, like floating gypsy caravans, he found whimsical and somehow romantic.

They sat down either side of a rickety metal table and she immediately dug out a packet of cigarettes, quite literally digging for them inside an oversized handbag. She then couldn't find a lighter and got up to ask at every table of diners until one was offered.

"My grandfather was a policeman," she said, as she sat down again.

"Here in London?"

"No - in Surrey." She appeared taken aback as though Ted had said something absurd.

"Did you ever think of following in his footsteps?"

She interrupted a drag on her cigarette. "Oh, no!" she said with a look of distaste. "I'd be far too pathetic." She spoke with what seemed to Ted a fake upper crust accent, with the over-the-top enunciation of someone desperate to impress. He wondered if she might be an unsuccessful actress and half expected her to start calling him 'darling'.

"Miss King -"

"Call me Becky." She rolled her eyes to heaven and tilted her head back, blinking repeatedly, fluttering the fingers of one hand in front of her left eye.

"Are you okay?"

"These bloody lenses!" she said.

"Ah," he said. "My girlfriend wears contacts. She hates

them too. Always drying out, apparently."

She tutted and lowered her hand; faced him again.

"So, Miss King -"

"Becky."

"Becky," Ted smiled, "how long is it since you last saw Warren?"

She gave a little shrug and a shake of her head. "You know we're not together?"

"No, I didn't know," he said.

"We broke up two months ago."

"Ah." Ted had a sinking feeling. "I'm sorry to hear that."

Dismissing his sentiment with a casual backwards flick of her hand, she took a long drag and held the smoke then let it trickle from her nostrils. Ted noticed the residue of yesterday's make up gathered at the corners of her mouth and in the lines on her forehead.

A waitress arrived and Ted ordered a grilled cheese sandwich which, according to the menu, would be served with quince jelly. Becky asked for a black coffee and some artificial sweetener.

"Have you heard from him since then?"

"Oh, yes," she said, frowning again. "He called me endlessly at first; several times a day." She drew out the word 'endlessly' in a way that Ted found annoying. "And we did go out once or twice - to dinner and the theatre." He almost winced at her ridiculously affected pronunciation of the last word.

"What is it you do for a living, if you don't mind me asking?"

"Not at all," she said. "I'm a journalist."

But something about the way she said it, the way her eyes evaded his, made Ted think she hadn't actually worked as a journalist for a long time, if ever.

"So how did you meet Warren?"

"Oh." She smiled but seemed disappointed by the question. "We worked together."

"He was a journalist as well?"

"No." She looked down at the table; picked absently at a dried-on morsel which Ted thought was probably bird droppings. "I used to work in PR. I did some work at Earls Court a few years ago - for the Boat Show. We met there." She looked up at him with narrowed eyes. "I wish you'd tell me what this is all about. Is Warren in trouble?"

The sandwich had arrived and he kept her waiting while he took a bite. It was delicious but he would have enjoyed it more if Becky King hadn't followed it with her eyes, staring like a starving man at a cake shop window. He gestured with his knife, offering to cut her a piece, but she turned him down and he didn't push it. Perhaps she had dietary hang ups on top of her other problems.

He swallowed. "Warren is missing," he said abruptly. "His boat was found wrecked off the north Kent coast."

She seemed at once astonished and bewildered. Her eyes began to well up with tears. Suddenly Ted felt remorseful for having broken the news so brusquely.

She made a choking noise and managed to say, "Is he . . ?"

"We don't even know if he was on board," he said calmly.

Still holding her cigarette, she put both hands to her face and began to cry. Her obvious distress attracted the attention of other diners. He handed her his paper napkin.

"I'm sorry to have to ask this but it is important. When did you last hear from Warren?"

He had to wait while she gathered herself.

"Oh," she said finally, sniffling. "I can tell you exactly." She dropped her half-smoked cigarette on the ground and began fishing around in her bag again.

Ted pressed his thumb and forefinger to his eyelids and squeezed hard then tilted his head back, blinking. He glanced down at the sandwich but didn't feel like eating any more. In his pocket, his mobile phone began to vibrate against his keys. He hoped it wasn't Caroline. Earlier that morning, he'd lain in bed pretending to be asleep until he was sure she'd left for her yoga class in Blackheath. Then he'd leapt out of bed, hurriedly showered and dressed, and driven north of the river to make his rendezvous.

He pulled out his phone and was relieved to see that it was DC Burns. Becky was still burrowing in her bag so he took the call.

"I thought you had the day off."

"I do but I got some very interesting emails this morning and I thought you'd like to know right away."

"Know what?"

"First of all, Warren Devlin's car turned up at Stansted."

"Really? Do we know how long it's been there?"

"Ten days."

So that was . . . he counted on his fingers, mouthing the days of the week - Tuesday or Wednesday before last, he thought. He turned to watch the ducks head back the way they had come. This meant that either someone else had parked the car or Warren Devlin had survived the wreck of his boat and then flown off somewhere. Another alternative, he supposed, was that someone else had been lost at sea.

"Okay. And what else?" he said.

"I think I know the whereabouts of our mystery flatmate, Paul Finch."

Ted sat bolt upright. "Where?"

"Italy."

"Why?"

"Because according to the Foreign Office a British guy called Steven Finch turned up dead in Italy two days ago and his body was officially identified yesterday morning by his brother, one Paul Finch."

Ted blew out a long breath. Things were supposed to become clearer as the investigation progressed, not the other way around.

"Want to know how Steven Finch died?" said Burns.

"How?"

"Murdered. Dissolved in acid."

Ted shivered. At least he'd never come across that in South London. "Do the Italian police have the killer?"

"Nope. They've got no idea, apparently."

Ted felt as though his brain was filling up. The inquiry was increasing dramatically in scope with each passing minute.

"There's more."

"Go on." said Ted, hesitantly, almost afraid to add any further intricacies.

"This is the big one. A man's body turned up on a beach in Kent this morning. A woman found it while she was out walking her dogs."

Images of the graceful lurchers sprinting along the sands flashed into Ted's mind.

"It was under a pile of seaweed. At a place called . . ." There was a swish swish swish as Burns leafed through his notes. "Birchington," he said with a hint of triumph.

Christ, thought Ted, turning to stare into the murky waters of the canal, I was just there yesterday, eating a sandwich. Maybe the body had been right in front of him, just below the surface.

"It's in pretty bad shape, apparently," said Burns.

"Where is it now?"

"Not sure. I can make some calls though."

"Do that first and let me know as soon as you find out. Then you need to try to get hold of Paul Finch in Italy. He must have a mobile phone with him. And don't let anyone touch that car until Simpson's had a look at it. I'll head down to Kent." He paused, his mind reeling under this sudden torrent of new information. He stared at a distant bridge, trying to relax, letting his vision blur. When he refocused he found he was looking directly at Becky King's tear streaked face. Something told him she cried a lot. She stared at him expectantly.

"Listen, this is great. Good work. I'd better go. I'll call you from the car." He hung up before Burns could reply.

"It was the Wednesday before last," said Becky, brandishing an old mobile phone. She held the screen in front of his face but it was cracked and unlit and the morning sun prevented him from reading it.

He frowned. "Sorry?"

"It was the Wednesday before last," she said. "The last time I heard from Warren. Ten days ago."

Ted raised his eyebrows.

SIXTEEN

A scrawny terrier skulked past nervously, pausing briefly at every quayside obstacle, giving it a sniff, perhaps in search of fish. A young man leaned over the gunwhale of a shabby old trawler, his sandpaper shushing and fizzing rhythmically as he rubbed down the timbers in preparation for a coat of varnish. Somewhere a radio played music; Martelli recognised Debussy's Claire de Lune. Now and again there was the distant screech of rent metal from the docks on the far side of the marina, where a luxury yacht, a mini ship really, maybe eighty metres in length, was undergoing a refit. Squinting at it, Martelli could just make out the tiny figures of the workmen, like ants on a huge, angular carcass. By day it was a tranquil place, the marina.

Four men sat outside the harbourmaster's office playing scopa. Their table was a large wooden cable drum, lying on its side. Three sat on rickety chairs and the fourth was perched on a pair of upturned beer crates. They were all deeply, almost comically tanned; their skin a rich mahogany from years spent by

the water. Around them, on the quayside, lay coils of rope and
heaped fishing nets along with dozens of brightly coloured plastic
containers adapted for use as floats to mark the whereabouts of
lobster pots and anchorages. There were also several stacks of
polystyrene boxes for keeping fish on ice in the sweltering heat of a
Ligurian summer. Behind the men, sunlight sparkled on the
chrome rails and polished cleats of numerous offshore power
boats. The boats bristled with aerials and antennas, radar pods
and whippy game fishing rods. Ropes clanged tunelessly against
the aluminium masts of the sailboats; little anemometers spun
lazily. A scattering of seagulls bobbed on the water, which was
crystal clear but for the occasional faint rainbow slick of diesel.
Martelli recognised all four men, though he knew only one:
Ricardo Orso, Loano's bespectacled and famously whisky-voiced
harbourmaster, brother of his old friend Giacomo, the cafe
proprietor. He wore dark blue shorts with neat creases down the
thighs and a light blue short-sleeved shirt, also neatly pressed. A
curl of gold braid, stained brown with use, dangled from his
pocket, attaching his keys to a belt loop.

Scopa means 'broom' and, as Martelli drew near, one of the
players did indeed sweep up all the cards, crying out in victory as
he did so. L'asso bello, the Ace of Coins, fluttered to the ground
and Martelli bent down to retrieve it.

"Hey, Mimmo! Ciao, bello!" said Ricardo, leaping to his
feet when he spotted Martelli and indicating that he should take
his place on the beer crates. "Sit, sit."

But Martelli remained standing. He placed the ace on the
table and gestured for the other card players to stay seated. The
three men nodded in silent greeting and then sat looking up at

him, open-mouthed in anticipation. To their obvious disappointment, Martelli asked Ricardo if they could speak in private.

"Of course, of course," croaked the harbourmaster, grinning. "Come into my office. I'll make coffee."

They went inside and Ricardo busied himself at the little kitchenette in one corner of the room while Martelli stood at the picture window overlooking the marina. He took in the rows of boats, flexing his aching jaw and wondering if it was a sign of anxiety or if he'd simply slept in an awkward position.

"Where's Aldo Bonetti?" he said over his shoulder. "Doesn't he usually play cards?"

"He hasn't been around much lately," said Ricardo, joining him at the window. As always he smelled of lavender and cigarettes, a combination which reminded Martelli of an elderly aunt long since dead. "How times have changed, eh?" He indicated the ranks of motionless vessels. "When we were boys it was all fishermen. And now it is mostly for pleasure. The fishing fleet is gone . . ." He let this sink in a moment before continuing cheerily, "I thought I'd be seeing you. Piero tells me you're in the market for a boat."

Martelli rolled his eyes to Heaven and shook his head.

Like Martelli, Ricardo had grown up in the caruggi. He and Giacomo had lived in a tiny apartment with their parents and five siblings. They were poor of course, but the children were fed and clothed and, in the decade after the war, that was all that mattered, to the children themselves at least. As a boy, Ricardo had been a champion swimmer and cyclist and somehow he had managed to retain that lean physique. He had a broad smile set in a small, wrinkled face; his thinning grey hair was cropped close but his moustache grew thick and tufty. His glasses were so powerful that they shrunk his eyes to little more than dots either side of his nose, and the bags under those eyes were piled high from years of smoking. His father had been a fisherman so he had spent his entire life on and around boats and there was no one in Loano better qualified for the job of harbourmaster, a position he'd held for more than two decades. He was a widower whose daughter - his only child - lived in Torino with her husband and two small boys.

"My grandchildren arrive tomorrow," he told Martelli, beaming. "I will take them fishing. They love to fish with their old nonno." He laughed, shaking his head. "Francesca worries they'll fall overboard but they're fearless, Mimmo, fearless, and Fabio, the eldest . . . Ah, you should see him! He swims so well, so strong. He'll be a champion like his grandfather, eh?" Ricardo swelled with pride, his eyes twinkling moistly and, for the briefest of moments, Martelli felt envy and regret. "So," continued Ricardo, changing the subject quickly, perhaps sensing Martelli's discomfort. "What sort of thing are you looking for? A fishing boat?"

"Actually, I wanted to talk to you about something else." Martelli turned to look Ricardo directly in the eyes. "You know there has been a murder up in Carpe? At the old Bar Reale?"

"Yes," said Ricardo, tutting and shaking his head, his face suddenly serious. "A terrible business."

"Well, the victim was a Steven Finch, an Englishman. He ran a boat charter service with a local guy called Mario Rossetti. They ran it from here. I'm trying to find out as much as I can about them."

Ricardo said nothing, his face impassive, his eyes searching Martelli's. Like everyone else in the old neighbourhood he was surely aware of Martelli's enforced retirement, and it was clear he had questions about what Martelli was up to. But the two men had a decades old mutual respect and Martelli, though prepared to give honest answers, was confident that the questions would remain unasked. He waited. The stovetop coffee pot gurgled and started to splutter. Ricardo glanced at it, pushed his glasses higher on the bridge of his nose. He turned back to Martelli, nodded once.

"You pour the coffee," he said, hauling his keys from his pocket, "while I dig out the file."

* * *

Give Ricardo the name of a boat owner and he might look at you blankly. But give him the name of a boat and he'll talk until you make him stop. Or so it seemed to Martelli as they stood on the quayside, hands on hips, gazing at the shallow transom of The Lucky Star.

"She was built in Genova in 1958, I think, and she spent most of her life in these waters. She was commissioned by an American and is American in style. What they would call a sportfisherman."

Martelli nodded.

"After the American died, she was sold by his widow to a Monégasque and she spent several years in Monaco."

None of this was in the file.

"She came to Loano in the early seventies and has remained here ever since. Rossetti bought her two years ago and is still the registered owner. I -"

Ricardo paused and raised his eyebrows as Martelli held up a finger.

"What can you tell me about Rossetti and Finch?" he asked. "What do they do exactly?"

Ricardo pulled a face and shrugged, suggesting he didn't think he could tell Martelli much.

"It's like you said, they operate a boat charter service. They rent out their vessel and a crew to paying customers. It . . ." He tailed off. Martelli looked at him askance. "Put it this way," he went on. "I don't think they catch very much when they go off fishing. They take guys out for the day, or for the night for that matter, rich guys, and . . ." He gave Martelli a lopsided grin. Martelli said nothing. "Well, they take girls with them. Not all of the time but . . . often I think."

"Girls?"

"Girls, you know . . . prostitutes." The word embarrassed him.

"I see. And how do you know they were prostitutes?"

The red flush of discomfort showed through Ricardo's deep tan. "I recognised one of them, Mimmo . . . you know, from Via Aurelia."

The road from Loano to Albenga was lined with small industrial units, wholesale outlets and vast nurseries for the propagation of house plants. Few people lived along it. At night, it played host to numerous working girls, several of whom had, over the years, ended up on the Frenchman's metal table. Martelli knew it only too well. He nodded.

"I recognise many of them too," he said in an attempt to put Ricardo at ease. "How often do they make these sorts of trips?"

"Oh, quite often. Once or twice a week. But I haven't seen them for a while."

"How long?"

"I don't think I've seen Mario for a couple of weeks now, maybe three."

"And do you speak to them much, Mario and Finch?"

"A little. There are fees to pay and occasional things to attend to. It's always Mario, though. I've never met Finch, although I've seen him from a distance, you know, coming and going." Ricardo nodded to himself. "They have a crewman too. A Polish guy, I think. His name is Tomasz. He's about twenty-five. I don't have an address for him but he has been to the office a few times with Mario. And also there's Estella."

"Estella?"

"Mario's girlfriend - such a nice girl, and always so smartly dressed. I can't believe she knows what they get up to. She works in Alassio at that boutique . . . I can't remember the name of it. It's opposite Valdini's. I saw her there one time," he smiled to himself, lost in thought for a moment, then suddenly he seemed startled. "I went to buy a gift for Francesca," he added quickly. "She has long blonde hair, Estella. I guess she's also about twenty-five. Tomasz has a girlfriend too, I think. Her name's Angela. She's a rough woman, uses foul language. She's thirty or so. Her hair is always a mess and she always looks like she needs a wash." He wrinkled his nose. "She was here a couple of weeks ago."

"Here on the boat or here at the marina?"

"Actually, she came to the office. She was looking for Mario. I told her I didn't know where he was. Why would I?" He snorted. "She was angry. She is always angry, that one. She seemed also . . . frightened, I think." He tailed off.

"Do you think . . ?" Martelli glanced down at the ground. "Look, I know this sounds a crazy question but do you think it's possible that Mario might have killed Steven Finch? Did you ever see them argue or fight?"

Ricardo blinked twice before answering, shaking his head as he did so. "Mario is . . ." He shrugged. "He's a gentle guy, y'know, a dreamer, always smiling. I can't imagine him killing anybody."

Martelli nodded and smiled. He could see that Ricardo was becoming a little overwrought and decided to bring their chat to a close.

"Ricardo," he said. "Your memory is exceptional. Thank you. And the address you have for Mario - is it in Castelvecchio?"

Ricardo nodded. He looked suddenly sad, as though he regretted their encounter. Two minutes later, outside the harbour office, he bade Martelli a quiet farewell and disappeared inside without looking back.

SEVENTEEN

In the depths of winter, viewed from a distance across the
plunging valley, draped in bulbous layers of snow, Castelvecchio di
Rocca Barbena looks like a bleak and impenetrable fortress, but
against the cloudless sky of that summer day, bathed in golden
sunlight, its shady streets were cool and welcoming, like a country
inn after a long day's hike. Martelli still remembered vividly his
first visit to the village as a child many years before. Then, as now,
his first glimpses of it were through the dense oak forest which
clings to the vertiginous mountainside as the road winds up and
up, turning back on itself more than a dozen times before cutting
through the outlying houses, spiralling upwards around a rocky
outcrop and finally opening out onto the small municipal car park.
His was the only vehicle. The villagers, he supposed, were all at
work in the nearby towns. He left his shabby Lancia, the metal
pinging and clicking as it cooled down, and entered the village on
foot.

* * *

Castelvecchio is perched on crags so high it often appears to be floating among the clouds; so high in fact that eagles sometimes circle effortlessly below the level of the houses. It has an otherworldly aspect to it and Martelli got the feeling that simply by walking its narrow streets he was somehow connected to past centuries. The little houses appeared to grow out of the hillside, to emerge from the rock and then tumble this way and that, a cascade of irregular boxes. They reminded him of the tiny silver cottage which dangled from his grandmother's charm bracelet, a gift, she had once claimed dreamily, from a foreign admirer long before Martelli's mother was born. The old castle from which the place took its name, was built to an altogether different scale. It dominated the centre of the village, a massive, forbidding and threatening presence, looming over every inhabitant, sitting at the summit of the crags, a gargantuan monolith with no visible entrance and no signs of life.

As he walked, he wondered how best to proceed when he reached Mario's house. He thought it highly unlikely that he would find Signor Rossetti at home; even more unlikely that he would be invited in and have his many questions answered. But what should he do if the house sat empty? Should he snoop about or try to gain entry? Nothing went unnoticed in these little towns, however sleepy they appeared. He decided that all he could do was play it by ear; find the house and then take things from there.

He headed first downhill, past the post office and a little restaurant, and then back up towards the central piazza. He encountered no one as he wandered around. One or two doors stood open but he was prevented from looking inside by curtains of multi-coloured plastic strips, designed to keep out flies and prying eyes.

He smiled as made his way up a steep, narrow passage with an uneven arched roof, smiled at the craftsmanship and at the remarkable fortitude of the people who, perhaps a thousand years before, and without the benefit of power tools or motor cars, had built this magical little place in the mountains. But as he stepped out into the sunlight and entered Piazza della Torre, he spotted something on the tooled granite paving which made his smile sag and his heart sink. It lay there like a tiny glossy torpedo, the fat end squashed flat and torn ragged under the heel of a boot. He fancied he could detect a hint of acrid smoke lingering in the still air. It was, unmistakeably, a discarded toscano cigar.

Instantly he regretted his decision to drive up there. He closed his eyes and considered whether to turn on his heels, to tell Finch he'd changed his mind, to return the Frenchman's report, to revisit Ricardo and ask if after all he might simply seek advice about the purchase of a fishing boat.

"Buongiorno, Signor Martelli." The smug smile had gone. Rubini looked tired and strained. The pressure to solve high profile cases was immense, as Martelli knew only too well, and Rubini's friends in political circles would soon desert him if he failed to come up with a viable suspect quickly. It was clear the man had barely slept since they last spoke.

Martelli ignored the 'Signor'. He held his breath. From the opposite end of the piazza came the loud crackle of water gushing from a copper spigot into the massive stone basin of the village fountain.

"Quite a coincidence I would say, you turning up here." Rubini's voice was hoarse and low.

Martelli felt his face grow warm and hoped, pointlessly he later realised, that his anger and shame did not show. A young man, someone he didn't recognise, entered the piazza on the far side, looked around and began to stride towards them, his footsteps echoing off the ancient walls. Rubini glanced briefly in the newcomer's direction then spoke again, his voice lowered still further, seemingly savouring every word. "I understand how difficult things must be for you, Signor Martelli, now that you are a captain without a crew."

Martelli flexed his jaw muscles, mouth clamped firmly shut. He watched as a look of infuriating condescension grew on his former colleague's face, a movement almost balletic in its smoothness, ending with a little flourish as Rubini flared his nostrils and turned his nose up just a little, as though he'd caught a whiff of something unpleasant.

Rubini glanced over his shoulder before speaking again, rapidly this time, so as to get his words out before the young man was upon them. "I cannot have you undermining me, Martelli. It makes me look foolish and I will – believe me I absolutely will - have you arrested for interfering with a police investigation if I see you at one of my crime scenes again."

The new arrival, perhaps sensing tension, had stopped a few metres short. He looked from Martelli to Rubini and then back again. Had he heard anything? It seemed unlikely. All sorts of responses flitted through Martelli's head, a lexicon of foul-mouthed retorts, but, with not inconsiderable effort, he controlled himself, forced a smile, and said simply: "Arrivaderci,

Commissario. Good luck with your investigation."

They stared at one another for a moment, each searching the other's eyes, then, as Rubini opened his mouth to speak again, Martelli turned abruptly and walked away. Behind him someone snorted.

* * *

He grew quickly breathless as he hurried through the steep, hemmed-in streets. One alleyway, consisting of tall, irregular steps, was so narrow he had to turn sideways to pass through it, and yet there was a doorway, to someone's house he presumed, in a tiny courtyard at the top. His mind raced. How could he have been so stupid? Not only to come here but to let Rubini catch him in the act? A quick telephone call to Bracco would have told him Rubini's likely whereabouts. And what about Ricardo? Had he already received a visit but chosen to say nothing?

"Damn! Damn it all!"

Had he said that out loud?

Back on the main street he came to a broad, roughly triangular piazza at the very heart of the village. Beyond it was a small public park with wooden benches and picnic tables. On the far side of this space was a wall, beyond which the landscape fell away in a series of irregular terraces supported by ancient stonework. The views were dizzying and spectacular. He stopped to catch his breath, the look on his face a silent snarl. Off to the right a movement caught his eye. A number of uniformed officers were milling around outside what must surely be Mario Rossetti's house. It was on the outskirts of the village at the bottom of a dead end street, a street now filled with police vehicles. His heart was pounding and he could feel himself starting to sweat. He was momentarily tempted to flee the intense heat of the midday sun and return to the pleasant cool of the confined, stone alleyways. But if he turned back he would inevitably encounter Rubini again, and his anger had yet to subside.

What infuriated him most was not Rubini's blatant attempt at belittlement. No, what had him incensed was the hint of pity in Rubini's eyes – real and really unwarranted pity. That's what affected him, that's what dug a knife into his side, that's what made him want to yell at the top of his voice and smash something to pieces with his fists.

He made a snap decision and set off, walking quickly again, breathing heavily, putting more distance between himself and his former colleagues. He hurried across the open space, staring straight ahead, hoping no one would spot him, and made his way down a meandering street on the south side of the piazza. It was wider than most of the other streets, wide enough for a small car if the driver took it slowly. To the left, behind a high wall stood an ancient church; to the right were the main entrances to the grandest houses of the village. Between them, narrow passages and stone steps led down to the gardens at the rear of the houses. He caught glimpses of neat vegetable patches and splashes of bright crimson bougainvillea flowers. The gardens must face mostly west, he thought, out across the plunging valley, towards the sunset.

After a minute or so he stumbled on the uneven paving and almost ended up sprawling headlong. Shaking his head he reduced his pace. He slowed to a gentle stroll, and continued along the street, hoping to find a road or track to the left by which he might make his way back to the car park without having to pass through the centre of the village. Another minute after that, as the road straightened out and grew yet wider it became clear that there was no such turning. He stopped and hung his head in exasperation, furious with himself.

Immediately to his right the flickering flame of a candle caught his eye. The door to one of the grand houses was wide open, propped with an oddly smooth, black, octagonal stone for which he could imagine no function. He looked inside and was immediately enchanted by the tranquil beauty of the shady interior. The walls were a pale, chalky grey and the floors were smooth and shiny, like polished stone but with a sense of depth, as though they had been lacquered countless times. Curiosity overcame him, that and an unconscious desire to escape his current troubles. He took a step closer, leaned on the stone architrave and stuck his head inside. In the far left corner of the room a passage led through to a parlour overlooking the garden; immediately to the left of where he stood a tightly wound staircase, so narrow as to be almost unusable, descended into the gloomy depths. The furniture was quite dainty. A chaise longue, upholstered in a pale, creamy calico and no more than a metre and a half in length, appeared ancient but well-preserved. In the centre of the room sat a dark oak table, knee high, with magazines and knick knacks arranged on the surface; at its centre sat a goldfish bowl in which there floated a single white water lily in full bloom. Next to the bowl stood the candle, its flame dancing inside a glass cylinder. The smoke was scented with something familiar, cloves or cinnamon. He filled his lungs with its sweetness,

breathing deeply and finding that it calmed him. Either side of the
table, a pair of small armchairs had been covered to match the
chaise. An oblivious cat was curled up asleep on one of them.
Everywhere there were oddities and unusual objects, among them
some peculiarly phallic African carvings, several brass scientific
instruments of unguessable provenance, a shoal of fish made from
driftwood, a pair of stone lions and a rather forlorn looking stuffed
elephant missing its ears. Martelli found himself enthralled.
Without thinking, he stepped across the threshold, ducking to
avoid the low lintel, and then just stood there, a little hunched,
blinking as his eyes got used to the dim light, smiling again, his
anger subsiding, his embarrassment temporarily forgotten.

　　All at once there was a pronounced creaking noise from the
bottom of the stairs as someone mounted the lowest step. He
tensed his body, his immediate instinct to turn and leave. The
door was just a single pace behind him. He could be out of sight
before this person emerged from the shadows. But something
changed his mind; something gripped him and rooted him to the
spot. It was, he supposed, as he stood there waiting to face
whoever surfaced, plain old tiredness mixed with the knowledge
that few things could be more awkward than what he'd just
experienced in the piazza. There were more creaking sounds,
drawing nearer. He glanced at his shoes, frowned as he noticed
they were dusty, and then turned to look towards the stairway.
She stood at the top of the steps with one hand on the banister and
the other on her hip. Her hazelnut shell hair was tied in an unruly
ponytail, coming adrift at the sides. A pair of sunglasses was
perched on top of her head. She looked perplexed but, to
Martelli's great relief, he detected also a little amusement in her

eyes. He summoned a smile and said, "Hello again."

EIGHTEEN

In Cristina's hand was a set of car keys and Martelli swiftly realised that the door was propped open because she had just carried something into the house. Even in the dim light her grey green eyes shone with optimism and kindness, and also an inquisitiveness that was almost childlike, belied by her crow's feet and the matching wrinkles either side of her nose. Her angular cheeks were on the rosy side, giving her an outdoorsy air, and he saw immediately that she was quick to smile, although right at that moment her expression was more one of curiosity than welcome. Her hair had streaks of golden blond and her face and arms were peppered with copper freckles. She wore an ankle length, pale green linen dress, the straps tied behind her neck, revealing her smooth shoulders and back. He guessed that she was in her late forties but she could just as easily have been a young looking fifty-five.

He shook his head and raised his hands in surrender.

"I realise how this must look but honestly I had no idea it

was your house."

She raised her eyebrows at this, lowered her chin and looked at him doubtfully.

"I apologise", he said. "The door was open and it looked so . . . calm inside."

"Calm?" she said as though uttering the word for the first time. She blinked and turned to survey the room.

He nodded. "Yes, it seems a very . . . relaxing place to be." Slowly he began to lower his hands. "I am very sorry," he added, in what he hoped was a convincingly sincere tone. "I didn't mean to frighten you."

She frowned at this and said, absolutely pokerfaced, "You didn't frighten me. I have a gun."

He stared at her, motionless.

"But it's all right," she added. "You can put your hands down." Her expression remained deadpan.

They stood in silence for a moment then she said, "So what brings you here, to the village?"

He sighed heavily, looking down at his dusty shoes. "Folly really. I'm investigating a . . . a crime, only I'm not supposed to be."

She stared at him, reading his face, making an assessment.

"Well", she said, shaking her head and smiling, delighting him and finally putting him at ease with those brilliant teeth, "that makes no sense to me at all. I was just about to make lunch. Maybe you can explain while we eat."

Martelli was taken aback. She had wrong-footed him again.

"I . . . I'd love to", he said. "Eat lunch, I mean." And

immediately he regretted the eagerness in his voice. Dear god, he thought, I sound like a frisky teenager.

"Don't get your hopes too high," she said with a giggle. "I'm not much of a cook, I'm afraid." She nodded towards the street. "Can you pull the door shut?" Then she turned and headed back downstairs, calling over her shoulder, "The kitchen's down here."

He stepped outside for a moment, raised his eyes to the heavens and shrugged. Then he closed the door and followed her downstairs.

* * *

Martelli sat on a warm stone bench, elbows on a table made from old floorboards, looking out across the plunging valley and taking pleasure in the sound of birdsong and the perfume of the abundant flowers and aromatic plants in Cristina's magnificent garden. Around him gravel pathways criss-crossed between patches of lawn and beds filled with flowering shrubs and cacti. Everywhere there were stone basins and earthenware pots overflowing with herbs and blooms. He recognised nasturtiums, violets, roses and bright yellow calendulas, all, he seemed to remember, edible. There were several varieties of tomato, from tiny scarlet spheres to huge misshapen green lumps the size of his fist, and also chillies of all strains and colours including a tantalising red so rich and deep it was almost black in places. Way down on the garden's lower levels he saw full-figured avocados, swollen purple figs, glossy sour cherries and luminous lemons, limes and kumquats alongside beds of onions, and yellow and

orange flowering zucchini. It was, he thought, a paradise, a
Garden of Eden.

Way over on the far side of the valley sunlight glinted off the
windows of an ancient church perched in a clearing on the thickly
wooded hillside. He could just make out the line of a narrow road,
snaking through the trees towards it. Electricity cables looped
their way up and over the hills as though in the footsteps of a
giant. Overhead, the pale blue of the sky was unbroken: no clouds,
no vapour trails.

On the terrace immediately below where he sat, nestling
between bushes of rich, dark foliage, sat a deep tub formed from
sheets of hand beaten copper, folded, soldered and riveted
together and fashioned into roughly the shape of a giant tea cup
with a wide lip around its top edge. It was full of water, with a few
leaves and flower petals floating on the surface. Two people would
fit inside it comfortably, he mused. Jutting out of one side, where
the handle of the tea cup would be, was a coil of stainless steel
pipe, like the filament from a giant electric light bulb. Martelli
couldn't immediately fathom its purpose.

Looking over to his right, between the houses, he could just
make out the comings and goings outside Mario Rossetti's house.

"So you're a detective, then," she said, suddenly appearing
at his shoulder. He jumped. She smiled at this and nodded in the
direction in which he'd just been looking. "Are you with them?"

As she spoke, she placed a wooden board on the table in
front of him. It was laden with ham and cheese along with fruit
and vegetables and a little vase of flowers, all, he assumed, from
her garden.

"No, I'm not." Quickly changing the subject, he said,

sincerely, "You have a wonderful place here. The house is lovely and this garden really is extraordinary."

"Thank you. You wouldn't say that if you had to maintain it. It takes a lot of work."

"You do all this yourself?" he said, wide eyed.

"Of course," she said, bemused. "Who else would do it?"

"I imagined you had a . . . help." Did she think I was going to say 'husband'? he wondered.

She handed him a plate. "No. Just me."

She went back into the house and returned a few moments later carrying two glasses and a jug of water with wedges of orange floating in it.

"Would you prefer wine?"

Martelli shook his head and smiled. "No, this is perfect," he said. "Thank you." And, after he said it, he thought that in fact it really was close to perfect, not merely the water of course but the situation, lunch with this vivacious woman in a garden of splendour and serenity. His confrontation with Rubini, though not forgotten, was readily swept aside, consigned to another world in a matter of minutes.

A dog appeared from inside the house, a blue merle border collie with one pale brown eye and one milky grey one. It came and sat at the end of the table, looking expectantly at Cristina. She gave it a sliver of ham which it wolfed down immediately. It sat waiting for another.

"This is Cosimo," she said. "Named after my husband. I only feed him from the table when I eat outside. He looks good for nine, no?"

"Oh," said Martelli, trying not to sound disappointed.

"Doesn't that cause confusion when you call him? Don't they both come running."

She laughed. "My husband hasn't come running for twenty years. Not since we got divorced. He didn't come running much before that either."

She served him some ham and they lapsed into a comfortable silence while they loaded their plates.

* * *

"The police are looking in the wrong place, I think."

"What makes you say that?" said Martelli, leaning forward to scrutinise her face, and then reminding himself that she wasn't a suspect or a witness, and that he wasn't even a policeman. He leaned back again.

"Mario has a place in the woods, high up above the village, an old farmhouse with a barn and a chestnut drying house a few kilometres from here. I've seen him up there." She saw the puzzled look on Martelli's face and added, "I go foraging in the woods, for funghi - mostly porcini but I have high hopes of Cosimo sniffing out some white truffles." She smiled and reached down to stroke the dog's head.

"Did you see him there just once or . . ?"

"No – several times. He drives up there in that noisy old Land Rover of his. There's no road, just a track, and it's pretty steep in places. He revs the engine like crazy. I've seen him with his mate, who's Polish, I think. That's what Mariella in the shop told me anyway." She shrugged and took a sip of water.

"Could you show me this place?"

123

She nodded. "Of course. It's a long walk though. And you'll need boots. And we can't go today because I have to be in Finale at four. In fact . . ." she ducked her head and squinted, peering in through the kitchen window, "Ooh – I have to get going. The time has flown."

And it had, he thought. They had talked about many things, from Martelli's upbringing in Loano, with his tannery worker father and schoolteacher mother, to hers in Amsterdam, with her artist mother and absent Italian father, in whose carefully cultivated garden they now sat. He had left her the house upon his death five years previously. She explained her surprise that 'the old Lothario' as she called him, though fondly, had somehow failed to father any other children with his 'numerous women'.

Like Martelli's mother, Cristina was a schoolteacher, at a Montessori school in Amsterdam. This was her first full summer in Castelvecchio and she intended it to be the first of many.

She drove him up to the car park in her creaking but elegant old Citroën DS. He struggled to enter her number into his phone as the car juddered and lurched on the unmade road.

"I love the name DS," she said, after giving him the last digit. She turned to face him, smiling. "Déesse is the French word for goddess."

Martelli chuckled but didn't tell her what he was thinking. They made a date for three days hence to trek up into the forest for a look at Mario Rossetti's hideaway. He was eager to get up there but Cristina couldn't do it any sooner because she had a friend coming to stay. He had wanted to ask if it was a male friend but held his tongue.

She kissed him goodbye, just a peck on the cheek really

but, as he watched the old, white car roar off, wallowing on its famed hydropneumatic suspension, he fancied he could still feel where her lips had touched him.

NINETEEN

Ted counted seven vapour trails in the otherwise clear blue sky on what was certainly the best day so far of a disappointing summer. It was warm and sunny with high humidity and just a hint of a breeze rustling the leaves on the lime trees in the hospital grounds. He weighed his mobile phone in his hand, wondering whether to return Caroline's call. They were, she had said in her message, supposed to be buying paint for the spare room, which he was then to decorate. Why they were planning to decorate the spare room of their rented flat when she was so keen to move out, he could not fathom. She had sounded angry. He scanned the undulating trees, turning on the spot, looking for nothing in particular. No, he thought, he would do this first; he would get it over with then clear his head before calling her.

He had left Becky King's place in a hurry, pausing only to ask her if she had a recent photograph of Warren Devlin. The holiday snap that she had handed over featured two men grinning broadly on a tropical beach. Becky herself stood between them, pouting drunkenly, wearing a white bikini more suitable for a woman twenty years younger and twenty pounds lighter. Ted couldn't help but wonder if she had chosen the picture because she featured so prominently in it. It had been taken in Thailand, Becky had said, five months previously. All three were smoking and drinking beer. They held their bottles towards the camera as though making a toast. In the middle distance, a pair of brightly coloured long tail boats had been beached on the wide expanse of pale sand. He could clearly see the many ribbons and braids tied around their high stems. In the background of the picture, towering over everything, like a colossal primitive arrowhead pointing at the sky, was a karst limestone rock formation hundreds of feet high, its lower slopes a dense mass of emerald palm fronds. Ted recognised it as West Railay Beach on the Andaman coast in Krabi Province. He and Caroline had been there a few years previously. According to Becky, the other man was Warren's best friend, Paul. Compared to Warren, Paul was pale and fleshy, his shoulders raw with sunburn. The cigarette in his hand was unmistakably a joint. Ah, Ted had thought. Was this the elusive Paul Finch?

* * *

The pathologist was much younger than Ted had expected, with a neatly trimmed beard and drainpipe trousers. A badge on his white lab coat said his name was Alan Moody. He smiled broadly and welcomed Ted into his tiny office in a broad Scots accent; east coast, Ted guessed. They shook hands and Moody led him across the corridor and through a pair of double doors into a large room with no windows.

The smell of disinfectant was sweet and sickly and so immediately and powerfully reminiscent of his previous mortuary visits that Ted clenched his stomach involuntarily. In the windowless chamber the day's warm sunlight was replaced by stark, white, characterless fluorescence; vents in the ceiling kept the air chilly and dry. Work benches ran along each of the four walls but the room was dominated by three examination tables, equally spaced, with an array of task lights hanging low over each of them, putting Ted in mind of a macabre pool hall. Two of the tables were empty but on the third, the furthest from the door, lay a bloated, partially consumed corpse the like of which Ted had never seen. The skin had taken on the appearance of wet papier-mâché - grey and moist and waterlogged - and it seemed to have come adrift of its moorings. There was a soggy looseness about it, which Ted found revolting but also compelling. Great chunks of flesh were missing from the arms and legs and crucially also the face. He swallowed. More than anything else it was the smells that he found most difficult to tolerate. The vinegary aroma of decomposition in combination with the foul gases of the gut made him want to retch. But the noises too were something to which he would never grow accustomed - the sucking and squelching as the body's cavities were explored. His mouth felt dry and his feet heavy. As they drew closer he reminded himself that he didn't have to do this. He could simply wait for the report then glance briefly at gruesome photographs and see the stomach contents as a list rather than something slopped into a bowl. But he always felt he owed it to the victims in his charge to attend their final examinations.

The pathologist was still smiling, a little too cheerily for Ted's liking, but then he supposed they had to get by how they could, those who dealt with the dead, and he should just be grateful that there were people in the world prepared to do it.

As they arrived at the table, Ted grimaced and suppressed a shudder. He tried to breathe only through his mouth.

"We'll have to identify him from his dental records," said the pathologist. "Assuming he's British, that is. If he's a foreigner it's going to take a lot longer."

"Can you give me anything at all?" said Ted.

"Well, he's a Caucasian male, between thirty and forty years old. He is one hundred and eighty centimetres tall – that's six feet. He has dark brown hair and brown eyes and he was pretty athletic I'd say, probably spent a good bit of time at the gym."

Ted wondered if he'd ever encountered Warren Devlin working one of the heavy bags or lifting weights at Harry Jay's club. He had recognised neither the face in the bogus passport photos nor the man in the picture found in Warren Devlin's ransacked flat but there was something vaguely familiar about both of the men standing on that beach in Thailand.

"He drowned, I take it?"

The young pathologist hesitated so long that Ted was on the brink of asking the question again.

"Well, he did drown . . ." The young man faltered, his smile subsiding.

"But?"

"But he didn't *just* drown . . ." Ted inclined his head. "I'm not sure how exactly," continued the pathologist. "But this man was unwell."

"What do you mean?"

"I'll have to carry out a few more tests. In fact, I've been in touch with a colleague of mine at Guys and St. Thomas's in London . . ."

"What sort of tests?"

"Well . . . this sounds rather vague, I know, but I think he might have been suffering from . . . some sort of sickness."

"So he was ill when he drowned?"

"Yes."

"Ill how?"

"I'm afraid I don't know that yet."

Ted sensed that the young doctor knew more than he was letting on.

"Well, was it just a cold or was it cancer?"

Moody sighed and inclined his head, his gaze fixed on the body.

"Look . . . I . . ." He raised his eyes. "Give me a day or two and I'll make him talk."

Ted jerked his head back, frowning deeply.

Moody shrugged. "That's what we do here," he said. "We're magicians – we make dead people tell tales."

TWENTY

Martelli placed his coffee cup on the parapet wall, put his hands flat on either side of it and leaned over, breathing in the nutty aroma while looking down into the teeming caruggi. The residents were mobilising, heading out to church and to visit relatives on what looked set to be another day of record temperatures. He watched, feeling as though he might throw up at any moment; wondering if any of his neighbours were in a similarly dissolute state. The Trigianis, he knew, liked a drink, and Signora Miconi was frequently to be heard lecturing her chickens after polishing off a bottle or two.

Four hours earlier, he had woken sprawled awkwardly on his rooftop bench to find that he'd vomited copiously during the night. A vile-smelling orange slurry was slopped over the teak table and his clothes; crusted on the side of his face and in his hair. He had a terrible pain in his neck, a trapped nerve, and his lower back ached from his having lain with it twisted. His vision had spun freely as he hauled himself gingerly to his feet, and he'd feared he might be sick a second time as he slowly made his way down the clanging spiral staircase and into the bedroom. Undressing consumed the last dregs of his energy. He crawled onto the bed, sunk into the pillows and was asleep.

When he opened his eyes, they burned as though stung by soap and his throat felt parched and brittle. Any movement triggered spasms in the muscles of his neck and once more his jaw ached as though he had been grinding his teeth in his sleep. There was a thumping in his head which started somewhere high up at the back of his skull, lanced through the centre of his brain and finished as intermittent pressure behind his eyes. He reached a hand to his face and found that his fingers throbbed painfully. The knuckles felt swollen and stiff.

In the bathroom, he held the edge of the sink with one hand, squeezed his eyes tight shut and breathed deeply, taking his time, filling his lungs to capacity. The air felt cool on the back of his throat. Opening his eyes again, he stared into the plughole for a few seconds, tutting and letting his shoulders sag with the weight of his self-loathing. Bleakly he reached for an expensive bar of soap, a gift from an ex-girlfriend long ago. Handmade, purchased in a little shop just a short walk away, it smelled of rosemary. He held it to his nose, savouring the aroma, and was reminded of his mother.

At a loose end the previous evening, and once more furious at himself for having allowed Rubini to catch him out so easily, he'd opened a bottle of wine, and then another, and the last thing he remembered clearly was losing his temper and punching the wall next to the bathroom door. At some point, he'd somehow made it up the spiral stairs, and presumably he'd managed to roll a joint or two, which would explain his ragged throat, but he couldn't recall having eaten anything or indeed the reverse of that process.

In the shower he leaned heavily against the tiles, letting the water flow over his body for a long time. Twice he experimented with a dramatic drop in temperature in an effort to perk himself up but he was unable to stand it for more than a few seconds each time. Noticing blood under a toenail, he frowned, before remembering that he had, for only the second time since abandoning it on the stairs all those years before, stubbed his toe on the stone head. As he stepped out of the cubicle he was barely able to raise his head to look into the bathroom mirror.

In a towelling robe, he made his way downstairs, wincing at the pronounced clicking of his knees. He opened the kitchen windows, pushed the shutters aside and, as the bells of the clocktower struck seven, hunted for painkillers. Finding none, he swore quietly and put on a pot of coffee, spilling grounds all over the counter top as he did so.

Outside, the neighbourhood was already approaching full song, the residents eager to get going before the onslaught of the wilting summer heat. Across the street, old man Trigiani, great-grandfather to the miscreant brothers, made bestial moaning noises. He had always been a colourless man, a diluted version of a human being, but now, aged ninety-something he was a shrivelled wraith, who announced to the world his continued existence with an occasional bout of energetic coughing and these degenerate lowing sounds. He had lived in that same house for as long as Martelli could remember, and that, Martelli reminded himself, was a very long time.

From below the kitchen window came the familiar discordant chiming of wine bottles as Eduardo began rearranging his shop. Martelli closed one eye at the inharmonious racket and, as he waited for the coffee to boil, went through the motions of tidying up, sliding dirty plates through the amber lenses of grease floating on the cold, cloudy water in the kitchen sink. The plates clunked against glass tumblers and settled on dishes from . . . The night before? He couldn't remember. He shook his head and tossed a fork in after them. As the competing clock began to strike seven, he was saved any further feeble pretence at domesticity by the spluttering of the tarnished aluminium coffee pot.

* * *

By the time Martelli leaned over the parapet, Marco the florist was already pedalling past - squeak, clunk, squeak, clunk - on the way to his shop on Via Garibaldi, and the queue at the bakers was beginning to clog the far end of the street. Martelli watched, wanly amused, as Signora Trigiani conducted her reluctant father, yawning husband and disobedient sons from third floor to street level and off to church. She had long since given up trying to persuade the old man to accompany them. These days she simply left him slumped, unblinking in front of the television.

An elderly lady, whose face and gait Martelli recognised but whose name he did not know, made her way down Via Richeri, a huge canvas shopper in tow. He was struck, as always, by her peculiar walk, an eccentric dance, in which she swung one leg as though the hip were frozen and then stamped the foot down hard. She paused and licked her lips after every step, steeling herself for the next one. Her hair was dyed that peculiar dark ochre colour favoured by women of a certain age and generation, and she was dressed as always in mourning. To Martelli she appeared constructed from little more than twigs and twine. A young man strode past and bid her a cheery 'Buongiorno!' She smiled and said something quietly in return, raising a bony hand in greeting too late for him to notice. There was a general air of determination about her, a stoicism Martelli couldn't help but admire.

As he watched the comings and goings, he thought how much he would miss Bracco's company; his unflinching cheerfulness and enthusiasm. In naive moments, dreams really, Martelli had imagined one day handing over the reins to the young detective. He also thought, though guiltily, how relieved he was he didn't have to face Nardi's questions that morning. His old friend preferred a lie in on Sundays, gathering his strength before visiting his mother in Dolceacqua, a small town north of Ventimiglia, where she lived with her sister and, if what Piero said was to be believed, did little but drink Rossese and totter about breaking things.

By a quarter to eight, it seemed the entire population of the old town was out on the streets. Adults marshalled toddlers, older children were yanked into formation, stragglers were rounded up and given a finger-wagging, pushchairs were carted outside and elderly relatives aided down steep stone steps. Entire families emerged in loose knots; watery-eyed, hair still damp from the shower. Harassed mothers nipped back inside to retrieve forgotten purses, bags, hats, glasses, handkerchiefs and even shoes, before returning to lead their charges to Mass, all in the summer version of their Sunday best.

Martelli took the wrapper off the little biscotti he'd brought
to dunk in his coffee and considered the fate of Steven Finch. If
your intention is simply to kill a man, he thought, to eliminate
him, then you do so as quickly and cleanly as your resources will
allow. You leave as little evidence as possible. You may even
dispose of the body - not too difficult a task in a coastal town. But
Steven Finch had not merely been killed, he had been subjected to
the most brutal, the most depraved, the most unspeakable torture.
And no effort had been made to conceal that fact. So either his
killer, or killers, had been trying to extract information from him
or they were making a statement, warning others not to cross
them as Steven had. Had the Englishman inadvertently stepped
on the toes of one of the large crime syndicates – the Nuova Mala
del Brenta or the Unione Corse? Or a North African ring?
Certainly there was organised crime in Loano and all along the
Riviera, the smuggling of drugs and cigarettes being among their
key sources of income. The coastline was like a leaking sieve and,
short of putting a line of Carabinieri along the beach at night there
was simply no way of keeping track of all the comings and goings,
of either people or merchandise. Despite the best efforts of the
Polizia di Stato and Guardia Costiera, smuggling was an industry
almost rivalling manufacturing. And the competing groups meted
out their own form of justice with depressing though relatively
infrequent regularity. He thought back to a past case, the brutal
murder of a middle-aged couple at their home in Boissano. The
wife had been tortured in order, it had been supposed though
never proven, to persuade the husband to give up his contacts.
Their killings had been linked to organised crime though the case

was never solved. At the time of the incident, he had been a police officer for just a few months. On first seeing the couple's remains, he had rushed outside to vomit. But Martelli had seen nothing even close to the level of cruelty inflicted upon his client's brother. Simple murders, yes – far too many. Punishment killings too, and even occasionally, as in the Boissano case, torture. But nothing quite like this, nothing quite so . . . He stared out over the rooftops. Personal. He twisted the biscotti wrapper into a chord and tied a knot in it, a habit he'd developed as a boy. That was it, he thought, pushing the crackling plastic into the pocket of his robe. There was something almost intimate about the way in which Steven Finch had been killed. His tormentor must have spent a long time with him, especially if he'd waited to make sure Steven was dead. He wondered if Finch had been terrorised before his death, told in detail what was about to happen, perhaps given a taste, a quick splash of the acid to whet his appetite for what was to come. He shuddered and felt his gorge rising. He needed to find out more about these businessmen with whom Steven took his late night boat trips, and he needed to find Steven's partner, Mario Rossetti.

A stooped old man with a stick - sole resident of a gloomy galleon of a house several streets away, its tattered awnings like the ragged sails of a ghost ship – appeared at the end of the street. He walked with agonizing ponderousness, bent as a question mark, parting the crowds like a rock in a stream. He had the waxy complexion and permanent hangdog expression of someone not long for this Earth, with a hint of yellow as though he'd been mildly smoked. His navy blazer had a pink silk handkerchief escaping from the breast pocket; his wheat linen trousers were stained on the thighs. Martelli was able to lean back, take a sip of coffee, replace his cup on the wall and resume his stance without the old man making any discernible progress in the meantime. A young woman jogger, a tourist by the look of her, stepped out of a doorway and began weaving through the throng on her way, Martelli presumed, to the lungomare. As she passed by, the old man turned to watch her bounce effortlessly out of sight, and continued watching long after she was gone, smiling to himself. Martelli chuckled. There was blood still pumping through the old boy's veins.

The sun was already high in the sky and it warmed his arms and the back of his neck. Soon the roof would be too hot for bare feet. He glanced around at the terracotta pots arrayed around the walls of his sanctuary, the remnants of an attempt, two years previously, to grow a small crop of fruit and vegetables along with a few decorative plants. Only the cacti had survived, thriving in the heat, the rest had withered and died, neglected and unwatered; their corpses lay crisp and brown on soil so arid it had contracted to leave a pronounced gap around the edge of the pots. Perhaps he would ask Cristina's advice about rooftop propagation, he thought. It would give him an excuse to invite her over. The prospect of their trip into the mountains lifted his spirits and galvanised him into action. He threw back the last of his coffee and headed downstairs.

Back in the bathroom, he splashed water on his face, slicked his hair back and scooped some clothes from the floor, examining the trousers for stains and sniffing under the arms of the shirt before putting them on and heading downstairs. He left his coffee cup bobbing in the sink and made for the door but, halfway down the stairs, had a thought, returned to the living room and picked up a dusty and rarely used pair of sunglasses from the hexagonal table. Wiping the lenses on his shirt, he put them on, took a deep breath and, mustering what determination he could, launched himself into the noisy torrent of people. He was due to meet his client the following day and was determined, in the intervening time, to make some progress.

TWENTY-ONE

Sunday started badly in south east London. It had dawned dull with a nip in the air and leaden clouds threatening rain, and Ted had crept outside to find that he had a flat tyre. He had then skinned his knuckles badly while changing the wheel and had had to return to the flat to wash his hands and apply some antiseptic. Hunting through the medicine cabinet, he'd knocked over a glass bottle, which had shattered in the sink, waking Caroline, who'd appeared at the bathroom door with a murderous expression.

They had rowed the night before. Chester had failed to turn up for his dinner and Ted was worried that his old cat might be lying injured somewhere, scragged by a fox in the thistly wilderness at the bottom of the garden they shared with two other flats. Either that or he was locked in a greenhouse or garage, where he would starve while the owners sunned themselves on the Algarve. For most of the evening Ted had walked the nearby streets looking for him, much to the annoyance of Caroline, who kept repeating that Chester would 'come home when he's hungry'.

She was already angry at Ted for spending the day working. And so they had fought, Caroline returning to the familiar themes of his job and its demands, along with the newer unfavourable comparisons of their own home life with that of their friends. They'd gone to bed still at loggerheads, a chasm between them. Ted had been awake when the birds started their chorus. He had hoped to leave for work without rousing her.

* * *

On the way to the station, he made a call, expecting to leave a message, but Simpson picked up after just three rings.

"Jim. It's Ted Logan here."

"Hi, Ted." He sounded wide awake.

"Hi. Listen – sorry to call so early on a Sunday. What can you tell me about Warren Devlin's car?"

"Not a lot, I'm afraid. It's clean."

Ted frowned. "What do you mean 'clean'?" he said irritably. "I thought that only happened on the telly. There must be a print or part of one somewhere, surely?"

"Nope, nothing at all. The driver must have worn gloves. In fact he must have worn gloves every time he drove the car. Some people do, you know," he finished testily, clearly annoyed at Ted's tone.

Ted took a deep breath. "Look, Jim, I'm sorry, it's just that I could do with a break on this case. At the moment it's a bloody mystery. Are you telling me that there is not one single fingerprint in or on the entire car?"

"That is exactly what I'm telling you. It looks like the driver or

141

drivers never touched the vehicle with bare hands. There are no prints on the passenger's side either, and it's obviously just been through a car wash because there's nothing on the bodywork, not even any kids' sticky finger marks." Simpson cleared his throat loudly.

"So the car tells us nothing, basically."

"No, the car tells us plenty. We have blood, mucus, skin, hair and what appears to be part of a contact lens, so an ID of the driver isn't completely out of the question. You'll have to give me a bit of time to process it but it's likely all we'll learn is that Warren Devlin wore contacts, picked his nose, cut himself shaving, was losing his hair, and parked his car at Stansted ten days ago and didn't get on a plane."

"Didn't?"

"Didn't. There's no record of anyone by that name having boarded a plane. Not at Stansted anyway."

"I see," said Ted, sighing deeply. "Okay, well, he might have been travelling under an assumed name using a fake passport. We're going to have to get someone to look through all of the security camera footage and see if he's on there. I'll get DC Burns to give you a call. Can you put him in touch with the officer in charge there?"

The mournful wail of a siren drowned out Simpson's response. Ted waited for it to pass before continuing.

"Jim?"

"I said, 'No problem'."

"Okay, Jim. Thanks for that and sorry to be grumpy."

"No worries. Speak to you later."

Ted hung up and immediately dialled another number. It

felt like an age before Alan Moody, the young pathologist, picked up.

"Have you had any luck identifying the body on the beach?"

"Not yet," said Moody sleepily. "I told you it might take a bit of time." He chuckled and stifled a yawn. "And luck has nothing to do with it."

Ted winced. "You did. I apologise. Do you know if he was wearing contact lenses?"

Moody considered this for a moment. "Well, he's not wearing any now but they might have been washed away. He was in the water for a while. I'll check again to make sure there's nothing around the sides of the eyeballs."

Ted let that image fade before thanking the young pathologist.

"No worries," said Moody. "Of course, as soon as we know who he is, I'll be able to confirm whether he needed glasses and if so, whether or not he ever wore lenses."

Ted thanked him again and rang off.

* * *

Sitting at his desk, with half an hour to go before the progress meeting was due to begin, he called DC Burns.

"Have you managed to get hold of Paul Finch?"

"No. I've left loads of messages on his voicemail but he hasn't got back to me. Maybe he doesn't pick them up when he's abroad."

"You'd think he would though, wouldn't you? This week, I mean. His brother's been killed. Surely he has to keep in touch with the Italian police?"

Burns thought about this for a moment. "Maybe not, maybe he just checks in with them every day. Maybe he's staying right next door to the police station."

"What's the name of the town again?"

"Loano," said Burns slowly, unsure of his pronunciation.

"And where is that?"

"North west. About sixty miles from the French border."

"What do the local police say?"

"I spoke to a bloke called Bracco, whose English isn't great. The officer in charge of the investigation's called Rubini but he doesn't speak English at all."

"And?"

"He gave me an address but no landline phone number, so all I've got is a mobile and an email. I'll keep trying but short of flying out there and knocking on his door . . ." Burns sniffed loudly.

"Can't the Italians send someone to knock on his door?"

"I did ask that."

"And?" said Ted impatiently.

"I'm not sure I got the message across."

"Do we know when he's due back here? Is he booked on a flight?"

"Nope. He drove there. Got the ferry from Dover to Calais. One way ticket."

Ted pondered this information for a few moments.

"Okay," he said, resignedly. "Where are you now?"

"I'm on my way in. I'll be there in a minute or two."

TWENTY-TWO

Flavia Buonanno was a plump, baby-faced woman, with rosy apple cheeks, a halo of curly bleached hair and stubby fingers adorned with around a dozen tarnished silver rings. In her short, white, toga dress she looked like a cherub fallen from a chapel ceiling, although the tattoo of a dolphin on her ankle, revealed when she stepped out from behind the counter, rather spoiled that image.

Thinking Martelli a customer, she greeted him with a lukewarm smile and an expression somewhere between apathy and indifference.

"Buongiorno," she sighed. "How can I help you?"

The shop where Estella worked was exactly where Ricardo had described: directly opposite Valdini's car repair workshop on Via Mazzini in Alassio, a few kilometres south west of Loano. It was a smart boutique selling crockery and napiery, fabrics and tassels, cake stands, vases, storage jars, scented candles and other accessories for the home – what Martelli would have termed bric-a-brac had it not been new and expensive. There were also numerous items of furniture, mostly distressed, and a selection of handmade greetings cards. A pair of thin, middle-aged women wearing oversized sunglasses was browsing at the far end of the shop, occasionally muttering to one another but other than that and the faint strains of Elgar's 'In the South' emanating from hidden speakers, the place was quiet.

The prices struck Martelli as unusually high, even for a wealthy town like Alassio, but what seemed to him most unusual of all were the proprietor herself - the overweight cherub, Flavia - and an older woman crouched behind her, slowly unpacking a cardboard box filled with smaller household items wrapped in newspaper. She had the glassy eyes and slow, deliberate movements of a habitual heavy drinker; her long, iron grey hair was tied in a loose pony tail. Both women seemed out of place in an establishment which surely relied on a veneer of sophistication when attracting customers.

"I'm looking for Estella," he said, smiling. "Do you know where I might find her?"

Flavia glanced nervously at the customers, tapped the older woman on the shoulder then gestured for Martelli to follow her.

"I've no idea where she is," she hissed, once they were in the office at the back of the shop.

Martelli found his gaze drawn to her teeth, small and pointed and thick with morsels of food. She must have noticed because she clamped her lips shut. He guessed that she was in her late twenties; in age if not physical resemblance, the older woman might have been her mother. She sat down behind a desk and he, though not invited to do so, sat down in the chair opposite.

"Do you have a phone number for her?" Martelli smiled.

"Who are you exactly?" said Flavia, glowering at him.

He was momentarily caught off guard by her animosity. "I . . . I'm investigating the murder of an English man called Steven Finch. He was one of Estella's friends."

She shook her head vigorously. "Never heard of him. I can't help you." Her words came at him like poison darts.

"You never know what might turn out to be important," he said, quickly regaining his composure and trying to maintain a measured, polite tone.

"I haven't seen Estella for weeks. I've no idea what she's up to."

"You're not in touch with her? She hasn't called?"

She shrugged.

"Do you know where she lives?"

"She's looking after her mother. Her mother's sick, apparently." Flavia clearly doubted this assessment.

"And where is her mother? In hospital?"

"At home."

"And where's that? Here? In Alassio?"

"Tuscany - a place called Barga."

Martelli knew Barga. It was in the north of Tuscany, in the Garfagnana. He had been there, many years previously, with his wife, though before they were married, while things were still good between them.

"And Estella's staying with her, is she?"

Flavia shrugged. She tilted her head to look through the open door, caught the older woman's attention and nodded towards the customers. She then made a deliberate show of looking at a wall clock, a gesture which Martelli countered by slouching and crossing his legs, letting her know that he was settling in, that he had the measure of her.

"So," he said, amiably. "Is Estella in danger of losing her job here . . ?" He tailed off with a wave of his hand.

Flavia frowned deeply. "Her job?"

"Yes. I mean, if she hasn't showed up for work for two weeks, presumably you're thinking of finding a permanent replacement. No?"

Flavia looked at him pityingly. "But this is Estella's place. She owns it. I'm just the manager."

* * *

Martelli left with Estella Ramazzotti's mobile phone number but no address for the ailing mother. However, the charmless Signorina Buonanno, after a little sighing and eye-rolling, had given him rough directions to the house in Barga, perhaps seeing some advantage for herself in having Martelli find her absent boss. Estella's apartment in Alassio had been sublet, apparently, to a distant cousin.

Outside, instead of crossing the street to his car, he turned left out of the shop, then left again, walked past a beautifully manicured public garden and took a stroll down the Budello, the pedestrianised, granite-paved street which wound its way through the centre of the old town, running roughly parallel to the shore just a few metres away.

Little more than a passage by modern standards, the Budello was bustling with holidaying families seeking shade and a bite to eat after baking on the beach. He smiled at children in pushchairs as they gazed wide eyed at the multitude of delights on display. Mingling with this throng a few heavily tanned yachtsmen in pristine white linen strolled arm in arm with their bejewelled, and more often than not much younger wives, stopping to take in the window display of every boutique. He smiled at them too, the wives, when they caught his eye.

He passed through a square packed with restaurant tables, every chair occupied. Palm trees so tall they seemed spindly reached for the sky between the buildings, their foliage hanging limp and motionless high above his head. Not a breath of wind, he thought, even here, just a few metres from the sea.

There were a few gelaterias along the Budello, and a handful of the usual seaside shops selling brightly-coloured inflatables and beach toys for the kids, but most of the street was given over to designer boutiques and jewellery stores aimed at the kind of tourists once referred to as the 'jet set'. That had been Alassio's heyday, the era of the jetsetters in the boom years after World War Two. The town had grown then, exponentially, into a year-round resort, and everywhere were the architectural characteristics of the fifties and sixties. It still attracted enough well-heeled visitors to keep the more exclusive shops afloat but Martelli found the town peculiarly characterless. It seemed trapped in time, the wrong time, no longer popular, neither overtly historic nor sleek and chic. Nowadays it relied more heavily on the ordinary Italian tourists who filled the many bars and restaurants along the seafront and in the streets and squares through which he passed. Those tourists packed the slender, sandy, fee-paying beach, while the town's residents tended to hang out at the eastern end of the bay, the public areas, around the pier - the Pontile

Bestoso - and beyond.

By the time he reached the third gelateria, Martelli could no longer resist and stopped for an ice cream. Thinking of his client, he plumped for two scoops of the peculiarly-named Zuppa Inglese - English Soup: custard yellow with pieces of fruit and chunks of chocolate, the flavour vaguely reminiscent of trifle, a dessert to which he was partial and which Nardi's Anglophile wife, Lena, served whenever he went to their place for dinner. Having had no breakfast, he tore into it greedily, and despatched it, cone and all, in the five minutes it took to stroll back to his car.

He'd parked directly outside Valdini's, the garage of choice for those Alassini fortunate enough to own exotic or classic cars. It had been in business since he was a little boy. Valdini's folding doors had been closed when he arrived but they now stood wide open and the unmistakeable smell of engine oil recalled the endless summers of his boyhood, he, Piero and Aldo on bicycles, stopping to gawp at the curvaceous Ferraris and gleaming Maseratis in for a tune up and tyre change.

He couldn't help but smile when he saw a scarlet Testarossa – a Redhead – up on the hydraulic lift. An old boy in tatty, oil-stained blue overalls stood underneath it, brandishing an inspection lamp and peering at its innards.

"Che bella macchina!" said Martelli, smiling broadly, wiping his fingers on a paper napkin.

The old boy shrugged, still looking up at the car. "You wouldn't say that if you had to pay the bills, Commissario."

Martelli frowned and ducked his head. Did he know this man?

The mechanic put down his lamp and stepped out into the

sunshine, wiping his greasy hand on the leg of his overalls and extending it in greeting. Martelli was astonished to see that it was old man Valdini himself, withered almost skeletal, his skin the colour of a freshly baked croissant and glossy with perspiration. The only marked change was a small V-shaped piece missing from his right nostril, as though a bird had taken a bite out of him.

They shook hands.

"Signor Valdini?" said Martelli, wide-eyed.

"Si," said the mechanic emphatically. Then he laughed. "I'm Vito, his son. My father passed away a few years ago. My brother and I run the place now."

Martelli chuckled as he realised his mistake, nodding while shaking the mechanic's hand.

"Well, I'm sorry to hear about your father but I'm glad to see this place is still going. I used to come here as a boy, to look at the cars."

"Oh, I remember," said the mechanic. "I was here. I did the washing and polishing." He nodded towards the kerb. "Right here on the street."

Martelli had vague memories of a sudsy teenager, his slicked back hair lustrous with pomade, shouting 'Ciao, bella!' to every girl who passed by, a cigarette hanging from his bottom lip. He smiled again.

"And whose is the Testarossa? I guess these are a classic now."

The old boy sighed. "It belongs to the Marchese di Zuccarello. His man brings it in for a service once a year." He shook his head. "I swear the only kilometres it clocks up are between here and the palazzo. He never drives the thing."

Martelli raised his eyebrows.

"I could probably buy my granddaughter a nice apartment for the price of this car," continued the old mechanic, still shaking his head. "And it was built to be driven. Honestly, to let it sit idle is madness." He clicked his tongue.

It was the exactly the sort of madness, the rich man's folly, that characterised this part of the world, thought Martelli, as he bid the old mechanic farewell and returned to his boat-like, ageing Lancia.

* * *

He drove through Albenga, past hectares of houseplants lined up under plastic canopies opaque with steam. Vast arrays of dribbling sprinklers, their nozzles linked by looping hoses, kept the plants alive. It was along this road - Via Aurelia - that the local prostitutes gathered after dark, loitering on street corners in groups of three or four. He pulled over at the entrance to a dusty farm track and took out his mobile phone. Barga was too far away, a journey for another day, so Estella would have to wait. And that left him with just one option - the Polish boy's girlfriend. He had to find Angela.

TWENTY-THREE

By noon a stiffening breeze had dispersed the cloud and the sun was streaming through the windows at Plumstead Police Station, lighting shafts of drifting dust in the large open plan office. Ted sat at his desk in the corner furthest from the door, stifling a yawn as he listened to his colleagues relate progress in the various investigations arising from the raid on Harry Jay's boxing club. Those not speaking shifted uncomfortably in their seats as the meeting progressed and the atmosphere grew more and more oppressively airless. Ted let his gaze wander idly around the room. A few feet from where he sat, a potted plant had entered the twilight of its life, its foliage curling and crisp at the tips; at its base what appeared to be a coconut kernel had begun to rot and collapse. Hanging from the bottom of his computer monitor, a yellow Post-It bore the words 'wine' and 'eggs' in his own writing. He read it and rolled his eyes. The blue carpet tiles were stained and worn beneath his desk and a black, shiny patch appeared to be compressed chewing gum brought in on either his or a predecessor's shoes. He wrinkled his nose. If it had been transferred from a predecessor's shoe, he thought gloomily, then it was at least seven years old. He puffed out his cheeks and leaned back. Overhead, the suspended ceiling tiles were stained yellow where the sprinkler system had leaked and there was a faint musty odour reminiscent of a pet hamster he'd had as a child. Mice, he thought, are an inevitable consequence of too many people too often eating at their desks. He remembered his flat tyre and itched to write another Post-It reminding him to get it replaced. The meeting dragged on, the voices fading to a drone. He stifled another yawn and found himself thinking of his gran in her little terraced house in Upper Belvedere with her ornaments and her smelly poodle. His monthly visit was always spent yawning and trying to stay awake while she chuntered on, the gas fire turned up way too high and every window locked, his grandad, when he was alive, constantly shushing her: 'Wheesht, woman! Can you not see I'm watching this?' But there was something about his gran's house - the warmth, the welcome, the reassuring familiarity, and, yes, the ceaseless prattle - that melted away his anxieties. He would always drop off in one of their turquoise Dralon armchairs, only to wake up and realise, shamefacedly, that she'd asked him a question: 'Can you put the immersion on? I'm going to have a bath later.' And from the tone of her voice he could tell that she was repeating it for the third time.

"Ted? Hello? DI Logan, are you awake over there?"

He opened his eyes to find everyone staring at him expectantly and his boss, Detective Superintendent Andrew Nichols, leaning against a desk near the door, gazing at him, eyebrows raised.

"Sorry, sir," he croaked. "I didn't sleep last night and it's quite stuffy in here." He shuffled upright in his seat, glancing around the room, catching the eye of a few colleagues as he did so. Some, he noticed, were amused, others relieved it wasn't them who'd been caught napping. How like school public institutions are, he reflected ruefully.

Nichols, not wearing a tie because it was the weekend, nodded impatiently. "How are you getting on with the elusive Warren Devlin?"

Ted pulled a face that said: Where do I start? "Well," he said. "I -"

"I had a call yesterday from a Detective Superintendent Henderson of Kent Constabulary. Apparently you've been poking about on their patch without telling anyone what you were up to. He only found out you'd been down there when a pathologist happened to mention it."

Ted looked sheepish but said nothing. His boss tilted his head and held out his hands, palms upward. An explanation was expected.

"Well, sir, Warren Devlin has a boat – The Jackpot – which ran aground off the Kent coast a couple of weeks ago. Then, yesterday, a body washed up on a beach not far from where the boat was wrecked. So I went down there to have a look at what's left of the boat and also to see the body. I -"

"Couldn't you have just called them? Kent, I mean."

Ted looked pained.

Nichols shook his head slightly. "Never mind. So it's him is it? Devlin?"

"We don't know yet. The body's in bad shape and they're

155

dragging their feet over the ID. Also . . ."

He glanced around the room again. Everyone was still staring, except DC Burns, who was consulting his notes.

"Go on."

"Also, Devlin's girlfriend, Rebecca King, claims to have spoken to him after the boat was wrecked. If that's true, then it can't be him at the mortuary in Margate."

"So we're waiting to find out the identity of the dead man," said Nichols. Ted nodded. "And Devlin's car has turned up in long term parking at Stansted?"

"Yes, a Porsche Boxster, but no one with the name Warren Devlin flew out of Stansted and he's not booked on any flights into the UK."

"You think he might have used a different passport?"

"Maybe. We're going through the security footage to see if he pops up."

"And what about the car?"

"He bought it from a dealership in Kendal, in the Lake District, about six months ago. Paid cash. Before that he drove a tatty, ex-army Land Rover. That's quite a leap: from an old rust bucket to a Porsche in one move . . ." He looked around the room; one or two people nodded assent. "Jim Simpson's giving the Porsche a going over down at Lewisham. He found part of a contact lens but no fingerprints."

Nichols raised an eyebrow. "No fingerprints at all?" Ted shook his head. "And does Devlin wear contacts?"

Ted shrugged. "There weren't any at his flat." He frowned, trying to remember something.

"Okay," said Nichols, breaking Ted's train of thought. "Is

there anything else?"

"The flatmate: Paul Finch. According to the FCO, he was in Italy last week. His brother was murdered and he formally identified the body."

Nichols folded his arms. "Right, and have you any idea how all of this fits together? What about the break-in at Devlin's flat?"

Ted folded his arms too, unconsciously mimicking his boss. He shook his head. "Someone really turned the place over. Maybe they were looking for the money, maybe something else. We just don't know. There was blood on the kitchen floor. Hopefully we'll know today or tomorrow whether it's a match for the body in Kent. I'm told we'll definitely have an ID by tomorrow."

"There's a lad called Lombardi, a Detective Sergeant, down at Lewisham," said Nichols, half to himself. "He speaks Italian." He stared down at his shoes for a moment then looked up and said, "I want you to focus on the club in Plumstead – you and DC Burns. You'll have a young lad called Dean Wilson to help you. Dean's new. He'll be with us from tomorrow." Ted glanced at Burns, who caught his eye and gave a swift, almost imperceptible shake of his head. "Dean can chase the hospital as well; find out if that security guard from the wholesalers is fit to answer any questions. You speak to the club members, find Devlin's friends; see if any of them can tell us what he's been up to. And talk to the girlfriend again, to . . ." He unfolded his arms and fluttered his fingers.

"Rebecca King," said Ted.

Nichols nodded. "Did she say she spoke to him in person or on the phone?"

"Phone."

"Find out if that's true. I'll get DS Lombardi to call Italy and see what's going on with this Paul Finch character."

TWENTY-FOUR

Angela's apartment was considerably more upmarket than
Martelli had expected. It was in a small block of just twelve
residences in Ceriale, a few kilometres along the coast from Loano.
Each apartment had a generous terrace big enough for al fresco
dining and there was a private parking area behind the building
where, after some indecision, he'd left his car. The apartments, he
guessed, dated from the late sixties or early seventies - the foyer
was a shock of thickly glazed tiles in bright orange and golden
yellow, the stairwell a tower of glass blocks. There was no lift, and
Martelli was heading for the top floor. As expected, the day had
grown formidably hot; the communal spaces were airless and
parched and generously salted with the dried-out carcasses of
flying insects. Sweat ran in rivulets down his temples and onto his
cheeks, gathering at his chin and dripping onto his shirt as he
dragged his weary legs up the six short flights of stairs. He paused
at the top of the sunny stairwell where the light was almost
blinding, magnified by the thick glass. A killer doesn't belong in a

scorching summer like this, he thought, a killer belongs in a cold, dark place. Of course he'd had the same thought many times over the years - too many times.

A single phone call was all it had taken to find out where Angela lived. Having spent a lifetime among those on the margins of Ligurian society, Martelli had long been acquainted with the pimps, prostitutes and petty criminals of the towns on his patch. His contact had been most helpful, explaining that someone had set Angela up in an apartment, 'a nice place, expensive'. Angela had been pregnant, of course, and doubtless 'the fool' was convinced the child was his. Whether the fool had convinced himself was another matter. It was a depressingly familiar tale and, predictably, Angela had been back at work just a couple of months after the baby was born; probably looking for money to buy drugs. Angela's sister took care of the child while she worked, took care of him for days at a time if the gossip was to be believed.

He had been unable to find out Angela's door number, just the building, but of the twelve names on the slim aluminium post boxes just inside the entrance only one included the first initial 'A', so he began with Apartment Nine.

There was a muffled shout in immediate response to the buzzer but it was an age before he heard the dull hammer blows of bolts being slid back and the door finally opened to reveal an elderly woman wearing a bright yellow, sleeveless summer dress. The skin on her arms collected into pleats in the crook of her elbows; her dyed hair was an iridescent blue. A faint whistling at the very limit of perception emanated from a hearing aid hanging useless at her neck. She beamed at him, clearly pleased to have a visitor.

"Buongiorno!" she said loudly in a southern accent, her voice echoing in the empty hallway.

"Buongiorno," he said, taking off his sunglasses and returning her smile. "I'm looking for Angela."

In an instant the smile disappeared and was replaced by a livid scowl.

"You should know better," she spat, her voice still raised. "She's young enough to be your daughter. Filthy bastard!" She leaned towards him, squinting, getting a proper look, as though memorising his face. Then she pulled back swiftly, almost flinching, eyes wide with surprise. He wondered if she recognised him from somewhere. With her chin, she gestured towards the apartment opposite before slamming the door in his face.

Martelli stood blinking as dust drifted down from the architrave. He looked at the floor and blew out a long sigh. As he did so, he noticed that a droplet of sweat had fallen onto the toe of his shoe, forming a pristine, shiny, black splash mark in the pale dust.

* * *

If Angela Vaccarezza was, as Ricardo had guessed, only thirty years old then she'd had a tough time getting there. Her skin was pale and pocked, her teeth yellowing and one lower incisor was brown where her cigarette sat, or possibly her crack pipe. Her mop of hair had been bleached and then dyed orange but it had grown black at the roots, threaded with strands of grey. Her scarlet nail varnish was chipped and patchy where she'd picked at it. She wore a short, black denim skirt and a stained, limp vest, which hung loosely, revealing too much of a bra gone chewing gum grey in the wash. But what aged her most was the anger and suspicion in her eyes. She would be quick to scoff and sneer, he thought, quick to pour scorn on others and their endeavours, and she would be defensive at all times. He recognised it in her immediately - it was apparent in the briefest eye contact - so he would have to tread carefully.

She eyed him with undisguised disdain, wrinkling her nose and curling her lip like a spoiled teenager.

"What do you want?"

"Angela?"

She said nothing.

"I'm investigating the death of Steven Finch," he said in what he hoped was a calming tone. "I just want to ask you a couple of questions."

"I don't know anything about it." She began to close the door but found it blocked by Martelli's foot.

"I know you don't," he said. "I just wanted to ask you about him. I'm trying to speak to everyone who knew him. I'm not with the police. I'm retired. I'm just trying to help Paul - his brother."

At the mention of Paul, her expression softened substantially. She relaxed the pressure on the door while she considered Martelli.

"Aren't you a little bit old?"

He frowned. "A bit old for what?"

"You know - a bit old to be chasing criminals."

Martelli blinked twice, wondering if perhaps she had a good point. He shrugged. "Well, when it comes to the actual chasing, I'll probably leave things to the police. All I'm doing is trying to find out if Steven was in any trouble."

Her eyes narrowed as she attempted to gauge whether or not he was trying to fool her somehow. She snorted, shook her head and said quietly, "Steven *was* trouble."

She pushed the door open.

* * *

Martelli sat on a small, wicker sofa facing floor-to-ceiling glass sliding doors which opened onto the generous terrace. Angela took a seat opposite, all but silhouetted against the bright morning light. Behind her the sun sparkled on the gently heaving sea. He had hoped for a cool drink but nothing was offered. In one corner of the room, a baby boy slept peacefully in a Moses basket, his mouth hanging open, his tiny hands pressed either side of his face. Martelli guessed he was no more than four or five months old. The child made the occasional squeaking noise but was otherwise silent.

As his host lit a cigarette, Martelli looked around. Cardboard boxes were heaped against the wall to his left. A few had been labelled with a black marker pen: 'Bedroom', 'Bathroom' and 'Kitchen'. On one box it simply and imprecisely said: 'My stuff'. The sofa cushions were stained and coming loose at the seams; a row of pistachio shells nestled in the gap between them. The rug on which he rested his feet bore a cigarette burn the size of a euro coin through which he could see the cool tiled floor. On the glass table between them, three empty beer bottles sat alongside a plate smeared with ragù.

"Have you lived here long?" he said, as she leaned back and took a long drag.

"No," she said with finality.

He nodded. "As I said, I'm trying to find out as much as I can about Steven Finch and his business -"

"I don't know anything about his business," she replied sharply. She held the cigarette with her right hand; with her left she fiddled with her hair, tugging anxiously at a greasy lock hanging next to her ear, winding it around her forefinger again and again. Nervous, he thought; frightened even.

He smiled. "I wondered if there's anything you can you tell me about Steven and Mario's customers? Who were they? Were they Italians or foreigners?"

"Have you spoken to Mario?" she said, ignoring his question.

"No, I haven't but I intend to."

"Where is he?"

Martelli was a little taken aback but tried not to show it. According to Ricardo, Angela had been down to the marina looking for Mario just two weeks ago and he had thought that, in the intervening time, she would have found him. "I don't know," he said. "I'd hoped you might be able to tell me that. Or at least tell me where I can find Tomasz." He gave an almost imperceptible shrug. "I've never met Mario. Why? Does he owe you money?"

She laughed, a harsh cackle, forced and malicious.

"He said he'd take care of us," she gestured towards the sleeping infant. "But he's gone - typical man." Her scowl made it clear that she included Martelli in that brotherhood of the unreliable. She tapped ash into a dish perched precariously on the arm of her chair. It was already full of cigarette butts.

He wondered if Ricardo had been mistaken about Angela being Tomasz's girlfriend.

"When did you last see him?"

She snorted. "About three weeks ago."

"And you've tried calling him?" Martelli knew it was the wrong thing to say, even as he was saying it.

"Of course I've tried calling him!" she spat. "What? Do you think I'm an idiot?" She shook her head and took another greedy drag.

"No, no." He patted the air with his hands. "I apologise. Have you seen Tomasz or Steven in that time? Have you spoken to Estella?"

At the mention of Estella she bristled again.

"That snooty bitch! Why would I talk to her?"

"I . . . well . . ." he dithered.

"Do you really think she'd speak to me? She wouldn't lower herself. She thinks she's better than everyone. Anyway – they've all done a runner."

Martelli leaned forward in his chair. "What do you mean?"

"I mean they've all done a runner." She thought it was a stupid question.

"Who? Who's done a runner?"

"Mario, Tomasz, Steven, that bitch Estella, even Paul . . ." She took another long, trembling pull on her cigarette.

"So you haven't seen any of them for three weeks?"

Angela watched him warily. She turned her palms upwards, staring at him as she blew out a long, steady stream of smoke.

"Have you any idea at all where they might have gone? Could Tomasz have returned to Poland?"

"I doubt that very much." She snorted.

"What's funny?"

"Nothing," she said, looking down at her bare feet. She doubled over and began to pick at the varnish on her left big toenail.

"What about Mario? I understand he has an old farm up in the forest above Castelvecchio. Could he be staying there?"

This piqued her interest. She forgot the big toe and scowled at him. "Where is it?" she demanded.

"I don't know," said Martelli truthfully.

She raised an eyebrow, clearly doubting him.

"And Estella?" he persisted. "Have you any idea where I'd find her?"

She shook her head and took another crackling drag, sucking hard until the glowing ember grew to a fierce orange rocket of almost unsustainable length.

"And when did you last see Steven?"

She shook her head. "About a week ago."

"Really?" he said, surprised. "Where?"

"I was visiting a . . . friend who lives on Via Monte Pasubio. I saw him there."

"Where exactly?"

She raised that eyebrow again.

"Please," he said. "It might be important."

"He was standing on someone's terrace. The small apartment block at the end of the street." She sighed. "It might have been his terrace for all I know. He might live there."

Martelli nodded. There was only one apartment block on Via Monte Pasubio. "He does live there. Or rather he *did* live there."

She smiled. There was evidence still of suspicion in her eyes but that initial anger had shrunk to a background murmur.

"You don't seem too upset that he's dead," he said.

She leaned towards him conspiratorially, shuffling forward in her seat. "Steven was a bastard, a psycho, a real nasty piece of work. He got what he deserved. He put one of my friends in the hospital; beat her black and blue. She nearly died."

Martelli made a mental note to ask Bracco if he knew whether Steven Finch had a criminal record in Britain. "Was he arrested?"

She sneered and flopped back in her chair. "Arrested? You're joking aren't you? Who cares about working girls in this town, eh?"

"Was it at least reported to the police?"

"No. No it wasn't," she said quietly. "I think he paid her to keep her mouth shut. Or Mario did." She shrugged.

"Well, maybe somebody decided that money wasn't enough. Steven was tortured before he died – burned with acid. Do you think your friend or someone who cares about her might have been responsible? Is that possible?"

She shook her head. "It was ages ago - two years or more. She's long gone."

"Gone where?"

Her anger bubbled to the surface again. "Home," she snapped. "Montenegro. What does it matter?"

"Okay," he said softly. "And do you know anyone, anyone at all who might have access to large quantities of acid."

She glared at him but said nothing.

The silence grew and yet still she glared.

"Fine, fine," he relented. "It was just a thought. Anyway, you disliked Steven; hated him even."

"Everybody hates Steven," she said. "They're all frightened of him."

She held his gaze for a few seconds then laughed and turned to stub out her cigarette. Martelli eyed her thoughtfully, weighing the little indications by which we all gauge a person's credibility. He took in the scratches on her arms and the frayed stitching of her tatty bra. He wondered how much she was holding back.

He licked his dry lips. "Could I have a glass of water?" he said.

* * *

Martelli stood sweating in the oppressive heat of the foyer. A wasp, a huge thing with long, trailing back legs, crawled along the thin metal window sill, rocking from side to side, almost rolling over with each step, its segmented body a cumbersome burden. As the creature struggled onward on its seemingly pointless journey, he mulled over what he had learnt from Angela and wondered why his client hadn't mentioned her. According to Angela, she'd met Paul Finch on several occasions, most notably at a party in this very building, at which Paul had become roaring drunk and staggered about on the terrace serenading the neighbours. She had smiled at this memory, the only time Martelli saw her do so during his visit, and it had transformed her, taken ten years off her in an instant. She had then asked how Paul's Italian was coming along and had told Martelli to send him her regards. She spoke of him almost fondly, describing a kind man with a ready smile and a good sense of humour. 'Was Steven invited to the party?' he had asked. 'No', she had replied, shaking her head emphatically. As for the nature of Steven and Mario's business, she had no idea, though there was clearly more to it than simply boat charters and fishing trips. In fact, although money did often change hands during the 'jaunts', as she called them, there were also bags and boxes and packages, though she claimed to have no notion of their contents.

He'd asked her directly if she thought that Mario could have killed Steven, and her answer had been an immediate and unambiguous 'No'. Mario was no killer, she had insisted. He was a loser and a coward but he was far too gentle a soul to commit murder. Under pressure she had speculated that the killer might have been a business rival or a disappointed customer – Steven had, after all, clearly got involved in some dodgy dealings – but the truth was she had no better idea than he did who might have murdered his client's brother.

Unsurprisingly, she had no photos from the 'jaunts'. Steven had confiscated all mobile phones at the beginning of each trip.

Martelli had left when Angela's sister showed up to collect the baby. The little boy had snuggled into his aunt's shoulder with barely a murmur, briefly opening eyes the colour of a hazy summer sky. His mother hadn't even kissed him goodbye.

His talk with Angela had raised more questions than it had answered, questions he would ordinarily have been able to assign to Bracco and other junior officers. Now however he had his work cut out. He sighed, looked down at his dusty shoes and found that his thoughts immediately switched to Aldo and his financial predicament. His old friend was due back from Napoli that very afternoon and he knew that he must keep his promise to Valentina and pay her father a visit the following morning. He shook his head, eyes closed. And before Aldo, he thought, I must endure breakfast with Piero, who will no doubt be furious at my having taken on a private client. Life, it seemed, grew more complicated as one grew older.

The bulbous wasp had by now made it to the end of the window sill and was tapping out a frantic tattoo with its antennae. Martelli watched and was on the point of feeling sorry for it when suddenly it launched itself into the air and flew directly at his face. He ducked out of the way and turned to gaze after it as it disappeared up the stairwell, shaking his head as it dwindled to a dot and disappeared from view. He had assumed the creature was exhausted but it had fooled him.

Out in the car park he saw to his irritation that his tatty foil-covered windscreen blind had fallen onto the seats, exposing the interior of the car to the fierce rays of the Mediterranean sun. Doubtless the steering wheel would be too hot to touch. He climbed in, started the engine, turned on the air conditioning and considered what he'd learned. Estella was not merely a shop assistant and Angela was not merely a friend; Steven was dangerous and violent, Mario was a loser and Paul was the only person about whom she'd said a kind word.

Later, stopping for petrol in Borghetto Santo Spirito, now a suburb of Loano, he looked around at the dozens of blocks of holiday apartments. They were crammed in as close to the beach as possible: concrete towers in white, grey and salmon pink, with smoked glass balconies and striped awnings. Packed now, in August, when so many Italians took their annual holiday, they sat empty most of the year - unoccupied yet obscuring the sea view which might otherwise have been enjoyed by the ordinary citizens of Borghetto Santo Spirito. More madness, he thought, more rich man's folly.

He paid for the petrol, climbed back in behind the wheel and sat staring straight ahead. The toot of a horn made him jump. He started the engine and pulled forward, no idea how long he'd been sitting there.

TWENTY-FIVE

Ted stood gazing at the haul of cash from Warren Devlin's locker
at the boxing club; dozens of bundles of bank notes loosely stacked
on the table. Altogether there were one hundred and eighty-seven
thousand, two hundred and forty-six euros. All denominations
were represented, including a thick wad of five hundreds, known
in some quarters as Bin Ladens and no longer available in the UK.
Next to them sat the cheap, brown sports holdall in which they'd
been found. It was well-used with cracked handles and fraying
bottom corners; in places the piping was coming adrift of the
seams. Not the sort of bag in which you'd expect to find a fortune,
he mused. And presumably that was the idea.

Beside the holdall lay a pair of jeans – a cheap brand
unknown to Ted – and a grey sweatshirt, along with thick, white
socks, a pair of checked boxer shorts and black, slip-on shoes.
Among the toiletries, there was a tube of toothpaste, still in its box,
and a toothbrush, also unopened. There was also a brand new
razor. Both packets of hair dye were black. Ted took out his

phone and, rather than risk calling him while he was in conference with officers from Kent Constabulary, sent a text message to Alan Moody, asking if it was possible to determine whether the dead man found on the beach had dyed his hair. He then looked at the passports. In the first, Warren Devlin was pictured exactly as he looked in the photograph pinned to the board in his kitchen, much the same as he did on the beach in Thailand. In the second picture he sported a moustache. The third showed a much younger Devlin, head shaved, the bags under his eyes considerably less pronounced.

At the end of the table was a plastic tray containing the other items from the holdall: a ballpoint pen, a pack of chewing gum, a few coppers and a crumpled blank envelope with directions written on the back in a barely legible scrawl. The first line read: 'A10 W, R on 582, 44, signs to village'. The '8' might well have been a '6'. The second line began: 'R at car park' and culminated, via a series of 'L's and 'R's, with the word 'house'. Using his phone, Ted took a photograph of the envelope, which he then emailed to himself. He would trace this route on a map later, he thought; find out where Warren had been, or had planned to go.

Pursing his lips, he clenched his fists, pressed his knuckles on the edge of the table and stared, more at the surface than the evidence, allowing his focus to shift - two separate images drifting apart in front of him.

The door opened and he looked up.

"How're you getting on?" said the evidence clerk.

Ted breathed out wearily and smiled, wanly. "I'm done."

* * *

DC Burns stared at the screen, watching grainy closed circuit footage of the entrance barriers at Stansted Long Stay Parking, thankful that the ticketing system had allowed him to narrow down his search to a one hour section of the endless video file. Otherwise it would have been a very tedious task indeed.

The cramped, windowless room smelled strongly of mint chewing gum and cigarettes, the technician having just been outside for a smoke. DC Burns sat hunched awkwardly over the corner of the table. Boxes of printing paper prevented him from stretching out his legs and a filing cabinet far too large for the limited space hemmed him in so he was unable to shuffle his chair into a more convenient position. The technician, oblivious to Burns' discomfort, typed two numbers into each of three fields at the bottom of the screen. As he tapped 'enter' the image jumped and was replaced by one much the same but for a dozen rabbits, frozen on the grass verge in the middle distance. He spun the shuttle wheel, causing the rabbits to hop about furiously, their progress jerky and comical at many times normal speed. In the blink of an eye they were gone, scattered in all directions.

There followed a period of stillness during which Burns stared at the featureless concrete road surface, almost mesmerised by the lack of movement. A newspaper caught his eye as it tumbled past in the distance, disappearing behind the bushes and then reappearing again, flitting across the mini roundabout, carried swiftly on a gentle breeze made gale force by the technician's finger. A man's legs lurched into view, close to the camera, in jeans and pale Timberland boots, and in a fraction of a second they were gone. A family emerged from a gap in the bushes, tiny in the distance, two adults and three children, wheeled suitcases trundling behind them. The youngest child carried a teddy bear. With twitchy movements, rocking from side to side like clockwork toys, they sped past and headed out of shot.

As the technician spooled more quickly through the footage, cars began to appear and disappear, each one visible for less than a second, flashing by like images in a child's flick-a-book – a Range Rover, a Mini, a BMW, a silver Japanese car that Burns wasn't able to identify. And another, and another, faster and faster, until the images blurred together into one supernatural vehicle swelling and contracting, stretching and shrinking, changing in the blink of an eye.

"There!" said Burns, pointing excitedly at the screen. The technician paused the cascade of cars, freezing an image of a white Toyota. "Go back," said Burns.

The technician turned the shuttle wheel with the tip of his forefinger, rolling the footage slowly backwards, slow enough that each vehicle dwindled into the middle distance before sliding to the left and out of the frame.

"There!" Burns exclaimed again.

The technician yanked his hand away from the controls as though electrocuted. Burns held his breath and leaned in close to the screen.

The driver had stopped the silver Porsche Boxster too far away from the ticket machine. Unable to reach, she had been forced to undo her safety belt and heave herself half out of her seat to stretch an arm out of the window. Even then it was only with leather-clad fingertips that she managed to grasp the ticket.

"Hold it there," said Burns. "Can I have a print out of that?"

He took out his phone and dialled. When Ted answered, he said excitedly, "Guess who drove Warren Devlin's car to Stansted."

TWENTY-SIX

Martelli hurried past the old, brass pump, once the sole source of drinking water for an entire street. He turned right, headed past Il Bagatto and emerged from the cool shade of the narrow passage into the glorious faded grandeur of Piazza Palestro - a tranquil, sunlit square. Squinting, he hastened to the far end and turned left into Via Doria, passing the pelleteria where the owner was already at work making handbags and wallets, doors wide open, radio blaring; the rich, creamy smell of new leather filling the air. Martelli glanced inside as he strode past. Catching the man's eye, he bid him a breathless 'Buongiorno!' I must be very late, he thought, the shop ordinarily didn't open until after eight. On Via Doria, the green, electronic sign at the pharmacy already showed thirty degrees. No wonder he was struggling to catch his breath. It was going to be another fiercely hot day. A dozen pigeons took to the air in panic as he charged into Piazza Italia. They flew in a circuit, anti-clockwise, passing directly over the tables outside Giacomo's cafe, where their usual spot beneath the trees was . . .

unoccupied. Nardi was gone. Martelli stopped dead, flung his arms out in exasperation and stood there with his chest heaving. He swore out loud through gritted teeth.

"Just be grateful you missed him. He's in a foul mood this morning." Giacomo put his cigarette out as Martelli approached. "You want coffee?"

Martelli shook his head. "I've got to get going. I've got a lot to do today."

He sat down at one of the tables and began retying his shoelaces.

"What's wrong with your eyes?" said Giacomo, unaccustomed to seeing Martelli in sunglasses.

"Nothing," said Martelli without looking up. "Did he arrive in a bad mood or was he annoyed because I stood him up?"

Giacomo shrugged. "Both."

Martelli snorted as he pulled the second knot tight. "It's the first time I've overslept in years." He glanced at Giacomo and sighed. "I suppose I'd better call him."

Giacomo looked doubtful. "Maybe leave it until this afternoon." He laughed. "And don't worry about being late. It's just your mind unravelling a bit. You're loosening up, Mimmo. Enjoy it. Enjoy retirement." He pointed at his own chest. "Look at me. The way things are now, I'll have to work until I drop dead."

Martelli left a disappointed Giacomo to preside over his empty cafe and walked quickly to the north end of the piazza. The warning bell was clanging at the railway crossing and he had to quicken his pace and weave through a knot of milling tourists before ducking under the free end of the barrier just a second or two before it settled on its yoke. The tourists gazed open-mouthed as he walked slowly across the railway line and crouched to shuffle under the opposite barrier. He was across the road and out of sight long before the slam and whoosh of the westbound train.

His car was parked in the market square, off the roundabout at the top of Via Simone Stella, the caruggi, of course, being impassable for all but the smallest of motor vehicles. He still felt woolly-headed and sickly as he started the engine, a feeling not improved by the stifling hot breathlessness of the car's interior and the sour smell of stale laundry blown in through the vents as the air conditioning started up. He'd slept badly again. A few dark beers and a loaded joint on his rooftop bench, far from relaxing him, had induced unsettling dreams in which Rubini's smug, tanned face had featured all too often. Several times he'd woken up to find the sheet bound tightly around his legs and his eyes stinging with sweat. In the end he'd headed downstairs for a glass of water and had settled on the sofa, where it was cooler, just for a few minutes.

He'd woken three hours later at about the time he should have been considering a second coffee with Piero and now he felt it imperative to get going. He would apologise at dinner – he and Piero were due to meet the Frenchman outside Il Bagatto at ten that evening. Before that, at around eight, he was supposed to see Paul Finch. But right now there was someone else he needed to speak to. He was going to keep his promise to Valentina. His stomach growled as he selected first gear.

* * *

Aldo lived in a crumbling house of honeycomb limestone overlooking the sea a short distance from the marina. It was an easy stroll from the centre of the old town but Martelli needed to move the car anyway, to make way for a crafts market the following morning, and Aldo's was as good a place as any to leave it for a day. He parked in the dappled shade of a laburnum, its pendulous chains of yellow flowers swaying gently in the scant breeze. He then spent a few minutes faffing around with the windscreen blind, delaying the inevitable. Eventually he gave up, chucked the blind in the back seat and dragged his feet towards the house. At the gate he stood with hands on hips and gazed up at the building in which, but for the duration of his military service and an abortive few months at a college in Genova, Aldo had spent his entire life. Smiling faintly, Martelli took in its diseased woodwork and corroded iron balustrades, its bubbling paint and lolling drainpipes. The roof was bowed and the stonework, once precise in its geometry, had been so eroded by the sand and salt-laden breeze blowing in off the sea it was as if the building was being erased.

Aldo had inherited the house in the early nineteen seventies after the premature deaths of his parents, both of whom had succumbed to cancer. He married Margherita, raised two children - Valentina and her brother, Giulio - buried Margherita, also a victim of cancer, and continued to live in the house. And during more than six decades spent within the same four walls, he had made no changes to the building other than to add, at Margherita's insistence, an indoor toilet and a modern shower cubicle, in which, since her death, he kept his rods and nets.

The heavy, brass door knocker was shaped like a

squirming, rather angry looking fish. Martelli lifted it and took a deep breath. The moment had arrived and what had been a constant, niggling uneasiness erupted into a dizzying, almost nauseating anxiety. He let the squirming fish fall against the striker.

* * *

Gone were the neatly pressed trousers with their razor-sharp creases. Aldo was wearing shorts and Martelli was treated to a close up view of his old friend's varicose veins as they trudged up a steep and ill-lit flight of stairs into a kitchen garlanded with damp laundry.

"What's wrong with your eyes?" Aldo said over his shoulder.

Martelli sighed. "Nothing," he said, taking off his sunglasses.

Aldo turned to look at him. "You look tired."

Martelli rolled his bloodshot, baggage-laden eyes.

"As do we all," said Aldo with a placatory chuckle. "You want coffee?"

Martelli nodded. "Si. Grazie. I'm not sleeping so well these days."

Aldo busied himself at the kitchen counter while Martelli looked around.

The remains of a quartet of grilled sardines lay derelict on a plate next to the sink. Their smell pervaded the entire house and Martelli was silently thankful when Aldo reached for a packet of Nazionali, the brand he'd smoked since childhood. He lit one and

it wiggled in his mouth as he unscrewed the coffee pot with one
eye squeezed shut against the smoke. It had been weeks since
Martelli had seen him and he appeared to have aged three decades
during that interval. He shuffled around like a nonagenarian with
arthritic hips.

The air quickly grew thick with smoke, so much so that the
far end of the room became indistinct, as though viewed through a
silk scarf. The lack of daylight didn't help – the shutters were
closed and a curtain of beads blocked all but a faint light from the
adjoining living room. As Aldo clattered about at the counter,
Martelli took a seat at a Formica-topped table, the surface pale
yellow with flecks of black and baby blue. One end bore the treacly
scars of numerous cigarette burns, where Aldo's father used to
perch his Gitanes sans filtre while fiddling with some old clock or
music box. He had been an inveterate tinkerer, old man Bonetti, a
lover of intricate mechanisms, a painter of miniature soldiers and
a rigger of ships in bottles and, though not quite the accomplished
fettler his father had been, Aldo was nonetheless quite handy and,
after leaving the army, had become a teacher of subjects such as
basic metalwork and woodwork. His hands told the tale – chipped
nails, scarred and calloused fingers – as did the numerous
soldered copper ashtrays and wooden trinket boxes sitting on
every surface in the large, dingy kitchen. Not that there was much
space for them. Margherita had obsessively populated their house
with knick knacks and ornaments, especially after the children had
left home, and since her death Aldo had done nothing to thin the
clutter. On just one shelf of the heavy oak dresser directly
opposite where Martelli was sitting there was a brass bell, a
delicate porcelain Virgin Mary, a sepia bride and groom - both

scowling, half a dozen nutcrackers, a pocket watch missing its pointers, a bundle of unopened bills, a trio of pewter jugs, a stack of old football programmes and a book about Napoleon propped against a basket of eggs.

Martelli smiled and directed his gaze at the tabletop, letting his eyes lose focus and his mind fill with memories evoked by the burn marks, the curling blue smoke and the smell of the coffee. He floated back half a century to a sunny day when Aldo's father had caught them up to no good. The nature of their transgression was long forgotten, but he recalled quite vividly being chased through the old town, his heart thudding staccato in his chest, his feet sliding on the dusty paving as he tore around the corners in the maze of streets, Aldo falling, his father catching hold of his collar and flogging him with a belt until he bled, all the while shouting, 'Shame, shame, shame, shame!' at the top of his voice until every window in the neighbourhood had been flung open and the mothers of the caruggi had pleaded with him to spare the boy. He smiled to himself.

Aldo delivered the coffee with shaking hands, the all but imperceptible movement signalled at the interface between espresso cup and tiny matching saucer. Their eyes were drawn simultaneously to the tinkling of the crockery, and then they looked at one another, Martelli searching his old friend's face and finding sadness and shame. The latter he recognised only too well, having floundered in it himself just the day before. Was that right? he wondered. Was it just one day since his encounter with Rubini? Or was it two? He shook his head and squeezed his eyes shut. When he opened them he saw a look of horror on Aldo's ashen face and realised that the shaking of his head had been misinterpreted. Clearly Valentina had warned her father of his involvement and the solemn gesture had been taken as a devastating update on the situation.

* * *

"Antonio has always resented me," said Aldo sadly.

"Antonio has always been a fool," Martelli replied. "You've been more than good to him over the years. You paid him far too much for his half of this house and you've been letting him get away with bloody murder ever since." He shook his head and took a sip of wine, trying to be judicious in his consumption, though not refusing it altogether as Aldo was clearly in the mood for drink. "When did you last hear from him?"

Aldo snorted, topping up Martelli's glass from a fiasco of Chianti. "Oh, months ago. God knows where he is. I'll probably never see him again."

"Oh, he'll be back," said Martelli. "As soon as he runs out of money he'll be knocking on your door. And I hope," he said pointedly, "you tell him to sling his bloody hook."

"He's my little brother, Mimmo. My flesh and blood."

"Valentina and Giulio are the only flesh and blood you need to worry about. And you'll probably have grandchildren soon. Think of them."

Aldo nodded, unconvinced, despondent.

"So," said Martelli, sighing. "How bad is it?"

Aldo pressed his forehead into the palms of his hands and leaned his elbow on the table. His voice dropped until it was almost a whisper. "About a quarter of a million."

Martelli was dumbstruck and dismayed. What could he say? Aldo was a proud and self-reliant person, always had been, even when they were kids. He was intelligent and cautious too. How had he allowed himself to be duped to such a degree? He took a deep breath as he pondered this bombshell. As he did so the thick smoke tickled the back of his throat and offered him a much-needed distraction. Pushing back his chair, he strode across the room, opened the doors to the terrace and folded back the shutters. He then opened the window above the sink and folded those shutters back too and instantly the room was flooded with sunlight.

"Let's get this laundry outside," he said. "Otherwise it'll stink of fish and fag smoke. Where's your drying rack? In here?"

Before Aldo could muster a protest, Martelli had circled the table and swept aside the bead curtain.

"Wait, Mimmo!" said Aldo, too late. He leapt from his chair, knocking the edge of the table and toppling both glasses of wine.

Martelli spun round, startled by the screech of the table legs on the tiled floor. Aldo stood frozen in the act of catching one of the wine glasses, bent double, cradling the intact vessel in both hands as though it was a baby bird. He was staring aghast at the other, which lay broken at his feet. Neither man moved and in the two seconds of silence that followed they both heard the dripping as the red puddles of Chianti merged and found the gap between the leaves of the old Formica-topped table.

They gazed at one another.

"Mimmo . . ."

Martelli turned to look into the living room. A sofa and two tatty armchairs faced the fireplace. The shutters were closed but the room was lit by a reading lamp brought from one of the bedrooms and perched on the edge of a small table in front of Aldo's favourite chair. On the table, at the centre of the pool of yellow light, were a bottle brush, a dirty cloth, a small can of oil with a flexible spout and, newly polished, a large, cumbersome revolver.

The gun was clearly an antique. The barrel was hexagonal in section, the release lever for the chambers crudely cross-hatched, a metal ring on the bottom of the handgrip would once have been tied to a leather lanyard. Martelli guessed it was at least seventy years old. The brown leather holster propped against a plantpot looked like an item of luggage. A cluster of bullets lay next to it. Martelli stood on the threshold and took all this in, mulling the possible explanations and coming up with nothing good. He was unsure quite what to say.

"So," he said finally, turning to face his old friend. He forced a chuckle and was uncomfortably aware of how hollow it sounded. "Are you planning a robbery?"

Aldo blinked twice before responding. "No," he said, matching Martelli's empty laughter with an insincere grin. "I was just cleaning it. I thought I might sell it."

Martelli tried and failed to hide his disbelief. "You know," he said, thinking quickly, loosening his stance. "I've a colleague on the force who collects old guns. I'll take it to him if you like, see what he thinks. He could tell you right away if it's worth anything. He might even buy it." I'm talking too quickly, he thought. He scanned Aldo's face, his gaze flicking from eye to eye.

Aldo opened his mouth but was slow to respond. "I . . . I don't want to put you to any trouble," he said, his voice thick with reluctance.

"Don't worry," said Martelli, looping the bead curtain over a coat hook fixed to the architrave. "It's no trouble at all. I've got to see him tomorrow anyway."

Aldo raised his eyebrows. "Oh?"

"About my pension," Martelli added hurriedly.

"I see." Aldo's face reddened. Then he nodded, his shoulders sagging, and flapped a hand, a gesture of defeat. "Sure," he said. "Take it."

Martelli, strode into the living room. "I'll let you know what Beppe says tomorrow," he said over his shoulder.

He quickly slid the pistol into its holster then scooped up the handful of bullets and put them in his trouser pocket. Of all his former colleagues on the force, he thought, as he fastened the holster shut, Beppe was the least likely to have a collection of firearms. Crucially though, he lived in Savona, so it was unlikely he and Aldo knew one another.

When he returned to the kitchen, Aldo had resumed his seat and was staring at the table.

"So," said Martelli, placing the revolver on a chair and crouching to pick up the broken glass. "Tell me about your dealings with Aricò." He spoke bluntly and loudly too, signalling an end to their tiptoeing around the subject. But then, he thought, why not? The cat, in the shape of a pistol and two hundred and fifty thousand euros, was well and truly out of the bag.

Aldo's cheeks flushed crimson; anger flashed in his eyes and for a second Martelli thought he'd overstepped his authority. But the anger subsided just as fast and was replaced by such obvious humiliation that Martelli feared his old friend would burst into tears.

"I never intended for things to go this far," said Aldo, unable to meet Martelli's gaze.

* * *

It had been a scam from the start - that much was obvious. Aricò had simply wanted Aldo's house, sitting as it did on a prime plot at the eastern end of the lungomare. How Antonio came to be involved in one of Aricò's bogus developments was unclear but, as things had unravelled, it had become apparent that he'd known from the start that his brother was being ripped off, and that, for Aldo, was the cruellest blow.

As Aldo reached the end of his sorry tale, Martelli tipped the last of the Chianti into his old friend's glass and said, rather rashly and with a sense of conviction that he simply didn't feel, "We will sort this out."

"How, Mimmo?"

"I don't know but you will not be forced out of this house. Not by Aricò and certainly not by Antonio."

Aldo raised his eyebrows and, for the first time since Martelli's arrival, looked like he might smile and actually mean it. "So – you'll speak to . . ?"

"Yes," said Martelli firmly, nodding for emphasis. "I will. Wait . . . Aricò, you mean?"

"Yes."

The wine, he reflected later, must have guided his response. Aricò was renowned for ruthless vindictiveness, a person best avoided. He didn't speak, simply nodded once then drained his glass, eyes closed.

"Thank you, Mimmo," said Aldo, with relief but also, Martelli noticed, the barest hint of triumph in his voice. "I knew I could rely on you."

A cynic might have wondered at those words, with which Aldo skilfully nudged him past the point of no return. They sat in silence for a moment then Aldo made a jarring change of subject, asking almost cheerfully, "Are you hungry? When you arrived I was about to make madeleines."

It was as though he'd achieved his goal and didn't need to discuss it further. The subject was now closed. And Martelli couldn't help but wonder to what degree he had been manipulated, by Aldo and also possibly by Valentina, who, he reminded himself, had had him wrapped around her finger since the day she was born. But the pistol told another story. He looked at Aldo and wondered. Were you 'about to make madeleines'? Or were you about to blow your brains out? He frowned, feeling suddenly light-headed at the thought of it. His diaphragm fluttered and he shifted uncomfortably in his seat.

"Mimmo?"

"Eh?"

"Hungry?"

"Oh, yes, yes. Madeleines would be great, thanks. I missed breakfast. And more coffee. Otherwise this wine's going to knock me out by lunchtime." He was aware he might have slurred the last word.

Aldo stood and began gathering ingredients and equipment: eggs, butter, flour, sugar, baking soda, a madeleine tin.

Martelli sat staring into space. Suicide suddenly seemed ludicrous. Perhaps Aldo really did plan to sell the pistol? He tilted his head to read the title of the book propped on the dresser. Aldo caught this movement and followed his gaze.

"He looted our nation's artworks, Mimmo," he said blithely, as though such actions were a mere bagatelle. "Like the Nazis looted Europe a hundred and fifty years after him." Crouching, he opened a cupboard and, amid much clattering and clanging, pulled out a large copper mixing bowl. "Of course," he continued, "if Napoleon had been born a year earlier, he would have been Genovese." He banged the bowl down on the table, smiling. "Like these cakes."

Martelli frowned, said slowly, "I'm not sure I -"

"Madeleines, Mimmo. The mixture's basically a Genovese. Can you do me a favour?" From a hook on the wall next to the window he retrieved a balloon whisk with which he pointed towards the open door. "Get me a lemon from the tree on the terrace. The biggest you can find."

* * *

They ate the madeleines hot and eggy, laughing as they both sucked in air and fanned their open mouths to save burning themselves. Aldo produced a bottle of grappa, unlabelled and of Heaven alone knew what provenance, and soon they were chatting animatedly with their mouths full. As they polished off the last of the twelve cakes, Martelli raised his glass to make a toast. Aldo looked at him expectantly.

"To the future."

Aldo hesitated.

Martelli nodded encouragement.

His old friend raised his glass and together they said it.

"So," said Aldo as they banged their little glasses onto the table. "Are you seeing anyone at the moment?"

It was Martelli's turn to hesitate. In his mind he quickly ran through the events of the past few days. Could Aldo have heard something? Had someone in Castelvecchio spotted him eating lunch with Cristina? Was the word out?

* * *

He walked home with the pistol in a plastic carrier bag, its hammer clinking loudly against the half empty bottle of grappa, which Aldo had insisted he take. With the paranoia of the daytime drunk he imagined that everyone he passed smelled the booze on his breath and started muttering about him as soon as he was out of earshot.

Via Richeri was mercifully quiet; just a few people strolling in the shade. Through the window of the enoteca, he gave Eduardo a brisk wave but was spared any conversation by the timely arrival of a customer.

Inside, he placed the pistol on the hexagonal table, scattering the bullets next to it along with his keys and a few coins. Walking unsteadily to the sink, he turned on the tap and let it run for a few seconds, listening to the water clunk and gurgle in the pipes, rolling his eyes and following the noise across the ceiling. He gulped down two full glasses then lay on the sofa and slid rapidly into sleep, recalling somewhat regretfully the tail end of his conversation with Aldo. On the subject of Cristina, he felt he'd given too much away when, after some thought, he'd answered, "Have you ever met someone who simply stopped you in your tracks?" And now his candour felt ill-advised, as though, by putting his feelings into words he'd exposed himself to potentially painful consequences. And with that worrying final thought, he lapsed into oblivion.

* * *

Something roused him, something not right, an unfamiliar noise that set the hairs on the back of his neck standing on end. Keeping his eyes closed, he tilted his head, listening keenly, suddenly alert.

There it was again, a clicking noise, not an insect, something else, something . . . mechanical? It was like the delicate snick-click of an old-fashioned alarm clock just before the clamour of the bells. He opened his eyes to find Paul Finch standing over him, pistol in hand.

TWENTY-SEVEN

Martelli held his breath; heard his own pulse pounding in his ear where it was pressed hard against the cushion. They stared at one another, Martelli blinking, bleary-eyed, wondering momentarily if he was having a dream; Finch lost in thought, pouting, his jaw muscles working rhythmically. Between them the gun hovered in the air, aimed at a spot uncomfortably close to Martelli's head.

After a few moments Finch blinked as though waking and slowly tilted the pistol until it was pointing at the ceiling. Viewed end-on, the gun had been unfamiliar but Martelli now realised it was Aldo's, the vintage hand cannon he'd carted self-consciously through the streets a few hours before.

"Your door was open," said Finch.

"Was it?"

Grunting, Martelli heaved his body into a half sitting position, strained to go further, failed, and slumped back into the cushions. Hooking a foot under the edge of the heavy table, he levered himself upright.

"Wide open," said Finch. He turned the pistol over, examining it. "This was sitting on the table at the top of the stairs. How old is it?"

Martelli stood. "I don't know," he said softly, reaching for the gun. "It belongs to a friend of mine."

"But it still works?"

Martelli shrugged, shaking his head. "I doubt it. Why? Do you want to shoot somebody?"

"Maybe," said Finch quietly. He chuckled to himself and smiled.

Martelli nodded at the pistol. Finch handed it to him.

"Sorry," he said. "I didn't mean to disturb you. It's just it's gone eight o'clock and, when you didn't show up, I thought I'd call in and see if you were at home."

"Eight? Really?" Martelli couldn't believe he'd slept so long.

Finch glanced at his wristwatch. "Eight twenty." He walked to the open window and leaned over the wide sill to stare down into the street. Watching him warily, Martelli shivered despite the heat. The gun felt heavy in his hand. Looking down, he saw that Finch had inserted the bullets into the chambers – snick-click, snick-click. On the low, square table in the centre of the room, the envelope containing Lelord's report had been opened. The gruesome photographs of Steven Finch's remains were laid out beside it.

* * *

The sun was setting behind the hills, bathing the beach and the lungomare in a pale crimson light. The promenade was packed with people leaning over the railings, looking down at a sea growing darker and more forbidding. The beach itself was crowded too; hundreds of people spread out along the shore, bunched together in groups of friends and family. Children chased one another while adults stood chatting, drinking from glasses of wine and bottles of beer. The warm night air was filled with the heady aromas of cooking, mingling with the faint smells of the sea, the sand and the people themselves, their perfumes and colognes, their freshly laundered clothes. It was filled too with talk and laughter and children squealing and crying.

In Loano, Ferragosto – the mid-summer holiday - has a special significance, combined as it is with the Diecimila Luci nella Notte, the Ten Thousand Lights in the Night, a memorial to those fishermen and sailors who've lost their lives at sea. A procession of brightly lit boats slowly makes its way along the coast while the people of the town light candles, for loved ones or for fun, and float them on the water. The candles are drawn out to sea, and gradually, as the stars pierce the night sky, the ten thousand lights drift and spread, rising and falling on the swell until the Ligurian Sea is a gently undulating blanket of flickering fires.

"It's beautiful," said Martelli. "We should light a candle."

If Finch was at all enthusiastic, he hid it well.

They were sitting at a table in Piatti Spaiati, the restaurant at Bagni Perelli beach club, Martelli with his back to the sea. Every seat was taken, every table packed with delicious dishes, every conversation conducted over the clatter and scrape of cutlery on china and the clinking of glasses. Martelli's stomach growled at the scent of sweet basil and garlic as a man at the next table was served a plate of Trenette al Pesto. It positively snarled when the man's companion received a plate of Involtini di Pesce Spada – swordfish rolls stuffed with capers and olives.

The waiter had been crestfallen when Martelli explained that he and his guest would be ordering aperitivi only. It was a disappointment that Martelli shared but he had decided to hold out until dinner with Nardi and the Frenchman.

Finch wore the same clothes - white linen, short-sleeved shirt, khaki trousers and sandals – but he'd added a faded grey baseball cap, pulled down low, and his eyes were hidden behind the sunglasses which normally hung at his neck. His chin bore a few days' growth, silver along the jaw line, and Martelli guessed he hadn't shaved since their last meeting. His mouth was fixed in a tight-lipped grimace and he appeared harried, uneasy.

Their drinks arrived and Martelli began to bring his client up to date, describing first his visit to the shop in Alassio and his conversation with Flavia.

Finch nodded eagerly; clearly impatient for more. "Did you go to Castelvecchio?" he said, interrupting. "Did you search Mario's place?"

Martelli was a little taken aback. He shook his head, smiling. "I drove up there but of course the police were still busy in the house. As far as I know they didn't find anything."

Finch didn't hide his disappointment. Sulkily he picked at the label on a tall, blue bottle of acqua frizzante, peeling it away in soggy strips.

"What did you think I would find?" said Martelli.

Finch exhaled noisily. "The money," he said.

"Money?"

"Yes. The money Mario stole from my brother."

"You're convinced he killed Steven?"

"Yes."

For a moment neither man spoke.

"Mario's girlfriend is in Barga, in Tuscany," said Martelli. "I'll drive there tomorrow and have a chat with her, see if she knows where he is. You know her I take it?"

"Yes. She can't help you." Finch stared at him intently.

"Why not?"

"She doesn't know where he is."

"You've spoken to her?"

"Not exactly."

Martelli frowned, leaning forward to rest on his elbows. "So what makes you say -"

"They split up."

"Estella and Mario?"

Finch nodded. "Yes."

"Because of the baby?"

Finch was taken aback. "What baby?"

"Angela's had a baby, a little boy."

Finch's eyebrows shot up. His sunglasses fell to the tip of his nose and he hurriedly pushed them back into place. "I see," he said. "I didn't know that."

"I'll find out who the father is when I speak to Angela again in a couple of days."

Martelli poked at the ice in his lemonade with the tip of his index finger, watched himself doing it, aware that Finch was watching too. He looked up suddenly, causing his client to shrink back ever so slightly.

"By the way, Angela sends her regards," he said slowly.

"Who exactly is this Angela?"

Martelli stared at his reflection in Finch's sunglasses. "She's one of the girls who used to go on the boat trips with Mario and your brother."

Finch remained impassive. "I don't think I know her."

"She said you'd been to her apartment in Ceriale, for a house-warming party."

Finch shrugged nonchalantly and raised his glass to his lips.

"According to her, you had too much to drink and serenaded the neighbours."

Finch forced a grin. "I don't remember that. Where does she live?"

Martelli described the apartment on Via Orti del Lago. "It's on the far side of the old town, a short walk from the sea, next to the railway line. Apparently you danced around on her terrace, singing at the top of your voice. Very drunk, she said." Martelli raised an eyebrow.

"Well, that's probably why I can't remember," said Finch with a hollow chuckle. "Too drunk." He grimaced and glanced around the restaurant.

Martelli watched him, unable to account for his client's foul mood, which contrasted so sharply with the tone of their earlier encounters. He supposed it must be a result of his recent bereavement. One had to make allowances. He took a sip of lemonade and tried again.

"Did you know Mario had another place up in the mountains? An old farmhouse?"

Finch sat suddenly upright. "That's it!" he exclaimed loudly. The diners at the next table stopped and turned to stare, their forks hovering. Finch banged the table with the flat of his hand. "That has to be it."

"What?" Martelli caught the eyes of their neighbours, who hurriedly resumed their meal.

Finch wagged a finger, angry now. Leaning forward, he hissed, "That's where Mario's hiding and that's where my brother's money is."

Martelli pushed away from the table and leaned back in his chair, sighing deeply. "Now wait, I have no idea where Mario's hiding or if he's hiding at all. Okay, it's suspicious that he hasn't been seen since your brother was murdered but there may be a perfectly simple explanation. He might be abroad. He might be staying with Estella -"

"I told you -"

Martelli raised a hand. "He may even have been murdered himself. Possibly by the same people who killed your brother. We simply won't know until we find him. And I'm afraid I have no idea where this farmhouse is. That's why I need to speak to Estella."

"But this Angela woman might know - especially if she's the mother of his child."

"Maybe," said Martelli, waggling his head. "But I don't know if Mario's the boy's father. And she said she didn't know the place."

"And you believed her?"

"I saw no reason not to but, as I said, I'll pay her another visit in a day or two and find out if she was holding anything back."

Finch leaned forward. "Go and see her tonight," he said insistently. "Forget Estella."

Martelli held his client's gaze. He spoke deliberately. "I have a dinner engagement tonight. I'll go to see Angela again in a day or two. Believe me, it's best to leave her alone for a -"

Finch snorted impatiently and flung himself back in his seat. "Okay, okay," he said. He leaned sideways and delved in a trouser pocket, producing a fat envelope. "Here. You'll need this." He placed the envelope on the table and pushed it across to Martelli.

"What is it?"

"Money."

Martelli stared at it. Up until that point the notion of working as a private detective had been just that, a notion. If money changed hands then things became serious.

"I can't accept payment until I'm issued a private investigator's licence by the Prefettura. If I take your money then I'm breaking the law and liable for prosecution. I haven't even applied for a licence yet. And when I do, it'll be a slow process. They'll want to go through my credit history and things like that. It could take weeks, even months."

Finch shook his head. "Keep it. You'll need cash for expenses. If it makes you feel better then don't open the envelope until the licence comes through." Martelli nodded but left the envelope where it was. After a few seconds Finch sighed with impatience. "Suit yourself," he said, pushing his chair back. "I'm off to London for a few days. I have to tell my mother that her favourite son is dead." He laughed bitterly. "She's old,

Commissario - old and unwell. She needs constant care. Without Steven's money I won't be able to keep up with the bills. I need to find it. Forget Barga — it's a waste of time. Speak to Angela. Concentrate on finding Mario and this place of his up in the mountains. And Tomasz. See if you can find out where he's hiding." He took the envelope from the table and stood up. "I have to get going. I'm leaving tonight."

* * *

He and Finch parted company outside Vittorino's wine bar on the lungomare. Watching him go through narrowed eyes, Martelli felt troubled at having had such an unsettling encounter. At previous meetings, he had found his client personable, easy-going, good company, much the same as Angela had described him. But this time Paul Finch had been taciturn and rude. And his claim that he didn't know Angela and had never set foot in her apartment simply didn't ring true, though often, Martelli reflected, people make an impression on an acquaintance which far outweighs the impression the acquaintance makes on them. They had arranged to meet again at Steven's apartment in three days, by which time the Englishman would, he had said, be back from breaking the terrible news to his mother.

As Finch disappeared from view, Martelli turned around and hurried back down to the beach, where he slipped off his shoes, waded into the shallows and lit a candle, setting it adrift in its delicate paper boat. For luck, he thought, watching the little beacon rise and fall on the gentle waves as though on the chest of a sleeping animal. The change in Paul's priorities made him uneasy.

Clearly his brother's killer was now a secondary concern, it was the money he was after. The candle spun and wheeled as it was carried further and further from the shore. Martelli felt relief that he had not taken the envelope.

"Buonasera, Mimmo. Come stai?" Ricardo smiled, the lenses of his spectacles filled with myriad tiny flames.

"Buonasera, Ricardo. I'm . . . I'm very well. How are you?"

Ricardo studied him for a moment before glancing out to sea. "The lumini are beautiful, eh?"

"Si. Always."

"Do you have a few moments, Mimmo? To talk."

"I . . . Sorry, Ricardo, I have to get going. I'm late for dinner. Can we speak tomorrow?"

Ricardo looked disappointed but nodded. "Okay."

* * *

At home, five minutes later, as Martelli slid Aldo's revolver into its holster and stood it between two heavy volumes of history on his bookcase, he put aside his doubts about his client and focused on dinner. Above all, he told himself, he had to remain calm and leave the histrionics to Nardi. Let him get it off his chest, burn himself out. Arguing would only make things worse. Changing his shirt, he smiled to himself. Things would be fine. They had been friends for a long time, a lifetime. It would take more than a missed breakfast and a difference of opinion over his retirement to drive a wedge between them.

TWENTY-EIGHT

"You are an idiot, Mimmo, an idiot! Do not do this. It will not end well." Nardi banged the table repeatedly with his fist, giving emphasis to each word. "No wonder you have been avoiding me. Do you remember, Mimmo? Do you remember thirty-five years ago I said to you, 'Do not marry this woman'? I was right then wasn't I? And I am right again now. Do not get mixed up in this investigation. I am telling you - it will not end well."

They were sitting outside Il Bagatto, under the streetlight, and Martelli found himself staring up into the whirling galaxy of moths as he struggled to conjure up the justification for his actions. Nardi and Lelord sat looking at him expectantly. Nardi had heard all about the embarrassing encounter with Rubini in Castelvecchio, and if the rumours had reached the top of the Carabinieri tree then they were surely circulating among the lower ranks. It was a disappointing though unsurprising development.

He thought back to his wedding day, thirty-five years ago. It had rained, he remembered, and the wind had been blowing in hard from the east; a few boats had dragged their anchors. She had looked determined, his bride, her pretty face rigid and unsmiling, as though she knew she was not his first choice. Nardi had been slim then, as had he, the pair of them just boys really. They had stood around outside the church, gawky and awkward, smoking cigarettes, uncomfortable in their ill-fitting military uniforms; children dressed as men. Nardi had pleaded with him, had begged him not to go through with it. He had said that what Martelli was doing was wrong, marrying one woman in order to forget another. And he had indeed said that it would not end well. The beseeching look had lingered in his eyes long after the vows had been taken.

She lived in Australia now, his bride, Marilena - Melbourne, perhaps, or Brisbane. He couldn't remember. Thinking back, it felt like she had left soon after the wedding, though in reality it was probably as long as a year. He had heard that she had four grandchildren now, all girls. She had probably shrunk, he thought, like all Italian women seemed to do in late middle age, much more so than other nationalities. He hoped that she was happy. He doubted that she had similar hopes for him.

His earlier hunger forgotten, Martelli picked idly at his linguine. It crossed his mind that their hosts would not be best pleased at his having left food on his plate. Lelord he noticed had also failed to make much of an impression on his dinner. Nardi was still speaking, still fuming, still pounding the table. Beads of sweat sparkled on his forehead. Martelli's brain was filtering out the words until, with a start, he snapped back into the present.

"What did you say?" he said gruffly.

"What?" said Nardi, slightly taken aback, his fist hovering

unsteadily.

"What did you say?" demanded Martelli. "Just then?"

"Mimmo, I said 'I know how you must feel now that you are a captain without a crew'. It must be -"

Martelli held up a hand. He felt a flush of anger rising in his face, as though someone was topping him up with warm blood. The Frenchman shrank back in his chair, flinching in slow motion. He looked ready to flee. Martelli opened his mouth to speak but faltered and fell silent. His pulse began to race; he was suddenly too hot. He stared into his old friend's eyes, his gaze switching rapidly from the left eye to the right, and back again. His face clenched like a fist.

All at once Nardi seemed to deflate, to wither in his seat, his bluster spent. He placed his hands flat on the table, tilted his head and adopted an expression Martelli recognised as intended to indicate compassion. It looked more like constipation. He struck the same pose, mimicking his old friend, mocking him, then he too placed his hands flat on the table, lurched forward and pushed himself upright. Lelord recoiled. Nardi watched wide-eyed. Martelli's chair scraped on the paving as he stood. A dog barked twice. He gave them a conclusive shake of his head then turned and walked away.

A few minutes later, as he stood in his kitchen, panting, arms folded, in darkness, there was a knock at his door. He supposed it was Nardi come to make peace, or Lelord to persuade him back to the table. He turned towards the stairs but remained silent. Again there came a knock. Martelli frowned. Would Nardi knock twice? Would the Frenchman? But who else could it be? He waited, counting the seconds, listening, his neck still twisted towards the stairwell. Nardi would shout, he thought. He wouldn't care that it was late, wouldn't care who heard him. He hurried to the window, pushed open the shutters and bent double over the wide sill but the visitor had gone.

As he turned back to the kitchen, something on the dining table caught the light from the streetlamp and glinted in the darkness. It was a flat, rectangular parcel, wrapped in crinkly, shiny paper. Eduardo must have brought it in for him. He frowned as he tore it open, wondering what on Earth it could be.

The photograph, a rare shot of Martelli in police uniform, had been taken shortly after he joined the force nearly four decades before. Around the picture, on the generous expanse of white mounting board, many of his current and former colleagues had written a message and signed their name. He recognised Bracco's neat script and Lelord's illegible scrawl. Paola, their endlessly patient receptionist, had written that it had been wonderful to work with him; even Leggiero, in Savona, had taken the trouble to write a message. His boss, as he might have predicted, had attempted a witticism. And there at the top, right in the middle, in a beautiful, cursive hand from another age, it said: *To my oldest and best friend on the occasion of his retirement. If this change in circumstances allows us to spend more time together then Italy's loss will be my immeasurable gain.*

Martelli stared at the message for a long time, reading it again and again, blinking repeatedly as he did so.

* * *

When he returned to Il Bagatto, Lelord was sitting by himself, nursing a limoncello, an expression of resignation on his face. The bottle sat where his plate had been. It was half empty and Martelli wondered if the Frenchman had polished off half a bottle of the ice cold, syrupy liquid on his own.

"Thank you for the photograph," he said, taking a seat. "When did that circulate?"

Lelord smiled. "A few weeks ago. I can't remember what I wrote."

"Well I can't read your writing," said Martelli, "so perhaps we'll never know."

The Frenchman laughed. "They'd planned some sort of presentation with speeches and other embarrassments but then . . . well, the body was found in Carpe. They asked Rubini to try to keep you out of it but then surprise, surprise you showed up anyway."

Martelli narrowed his eyes. Was that why Rubini hadn't contacted him? He grunted. "Piero called me."

The waitress brought Martelli a glass and he poured himself a drink.

"How old were you when the picture was taken?"

"Twenty-two, I think. My wife had just left me. I had no money and nowhere to live."

Lelord raised his eyebrows and took a sip from his glass. "Sounds terrible."

"It was the happiest summer of my life," said Martelli, raising his glass and swallowing most of its contents.

"All downhill since then, eh?"

Martelli shrugged but he was smiling. "I suppose Piero

was responsible for the photo," he said. "Where did he go, by the way?"

Lelord nodded. "He just marched off. I thought he'd gone to look for you."

So it had been Piero knocking.

"Were you at the team briefing this morning?"

The Frenchman nodded.

"How did it go?"

"Dismal," he said. "They found a rental car apparently abandoned in Bardineto. It was hired in Genova last week by a couple named Schmidt so Rubini had the whole team chasing around the countryside looking for German tourists. Complete waste of time. Then he changed his mind and decided it must be the business partner, Mario Rossetti." He sighed. "I suppose that makes sense."

"What about the owner of Bar Reale?"

Lelord shook his head. "No help at all."

"Someone's tracking down Finch's associates?"

"Sure, sure but they're hard to find it seems. No one's seen Rossetti for weeks."

"What about Valli? Did he get anywhere with Banca Carige?"

"Nothing. Infrequent deposits and not much money in Finch's account. You'll have to speak to young Bracco if you want any more detail than that."

Lelord knocked back his limoncello and banged his glass clumsily down on the table. As he reached for the bottle and poured himself another, Martelli watched him and tried to remember exactly when he'd first realised that Lelord was gay. He wondered too, for the umpteenth time, if Allegra, whom no one had ever met, rather than being the last *woman* in his old friend's life, had actually been the first *man*, renamed as a means of including him in the conversation. It seemed to Martelli that he and Nardi, and the one or two others with whom they occasionally spent time, had come to mention their own, heterosexual liaisons, such as they were, less and less, perhaps subconsciously sparing the Frenchman from exclusion.

As Lelord waved for the bill, Martelli watched him thoughtfully. The Frenchman had fled his life in Paris and reinvented himself among strangers on the Riviera. He had assumed another identity – albeit his true one. Had Steven Finch undergone a similar reinvention when he arrived in Loano? Had he become a different person?

Lelord topped up Martelli's drink. "About the investigation . . ." he said. "Do you think Piero will come round?"

"Well . . . put it this way," said Martelli. "He never has before."

Lelord started to laugh and it wasn't long before Martelli joined him. They raised their glasses in salute to their friend.

TWENTY-NINE

"You're sure?" said Ted.

"A hundred per cent," said Moody. "It's him. No doubt about it."

Ted fell silent.

"Hello?"

"Yeah, I'm . . . I'm still here," said Ted. "Thanks for letting me know."

"No problem. Sorry to call so late but you said you wanted to know as soon as the ID was confirmed. And listen, I may have dropped you in it a little bit. I happened to mention to one of the local boys that you'd been down here and he didn't look too happy."

Ted snorted. "Don't worry. It's fine. My boss has sorted it out. And I'm glad you called. Did you hear from your mate at Guys and St. Thomas's?"

"Not yet. I'll give you a ring as soon as he gets back to me. In fact I'll speak to him tomorrow morning."

Ted thanked the young pathologist and unplugged his phone charger from the cigarette lighter.

There were spots of rain on the windscreen and the trees at the end of his street were thrashing about, leaves waving like hands. It was going to be another stormy night. He gazed up at their bedroom window, wondering if Caroline was asleep or if she'd heard him pull up outside and was lying fretting, waiting for him to come in, growing angrier by the minute. Pursing his lips, he got out of the car and entered the house as quietly as he could.

At the top of the stairs he winced as his phone pinged to signal the arrival of a text message. Eyes on the gap at the bottom of the bedroom door, he held his breath and tiptoed down the hallway to the kitchen. Closing the door with barely a click, he got a beer from the fridge, unscrewed the cap and sat down at the table. His heart leapt when he noticed that Chester's bowl was empty but he quickly realised, with great disappointment, that it had been emptied and washed - the old tomcat had not returned. Doubtless Caroline was secretly delighted. He took a good swig of the beer, closed his eyes and tried to imagine the tension draining from his body and evaporating. He pictured a meadow, a tranquil place, warmed by late summer sunshine and silent but for birdsong and the rush of a gentle breeze through the long grass. He sat at the edge of the meadow, on the bank of a stream, fishing but not worried about catching anything; a cold bottle of beer in his hand, several more cooling in the water and a well-thumbed Harold Robbins beside him. He sat immersed in this dream world for ten minutes, luxuriating in the drowsiness brought on by alcohol at the end of a long day. He'd spoken again to all of Devlin's neighbours and visited Harry Jay's club and the few shops thereabouts. Tomorrow he would drop in again on Rebecca King and find out what the hell Warren had been up to. He was certain there was more to it than sailing charters and teaching. The new lad, Dean Wilson, had confirmed that Rebecca had told him the truth about the phone call. She had indeed spoken to Warren ten - now twelve - days ago. Ted had left messages for Miss King but she had yet to respond. He would head down to the Kingsland Road in the morning, take Burns with him; treat the Detective Constable to a toasted cheese sandwich at The Towpath cafe. Another thing he must remember to do was get his road atlas from the car and trace the directions scrawled on the envelope in the evidence locker. Maybe they'd lead to Warren.

He jumped as a car horn sounded in the street. His tranquil meadow forgotten, he got up and fetched another beer, checking his phone as he did so. DC Burns had written: *Any news from Margate?* Ted didn't reply.

Something caught his eye and he froze, staring at it, hardly able to believe that it had taken him twenty minutes to notice it. It was a square, white envelope propped against the toaster. She'd written his name on it in red ink. And he knew without having to open it that he didn't need to worry any more about making a noise. He had the place to himself. Caroline was gone.

THIRTY

The road from Loano to Genova sweeps along the coast as though drawn by the hand of the Almighty himself. High above the sea, it cuts through mountains and rocky spurs and leaps across the steep-sided valleys between. The Ligurian Apennines dip their toes into the blue crystal seas for sixty kilometres and more and the road is, by necessity, an engineering marvel incorporating dozens of echoing tunnels, or gallerias, and many gracefully curved bridges, all named for saints and long-dead dignitaries. Beyond Genova the road continues to Chiavari and onwards past La Spezia to Viareggio, where it curls inland and forks to Florence and Pisa. But Martelli wasn't going that far. He was heading to Barga.

Despite its age, the Lancia felt powerful beneath his right foot, giving a full-throated roar in the tunnels and a healthy rumble on the bridges. But it no longer kept pace with the newer cars, many of which sat on his bumper, the drivers impatient to get past, looming so close in his rear view mirror that he could see the gold in their teeth. Either that, he thought, as yet another driver jostled for position, or he himself was stuck in second gear. He changed lanes and watched as the other car sped past. A four wheel drive with steroidal haunches, it dwarfed the Lancia.

He stopped for lunch in Camogli, west of Rapallo, where once, as a boy, he'd stood with his father and older brother, Gennaro, and watched as ten metre waves pounded the little harbour until the fishing fleet was matchwood and the buildings on the quayside were uninhabitable - a rare occurrence but still a potent threat. At a little restaurant overlooking the sea, he ordered a locally made sanguinaccio – a blood pudding - and, mindful of his waistline, a citrus salad to counter its rich, creamy texture. Along with his food, the waitress brought an ice-cold beer and a shy smile, which he was delighted to return.

After lunch he strolled along the sea wall eating an ice cream, a Malaga - Italy's answer to rum and raisin. An elderly woman stood at the end of the inner mole, watching a boat ferrying tourists to the abbey at San Fruttuoso di Capodimonte. He watched as she crossed herself and wondered what it felt like to believe in God. Did the sea air taste fresher? Was the sky a richer blue, food more delicious, life altogether a more satisfying experience?

His tape of Bob Dylan's *Blood on the Tracks* developed a squeak somewhere near Fivizzano, so from there on he drove in silence.

By two o'clock he was on the outskirts of Barga Giardino, the new town, and by ten past he was parked next to the mediaeval Porta Mancianella, gateway to the ancient heart of the city, where he sat for a minute with the car door open, suddenly weak and trembling. He wondered if he was coming down with something or, more likely, if his recent heavy drinking had taken a greater toll on his body than he realised. He felt as though he'd lost the ability to think straight. Perhaps Giacomo was right, he thought, perhaps he was just unravelling a bit, loosening up after a lifetime of deeply felt responsibility. He could only hope it would pass. His need to escape the heat stirred him into life again, sending him hurrying into the shady streets to shelter from the sun's unrelenting rays.

It was nearly forty years since his last visit and he was pleased to see that the city had not changed at all. He slowed his pace, put his hands in his pockets, breathed deeply and imagined a weight being lifted from his shoulders.

Barga is Italy's smallest city, the central quarter of which is a walled citadel perched on top of a hill overlooking the Serchio valley. In the heart of the Garfagnana, it is an ancient place with streets perhaps a thousand years old, paved in hand tooled granite. That afternoon the scent of orange blossom hung in the still air and from the open doors and windows there came the laughter and animated chatter of the city's residents, the Barghigiani, who struck Martelli as a singularly happy crowd.

In the Via Pretorio, dazzled by sunlight reflecting off the smooth, grey paving stones, he heard Mozart's *Le Nozze di Figaro* along with the unmistakable click and crackle of a stylus on vinyl. Stopping to listen for a moment, he looked up, turning three hundred and sixty degrees and gazing at the beautiful buildings with their decorative architectural flourishes and brightly coloured facades. Somewhere a toddler started crying and was shushed into silence. An unseen man coughed raggedly. A motor scooter spluttered and parped and was gone. A clock struck three. He followed Flavia's directions but took time to browse at the windows of the little shops and to read the list of forthcoming events at the Teatro dei Differenti and also at the excellent bookshop. The Barghigiani, it seemed, were fond of jazz and opera. He indulged himself in a little fantasy, imagining one day bringing Cristina to a concert here.

Of course he had to keep an eye out for buzzing scooters and high–revving three–wheeled Ape pick–up trucks but nonetheless he found himself calmed and quite charmed by Barga's cool, tranquil, almost traffic–free piazzas and its steep, narrow, higgledy–piggledy streets.

Straying from his route, he climbed a long flight of stone steps to a piazza at the very summit of the citadel. At its centre stood a magnificent Romanesque cathedral, the Duomo di San Cristoforo, formidable in pale grey limestone, its construction an improbable undertaking in any city, but here, perched on this hilltop, its square tower so high above the plain, a marvel, a towering achievement. A little out of breath from the climb, he stood and took in the view of the valley, which stretched away into the dusty distance, lush and verdant, the nearly dry riverbed a pale, jagged backbone at its centre. To his left, high above the mountains, a pair of eagles wheeled and turned on columns of warm air. To his right, olive groves and vineyards transformed the rolling hills into a heaving quilt of greens and browns, regimented lines interspersed with billowing softness. Behind him a man in the overalls of the local comune - the city council - sat on the steps of the duomo, equally engaged in the Corriere della Sera and a foul-smelling cigar, its rancid odour noticeable even to Martelli several metres away. As he turned and walked towards the cathedral's great entrance, a helicopter flew low overhead and he leaned back to watch it pass.

"They're looking for smoke," said the man with the cigar, lowering his newspaper as Martelli drew near.

Martelli nodded. The threat of forest fires hung over the people of this region as it did the people of his own. The undergrowth was dry as tinder and liable to erupt into a storm of fire at the slightest provocation; a carelessly disposed of cigarette was all it would take, or sunlight magnified through the lens of a discarded glass bottle. And the resulting conflagration could consume countless hectares of woodland in a matter of hours, leaving the landscape scarred for years. And then there were the firestarters, those lunatics who deliberately set the forest ablaze. It was a constant source of anxiety during the summer months, even more so further south.

On a whim, he asked the man, "Do you happen to know the Ramazzotti family? I'm trying to find Estella."

And just like that, without a moment's hesitation, the man rattled off the address, pointing vaguely with his cigar as he did so. "She's always sick, the mother," he said. He spoke gravely but in a way that conveyed his doubts about the true nature of Signora Ramazzotti's ailments.

Thanking the man and bidding him a cheerful goodbye, Martelli mounted the steps and headed into the cathedral, where he sat down on a wooden chair beneath the ornate twelfth century pulpit. The faint smell of camphor and cloves took him back to the Sundays of his childhood and those interminable church services, the only hope of relief the possibility that Giacomo Orso, standing sentinel beside the altar, might faint, something which he did with alarming regularity and which Martelli's grandmother attributed to his shoes, formerly his brother Ricardo's, which she insisted were so tight they cut off the delivery of blood to his brain. After each of these disruptive episodes, the priest would suggest that Giacomo relinquish his position - essentially that of magician's assistant - only to be persuaded otherwise by the heartfelt entreaties of the boys' mother. He smiled at the memory and tried to marshal his thoughts.

Suspicious of his client's insistence that meeting Estella would be a waste of time, he'd decided that she was exactly the person he needed to speak to. So he'd left a message for Nardi, cancelling breakfast, not that he'd expected to see him anyway, and set off shortly after the morning rush.

Including the stop for lunch, the journey had taken four and a half hours, during most of which he had been able to forget Steven Finch and his brother Paul, to forget Angela and Flavia Buonanno and Commissario Rubini, and to forget Aldo and his, let's be frank, he'd inwardly admitted, absolute stupidity. And instead he'd lost himself in the simple pleasure of driving as though just for the sake of it, relishing the curves and the plunging hills, crossing lanes for a racing line in the bends and winding down his window to hear the roar of the engine as it echoed off the walls of the tunnels.

Now, as he looked around at the soaring curved arches and the gleaming floor of russet marble, he wondered at the wisdom of getting involved with Paul Finch and once more felt relief at having refused to take the envelope of money.

* * *

Three kilometres away, Estella Ramazzotti stood with her back to the tall crucifix in the grounds of the church of San Giusto and stared a little wistfully at the countryside of her childhood. It was hazy down in the valley, as though a fine mist was rising from the Serchio itself, although the riverbed, as always at this time of year, and particularly when temperatures were breaking records, was a bleached, rocky, boulder-strewn channel, with little more than a stream snaking along its centre. Around her the voluptuous hills bounded in all directions, dense with oak and chestnut, rich with wildflowers and fruit. Leaning back, she stared into the flawless, watercolour blue sky, narrowed her eyes and took a deep breath, savouring the fresh fragrance drifting from the stone pines as the sun warmed up their oily foliage. She found the aroma deeply invigorating. A royal eagle circled high above, the feathers of its wingtips upturned and splayed like fingers, as though the bird was stretching after a deep sleep.

She'd come to put flowers on her father's grave, to pull the weeds and light a candle for him, something her mother used to do but was now no longer capable. She'd also helped out a little inside the church, had swept the floor, done a little dusting and polishing, and rearranged the tatty bibles stacked in the vestibule.

At a crunching noise behind her she turned in time to see Fra Benedetto's dusty, white Fiat Panda bounce and sway into the gravelled car park. The old priest had first come to the church on the hilltop at Tiglio Alto as a seminarian nearly five decades before. He had fallen in love with the place and contrived to have himself posted to what at the time of his appointment must surely have been regarded as a backwater. Estella smiled and waved at him. She took one last look at the glorious view before mounting her Vespa and firing up the engine. Trundling slowly along, plunging into the potholes, suspension shrieking, she pulled up alongside Fra Benedetto and greeted him as he unloaded groceries from the boot.

"Ciao, Estella," he said. "How's your mother?"

"Oh, still clinging to life," she replied cheerily.

Her mother had been ill for as long as anyone could remember; a succession of hypochondriacal fantasies which had served the teenage Estella well on days when she didn't feel like going to school but which had since become the unremittingly tedious theme of their thrice weekly telephone calls.

The priest gave her an understanding smile. "Well, that *is* good news," he said. "I'll call in to see her next week sometime."

Estella chuckled. "Thank you," she said. "That will be a great comfort to her."

He flashed a mischievous grin. "Are you here for long this time?"

She frowned. "Yes," she said with uncertainty. "Well, for a while at least. I think I'll still be here next week when you visit."

He searched her eyes and for a moment appeared on the brink of asking what was troubling her. The return of her smile changed his mind and he decided to leave it but, as she buzzed away, engine spluttering, he scuffed the baked ground with the toe of his shoe, wondering what Estella had got herself into this time. He stood listening as the sound of the little engine faded to nothing.

* * *

Estella relished the wind in her face as she rode the scooter along the mountain roads. She headed down into the valley and then back up again, around the hairpin bends towards Barga and her mother's house. Her route took her through the main gate, where Martelli had left his car, and into the shadows, the loud, faltering note of her engine echoing off the pristine walls. By now the city appeared all but deserted, the residents having retreated indoors for an afternoon nap. She shot down a slope into the Piazza Santa Annunciata, past the ice cream shop, and uphill again towards the western quarter of the city.

A stranger was waiting outside the house. He stood with his hands in his pockets watching her arrival. Taller than average, he looked strong despite his age, which she guessed was about sixty. His short hair, once dark but now mostly grey, stuck out at the back where he'd slept on it. He hadn't shaved and she noted that his clothes needed ironing.

Estella brought her scooter to a standstill a metre from his feet. She dismounted, hauled the machine backwards onto its stand and stood, hands on hips, staring at him.

The man took off his sunglasses to reveal eyes heavy with fatigue.

"Hello," he said softly. "I'm Domenico Martelli and I'm trying to find Estella Ramazzotti."

THIRTY-ONE

Lelord grimaced as he kneeled on the hard tiled floor and leaned into the bath tub. He had knee pads in the car for those occasions when the crime scene was strewn with broken glass but he wasn't going to traipse down and back up six flights of stairs to get them.

Without turning round he said, "So where's Commissario Rubini?"

"There's a procurement meeting, Doctor," said Bracco from the doorway.

Lelord tutted and shook his head in disbelief.

Bracco blew out his cheeks and shrugged. "He doesn't schedule the meetings," he said in defence of his new boss. Changing the subject, he added, "I heard on the radio it's forty-six degrees in Torino. Shit, that's hot."

Lelord grunted. He inserted the spike of the thermometer and gently pressed it home, feeling for the change in density as the tip pierced the liver. Bracco glanced around the room, looking anywhere but the bathtub; finally letting his gaze settle on the ceiling. On the inside of the glass lampshade he counted seven dead moths. He wondered how they'd got in. He took out a handkerchief and mopped his brow. It was stifling hot in the little bathroom and the smell was atrocious. He was trying to breathe through his mouth.

"I'm just going through the motions here," said Lelord. "She's cold. And in this heat that means she's been dead for at least twenty-four hours. Any less than that and the temperature of the water might have given us a false reading anyway."

He withdrew the thermometer and stowed it in a plastic container before shuffling to the end of the bath and gently gripping the dead woman's left foot with both hands. Bracco held the handkerchief to his nose, moved in closer and watched with interest as Lelord tried flexing the woman's toes.

"The feet are always last to stiffen," the Frenchman explained. "But like I said, I'm just going through the motions." He shook his head. "I'll be able to tell you more when I get her to the mortuary." Gently, he tugged at the chain wrapped tightly around the woman's ankles and leaned closer to inspect the wounds where the metal had dug into the flesh. "She put up a hell of a fight."

He straightened up, wincing and arching his back. As he got to his feet, his knees made a pronounced popping noise.

"So what are we looking at?" said Bracco, retreating to the doorway.

"Well, my guess is that her heart gave out." Lelord stared at the woman's body, the look on his face one of profound sadness. "The pain must have been indescribable."

"What caused these injuries?"

"Well, she was beaten but most of the damage was caused by boiling water."

"Boiling?"

The Frenchman nodded. "Put simply - she's been scalded to death."

Bracco stared at the Frenchman, shaking his head in disbelief. "So someone stripped her, tied her hands behind her back, chained her ankles to the taps and then turned the hot water on?"

The Frenchman shook his head emphatically. "No, no - whoever did this used water boiled in the kettle or else in pans on the stove, or both. And they made sure to pour it directly onto her face and chest."

Bracco was horrified. He looked from the Frenchman to the body and back again.

"Yes," said the Frenchman, removing his rubber gloves with a snap, snap. "It must have taken a long time, possibly hours."

They stared at one another, each imagining how much the young woman must have suffered.

A clatter startled them, made them both jump. Two young men appeared behind Bracco, red-faced and panting. It was the ambulance crew, breathless from carrying a stretcher and a heavy bag up six flights of stairs.

Lelord held up a hand. "Be with you in a moment, lads." The two men dumped their gear and headed straight out onto the terrace on the far side of the living area. Eyeing Bracco, Lelord said, "Who found her?"

"The sister was looking after her baby boy - had him for a

couple of days. She found the body this morning when she brought him back. She has a key."

Lelord put a hand to his throat and returned his gaze to the dead woman in the bath. So she was a mother, he thought.

"And the father?"

Bracco shrugged. "No idea but the apartment's rented in the name of Mario Rossetti.

Lelord turned. "Isn't he . . ?" He tailed off, eyes narrowed.

The younger man nodded. "Steven Finch's business partner."

Lelord tutted. "What the hell is going on in this town?"

"There's no sign of forced entry," continued Bracco, ignoring the question. "So she must have let the killer in." He glanced at his watch. "I'd better start knocking on doors. See if one of the neighbours remembers any visitors."

The Frenchman returned his gaze to the dead woman. "'Hell is empty and all the devils are here'," he said quietly. When he looked up again, Bracco was gazing at him, uncomprehending. "Shakespeare," said Lelord. "La Tempesta."

Bracco nodded blankly and looked at his shoes. "The Chief said something about that," he said. "About the banality of evil. He said it hides in ordinary places."

Lelord sighed. "Sadly true."

Bracco looked at him. "Is he . . ?"

Lelord inclined his head. "What?"

"Is he okay? The Chief, I mean."

"Sure. Why do you ask?"

"I saw him yesterday on Via Garibaldi. I was in Marco's buying flowers and he went past. He was . . ." He let his gaze roam

225

a little before meeting the Frenchman's stare once more. "It was only midday but he seemed quite drunk. He was staggering about and he looked really rough. He looked like he hadn't slept for weeks. My wife -"

Lelord held a finger to his lips and eyed the door. He gestured for Bracco to come closer then nodded for him to continue.

"My wife," murmured the young detective. "She's friends with Michela Trigiani, who lives opposite the Chief. Her boys are in the same class as our eldest girl. Michela says he gets stoned every night and collapses on the roof in his clothes. She sleeps with her window open and she can smell the marijuana." He searched Lelord's eyes but the Frenchman gave nothing away. "When I saw him he looked terrible," he went on. "He looked like he needed a wash."

Lelord smiled, shrugging off the young man's concerns. "He'd probably been out celebrating his retirement." He shrugged, the corners of his mouth turned down. "And this woman, this Michela, is probably exaggerating," he said dismissively. He gestured for Bracco to get going. "I'd start with the old lady across the hall," he said. "Deaf as a post but I bet she misses nothing. She was outside on the balcony when I arrived and standing in her doorway by the time I got upstairs."

Bracco nodded moodily. He didn't need to be told how to do his job.

Lelord watched him leave then stood for a minute, his brow drawn low over his eyes, tapping a finger on his lips.

"All set in here?"

"What's that?" said the Frenchman, startled.

"Is she ready to go?" said the paramedic.

Lelord nodded. Turning to look at the body, he said, "I'm afraid she is."

THIRTY-TWO

"Fish and chips?" asked Martelli.

"Two thousand kilos. Maybe more. For two weeks every year." She grinned half-heartedly. "Didn't you know? Barga's the most Scottish place in Italy."

Martelli looked around, momentarily at a loss. He and Estella had taken a seat at a picnic table at one end of the local football pitch. Around them dozens more tables were busy with diners, all tucking in to huge platefuls of battered fish and chunky chips. Beneath the corrugated metal canopy of the makeshift stadium a team of cooks, red faced and slick with sweat, laboured over bubbling vats from which great mushroom clouds of steam erupted as the batches of fish and chips were plunged into the spitting vegetable oil. There was ketchup, of course, but no vinegar. Diners were offered wedges of lemon, a fresh salad with a balsamico dressing and gallons of wine. Everything was served on paper plates and eaten with plastic knives and forks.

Many villages in Italy hold festivals – sagri - during the

summer and into the autumn months, celebrating everything from the humble onion to the grape harvest. Martelli had attended plenty of these events, frequently involving processions of people in mediaeval dress along with jousting, barrel rolling, horse races and curious acts of religious devotion. But he had never been served fish and chips by a man in a kilt on a football pitch in the stifling heat of a summer evening; had never even heard of the Sagra del Pesce e Patate, billed as a celebration of *'traditional Scottish fish'n'chips'*. He laughed aloud as a bagpiper, straining as though in a stranglehold, launched into a mournful, tuneless rendition of *Flower of Scotland* prompting the children on a neighbouring table to stick fingers in their ears.

Estella Ramazotti looked to be a little over thirty. She wore loose-fitting blue shorts, a white vest and dusty black flip flops. Her dark, shoulder length hair was tied in a pony tail and she seemed to be wearing no make-up, although Martelli didn't peer too closely. Her brown eyes were large and terribly bloodshot, as though she lacked sleep. A cold sore on her top lip, directly under her nose, had scabbed over. On the inside of her left wrist there was a tattoo, a constellation of five-pointed stars, outlined in dark blue. All that said, there was something about her, Martelli thought, which he couldn't quite define; a classiness perhaps, and a savvy nature that belied her scruffy appearance. He imagined she played her part well when dealing with customers in the boutique of which, he reminded himself, she was the owner. He shook his head. It was too big a commitment to simply abandon, a business like that, even temporarily. And it seemed too significant an asset to leave in the unreliable hands of Flavia Buonanno, if only for a short period. Something very important had brought her back to her mother's house. Martelli doubted she had developed a sudden renewed interest in the older woman's imagined illnesses. He wanted to know what she was hiding from.

"Are we going to eat?" said Estella, meeting his gaze.

"I'm in your hands," he said, smiling again.

* * *

"Don't listen to anything Angela says," said Estella, scowling. "She's devious and she's a druggie." She looked as though she might spit. Martelli took a mouthful of fruity wine. "Mario's a stoner. That's how he knows Angela. She used to get him weed from a friend of hers in Savona – some computer whizz." She took a gulp of wine. "And Paul's un pigrone – good for nothing," she went on. "And he's always drunk. They're both useless. Steven ran things." She pointed her fork at him. "And don't expect Paul to pay you. He never has any money."

Martelli turned his head and stared off into the distance, at the opposite goalmouth. He pursed his lips and allowed his focus to drift, trying to remember if Paul had sipped anything other than mineral water during dinner at Il Bagatto. Certainly that was all he'd ordered at Piatti Spaiati. He thought too of the envelope stuffed with cash. The Paul he knew certainly didn't behave like a penniless drunk. Was Estella really talking about the same man? Could she be misleading him for reasons as yet unclear? Or was his client not who he claimed to be? The piper coaxed a particularly piercing screech from his instrument, jolting him from this train of thought. He turned to face Estella, his expression impassive. She, he reminded himself, like Angela, had appeared neither surprised nor disappointed at the news of Steven's death, even though he was the business partner of her recent ex-boyfriend. "And what exactly did they do?" he asked. "Steven and Mario? Smuggling, presumably?"

She wrinkled her nose. "Cigarettes."

"Just cigarettes?"

She held his gaze for a moment before replying slowly. "Drugs. From Morocco, I think, or Tunisia. And other stuff . . ."

Martelli inclined his head, giving her a quizzical look.

"I don't know. People maybe." She said this with a casual shrug, as though it was a minor infraction. "But it was all Steven. Mario's just stupid. He's easily led. He was doing fine, you know, cleaning swimming pools, taking people on fishing trips. He doesn't owe any money on the boat. And then Steven came along . . ."

Martelli stiffened. "Swimming pools?" He narrowed his eyes. "Did he use acid for that?"

She glowered. "How would I know?"

"Did they all hang out together? Mario, Steven and Paul? Would you say they were friends?"

"No. Mario and Paul spent a lot of time together. And they hung out with Tomasz from time to time."

"The Polish guy?"

"Mmm," she took another gulp of wine, nodding. "But Steven was a real loner. They never saw him unless they were, you know, working."

"Did you know Mario has a place up in the mountains, above Castelvecchio?"

She nodded, a look of derision on her face. "His secret

hideaway. His uncle died and left it to him." She shuddered. "È molto sporco. It's a dump. There's no toilet and it needs a new roof."

"You've been there?"

She shrugged. "A few times. Not for ages. Why?"

"I wondered if he might be living there."

"What do you mean?"

"Well, he's not at home and nobody's seen him for weeks. When did you last hear from him?"

She shrugged, holding his gaze. "Months ago." But she was lying. The eyes will always betray you, thought Martelli, no matter how hard you try.

"Have you any idea where he might have gone?"

She speared a chip, avoiding his gaze this time. "He's probably getting stoned somewhere. He always said he wanted to retire to an island one day."

Another lie, he thought. "He's a bit young to retire, isn't he?"

"They had a big payday coming," she said, chewing noisily. "Or so he claimed. He's probably off spending it somewhere, wasting it. Try Ibiza." She gestured with her fork again. "Or London - he has friends there."

The money, thought Martelli, looking at his own plate. That's all my client's interested in. He's just using me to find the money. Or trying to.

"You know you're getting him into big trouble by telling me this?" he said. "I'll have to tell the police. If what you say is true then he might go to prison for a very long time. Paul as well. And Tomasz."

"What do I care?" she said, her cheeks reddening. But

clearly she did. Is this revenge? Martelli wondered. Is this payback for an affair with Angela? For the baby? If so then it seemed mercilessly out of proportion.

"So that's how you paid for the shop? With Mario's money?"

Estella was taken aback. "No, certainly not," she exclaimed. "What made you think that?"

He spread his hands and shrugged, shaking his head. "It was a question not an assumption."

Estella speared another chip, eyeing him irritably and with a degree of mistrust. "My aunt bought the shop for me."

"Your aunt?"

"Yes, my aunt." She nodded emphatically. "My mother's sister."

Martelli's expression was a question.

Estella sighed at this probing of seemingly unrelated aspects of her private life. "Mariacarmela Aricò. You might have heard of her. She's a business woman. She buys and sells properties."

The question was answered but the expression remained. Aricò? Estella's aunt? He shook his head. Using his fingers, he tore at the crispy batter on his piece of fish. It was very greasy and he thought it revolting. Letting it fall to his plate, he decided to change the subject. "Can you give me directions to the farmhouse?"

"If you like," she said. "There isn't a proper road though. You'll probably need a four-wheel drive. Mario got an old army jeep off one of his English mates." She stabbed at her chips. "But why don't you just get Paul to take you up there?"

"Paul?" Martelli exclaimed, unable to hide his bafflement. He shook batter from his fingers and reached for a paper napkin. "He didn't even know it existed until yesterday."

"What?" she said, leaning back, puzzled. "Cristo santo - he's there all the time. He practically lives there."

Since waking to find Finch standing over him, pistol in hand, the needle on Martelli's internal barometer had been oscillating wildly. It now swung towards 'storm'. Something was very wrong and somehow he'd ended up in the middle of it.

THIRTY-THREE

DC Burns' face lit up as the toasted cheese sandwiches arrived and he welcomed his plate with outstretched arms. Ted's stomach gurgled loudly. The waitress heard it and smiled, catching his eye. He didn't return the smile.

"What is quince, anyway?" said Burns, reaching for the open jam jar.

"It's a fruit," said Ted, cutting his sandwich in half. "It's like a sour pear, I suppose. My grandad used to make quince wine. I don't think you can eat them raw."

DC Burns eyed the viscous brown jam with suspicion.

"You don't have to have any," said Ted sharply, reaching across the table and dragging the jar towards his plate.

Sheepishly, Burns looked down at his sandwich. Ted grunted quietly, silently admonishing himself for letting his bad mood show. He bit into his own sandwich and glanced around as he munched.

The sun shone brightly, reflecting off the waters of the

Regent's Canal and throwing sinuous patterns of light onto the walls of the waterside buildings. Half a dozen mallards squatted at the water's edge, eyes closed, resting their heads on their wings. They displayed a masterful disregard of the foot traffic just a couple of feet away, remaining still even when a trio of long-haired dachshunds went trotting past. Ted envied them their wilful obliviousness.

He'd intended to visit Rebecca King first thing in the morning but the Blackwall Tunnel had been closed. Unable to get hold of DC Burns, he'd gone to the station instead. By the time the tunnel reopened, he'd been stuck in a media relations seminar – something he'd avoided for weeks and which dragged on for much longer than he'd been led to expect. He'd then sat at his desk for nearly an hour, trying to follow the directions written on the back of the envelope found among Warren Devlin's possessions and growing increasingly impatient as he failed to do so. Now it was past four thirty and he'd missed lunch. So, while he and Burns waited for Rebecca King to get home from work, he tucked greedily, if rather grumpily, into the toasted sandwich. Oozing with melted cheese, butter and the sugary quince jelly, it wasn't the healthy option.

"What are you going to ask her?"

"Well," said Ted, swallowing. "I'm going to ask her why she lied to me."

"What about?" said Burns.

"She told me they'd split up. So why did she drive his Porsche to Stansted? I'd bet you any money it was her contact lens Simpson found in the car. Okay – maybe they aren't together any more but I reckon she knows where he is, or where he was ten or twelve days ago at least."

"Do you think she's involved in whatever Devlin's up to?"

Ted rolled his eyes impatiently. "How would I know?" he snapped.

Again Burns looked cowed and Ted immediately regretted speaking harshly. He put down his sandwich.

"Look – I'm sorry." He pressed the thumb and index finger of his right hand to his brow and squeezed hard, eyes shut tight. "I didn't sleep too well last night and this business is really starting to get on my nerves." He yawned, diverting his thumb and forefinger to his closed eyes, digging hard into the sockets, relishing the discomfort. "And this afternoon I got caught up in one of those bloody awful media seminars, which went on for hours." He lowered his hand, blinking. "Then I tried to follow the directions written on that envelope from Devlin's gym bag and didn't get anywhere. They don't make any bloody sense." He reached into his pocket for his mobile phone. "Here – maybe you can figure it out."

Burns squinted at the photo on the proffered phone, cupping his hands around the screen. "The A10 is the Old North Road," he said. "Does that say 582? Where's that?"

"Preston," said Ted gloomily.

Burns frowned. "Does the A10 go as far north as that?"

"No," said Ted, returning his phone to his pocket. "It runs from London Bridge to Kings Lynn." He raised his hands, palms skywards, pulling a face that said: 'I give up'.

"Is it a 6, maybe?"

Ted shook his head. "The 562 runs from Liverpool to Warrington - nowhere near the A10."

Burns squinted at the screen. "That's not . . ." He stopped mid-sentence, suddenly thoughtful. "Wait a sec." He raised the index finger of one hand while reaching into the pocket of his jacket with the other. "Look at this." He pulled out a piece of paper, which he unfolded and lay flat on the table. On it was printed a small and rather fuzzy-edged map, the colours bleeding into one another. He spun it around so Ted could read it. "Here," he said, pointing.

Ted stared but didn't immediately grasp the significance of what he was looking at. He shook his head. "I -"

"Here," said Burns, tapping his finger on the map. "There's the A10. It runs along the coast. And look, here's the 582."

"Where is this?"

"Italy. Loano."

Ted sat upright. "Is that . . ?"

Burns nodded. "Where the flatmate's brother died."

Ted flopped back in his seat, still staring at the map, both hands flat on the table, forehead deeply lined, sandwich forgotten. "Has that Lombardi guy spoken to the Italian police yet?"

"He's supposed to be doing it today." Burns picked up the map and began folding it. "What time's King due back?"

"Her text said around five," said Ted distractedly, still focused on what he'd just learned. "But she'll probably be late. Listen, can I take that?"

"Sure," said Burns, shrugging and passing Ted the piece of paper. Ted weighed it in his hand before slipping it into the inside pocket of his jacket. Deep in thought, he turned and stared into the murky water. A narrowboat chugged past, its wake rippling along the banks, lifting a Mexican wave of flotsam. On the far side of the canal, at a spot only accessible from the water, a flash of bright pink caught his eye. Looking closer, he saw that it was a flip flop wallowing among the algae. "Come on," he said. "Let's speak to Miss Rebecca King."

ADAM BANE

THIRTY-FOUR

Martelli ran; his keys and loose change jangling wildly in his
trouser pockets, the slip-on sandals he'd chosen to wear that
morning wholly inappropriate for haste, the fish and chips sitting
in his stomach like a cannonball.

'He practically lives there,' Estella had said. What in God's
name was going on? Why would Paul lie to him about something
like that?

The answer was obvious: he wouldn't.

Martelli desperately needed to speak to someone – to
Nardi, Bracco or Lelord, even Rubini if he had to. But foolishly
he'd left his mobile phone in the glovebox of the Lancia, where it
had likely melted like a bar of chocolate in the late afternoon heat.

"Stupido! Stupido! Che sciocco!"

Three times he stumbled, cursing himself for a fool as he
charged up Via Giacomo Puccini, gesturing at passersby to step
aside. It was uphill all the way to the Porta Mancianella – one and
a half kilometres - and by the time he reached the Ponte Vecchio

his heart was racing and his shirt was soaked with sweat and sticking to his skin. On the old bridge he had to slow down to catch his breath before turning right onto Via Guglielmo Marconi, which snaked steeply around the perimeter of the old town.

When he reached the car his legs felt leaden and his throat raw and he had pins and needles in his feet. His hands shook violently as he dug his key out of his pocket and it took him three attempts to insert it into the lock. The air inside the car was warm and fetid; it rushed out at him as though swollen to twice its volume. As he leaned in and fumbled to open the glove box it felt hot enough to bake bread and he found himself struggling to breathe. His mobile phone hadn't melted but it was nearly out of juice and he cursed himself for having forgotten to charge it the day before. His knees started to tremble uncontrollably. He needed to sit down. It was too hot in the car to perch on the edge of the driver's seat so he leaned against the wing, still breathing heavily. As he dialled Nardi's number, he wondered briefly what Estella Ramazzotti must have made of his sudden departure, the remainder of his fish and chips forgotten, his cup of wine knocked to the ground. Had she stared after him as he hurried away? Had she sighed with relief and hoped never to see him again? Or had she wondered, perhaps with a hollow feeling in the pit of her stomach, what she had said to get him so agitated?

Nardi didn't answer and Martelli left a voicemail message so muddled, so breathless and wheezy, as to be all but incomprehensible. Bracco didn't pick up either - the call went straight to voicemail so either he was already engaged in another call or his phone was switched off. He left the young detective a message too, this one only marginally less muddled than the first:

"Ispettore . . . I mean . . . I mean Bernardo. It's Comm . . . It's Martelli. Domenico Martelli. Can you call me as soon as you get this? It's urgent. It's *very* urgent."

Next he rang Lelord and, to his relief, the Frenchman answered immediately. He spoke without preamble, as though he'd anticipated Martelli's call.

"Where are you?" he asked, gravely.

"Barga."

"What?" He sounded bewildered. "Where's that?"

"The Garfagnana. Tuscany. I'll explain later. Listen -"

"No, you listen -" said Lelord.

"No, Pippo, please, this is important. Who identified Paul Finch?"

"You mean Steven?" the Frenchman sounded out of sorts, uncharacteristically harassed. "His brother did. You know that."

"No. Not Steven. I mean the brother himself, my client. Who identified him? Who checked his credentials?"

"I suppose Rubini did. Why?"

"How? How did he check his identity?"

"I guess from his passport. Mimmo, listen, you need -"

"Did *you* see his passport?" demanded Martelli.

"Of course not," said the Frenchman, angry now. "It's not my job to question the identity of the bereaved. It would be -"

"Where's Bracco? Have you seen him today?"

"I was with him about an hour ago. Mimmo, listen to me. You need to speak to him."

"I know. I just left him a message. What's -"

"Mimmo!" snapped Lelord.

Martelli fell silent. He had never known the Frenchman to

lose his cool.

Lelord took a deep breath and continued, his words now drawn out, measured; the solemnity in his voice unmistakable, as when delivering terrible news. "He's at an apartment in Ceriale, on Via Orti del Lago. The girl's name is . . ." The Frenchman paused, checking his notes.

Martelli heard a roaring noise, like wind through a stand of trees. "Angela Vaccarezza," he said quietly and with a profound sense of foreboding. His head began to swim. He felt queasy. He lolled forward, caught himself just in time. The trembling in his legs, having subsided, started up again. The phone felt suddenly slippery in his hand as his palms began to sweat.

"That's right," said the Frenchman. "Whatever you do, don't go to her apartment."

"I've already been there," said Martelli almost choking on the words.

"Ah. In that case -"

"Is she . . ?"

"She's dead, Mimmo. The sister found her this morning."

The roaring grew louder. Martelli pictured the little boy, Angela's son, lying contented in his basket, snuffling occasionally in his sleep. He whispered, "Oh, Dio santo."

Neither man spoke for perhaps ten seconds. To Lelord it felt like as many minutes. Martelli closed his eyes and swayed gently, the top of his head describing a tiny circle. There was a faintly bitter, metallic taste in his mouth, coppery, like blood. Eventually he said simply, "How?"

"Very bad, Mimmo. She was tortured with boiling water."

Acid burned the back of Martelli's throat. He took a deep

breath and blew out through puckered lips.

The Frenchman changed the subject. "What did you mean earlier? Why were you asking about your client?"

"Because I think it's not him, Pippo."

"What do you mean? Not who?"

"Paul Finch," said Martelli with finality. "I think my client isn't who he claims to be. He isn't Paul Finch."

THIRTY-FIVE

"Paul Finch is dead," said Ted brusquely, staring intently at Becky King. "His body washed up on a beach on the north Kent coast, at a place called Birchington. It's pretty safe to assume he was aboard Warren's boat when it was wrecked two and a half weeks ago. I need to speak to Warren. So I need you to tell me, right now, where he is."

She blinked twice. Her cheeks grew quickly red, her lower lip began to tremble and tears welled up in her eyes. Ted looked away, not wishing to encourage any hysterics.

Two minutes earlier, he'd rapped loudly several times on the metal roof of her boat. Not really expecting a response, he'd been surprised when she popped up on the rear counter deck looking, if anything, even more dishevelled than during their first encounter. This time she wore a tight-fitting, blue denim mini-skirt with pink fishnet tights and training shoes with high platform soles; a bright red bra showed through her thin white blouse. Her smile had been nervous, but she'd invited them in nonetheless.

At six feet tall, Ted had had to duck to get below deck and once inside had remained stooped, constantly mindful of the low ceiling looming just above his head. The three of them had squeezed onto bench seats either side of a built-in pine dining table, Ted sitting awkwardly, straining to prevent his knees from touching hers, Burns sitting next to her, twisted at the waist, his legs sticking out into the narrow central aisle.

"Here," said Burns gently, reaching for a box of tissues as tears started to roll down her cheeks.

She turned to the younger man and smiled, accepting the box and tugging out a tissue, flashing Ted a wounded, accusatory look. As she bent forward to blow her nose, Ted eyed her thinning, bleached hair and flaking scalp with undisguised distaste. He averted his gaze, hanging his head and looking down at the stained and scratched tabletop, eyes wide with exasperation. He puffed out his cheeks and exhaled loudly. When he looked up again, Burns was glaring at him. "What?" he mouthed. Burns tentatively patted the air. Ted clenched his fists and mimed a fierce snarl, aiming it at the top of Rebecca King's head. Burns looked pained, though a little unsure of himself. Ted shook his head and let his gaze wander around the cluttered interior of the houseboat, taking in the shabby furnishings and ill-maintained fixtures, the bundles of clothes and piles of yellowed newspapers, the overtly penurious nature of Rebecca King's circumstances. At the far end of the boat, in the living area, she'd clipped a faded batik throw to the window frame in place of curtains; in the kitchen, where they sat, all but one of the cupboard doors was missing its handle. Around the sink the sealant was black with mould, above the gas hob the ceiling was caramel with coagulated grease and the whole place smelled strongly of stale cigarettes. Through the open door to the tiny bathroom Ted spotted a squat, white plastic bottle sitting on a shelf above the sink. It had a pale blue label and a small, conical screw cap. He grimaced. Caroline and Becky King used the same brand of contact lens solution.

"I need to know what's going on," he said irritably, focusing on Becky King once more. "Were you there to pick up Warren or someone else?"

"What?" she said, hesitantly. As she raised her head, he couldn't tell whether her confusion was genuine or not.

"Stansted. Did you go there to collect Warren or someone else?"

"I . . ." She started to cry again. Burns pulled more tissues from the box and handed them to her. She scrunched them together and hid her face in them.

"Oh, for goodness sake." Ted squeezed his eyes shut and tapped a clenched fist against his forehead.

"Shall I put the kettle on?" said Burns brightly.

She sniffed loudly and nodded, her face still buried in the tissues. Ted rolled his eyes again.

While Burns made the tea, Ted sat staring out of the window, watching the legs, dogs, bags and bicycle wheels of passersby. When Burns clattered the little tin kettle onto the hob, Becky King flinched but kept her head down.

"So, Miss King, Becky, let's start again," said Ted impatiently. "Presumably you'd already guessed that Paul had drowned since you knew it wasn't Warren on board the boat."

She nodded slowly, still slumped forwards. Thank Christ, he thought. Progress at last. He waited while she dabbed at her eye makeup.

"And you didn't think to tell us?"

She shivered but said nothing.

"Where is Warren?"

Again she gave no response. He glanced at the ceiling. He looked over at Burns but the younger detective had his back turned and was searching in the cupboards for teabags. "Is he in Italy?"

She stiffened. After a moment's hesitation, she gave a quick shrug.

"Can you explain to me why you left Warren's car at Stansted ten days ago?"

She looked up, puffy-eyed, a hand clasped tightly in front of her mouth, alarm showing through the tears.

"It's an airport, Becky. There are cameras everywhere. You parked the car and then you sat in arrivals for nearly two hours. I'm guessing you were waiting for Warren since you were driving his car. If you were waiting for someone else then I need you to tell me who. When Warren – or whoever - didn't show, you left. But you took the train back to London. Why? Can you tell me why you left the car?"

She shook her head and looked down again, reaching blindly for another tissue. Exhaling loudly, Ted pushed the box until it touched her hand.

"Why not? Why can't you tell me? Has someone threatened you?"

She flinched but continued staring at the grubby tabletop, fumbling tissue after tissue out of the box.

So, he thought, she has been threatened. "Who threatened

you? Was it Warren?"

She shook her head emphatically as she pressed the fresh bunch of tissues to her face.

He was surprised by this. "Who then? And where is Warren? Is he still in Italy?"

Once more she didn't answer.

"Becky, you have to tell me."

Again nothing. Ted snorted furiously.

"This is serious, Becky. Becky! Answer me! Where is Warren?"

The kettle started to whistle.

"Is Warren still in Italy?" he demanded again, louder this time. "Answer me! Where is he? Where is Warren? And who threatened you?"

The kettle whistle attained a higher pitch and he raised his voice yet further. "Tell me Becky! Tell me where he is! Where is Warren!"

The whistling grew louder and higher still. Ted slapped the tabletop hard. Becky King jumped in her seat and wrapped her arms around herself, her shoulders shuddering uncontrollably as the tears flowed ever more freely. Ted took a deep breath, leaning back, poised to shout his next question.

"Do you want tea, sir?"

Ted rounded on Burns, eyes ablaze. "What?"

"Tea, sir? Do you want tea as well or am I just making two cups?"

Ted stared at the little red kettle in Burns' hand. He thought of the disappointing camping trips of his youth; freezing cold and knee deep in clart, struggling for ages to get a fire going and for what, for some horrendous cup-a-soup with lumps of unmixed powder at the bottom? His clothes damp, everything damp; his book ruined and his torch packing in. Awful. Those trips had been awful. Like this stupid, snotty woman. He leaned his elbows on the table and pressed his face into his cupped hands. Why was she being so obstructive? Why didn't she just tell him what he wanted to know? Couldn't she see she was just wasting everybody's time? He shook his head, leaned back in his chair and dragged his hands down his face.

"No, thanks."

"Becky, do you have sugar?" said Burns.

Becky King looked up and shook her head. "I don't take sugar," she said weakly.

"I couldn't find any milk."

She shook her head again. "I'm out of milk," she whispered.

Burns placed a mug of tea on the table, turning it so the handle was towards her, then he sat down, folding himself awkwardly into the tight space, careful not to spill his own tea as he did so.

He blew into his mug. "So," he said softly. "Let's start at the beginning. When did you and Warren split up?"

Becky King gripped her mug with both hands and stared into it as though spellbound. The detectives remained silent. A lorry in an empty yard on the opposite side of the canal rattled into life and reversed slowly out of view, taking with it the long shadow that had been keeping Becky King's boat cool. By degrees, sunlight streamed through the grubby window above the sink, lighting dusty cobwebs on the brass wall lamps and giving the pink tissues a luminous quality.

"Warren went to Italy to speak to Mario," she said weakly, still staring into her tea. "To a place near Genoa."

Ted took a breath and opened his mouth to speak but Burns stopped him with a swift shake of his head.

"I was supposed to pick him up from the airport but he wasn't on the plane," she went on. "While I was at the airport, Paul's brother rang me. Steven." She choked a little as she said the name. "He threatened me, told me to keep my mouth shut, told me he'd find me if I didn't." She leaned forward and took a sip of tea without lifting the mug. "I panicked and left the car. Warren has another key. I thought he could pick it up when he came back."

"Well, Steven Finch is dead," said Burns. "So you needn't worry about him anymore."

Ted leaned forward, staring intently.

"Who's Mario?" he said.

THIRTY-SIX

Nardi always referred to it as the 'struggle for clarity', that phase of an investigation during which it became crucial to tie together the seemingly incongruent and tangential witness statements with the physical evidence. On television, detectives talked of 'solving the riddle' or of 'finding the final piece of the jigsaw puzzle', but Martelli saw things differently. In his opinion a criminal investigation wasn't analogous with a child's game. It was a much more emotional, immersive experience. He couldn't detach himself from the pain of the victims' families in that way; couldn't reduce those involved to mere counters on a board. He felt the fear of those in danger, felt the anger of those whose lives had been shattered. And it was that emotion, that empathy which for four decades had made him - in the words of Cesare Molineri, veteran Vice Questore, in his letter of recommendation proposing Martelli as the new head of Sezione III many years before - 'a supremely effective detective'. And the importance of that empathy, in Martelli's opinion, could not be over-estimated. It instilled in the hunter - and that's how he saw himself, a hunter, killers his quarry – a level of tenacity so unyielding as to be unstoppable.

But now, for the first time in those forty years, he found himself doubting his own abilities. Had he lost his capacity to read people's emotions? Or was it simply that the man he knew as Paul Finch had been unconvincing and therefore confusing from the start?

In his head he replayed the conversations he'd had with his client and realised that he'd asked very few questions; that in all probability he had been so wrapped up in his own grief at the loss of his career and the collapse of his life's structure that he'd neglected to make even the most cursory of background checks. The business with Aldo, the row with Gianpiero and the potential for romance with – no, his lust for Cristina - had all contributed to a lack of clear thought bordering on delirium; that and his own self-indulgent moping. He had been, he was ashamed to admit, a supremely *ineffective* detective.

And now Angela was dead.

He yanked back and forth on the steering wheel as though attempting to strangle it.

It was time to start thinking clearly again. His date with Cristina for their hike into the forest was fixed for the following morning. He must call her and make sure it was still going to happen. There was an urgency to it now. He had to find Mario Rossetti's hideaway. He had to find Mario himself. He had to find Angela's killer.

He pushed the Lancia hard, crushing the accelerator to the floor, desperate to be back in Loano. At a certain speed, well over the legal limit, the loose end of a piece of duct tape holding the driver's door mirror in place began to vibrate. It buzzed like a bee in a jar and the noise drove a wedge into the already confused plane of his thoughts, splitting it into fragments, rendering clear consideration impossible. The only way to remedy the situation was to slow down, which infuriated him as much as the noise itself. So he wound down the window, grabbed the tape and ripped it off, sending the glass from the mirror tumbling onto the road, where it shattered into a shower of glinting fragments. Behind him a horn sounded repeatedly, angrily, but if Martelli heard it at all it didn't register.

If he wasn't Paul Finch then who was he, his supposed client, this man of whom he knew . . ? What? Anything or nothing? Was it all invented? Images flashed before his mind's eye of his client, a supposed heavy drinker, peeling the label from the bottle of mineral water, of the baseball cap and sunglasses and the repeated wary glances at their fellow diners. Was there really an elderly mother in an expensive care home? Had there ever really been any grief at the loss of . . . Martelli paused. The loss of whom? If his client wasn't Paul Finch, if he was an imposter, then who was the dead man lying in the mortuary?

His head swam with the possibilities. He gripped the steering wheel still tighter, hunched forward, chin lowered, his entire body tense.

"Cazzo!" he shouted through gritted teeth. "Cazzo! Cazzo! Cazzo!"

THIRTY-SEVEN

Once she started talking, it was as though Becky King couldn't stop and neither Ted nor Burns felt inclined to interrupt her. Warren had called from Italy, she told them, to let her know he was on his way to the airport. Only he didn't turn up. The plane touched down, the passengers disembarked and Warren was not among them. She had hung around for more than an hour after the plane landed before guessing that he might have been collared for using a false passport. She had panicked then, had abandoned the car and returned to London, taking the train into Liverpool Street, from where it was a short bus ride and a few minutes' walk to her boat. She had had no contact with him since then.

"What was Warren doing in Italy?" Ted asked, taking a gentler tone now that she was cooperating.

As she answered, she was unable to meet his gaze, choosing instead to stare into her tea, which sat on the table in front of her, untouched but for that first sip.

"He went to find out what happened to Paul."

255

"His flatmate?"

She nodded.

"What do you mean? What did happen to Paul?"

"Paul was supposed to sail here."

"In Warren's boat? The Jackpot?"

She nodded. "He was supposed to drive from Italy to Dunkirk, where the yacht was berthed, then sail it across the Channel and up the Thames. Only he didn't show up. So Warren went to look for him. And to find his boat. It's worth a fortune."

"Warren didn't know the boat had run aground?"

"No," she whispered, shaking her head.

"And he flew to Genoa?"

"That's where Paul started from. Well - in a town not far from there."

"Loano?"

She raised her eyebrows. "Yes."

"So he thought something had happened to Paul?"

She didn't answer.

"Becky?"

"He thought Paul had ripped him off," she said. "And maybe stolen his boat."

"Ripped him off? How? What's in Loano?"

She closed her eyes.

"What's in Loano, Becky?"

She blew her nose, took a deep breath and told them about Mario and Steven, about the smuggling route from the Ligurian Sea to Loano, overland to the French coast and then across the Channel to one of several locations between Sandwich and Lime House Basin. They sat silently as she explained that Warren had started out smuggling cigarettes but had graduated to more profitable cargoes, the latest being so lucrative that he'd planned to take a year off on the proceeds.

"He was going to travel around the world," she sobbed. "He was going to take me with him."

"What was it?" said Ted, hoping she'd say counterfeit banknotes rather than high explosives.

She shook her head. "I don't know. He wouldn't tell me."

"He told you about the other stuff, the cigarettes?" She raised her head then, looked straight into his eyes. "But he refused to tell you about this latest shipment?" She nodded.

Ted tried to interpret the look on her face. It was somewhere between guilt and terror. With Paul dead and Warren missing, perhaps she was just worried she was next. Thinking of the break-in at Devlin's place, he said, "Did you collect the car from outside Warren's flat?" She nodded. "You have his spare car keys? Even though you're not together any more?"

She shook her head. "He keeps them in a drawer next to the bed. I still have a key to his flat." Her voice had dwindled such that her reply was barely audible.

"Only you didn't need a key to get in because someone had been there and trashed the place."

She nodded mournfully, once more fighting back tears.

His phone rang. He tutted and shook his head, leaning over to retrieve it from his pocket. As he did so, his knees collided with Becky King's and she flinched as though jabbed with a pin. Ignoring her, he looked at the little screen. His hand flopped onto the table and his shoulders sagged. Ordinarily, his boss never called. This wasn't going to be good news.

* * *

"Warren Devlin and Paul Finch have been smuggling cigarettes and something else – drugs maybe."

It was an hour later and Ted was sitting in the office of Detective Superintendent Andrew Nichols. Nichols was leaning forward on his elbows, hands clasped together, listening impatiently as Ted outlined what he'd learned that day.

"The whole enterprise is, or was run by Paul's brother, Steven. Warren was apparently paranoid about Paul and Steven, and a bloke called Mario at the Italian end of things. He thought they were conspiring against him, stealing from him. So he went off to Italy to have it out with them. While he was away, Steven phoned and told her to keep her trap shut. Since then she's been worried sick. She got the call while she was waiting for Warren at Stansted. She panicked and left the car. Warren has a spare key so he should have been able to drive it away if he'd ever turned -"

"Listen, Ted . . ." Nichols sighed and then sat back, stony-faced. He placed his hands flat on the desk and shook his head minutely. "It's out of our hands now."

Ted uncrossed his legs and sat forward. "What?"

"Have you spoken to the pathologist today?" said Nichols. "Down in Margate? Moody, I think his name is."

"No. Why? What's -"

Nichols stopped him with a raised hand. "The owner of the marina, the guy who salvaged the wreck, a Mr. . ." Nichols consulted a piece of paper on his desk. "Terrence Reid. He's dying. The doctors don't think he'll make the end of the week.

The son, Carl – the kid you spoke to – he's in hospital too. He's critical. He's not expected to make it either. They have radiation poisoning."

"What?"

"It's in the boat, Ted - Warren Devlin's boat. The cargo was radioactive pellets of some sort - key ingredient of a dirty bomb. The marina's been cordoned off and the case has been handed over to Counter Terrorism Command, SO15. They need to debrief you. There are two officers waiting in the meeting room. Ted, did you touch anything on board the boat?" Ted opened his mouth but his brain was so fully engaged trying to process this latest turn of events that he was unable to formulate an answer. He shook his head. "You'll need to go for tests to make sure you haven't ingested it. Are you sure you didn't touch anything?"

"No. I mean, yes. I mean I didn't touch anything. I . . . I'm fine."

Nichols flapped his hand as though parrying a fly. "Never mind. The doctors will ask you all of these questions."

"So the kid's going to die?" said Ted, trying to focus on one element at a time.

"I'm afraid it looks that way, yes," said Nichols gravely.

"Christ – he's only about twenty."

"Twenty-two. Just."

"So . . . they're terrorists?" Ted could hardly believe what he was hearing. He was thinking: Becky King?

"We don't know what they are. But there's no legitimate reason for smuggling radioactive material into Britain."

Ted raised an eyebrow more at Nichols' caginess than anything else. "What are they? The pellets, I mean. Polonium?

The stuff they used to kill the KGB guy?" Ted held out his hands and looked at them, front and back.

Nichols watched this gesture with narrowed eyes. He shook his head. "No – this is in fairly large quantity. It's more likely to be something like Strontium-90 - perhaps from a fuel cell. The Russians use it to power remote weather stations and navigation aids – lighthouses in the Arctic Circle, things like that. But we won't know until the tests have been carried out. It might not be Russian at all."

Ted flopped back in his seat. "And I might have radiation sickness?"

"It's unlikely but again we won't know for sure until they do tests. Terrence and Carl Reid had both been inside the wreck, they'd touched God knows what in there – maybe the pellets themselves - and the father had sat next to it all day everyday for more than a fortnight."

"There's a crane operator as well," said Ted. "The guy who lifted the boat off the beach."

"Already in hospital undergoing tests," said Nichols. "And the beach has been completely sealed off."

"So that's it, is it? We just forget about it?"

"Well, as I said, you'll be debriefed at some point. Probably this evening. And right now the officers from SO15 are going to take you to University College Hospital where a doctor's waiting for you." He paused. "It's just a precaution, you understand. If you didn't touch anything you should be fine."

Ted nodded, not really listening.

"And I want to say well done, Ted. If you hadn't spotted the shenanigans at your gym, well . . ." he inclined his head.

Boxing club, thought Ted. It's not a gym, it's a boxing club.

"So," Nichols continued, smiling now. "I want you to take some time off. Paid, of course. And it won't come out of your annual leave." Ted frowned and opened his mouth to speak but Nichols cut him off. "I insist. Take the time. Once you've been given the all-clear, go away somewhere. Visit friends or family." He glanced at the clock on the wall. "But right now you have to go, Ted."

Ted nodded but didn't move.

"Ted?" said Nichols. "When I say 'right now', I mean immediately."

THIRTY-EIGHT

By the time Martelli reached Loano, it was after ten o'clock and the
sun had long since sunk behind the hills. It was a sultry night.
Dense cloud had rolled in low from the sea, trapping the heat of
the day and charging the air with the electricity of the coming
storm. He left the car illegally parked outside the church at the
end of Via Monte Pasubio; two wheels on the grass. As he crossed
the road, the first flash of lightning lit up the sky and he counted
three crocodiles – tre coccodrilli - before the clap of thunder rent
the air, the boom multiplied as it echoed off the hills beyond
Toirano. By the time he reached the front door to the pale yellow
building in which Steven Finch had his apartment, the wind was
picking up and the first heavy droplets were rattling in the trees
and making black marks on the dusty grey paving.

    Gaining entry to Finch's apartment proved easy. He
allowed himself to get a little damp in the rain then stood under
the portico, in front of the glass doors, holding his defunct mobile
phone to his ear, waiting for someone to arrive or to leave the

building. He didn't have to wait long. After only a few minutes, a young couple came down the stairs into the foyer, arm in arm, chattering excitedly, giggling as they prepared their large umbrella for immediate deployment. As soon as he saw their feet appear on the stairs, he took a couple of hasty steps towards the door, thrusting one hand into his pocket as though searching for keys and speaking loudly into the inoperative handset.

"Yes, it's really starting to pour down. Yes, I'm just outside. See you in a moment."

He smiled at them as they stepped outside, rolling his eyes and looking aghast at the heavens. They returned his smile and held the door for him.

It was that simple.

Once inside, he made his way up the stairs, past Steven Finch's front door and up another level to the flat roof, which he was able to access through a fire exit. From the roof he lowered himself onto the large, L-shaped terrace which ran along the two outer walls of Steven's apartment, slithering down a drainpipe and dropping the last metre.

The windows were locked so he broke one with his elbow and let himself in.

It was dark but Martelli didn't turn on a light. He stalked slowly from room to room, taking in first the smells: the greasy overtones of the kitchen to the left of the entrance; the sickly sweet pine smell of disinfectant from the bathroom at the end of the corridor; the musty, fungal whiff of old books from the spare bedroom; in the lounge something indefinable, spicy and cloying - incense perhaps. The main bedroom smelled of black pepper, the unmistakable fragrance of his client's aftershave. In each room

Martelli closed the blinds and pulled the curtains.

Eventually, he sat at a desk in the corner of the lounge and listened to the storm. Those first sporadic raindrops had multiplied into a deluge which beat an increasingly frenetic rhythm on the green awning which spanned the full length of the terrace. He counted coccodrilli between the flashes of lightning and their accompanying cracks of thunder and by the time the gaps were indiscernible, the tumultuous roar of the downpour sounded like continuous gunfire, the beating on the flat concrete roof so loud that the drumming on the awning was reduced to mere accompaniment.

He got up and flicked on the main light; went into the other rooms and did the same. Then he walked his circuit of the flat again, taking in every detail, from the brown and beige patterned floor tiles to the textured ceiling. He opened drawers and cupboards, searching behind the piles of linen in the bedroom closets, feeling in the pockets of the clothes hanging in the wardrobe. In the kitchen, he raked through the cutlery, peered into every box and jar, flicked through the recipe books and emptied then restocked the freezer. In the bathroom, he lifted the lid from the cistern and examined all the bottles on the shelves and in the cabinet above the sink. In the spare room, he pushed aside the books in the bookcases and poked around behind them; in the master bedroom, he checked under the pillows and even heaved the mattress from the divan.

He found nothing incriminating and nothing unusual or obviously out of place. Bracco's assessment had been spot on. The place, he had said, was 'just . . . ordinary'.

Back in the lounge, he opened a tall cupboard and found dozens of bottles of spirits alongside glasses and tumblers in heavy lead crystal. He poured himself two fingers of scotch and resumed his seat at the desk in the corner of the room. In the drawers he found maps and guidebooks and instructions for arming and disarming the burglar alarm. There was also a file of invoices for the rental payments and a letter from the managing agents about rubbish disposal and scheduled repairs to the perimeter fences. In the top drawer, little more than a shallow tray, sat pens and pencils, elastic bands, paperclips, a small padlock for securing a suitcase, several books of matches and the key to a Porsche sports car. Martelli picked up the key and turned it over in his hand. He couldn't remember seeing a Porsche parked outside. Perhaps his client, his *former* client, had taken it. He replaced the key and pushed the drawer shut then knocked back the scotch, closed his eyes, leaned back in the chair and allowed the cacophonous rain to carry his thoughts high into the night sky.

THIRTY-NINE

By the time Ted got home it was after midnight and the street was quiet. His neighbours, he noted with a shake of his head, had put their wheelie bins out for collection the following morning. His own – the garden waste, the mixed recycling and the non-recyclable materials – were all so full he could no longer shut any of the lids. It was something Caroline had frequently nagged him about, bin night, one of the many things. He wrinkled his nose. They could wait. Right now he felt queasy and weary and ready for a hot shower to rid his body of the smell of the hospital.

He got out of the car and, as he reached for his house keys, dropped his mobile phone, swinging his arm in a vain attempt to catch it. He watched in dismay as it split along its length and went skittering along the pavement, shedding its battery in the process. As he crouched to retrieve the rear casing from the gutter, he heard a door open and turned to find Stephanie, his downstairs neighbour, silhouetted against her hall light.

"Hi, Steph," he said, giving her his best attempt at a smile.

"Ted." She sounded pained. "I'm sorry - I've got some bad news."

He clenched his stomach.

They'd tried to keep him in overnight, the doctors. Just to make doubly sure, they'd said. But he'd dressed himself and stomped down the corridor with an expression on his face like a man ready to punch something, or someone, so they'd let him go on condition that he return for further tests sometime over the next few days. It was a promise he had no intention of keeping. Nichols had signed him off for ten days and he intended to spend that time drunk, either at home in front of the telly or at his local, The Lord Herbert, where the lager was cheap and he was unlikely to get caught up in unwelcome conversation.

At the mention of yet more bad news, he closed his eyes, hung his head and stood up.

"Well," he said, bracing himself, thinking it must have something to do with Caroline. "I don't suppose it'll make my day any worse than it is already."

But he was wrong.

Stephanie had discovered Chester's body in the front garden, in the narrow gap between the boundary wall and the small metal shed in which she kept her bicycle. She led Ted to the spot and they stood for a moment, side by side, gazing sadly at the corpse.

It looked as though the old tomcat had simply laid down and died. Certainly there were no signs that he'd come off worst in a fight with a fox or a dog, or that he'd been hit by a car. At first Ted was a little annoyed that she'd simply left him there, still soaking wet from the previous day's rain, looking gaunt and ragged, as furry animals do when drenched, but he hadn't said anything. Steph had said sorry a few more times, as though finding the body somehow implicated her in Chester's death, then she'd retreated indoors and left Ted to it.

He wrapped his old companion in a moth-eaten, grey sweatshirt and buried him by torchlight at the bottom of the garden, at the foot of a lopsided sycamore. He covered the grave with a concrete paving stone to prevent other animals from digging up the corpse. After lowering the slab into place, he stood for a while among the thistles and nettles, wracking his brains for an appropriately eulogical phrase and coming up with nothing better than 'goodbye'.

In the kitchen he found another letter from Caroline, again propped against the toaster, this time written in purple ink, which he found unaccountably annoying. In it she explained that she was staying with Gemma and Adrian and that she would be over to collect her belongings at the weekend. Like her first note, it offered no apology, merely a spare explanation of the facts. In a post script, she asked if he would mind climbing into the loft for the cardboard boxes they'd used when they originally moved in. It had been a sunny day, he remembered, four . . . no, five years ago; his mate Dan had helped him unload the van and cart the boxes up the stairs.

He tore the letter into tiny pieces, which he scattered on the kitchen table for her to find on Saturday morning. He then stood on a stool and reached on top of the boiler cupboard for her precious flowery teapot, bought after much deliberation and numerous visits to different shops two summers past. Since then, much to his annoyance, she had used it only once, on the occasion of her grandmother's death. That interminable shopping trip had been a waste of time.

Standing there, his hair brushing the ceiling, he took the teapot out of its box and cast the box aside. Then he removed the protective bubble wrap and stood swaying as though in a breeze, staring at the thing, holding it in both hands as though making a presentation. As he did so, he thought about his life, one of conformity, distinctive only for its complete dearth of rebellious interludes. He stood there thinking until his arms began to ache then he turned the teapot over in his hands and threw it hard onto the kitchen floor, shattering it into hundreds of fragments. In the bedroom, he flung his clothes aside, lay down on the bed and slept soundly for the first time in weeks.

FORTY

A sudden eruption of thumping bass from the flat across the landing woke Martelli from a disturbing dream in which he recalled, with distaste, a previous case. It had been a murder suicide, in which a husband had killed his wife before putting the barrels of the shotgun into his mouth and pulling the second trigger. A note had explained that he'd felt unable to live with the shame of being a cuckold. The most cursory of investigations had revealed that the man had been mistaken. His wife had not been unfaithful; she had been covering for her errant sister. The couple's two children were just toddlers, newly orphaned. Martelli wondered what had become of them. In his dream, the wife had Angela Vaccarezza's face.

He rubbed his eyes, yawning. What I need, he thought, if I'm to properly investigate these murders, is a good night's sleep. The apartment was stuffy, short on oxygen, and the booze felt raw in his stomach. Pressing on the arms of the chair, he raised himself to his feet, head swimming a little despite the ponderousness of his movements. A wave of nausea passed through him, followed by an unexpected chill. He shivered, which seemed to shake it loose. Grimacing, he pressed a hand to his belly. The fish and chips were the last things he'd eaten, hours ago.

A cork popped, people cheered and glasses were clinked; someone guffawed loudly and voices were raised in lively conversation. Martelli got up and walked into the hallway, where he turned off the light and pressed his body against the inside of the front door. Cautiously, he twisted the cover from the spy hole and looked out. He flinched as a man's face loomed close, apparently staring straight at him. Cupping his hands around the little brass porthole, he looked again and saw that the communal landing was crowded with people and the front door to the neighbour's flat wide open. They were having a party. Someone turned up the music and he felt the door shudder beneath his hands.

"Merda," he mouthed.

Moving quickly, he went from room to room turning off all the lights. Then he stood in the centre of the lounge, breathless, pulse pounding. He could leave in full view of the revellers, he thought. It was after all his client's apartment. But when the break-in was eventually discovered and the police began asking questions, it wouldn't be long before his former colleagues came knocking on his door. He could wait, of course, until the party was over but he longed for his bed, especially since he was due to hike into the mountains the following day, and it didn't look like the celebrations would start winding down any time soon.

The alternative was to find another way out.

He slid open the glass door to the rear terrace and stepped outside where the gutters gurgled, the wet wind slapped his face and the noise of the rain on the canopy was deafening. Somewhere below, a metal bucket rang with heavy droplets. To his right a steel trellis reached from garden to roof, supporting a gnarled wisteria as thick as his wrist. Sliding the door shut, he took two paces forward and leaned over the railings. He shivered as the first cold fingers of rain found the nape of his neck and trickled between his shoulder blades. It was a six metre drop to the waterlogged lawn, at the centre of which stood a slender poplar as tall as the building. It danced as though possessed, shimmying and bowing to the rhythm of the wind, its tip whipping back and forth like a fly-fisherman's rod. Martelli scanned the surrounding buildings and was relieved to see they were all in darkness. On the far side of the lawn, almost out of sight behind a modest grove of orange trees, he could just make out the rear gate. He made one final, nervous assessment of the climb then swung his left leg into space and reached for the wisteria.

He fell. Not all the way but far enough to knock the wind out of him and leave him sprawling on his back, flailing his limbs like a flipped beetle. The ground had yielded mercifully, softened by the heavy rain, so nothing was broken, but when he righted himself he found that he was missing a sandal and a quick survey of the ground around him proved fruitless. Cursing under his breath, he limped to the far side of the lawn, ducked under the orange trees, unbolted the gate and emerged onto the street. There he took off his one remaining sandal and set off barefoot, smeared with mud, splashing through the puddles like a toddler on the loose. It was a liberating experience and he couldn't resist a

smile despite being quickly soaked through to his underwear.
Without a hint of regret, he chucked the solitary sandal in a litter
bin along with his scarcely worn sunglasses, which had snapped in
his pocket when he fell, or rather when he landed, crushed against
his mobile phone.

He wiped the rain from his eyes on his soaking wet sleeve.
Everyone else, he thought, everyone with their faculties intact
anyway, was either indoors or inside a vehicle. There were plenty
of cars on the road trundling cautiously along through water
twenty centimetres deep, wipers swishing double time. The
occupants paid him no attention.

The torrential downpour gave a blurry aspect to the town
and a constantly shifting texture to the vast expanses of standing
water. He walked as quickly as the conditions allowed, squinting
into the driving rain, wading ankle deep in places, the drains
overflowing, the gutters filled with floating palm fronds and pine
cones. Out on the main road, Via Aurelia, the raindrops blazed
beneath the fiery orange glow of the sodium street lights, forming
tall cones of flitting sparks beneath each one. To Martelli,
squinting into the rain, they looked like a row of Christmas trees.
At the roundabout a gaggle of teenage girls, giddy and coltish,
drunk but mostly on youth, came towards him, heading in the
opposite direction. Like him, they were soaked to the skin and
shoeless. They snickered as he drew level, lunging to be past him
before erupting into peals of laughter. He crossed the road then
the railway line and hurried down Via Simone Stella to the narrow
covered passage which led to Via Richeri. In the entrance to the
alley, a mangled black umbrella lay flapping forlornly in the wind.
As he stepped around it, a shout rang out ahead, the words

indistinct but the malicious sentiment all too apparent. He picked up his pace, out into the open again, around the dogleg and past the deserted bakery and the shuttered pasta workshop. His front door lay ten metres further on, on the right. Before him stood Signora Bartolotti's thuggish son, pounding on her door, demanding to be let in out of the rain.

"Open the door, you stupid old cow!"

Martelli stopped in the shadows. His breath caught in his throat, his arms hung loose at his sides.

"Open the fucking door now!" The thug took a step back and peered up at the darkened house.

Martelli's thoughts raced, images flashing through his mind, both real and imagined, glimpsed like passengers on a passing train, the brutalised corpse in the Frenchman's lab, Angela's scalded body, Rubini's smug face, the man he knew as Paul Finch standing over him, holding Aldo's gun, then Angela again, smiling that fleeting and beautiful smile. He lowered his chin and strode towards the younger man.

Bartolotti aimed a kick at the door. "Now, you cunt! I'm fucking soaking!" His eyes lit up as he caught sight of Martelli for the first time, taking in his sodden, muddied clothes and bare feet. "Hey, grandad, forgot your shoes?" He cackled harshly.

Martelli closed the gap between them - five paces, now four.

"Come on!" The young man shouted up at his mother's window again.

Three paces.

"Open up! Bitch!"

Two.

"Fuck!"

He turned.

"What the . . ?"

Martelli's punch caught the ingrate full in the face, breaking his nose and dislodging a tooth. He stumbled, tripped and fell on his backside. Martelli stood over him, face set in an angry snarl, breath hissing through his nostrils, right fist pulled back ready to deliver another blow. The boy rolled to his right, sprang to his feet and came at Martelli, arms raised, fingers splayed and curled like claws. He aimed a kick at Martelli's groin but Martelli sidestepped and caught him hard in the solar plexus with a left upper cut. The younger man folded at the middle, howling as the air was driven from his lungs.

A light came on.

Martelli grabbed a handful of collar, spun the boy round, hauled him upright and slammed him against the wall next to his mother's front door.

"What's going on?" said a shrill voice from above. It was Signora Trigiani.

More lights came on. Latches squeaked; shutters rattled open.

"You will treat your mother with respect! Do you understand? Or you will answer to me!" Martelli said loudly.

"Go fuck yourself, grandad!" He spat the words, struggling to free himself from Martelli's grip. "I heard about you. You're not a fucking cop anymore."

Once more Martelli rammed the thug's head against the wall then he leaned in close and whispered so his words weren't shared with the entire street. "That is precisely why you should be worried - because I'm not a cop anymore." He drove his knee swiftly and brutally into the younger man's groin.

As Martelli stepped back and let the thug sink to his knees, he was suddenly dazzled as a bright light came on directly in front of his face. Signora Bartolotti opened her front door and stood on the threshold, self-consciously clasping together the lapels of her dressing down. After a brief glance at her groaning son, she stared directly at Martelli, who looked into her tearful eyes and saw no relief, only anguish. Above them, out of sight, someone started a slow hand clap. He glanced upwards, turning on the spot, and saw a dozen people peering down, faces white as hotel china in the glow from the outside light. And he realised, to his utter dismay, that far from helping his neighbour, he had only added to her shame.

A voice called out, "Where're your shoes, Commissario?" He looked down at his bare feet. What was happening to him? He was once an upstanding member of the community, a police inspector, for goodness sake, respected, quietly dignified. And now what? Now he was someone who drank alone and brawled in the street.

He took a few steps towards his front door but stopped to examine his reflection in the darkened window of Eduardo's shop. His clothes were soaking wet and smeared with mud. They stuck to him, twisted uncomfortably, making his legs and arms look spindly. There was blood – Bartolotti's, he assumed – spattered down the front of his shirt; his hair was sticking out in all directions and had acquired a foliage adornment. Beneath his eyes there were deeply etched, puckered bags so dark as to give him a sinister aspect. He looked like the ghost of his own drowned self.

He was furious with himself, a maddening mix of anger and frustration. He felt like shouting, like roaring at the top of his voice, but refrained for fear that the neighbours would think he'd lost the last few of his mostly scattered marbles. And yet despite all this anger, he also felt oddly liberated, a great sense of relief at having let himself go.

With a last disdainful glance at Bartolotti junior, he dug his keys out of his waterlogged pocket and retreated regretfully indoors.

* * *

It was a little after three when his former colleagues came for him. He wasn't afforded any special treatment; no advance warning, no discreet knock from a cop in mufti. Instead Via Richeri was all at once crowded with uniformed officers who'd made their way through the caruggi on foot in the pouring rain. It was filled too with blue light from the police motorbikes stationed at either end of the street, their glow blossoming and fading to the throbbing rhythm of the engines, giving the faces of the sopping wet officers and the once more rudely awoken neighbours a spectral pallor.

Martelli was drifting in the limitless arena of sleep when the doorbell rang. In his dream, the sea was oily, black and extremely cold. The briny water stung his eyes; it burned his nasal passages and the back of his throat, his teeth chattered uncontrollably. He felt the fatigue in his lungs before it reached his limbs. He supposed the bitter cold was numbing his extremities. Somewhere a ship's horn sounded long and dreary, like the moan of a dozing drunk.

He woke with a start. His heart was beating quickly - too quickly for a sleeping man, he thought. He clutched at his chest. Had Doctor Bassi been right all along? The ship's horn sounded again, this time more high pitched and tinny. He switched on the bedside light, listening intently.

There it was again.

"Cristo santo!" he said, flinging back the duvet.

It was the doorbell.

He crossed the room, opened the shutters, leaned over the sill and frowned at the knot of police officers outside his door. Had they come for him because he hit the Bartolotti boy? Surely not. Could it be for the break in at Via Monte Pasubio? He doubted it, although someone might have seen him on the terrace, might have recognised him. Had he left anything behind? Perhaps the real Paul Finch had turned up. Or Steven, the tenant.

He pulled on a pair of trousers and a shirt and dashed down the two flights of stairs. By the time he reached the front door, someone was pounding on the other side of it. He switched on the outside light, put his eye to the spy hole and gasped as he saw who was on his doorstep. This wasn't about brawling or break-ins; it was about something altogether more serious. A rush of adrenalin hit him and he felt suddenly light-headed. He leaned heavily on the door and breathed deeply, counting slowly to ten as he did so. Taking a step back, he hung his head and couldn't help but smile. Well, he thought resignedly, I can hardly flee. Gathering his wits, he smoothed his bed hair with both hands, raised himself to his full height and opened the door.

In a demonstration of his power over both of them, Rubini

had sent Bracco to arrest the man he still called 'Chief'.

FORTY-ONE

Despite the look of mortification on the young detective's face, for
the benefit of the other officers Martelli spoke with all the warmth
and confidence he could muster.

"Bernardo! Ciao, bello. You'd better come in."

As he stepped aside to let Bracco enter, the young Ispettore
turned to the two uniformed officers flanking him and told them
to stay put, prompting an exchange of curious and disappointed
glances. He then entered the house, closed the door behind him
and followed Martelli up the stairs.

"I've been trying to call you but your mobile's switched off,"
he said, his voice laden with misery.

"Ah." Martelli tutted, flapping his hands. "The battery
died. I forgot to charge it."

In the living area, they stood on opposite sides of the low,
square table, staring at one another, Martelli expectant, trying to
maintain a smile; Bracco glistening wet, desperate, wringing his
hands as he struggled to come up with the right words.

Martelli said gently, "It's okay, Bernardo. Relax." He chuckled, shaking his head. "Difficult, I know."

"Chief, I . . ."

Martelli gave the younger man a little time but nothing further was forthcoming. He smiled again. "Rubini has sent you to arrest me," he said.

Bracco nodded.

"Because the old lady across the hall – the old lady with the hearing aid – saw me at Angela Vaccarezza's apartment. She recognised me?"

Bracco sighed and nodded minutely. He hung his head and swept his fingertips along his eyebrows as though squeezing the rainwater from them. "Si, Commissario."

"And Rubini's stomping about like a petulant child because I'm sticking my nose into his case, right?"

Bracco met Martelli's gaze and raised his hands in defeat.

Martelli smiled. "And you think the same. You think I should keep out of it."

Bracco didn't answer.

Out of habit Martelli started to count in his head, wondering when the ordinarily loquacious young detective would break his silence. But by the time he reached twenty, he still hadn't.

The thick walls and sturdy shutters kept out the noise of the storm and reduced the hubbub in the street to a mere murmur. Bracco stood there, water dripping from his raincoat onto the living room's smooth terrazzo floor, the sound of each tiny splash audible. He glanced down at the puddles forming at his feet and gave Martelli an apologetic look.

"Don't worry," said Martelli with a dismissive wave of his hand.

Someone hammered on the door with their fist.

Bracco lifted his gaze. Over his shoulder, he said, "Wait!"

From outside someone shouted, "Is everything all right, Ispettore?"

Bracco turned and yelled, "I said 'Wait'!"

"You brought plenty of guys," said Martelli. "Was Rubini expecting trouble?" He forced a smile again then attempted a chuckle. Bracco did the same but his was equally half-hearted. Neither man felt in the mood for mirth.

They fell silent again.

Martelli experienced a sudden, brief jolt of panic. "You know, Bernardo, when you search the place, you're going to find . . ." He puffed out his cheeks and directed his gaze at the brass buffalo standing in the centre of the table. "It's . . ."

"I know," said Bracco quietly. "I spoke to Colonnello Nardi." He unslung an Alitalia flight bag from his shoulder and held it out for appraisal. Martelli raised an eyebrow. He recognised the bag. Once upon a time Lena, Nardi's wife, had worked as an air hostess. He had been unaware that his old friend knew of his marijuana habit. He shook his head.

"Oh and also . . ." Martelli pointed at the bookcase, at the volumes of history between which he had slipped the hefty pistol in its sturdy leather holster. But he couldn't see it. "Also . . ." he said again, frowning and taking a step closer to the bookcase, bafflement etching its lines on his brow.

Hands on hips, he scanned the shelves, thinking for a moment that he was looking in the wrong place. But no, he wasn't.

The gap between the history books was empty.

"Figlio di puttana," he whispered.

"What is it, Chief?"

Martelli stood silent, considering the implications of the theft.

"Nothing," he said, blinking repeatedly. He glanced quickly at the ceiling. I must have left the trapdoor unlocked, he thought. That'll be how he got in. Unless he unbolted it himself while I was asleep.

So now he had a gun. Not only had he given him Angela's address, he'd told him where to find Estella too.

He wanted to sit down, to collapse, to fall backwards into the warm embrace of the Ligurian Sea and float, arms and legs akimbo, the sun beating down on him, the cooling water washing over his hot skin. He turned to find Bracco watching him, his expression combining curiosity and concern in equal parts. Martelli shrugged. "My mistake," he said.

Bracco nodded and reached for the brass buffalo. "We must be quick," he said. "May I?"

"Si, si - of course." Martelli nodded and made to help the younger man.

"It's all right, Chief. I've got it."

Their eyes met, up close, as they both bent down to grab the heavy ornament. For a second they held one another's gaze.

"It's going to be okay, Chief."

Martelli reached out and squeezed the younger man's shoulder.

"Thank you for this, Bernardo."

Bracco gave a tiny shrug.

The fist pounded impatiently on the door again.

"Come on," said Martelli, standing upright and sounding more emboldened than he felt. "We'd better go. Let me just grab a jacket and my book. No doubt I'll be expected to do a lot of waiting."

A minute or two later, as he stood outside his front door with his arms held out in front of him, palms together, he looked up at the narrow corridor of night sky, blinked against the downpour, and saw the delinquent Trigiani boys gawping at him, wide-eyed and open-mouthed. He gave them an exaggerated wink and one of them – he had no idea which - stuck out his tongue and blew a raspberry.

FORTY-TWO

Rubini had obviously insisted that Martelli be handcuffed and Bracco had averted his gaze as the uniformed officer, the one who'd beaten his fist against Martelli's front door, snapped them into place. Martelli had then been led through the caruggi, silent witness to the events of his life, beneath the bleary-eyed gazes of his curious neighbours, while Bracco attempted and failed to shield him from the rain with a small, asymmetrical umbrella.

A press photographer, an ill-tempered man whom Martelli recognised, was sheltering from the rain under a shop awning a few metres from the waiting patrol car on Corso Roma - his presence at this god-forsaken hour doubtless also Rubini's doing. Martelli, to his further dismay, was to be paraded, metaphorically speaking, before the people of the town. Under Italian law some suspects are afforded the peculiar and very public status of 'person of interest', though they might never be found guilty of a crime. It had ruined reputations. It had made some too. He was too muddled to imagine the headline in the next day's late edition but wondered if that was how he was to be described: 'a person of interest'. Would Rubini go that far? Blinded by the camera's flash, he banged his head painfully as he climbed into the back of the car.

* * *

To say that his former colleagues were shocked at his appearance as he was led into the police headquarters would be to understate the case. The few able to meet his gaze soon looked away again. Only Luigi Imbriani, the veteran sovrintendente on duty, who'd worked the graveyard shift for as long as Martelli had been a police officer, remained impassive, simply processing Martelli's personal effects as he might have done those of any other prisoner, smiling as he painstakingly noted that the copy of *Moby Dick* was damp upon receipt.

Despite Martelli's best efforts at cheerfulness, Bracco had appeared distraught throughout this process and had continued to do so as he shepherded his former chief to a cell. He had simply nodded when they parted company, unable to find any words. Martelli's 'Buona notte' sounded, he thought later, a little foolish.

The walls of the cell were plain brick, thick with pale blue paint, droplets of which spattered the bare concrete floor around the perimeter of the room. A caged incandescent bulb in the centre of the high arched ceiling was circled helter skelter by a squadron of insects. The small window high above his head was open but air did not circulate so the cell remained hot and stuffy. In the corner furthest from the door stood a stainless steel toilet pan but it was a low, metal cot furnished with a thin, lumpy mattress and a thick felt blanket which took up most of the floor space.

It was a bleak and soulless place, heavy with the melancholy of its previous tenants. It was reasonable, he thought, to assume that no one had been happy to spend time there. He knew of several murderers who'd passed their first nights of incarceration in that very room and over the years doubtless there had been many more. He could feel the terrible accumulated weight of their bad deeds.

At four in the morning or thereabouts, not long after he'd been brought in, a young officer he didn't recognise came to check on him. Perhaps they thought he might be suicidal. Martelli had asked if Commissario Rubini was even on the premises and had received a shrug and a shake of the head in reply. By this time, the faint pink light of dawn was visible through the small window. He'd asked for the light to be turned off in his cell and the young officer had obliged.

At first he'd lain in the semi darkness, eyes wide open, clicking his fingers softly and without rhythm, staring at the high ceiling, the coarse blanket rough on the back of his neck. Then he'd forced himself to take deep breaths through his nose, exhaling through his mouth, counting slowly to five each time, trying to remain calm at the prospect of the long night yawning ahead of him. The guilty sleep soundly on the night of their arrest, a former colleague had once told him; the innocent, on the other hand, lie awake fretting. Which am I? he wondered, thinking of Angela Vaccarezza.

His sleep in the end was irregular, inconclusive.

A roaring noise entered his dreams sometime around five,

growing ever louder until it sounded as though a jet airliner was in the room with him. When he realised the noise wasn't imagined, he leapt out of his cot and stood up, alarmed, only to laugh at himself a moment later. It was the sound of one of the municipal cleaning trucks: tiny vehicles with huge rotating brushes which scoured the gutters of the town to no discernible schedule. The roar was soon accompanied by an orange light, flaring and dwindling. He lay down again and watched as the light swept the ceiling, allowing himself to be mesmerised by it, just to pass a little time. He longed for a beer and a joint, for a few hours of blissful insensibility on his rooftop terrace.

Rubini turned up at seven. He smelled strongly of cologne but he looked shattered; puffy-eyed and pallid, and he'd cut himself shaving. Martelli knew only too well the pressure he must be under. And now, after this second killing, well, the young Commissario must be feeling hounded, cornered even.

He sat on the end of Martelli's cot, too tired to be smug, and spoke quietly, his words well-practised. "My old mentor, Commissario-Capo Massimo Pavone, once told me that a detective's greatest asset is a selective memory. That way he remembers only what may be useful to him, while forgetting the horrors and the disappointments. I want you to forget the disappointment of having to leave your final case to be solved by someone else."

For a few moments Martelli said nothing. He stared at the floor, letting his vision blur. Then, as Rubini took a breath to speak again, he interrupted him. "Who checked the Englishman's credentials?"

This caught Rubini off guard. "What?" he said.

"The man who identified the body of the first victim. The Englishman. Who checked his identification? Was it you?"

"I can't remember. Why?"

"You can't remember." Martelli gave a derisory snort.

"What does it matter?" said Rubini defensively.

"It matters because he's not who he claims to be."

"Well, he's your client, isn't he? Are you telling me you don't know who he is?"

"He's not my client and you haven't answered my question." Martelli lifted his gaze and stared.

In the street, in a bar, perhaps queueing next to you in the bank, in all likelihood, in these everyday situations you would barely notice Martelli. But if he got you into a room, an interview room, just the two of you, you would remember forever with whom you shared that space. His stare would pin you to your chair. A bead of sweat formed at Rubini's temple and rolled down the side of his face. He began to speak but thought better of it; began again but was once more cut short.

"If the man who identified the body is not Paul Finch then how can you be sure the dead man is his brother, Steven?" said Martelli gravely.

"Look," said Rubini. "If you know something about this case that you're not telling me then -"

"Then what? You'll have me arrested again? Have me dragged out of bed in the middle of the night?"

Rubini wiped the side of his face with his fingers.

"There's a woman called Estella Ramazzotti," said Martelli. "She was Mario Rossetti's girlfriend but they broke up a few months ago. I think she might be in danger. You need to take her into protective custody until you work out what's going on. She's staying in Barga with -"

Rubini gave a mocking laugh. "Oh, you 'think' she might be in danger? You 'think'?"

"That's right," said Martelli. "I think she might be in danger. I think whoever killed Angela might go for her next. I think the killer is after Mario's money."

Rubini considered this for some time. "Keep out of this," he said finally. "Keep out of it or I will have you arrested for operating without a private investigator's licence."

Martelli lapsed into silence.

"You have a good friend in Colonnello Nardi," said Rubini.

Martelli wasn't sure if this was a statement or a question.

"Yes," he said. "We've been friends since we were very young - six or seven. I can't remember exactly. Why do you ask?"

"Would you say that Colonnello Nardi knows you better than anyone else?"

Martelli blinked then nodded, wary.

Rubini looked down at his hands; flexed his fingers. "It's unusual for such a high-ranking officer of the Carabinieri to attend a murder scene. I was surprised, that's all."

Martelli wondered where Rubini was going with this. "Given the method, it was clear that it was going to be a particularly high-profile case. And Piero - Colonnello Nardi is the face of the Carabinieri afterall."

Rubini nodded slowly. Martelli narrowed his eyes. "What are you getting at?"

"Nothing. I just wondered if perhaps he thought you might need . . . Assistance."

"Are you questioning my competence?"

"No. No."

"What then?"

"Nothing." He flashed a weary version of that smug smile and held up an open palm signalling the end of that particular aspect of their discussion.

Martelli studied the features of Rubini's face: the even tan, the small, perfectly straight nose, the feminine lips and long eyelashes, all ordinarily marks of a handsome, healthy man but at that moment somehow failing to come together. Just for a second he contemplated telling him that in all likelihood his prime suspect was sitting outside a dilapidated farmhouse in the forest, drinking beer, smoking weed and piddling in the bushes while waiting for this - whatever *this* was - to blow over. But he thought better of it. Why steer him even further towards the wrong man? Better to let him exhaust his line of enquiry sooner. He closed his eyes and shook his head. "I want to go home now," he said firmly.

With a noncommittal grunt, Rubini stood up and beat the door three times with the heel of his hand. As it opened, Martelli said, "What about Angela Vaccarezza? You haven't even asked if I have an alibi."

"Oh, one has been provided," said Rubini cryptically as he stepped into the corridor. He turned and the two men stared at one another, a scornful expression on Rubini's face; Martelli with a question on the tip of his tongue. Then the heavy door was pulled shut and Martelli was alone again.

He stretched out with his hands laced behind his head and stared at the wall. His back and shoulders ached from his fall the previous night. They ached also from the stress, he supposed, both mental and physical, of spending the night in an uncomfortable cot on the wrong side of that heavy, steel door. Through the small window, the rising sun projected a beam of light, which terminated in an almost blindingly white square on the wall beyond his feet. It was so bright he was unable to look at it for more than a few seconds. He lifted a foot and held it in the beam, warming his toes and casting a stark shadow in the square. He stared at the shadow with one eye squeezed shut until a crimson-edged, turquoise shape was imprinted on his retina. Eventually, exhausted, he nodded off.

FORTY-THREE

There is a point beyond which the effects of fatigue are like drunkenness and Martelli, whose fitful, disrupted night had left him neither rested nor refreshed, reeled when he stood up. He staggered and reached out a hand to steady himself against the wall opposite his narrow cot. He sat down again.

He needed strong coffee. A cold shower and a decent breakfast would have been very welcome too but at that moment what he longed for was one of Giacomo's double espressos, made using his proprietary blend of beans. Martelli imagined he could smell it, that rich aroma with its earthiness and odd hint of caramel.

Raised voices in the corridor were closely followed by the crunching of a key in the lock. He stood again, more easily this time, though he felt an empty queasiness in his stomach. The heavy, steel door of his cell swung slowly inwards, propelled by a shiny black boot, and there stood Nardi, his ample girth filling the doorway, a paper espresso cup in each fist.

Martelli could have kissed him. In fact he would have embraced him but for the paper cups and the expression on his old friend's face, which was very sombre indeed. To Nardi they were a serious business, incarceration and coffee.

Nardi took a step forward and handed Martelli one of the cups, which he accepted and upended into his mouth in one swift movement. Nardi exchanged the empty cup for the remaining full one, which Martelli sank with equal despatch.

In the corridor, a junior officer, different from the night before and barely out of his teens, lurked uncomfortably, shifting his weight from foot to foot, jangling keys on a ring the size of a saucer.

"We're leaving now," said Nardi, his voice more than usually hoarse. He accepted the second empty cup and took from under his arm a large manila envelope, which he handed to Martelli. It contained his keys, his phone, his wallet and his copy of *Moby Dick*. Nardi tilted his head to see into the cell then he looked Martelli up and down. "Do you have anything else with you?"

Martelli shook his head. Nardi nodded gravely at this, realising the significance: Rubini had afforded Martelli no special favours.

Martelli asked, "What time is it?"

Nardi didn't answer. He took hold of Martelli's elbow and propelled him into the well lit corridor. "I have my car outside."

* * *

They passed only Paola, the receptionist, on the way out. She gave

Martelli an anxious smile before ducking behind her computer monitor. The rest of the staff were either out or had slyly made themselves scarce in order to avoid his departure.

On the passenger seat of Nardi's Carabinieri Land Rover sat a newspaper bearing the headline: *Former Murder Squad supremo arrested.* The accompanying photograph might have been of a startled troglodyte dragged from his underground lair. Martelli quickly scanned the article for the phrase 'person of interest' but it appeared that Rubini had refused to speak to the press, choosing instead to let the photograph and its accompanying headline speak for itself. Unnamed sources had told reporters that '*the recently retired Commissario Martelli, a detective with almost forty years experience, was seen visiting Angela Vaccarezza only hours before her body was found. He was later involved in an altercation in the street outside his house in Loano's centro storico.*'

Martelli folded the newspaper in his lap and sat slumped awkwardly. Nardi waited until there was some distance between them and the police station before speaking.

"You know Rubini has a handicapped child; a boy of eight. It must be hard for him and his wife and their other children. I'm told he has good days and bad days. Perhaps he takes out his frustrations on his colleagues."

"Didn't you describe him as 'an enthusiastic sniffer of arses'?"

Nardi frowned. "He is. But that doesn't make him a bad policeman. And at least he's made the effort to acquaint himself with the people who pull the purse strings. Did you know he's put in a requisition request for stab-proof vests for every member of the squad? And apparently it's been approved. He's also arranged for computer training for everyone on his team, and for seminars with Europol and Interpol. He . . . I suppose he's trying to stamp his signature on things."

Martelli said nothing. He turned his head and looked out of the window, staring absently at the shop fronts as they slid past. They were in a sleepy part of town free from the holidaymaking hordes; just a few locals going quietly about their business, running errands, taking time to greet one another properly and respectfully, and to exchange gossip.

Nardi waved a hand dismissively. "Look, Mimmo, I could carve a better man out of a panettone -"

Martelli interrupted frostily. "You just said he was a good police officer."

"No, I said that sniffing arses didn't make him a *bad* police officer. He's still a piece of shit and I don't like him. He's more interested in statistics than catching criminals but - mark my words - five years from now he'll be Vice Questore. In ten years he'll run the entire province and then where will we be?"

Martelli sank down even lower in the seat, stretching out his legs and leaning his head against the cool metal of the door pillar. He held out his hands and saw they were shaking. Must be the coffee, he thought.

"Pull yourself together, Mimmo. Dio Santo, can't you see everyone's watching you? They're either hoping you'll sort yourself out or, in Rubini's case, that you'll fall flat on your face."

Martelli exhaled noisily through his nostrils.

"And don't roll your fucking eyes!" said Nardi angrily.

"Please watch the road."

"I am watching the fucking road."

"And stop swearing at me."

"This is my car and I'll fucking swear if I fucking feel like it. Damn it, Mimmo!"

"It's too late," said Martelli loudly, swivelling in his seat.

"What? What's too late?"

"I've already fallen flat on my face!"

"What?" Nardi stared at Martelli as if his old friend had said something preposterous. "What the fuck are you talking about?"

"Just keep your eyes on the road," muttered Martelli, looking straight ahead.

Ignoring him, Nardi said, "You haven't fallen on your face. That stronzo Rubini -"

"Watch out!" shouted Martelli.

A horn sounded and Nardi gestured angrily.

"Aren't you going to say 'I told you so'?" said Martelli, regretting it even as the words left his lips, regretting too the whiny tone creeping into his voice.

"What? No!"

They fell silent. Nardi turned onto Via Aurelia, a street busy with passersby of an altogether different character. This was tourist territory. Women shambled along wearing bright bikinis under translucent tee shirts accompanied by shirtless men with tattooed arms. Everywhere flesh squelched out between items of clothing too small and too tight; unsightly bulges of blotchy, sunburned skin. Though he had never discussed it with anyone, Martelli thought it undignified, the modern family holiday, permissive.

Eventually Nardi said, "Did you punch Emanuella Bartolotti's boy?"

Martelli sighed. He put a trembling hand to his brow and found it damp with perspiration. "Giacomo thinks I'm unwinding."

"According to the Frenchman, you broke the boy's nose."

"He's a disgrace. You should hear how he speaks to her."

"What if he decides to press charges?"

"Let him."

"She chooses it, Mimmo. She chooses to have him live in her house."

"She doesn't choose it. He's her son. She's stuck with him."

Nardi threw up his hands. "And brawling in the street is the answer?"

"In this case, Piero, maybe it is. Anyway, I'm not going to make a habit of it."

Nardi sighed and cleared his throat raspily. "The brother is dead," he said, his voice a dull monotone.

"What? Whose brother? Bartolotti's?"

Nardi shook his head vigorously. "No. Steven Finch's brother, Paul. The British police called this morning. His body was found on a beach. He'd been dead for some time, two weeks maybe. Your man, Bracco has the details."

So he'd been right. Too late but right nonetheless. Eyes wide, he stared at the road, blinking repeatedly at the brightness of the day.

"How did he die?"

"He drowned but . . ." Martelli cocked his head. ". . . He

had been poisoned."

"Oh?"

Nardi nodded sombrely. "Radiation sickness. It seems he was trying to smuggle radioactive material into the UK. His boat was recovered. Others have become sick after contact with the cargo."

Martelli turned to stare. "What did it look like, this cargo?"

Nardi shrugged. "Pellets, I think. You'll have to speak to Bracco. He has all the details."

Terrorism? Was that it? Did that explain why Mario Rossetti had fled or gone to ground? They fell silent, Nardi concentrating on the road, Martelli contemplating this latest news.

Eventually, Nardi said, "What about your client? Where is he? And who is he?"

Eyes closed again, Martelli gripped the bridge of his nose, squeezing hard. "He's not my client. And he said he was going back to the UK for a while to see his mother, to tell her . . ." He ground to a halt, trying to remember the exact words. It seemed a long time ago, that awkward conversation at Piatti Spaiati.

"What?"

Martelli shook his head mournfully. "I've no idea. I don't even know who he is or if he even has a mother." He glanced at his old friend. "But when I find him I might just break his nose too."

Nardi tutted. "Do you think you've . . ?"

"What?"

"I was going to say, do you think you've . . . regained your equilibrium?"

"That sounds like something Pippo would say."

Nardi didn't reply.

"Did he say it?"

"Maybe. I can't -"

"What? Are you discussing me now? Am I a problem to be solved? A basket case?"

"He was just . . . *We* were just worried, that's all."

"Well don't be. I'm fine."

"Oh sure, Mimmo." He threw up his hands again. "You're fit as a fucking fiddle."

Martelli resumed his absent window gazing. After a long interval, he said, "I went to see Aldo."

"Okay." Nardi frowned at the change of subject, wondering where it was going. "How is he?"

"Not good. He owes a quarter of a million euros to Aricò."

"What?" Nardi was horrified.

"Antonio conned him into investing in some phoney apartment complex. Now Aricò wants his house."

"Are you sure?"

"Dio bono! Of course I'm sure."

"What's he going to do?"

"I don't know. I promised I'd talk to Aricò."

Nardi shook his head in disbelief. "Really? Aricò? And what are you going to say?"

"I don't know."

"Madonna mia! Do not get involved, Mimmo -"

"I know, I know - it will not end well."

They lapsed into silence again, the tension palpable. Nardi gripped the wheel tightly, concentrating as he turned onto Viale Libia. He accelerated hard towards the old roman bridge and took the tight bend too fast for comfort, flinging Martelli against the armrest and then jerking him back against the door. They emerged into Campo Luigi Cadorna, a wide boulevard given over mostly to car parking. From there they headed towards the lungomare, where they had to wait as the little tourist train, il trenino – a thinly disguised tractor hauling three trailers - toot-tooted and trundled past.

"Look, Mimmo, I know what happened. I know Rubini fucked up."

"Piero, I'm the one who messed up. I gave out Angela's address. And I told him where to find Mario's girlfriend, Estella."

"Rubini's to blame. Not you. He's the one who failed to check his ID."

Martelli sighed, shaking his head. He slumped against the door pillar again.

Nardi turned right onto Corso Roma and followed the train as it crawled along the seafront. "He thinks Rossetti's the killer, the business partner. They found chemicals at the house in Castelvecchio. Also a blue barrel and a sack truck for carting them around. He's absolutely convinced it's him." He looked at Martelli out of the corner of his eye. "But we know different, right?" He brought the Land Rover to a standstill near the arched entrance to Piazza Rocca, a short distance from Martelli's house. "Get some sleep, Mimmo. I'll call you later."

As Martelli opened the car door, Nardi called, "Wait!" He reached behind the passenger seat and pulled out the old Alitalia flight bag, struggling one-handed with the weight and the awkward bulk of its contents. Martelli caught his eye and blanched. He took the bag and glanced inside. When he looked up again, Nardi spoke quietly, his eyes fixed firmly on the road ahead. "Bracco called me on his way to your place, Mimmo. He's a . . . He's a good man."

"Piero, I -"

Nardi batted away his words. "You don't need to explain."

But Martelli felt he did. "It . . . Without it I would never switch off, I think. It was grown by a computer programmer in Savona. He told me it was engineered by the Soviets during the Cold War. 'Smoke one joint and you turn Communist'." He tried to laugh but it sounded forced, empty. "I confiscated it because the last thing we need in Italy is more Communists."

Nardi remained grim-faced. "Go, Mimmo. Sleep."

Martelli hesitated for a moment then said quietly, "What did you tell Rubini?"

Nardi looked at him from the corner of his eye. "What?"

"Rubini said an alibi had been provided. That's why I'm being released. What did you tell him?"

Eyes on the road again, Nardi muttered, "I told him we were together when Angela Vaccarezza was killed."

Martelli narrowed his eyes. "Were we?"

A quick shake of the head. "According to Pippo, the time of death was . . . Later."

For Martelli this was almost too much to bear. He felt hot, hotter even than a day well on the way towards record temperatures. He stood swaying, unable simply to leave it but unable to find adequate words. Once more Nardi came to his rescue.

"Find him, Mimmo. Find the killer. I'll help you if I can. And I'll have Signorina Ramazzotti taken into protective custody. I'll call Firenze this morning." He turned and gave Martelli a smile from which he was unable to eliminate the sadness. "Now go. Sleep. I think you're going to need it. And . . ." He glanced at the flight bag. "And try to keep a clear head."

Unable to meet his gaze, Martelli simply nodded and said, "Thank you, my friend, thank you." He felt close to tears, a symptom, he later preferred to think, of intoxicating weariness.

He watched Nardi drive away and then traipsed to his front door, the Alitalia bag banging against his hip, the heavy brass buffalo inside clunking and rattling with each impact.

* * *

His house was a mess; not quite ransacked but in considerable disarray. Books had been taken out of the shelves and replaced upside down and back to front, cupboard doors had been left ajar, drawers pulled open and rifled, his belongings moved, lifted, examined and tossed back willy nilly. Rubini's team had given the place a thorough going over. But he had neither the energy nor the inclination to care. His home, he thought, choosing to be philosophical about it, was long overdue a clear out.

In the bedroom he tried Estella Ramazzotti's number but it rang and rang and didn't connect to voicemail. He then lay down and slept what his father would have referred to as 'the sleep of the just', though of course, had anyone asked him, he would have insisted that the word 'just' didn't apply. That his oldest friend's career had been compromised to such a degree, that Nardi had willingly and readily committed perjury, weighed heavily on his laden, sinking conscience, along with his other sins of omission and commission.

ACQUA MORTA

FORTY-FOUR

When Martelli woke at two that afternoon, he immediately reached for the phone by his bed and dialled Lelord's number.

As always, the Frenchman picked up almost immediately. "Pronto."

"Pippo. Mimmo."

"Ah - the jailbird," said Lelord. "Have you slept at all?"

"Si," said Martelli, frowning at his friend's attempt to make light of events. "Where are you?"

"At work. Your picture in the paper reminded me of a line from Dylan Thomas: 'I hold a beast, an angel and a madman in me'." He laughed. "Two out of three isn't bad."

"That's a Meatloaf song," said Martelli, thinking that only Lelord would come up with such a pairing: Meatloaf and Dylan Thomas. He wondered which two of the three he represented in Lelord's view.

"What is?"

"Never mind. Listen," he said. "I want to talk to you about

my client."

It was the Frenchman's turn to frown. "You know that -"

"Yes. Paul Finch – the *real* Paul Finch - is dead. Piero told me."

"Okay. Look, Mimmo . . ." Lelord exhaled wearily. "I feel terrible. If I hadn't given him your address then maybe -"

"Forget it," said Martelli. "You said it yourself - he'd have found me anyway."

"But . . ."

"Forget it, Pippo. It's done. Let's move on. I need your help with this."

"Okay." The relief was evident in the Frenchman's voice.

"Was Angela Vaccarezza shot? Is that what finally killed her?"

"No. Why?"

"I'm pretty sure Paul . . ." He sighed. "I'm pretty sure my client broke into my house and stole a pistol."

Lelord was immediately uneasy. "You keep firearms in the house?"

"It's not mine. It belongs to Aldo Bonetti. I took it off him because I thought he was going to shoot himself."

"I see. Is he suicidal or just a bad shot?"

Again an attempt to make light of bad circumstances. Martelli wondered if his friend was perhaps over-compensating a little, if these efforts at humour were in fact an indication of anxiety. "Both."

"Ah. Anyway, you think our fake fringuello has the gun and that he killed Angela Vaccarezza?"

"Yes." Martelli sat up in bed and shuffled back until he was leaning against the headboard. "I'm pretty sure he hired me because he's trying to get his hands on Mario Rossetti and Steven Finch's money, or maybe he's after whatever it was they were smuggling." He puffed out his cheeks and breathed out sharply. "If it's not a crime of passion then the answer's usually money."

"Sure but why would he need you?"

"Because I know the town, I have contacts -"

"And maybe they know this guy," the Frenchman cut in. "Maybe people would recognise him. Maybe he knows they'd go into hiding if they learned he was sniffing around. You, on the other hand, are a friendly face."

When Martelli didn't respond, Lelord prodded him. "Mimmo?"

"That's it," said Martelli with a groan. He couldn't believe he'd been such a fool. "They must know him. That's why he couldn't go around asking questions. He needed some idiot to do it for him."

"How many people are involved in this smuggling business? Have you accounted for them all? What about the Polish guy?"

"According to Ricardo, Tomasz is in his mid-twenties."

"Maybe it's someone from the British end?" suggested Lelord.

"Possibly. You know, another reason he might have needed me is that he doesn't speak Italian. That might be part of it."

"Who doesn't? Your client?"

"*Former* client. But yes."

It was Lelord's turn to pause. When he spoke the wariness

was evident in his voice. "Mimmo – he spoke fluently with me."

"Did he?"

"Absolutely. Believe me - speaking as one who's had to learn it himself - the man's Italian was astonishingly good."

Martelli tapped two fingers against his temple. Gloomily he recalled his having to explain the menu to his client when they met for dinner at Il Bagatto. But it had all been a charade. The Frenchman interrupted this distressing train of thought.

"I spoke to Piero at lunchtime. It sounds like he's come round after all. He'd just been on the phone to a colleague in Tuscany."

Martelli grunted but his thoughts were elsewhere, on the trail of a killer. The degree to which he'd been duped left him smarting. "I really want to find this man, Pippo. I pray that I do."

Lelord paused for a long time before answering. "Be careful, Mimmo. Quando dio vuole castigarci ci manda quello che desideriamo. When God wants to punish us, he sends us what we want. He answers our prayers."

For a moment Martelli said nothing.

Lelord broke the silence. "Rubini's got half the uniforms scouring the countryside for Mario Rossetti."

"So I hear. Piero said the team found chemicals at Rossetti's house; also a barrel identical to the ones used in the first murder."

"Yes. Rubini thinks this lends credence to his theory that Rossetti's the killer. But he's wrong.

"What about?"

"Our first fringuello was murdered using sulphuric acid, which is diluted for use in batteries. The chemicals at Rossetti's house were for cleaning swimming pools. Not the same stuff at all. And the barrel -"

"Is a standard container found all over the world," Martelli interrupted. "I remember what you told us."

"I'm glad someone pays attention."

Here Martelli managed a brief chuckle. "Do you know if they got anything from the house to house enquiries round Bardineto and Carpe?"

"Not that I'm aware of. You'll have to check with Bracco."

"And nothing new from the old lady?"

"Again, you'll have to check with Bracco but no, not that I know of. By the way," continued Lelord. "I bumped into the harbourmaster at the opera recital last night." Martelli winced, remembering that he was supposed to have accompanied the Frenchman. "He needs to talk to you. Said it was about the case."

Martelli recalled the disappointment on Ricardo's face at the Diecimila Luci nella Notte. He pressed his cheek with a finger and chewed the inside. "I'll pop down to the marina sometime today."

"Actually I think he's going to come to you. Listen, Mimmo, if there's anything I can do to help . . ."

The buzzer sounded downstairs. "Thanks, Pippo. That's my door. I'd better go."

"Okay. Ciao."

"Ciao."

Martelli threw on a robe and tramped down the two flights of stairs. Nobody was at the door but sitting on the step was a bright orange, enamelled baking dish with a red and white chequered tea towel draped over it. Next to it was a pickle jar half filled with water in which there stood a flower – a white rose with green tinted edges to its petals.

His brow knitted, Martelli leaned out into the street and looked left and right. He saw a dozen or so people but none he recognised and no one was looking his way. Still frowning, he picked up the dish and the jar and carried them inside, pushing the door shut with his foot. At the kitchen counter, he lifted the tea towel to reveal a fine looking lasagna verde alla Bolognese, still warm from the oven, its surface an irresistibly crisp, caramelised landscape, its aroma so deliciously rich it set his taste buds tingling and his mouth watering. As his stomach burbled in sympathy, he picked up a spoon from beside the sink, dug in and took the largest mouthful he could manage.

The taste was as delectable as the smell and he chewed with his eyes closed, transported for a moment to a place free of responsibility. He took another spoonful and did the same again.

The buzzer ruined his daydream.

Still munching, he tramped reluctantly down the stairs again and opened the door to find Ricardo Orso, the harbourmaster, standing on the step, so near that his nose must have been nearly touching the woodwork, his small, close-set eyes blinking rapidly behind his powerful spectacles. As always, he was wearing a neatly pressed short-sleeved shirt and dark blue shorts with precise creases down the thighs. On his head he wore a weathered, sun-bleached red baseball cap; on his face a grave expression quite out of character. Martelli didn't hide his surprise. He swallowed the mouthful of lasagna, attempted a smile and said, a little hesitantly, "Ciao, Ricardo."

Unsmiling, Ricardo returned the greeting. Tentatively he

added. "May I come in?"

"Si, of course," said Martelli. He stepped aside to allow the harbourmaster past.

Before crossing the threshold, Ricardo held a hand in front of his face and described a small circle in the air with his index finger. There was a moment before the penny dropped, and then Martelli touched a hand to his chin and found a smear of Béchamel sauce. He hurriedly wiped his mouth on the sleeve of his dressing gown before following Ricardo up the stairs.

"So," he said, picking up his mobile phone from the little hexagonal table. "Can I offer you a beer? A glass of wine?"

Ricardo took off his cap and crushed it between his hands. "No, thank you." At a gesture from Martelli, he pulled out a chair and sat at the dining table.

"Sorry," said Martelli, brandishing the phone. "I must just plug this in. I let the battery die yesterday."

At the kitchen counter, he opened the odds and sods drawer and poked about until he found the charger, glancing at Ricardo as he did so. The harbourmaster, he noticed, raised a disapproving eyebrow at the tangle of knots in the cable. Martelli plugged the phone in, satisfied himself that it was charging, and turned to his guest. "So, what can I do for you?"

Ricardo breathed deeply and sighed as though pained by what he was about to say. "You remember what you came to talk to me about the other day?"

Martelli blinked twice. Just for a moment, just to make mischief, just because the question, though essentially rhetorical, sounded so ludicrous, he was tempted to say 'no'.

"Yes, of course."

"Well . . ." Ricardo tailed off, twisting the sun-bleached cap in his small, dry, callused hands as though wringing water from it.

Martelli took a step closer and noticed once again the strong scent of lavender from the harbourmaster's clothes; the reek of cigarettes on his breath. "Are you sure I can't get you a beer, Ricardo? It's hot out there."

"No, no, I'm fine. Thank you."

Martelli sat down in the chair opposite and waited.

"Do you know Salvatore di Natale?" Ricardo looked askance at Martelli. "He has the pesto shop on Via Garibaldi."

"Yes - he was playing cards with you at the marina."

Ricardo nodded. "He joins us for an hour or so at lunchtime."

With a sinking feeling, Martelli asked, "Is he in trouble?"

"Ah!" Realising the tenor of Martelli's thoughts, Ricardo raised a hand as if to say, 'Stop', his eyebrows leaping from behind his lenses. "No, no! He's fine. But I thought he might be able to help you."

"Oh?"

"With your investigation, I mean. Do you remember he used to be a boxer?"

Martelli squinted into an imagined middle distance. "Vaguely," he said slowly and with a shake of his head. "I didn't ever see him fight."

"Well, he still coaches down at Spinetti's in Borghetto Santo Spirito. Do you know it?"

"Is it the place that backs onto the railway line?" Ricardo nodded. "I didn't realise it was still going."

"Oh, yes. Anyway, he often sees your man Mario Rossetti

down at the club." Martelli stiffened, leaning forward. He felt a prickle of anticipation on his scalp. "Also Tomasz, the Polish guy," said Ricardo. "They lift weights and spar with a few of the local fellows. I thought maybe someone down at the club would know where to find them."

"When did he last see them?"

"Not for a few weeks but I thought it might still be worth talking to him. He doesn't like them."

"Why not?"

"He thinks they're not serious about boxing."

Martelli sat back. It wasn't the most illuminating of answers but this was certainly a step in the right direction.

"I told Salvo you'd be along to see him."

"At the marina?"

Ricardo shook his head. "He can't get away today but he said it was okay for you to call in at the shop."

"Have you spoken to the police about this?"

"No. A young officer, an Ispettore, erm . . ?" He raised a hand to his mouth.

"Bracco?"

He nodded. "Yes. He spoke to me the same day I saw you, but later. I didn't know about this then."

Martelli nodded and smiled. "Thank you, Ricardo."

They talked a little longer, the harbourmaster chattering proudly and with considerably less rigidity on the subject of his beloved and 'fearless' grandchildren – Ludovico, the youngest, and Fabio, the strong swimmer - with whom he had spent an enjoyable couple of days. When he left he appeared somehow lighter, unburdened perhaps. The spring had returned both to his step and his moustache, and that well-known smile was beginning to re-emerge. It was as though he'd undergone the Sacrament of Penance and attained Divine mercy.

After he'd gone, Martelli quickly showered and put on clean clothes. He then addressed himself to what, on any other day, he might have regarded as the difficult call. Butterflies beat their wings among his innards as he dialled her number.

"Hi," she said brightly. "What happened? Did you forget our date?"

"No," he said. He took a deep breath. "Did you read the newspaper this morning?"

"I seldom read the papers. Too depressing."

His feeling of relief was tempered by the knowledge that he would now have to furnish her with an explanation. He should have taken a leaf out of Rubini's book, he mused; practised what he was going to say. Instead he faltered. "I . . ."

"Come on. Come here," she said in a sing-song voice.
"Sorry?"

"I was talking to Cosimo," said Cristina.

He pictured her sitting at the table in her fecund garden, patting her thigh and beckoning for the dog.

"So?"

"So," he said.

In the end she was forgiving and invited him over for dinner, although all he told her was that he had been involved in a police matter, a murder investigation, and had been unable to get away or even to call. In addition to the dinner invitation, she suggested that they reschedule their hike into the mountains for the following morning. She said this plainly, with no fanfare of girlish laughter, no coy giggle, but significantly without a clear invitation to stay the night. And it dangled before him, this possibility. Should he pack a change of clothes, he wondered as he hung up the phone, his diaphragm convulsing minutely, or would such presumption jinx things and guarantee him a late drive home? Whether sixteen or sixty, he reflected, when it came to matters of the heart the uncertainty, the danger of misinterpretation remained the same.

After a bout of markedly irresolute dithering, he told himself that fortune favoured the brave and packed his walking boots, a change of clothes and a toothbrush in the Alitalia flight bag. He would leave it in the car when he got to Castelvecchio di Rocca Barbena, he decided. See how things went before confessing his bold presupposition.

In the living room, he replaced the brass buffalo at the centre of the low table then stood awhile, staring at it, letting his thoughts meander. After a minute or two, he reached over, pulled out the pin, lifted the hasp, opened the back and took out the old tobacco tin. Holding it in both hands, he marched upstairs to the bathroom, removed the lid and emptied the contents into the toilet. He did this with an exaggerated degree of formality, his movements precise, almost ceremonious. He watched the flowers and buds and shrivelled shreds of leaf soak for a moment, as though steeping an exotic tea, then touched his thumb to the chrome button on top of the cistern, took a deep breath and pressed it home.

Before leaving the house, he put the orange baking dish containing the lasagna in the fridge. As an afterthought, he yanked the chain attached to the plug in the kitchen sink but didn't stay to watch the cloudy water drain away.

In the street, he found Eduardo washing the windows of the little wine shop, slopping his cloth into soupy, grey water in an old tin bucket. He stopped when Martelli appeared; stood staring at him with his arms lifted from his sides as though expecting his landlord to keel over at any moment.

"Ciao, bello," said Martelli cheerily, his mood buoyed at the prospect of an evening in Cristina's company.

"Ciao, Mimmo. Va bene?"

Rather than say 'No – things are definitely *not* going well', Martelli held his tongue. He simply smiled wanly and shrugged his shoulders in slow motion, arching one eyebrow and raising his palms as though checking for rain.

Eduardo chuckled. Crouching to wring out his cloth, he nodded at the flight bag. "Going away somewhere?" he said. From his tone it was clear he thought this a good idea.

Martelli shook his head. "Probably not," he said, closing the subject. "You didn't happen to see who left a baking dish on my doorstep this afternoon, did you?"

"Michela."

Martelli inclined his head, a curious look on his face. He didn't know Michela.

"Michela Trigiani," said Eduardo, jerking a thumb towards the house across the street.

Martelli considered this for a moment, making no effort to conceal his surprise. He wasn't sure what to say; finally settled on "Why?"

Eduardo dropped the cloth into the bucket and stood, fists on hips. For a moment he simply stared open-mouthed then he said, "For sorting out Bartolotti's son. The whole neighbourhood was watching." He laughed and shook his head. "I wish I'd seen it myself."

"Have you seen her today? Signora Bartolotti?"

"Sure. She went out shopping this morning; stopped for a chat."

"How did she seem to you?"

Eduardo wobbled his head, tossing his mop of unruly hair from side to side. "Fine, I suppose. Almost cheerful."

"Almost?"

Eduardo chuckled. "She's a bit of a dour old bird anyway, I reckon – hooligan son or no hooligan son."

Martelli stood pondering this, chewing the inside of his lip.

"Where're you off to?" said Eduardo, looking again at the bag.

"Actually, I'm going to see Salvatore di Natale."

"The pesto man?" Eduardo scowled comically and shrank back.

"What?"

"I've met him at the local traders association. He's another miserable old bugger."

Great, thought Martelli. That's just what I need: yet more wretchedness.

FORTY-FIVE

The heat hit Ted like the pressure wave from a passing train.
Within a minute it had shortened his breath and was soaking his
clothes under the arms and down his back. And he loved it; was
happy to bask in it. The dreary British summer had blackened his
mood and flattened his enthusiasms for too long.

He grinned as he clumped down the aeroplane steps and
onto the tarmac, where he stepped to one side and put on
sunglasses, unable to remember the last time he'd worn them.
Unaccustomed to Italian airports, he then strolled at a leisurely
pace instead of joining his fellow passengers in a frantic dash for
the terminal building. As a consequence, he soon found himself at
the back of a very long queue for the passport control booths. But
he didn't care. He was happy; happy to be away from London and
away from Caroline, who, if not forgotten, was definitely at the
back of his mind.

While he waited to be waved through immigration with
barely a glance, he passed the time studying the expectant faces of

the people around him. Most were Italians heading home, swarthy and stylish, notable for their coats and scarves despite the heat, but there were a few Britons among them, pasty-faced like him, heads hung wearily, shoulders slumped, sighing impatiently at yet another unwarranted delay to their journey.

Once through customs, picking up the hire car was quick and easy. Genova Cristoforo Colombo Airport is small, everything within easy walking distance, and Ted's car was parked only a few metres from the arrivals hall, so he was soon on the Autostrada dei Fiori – the Motorway of the Flowers – which linked Genova to Ventimiglia and thereafter headed past Monaco and onto the French Riviera. He passed the industrial installations next to the airport: silos and towers, chimneys and radar installations, globular shapes for which he couldn't guess a purpose, all painted in bold red and white squares. Beyond them, to the south and west, a vast silver seascape stretched off to the horizon. He cast glances heavy with longing at the white yachts, the motor launches, the cargo ships indistinct in the distance, the sun glinting gold on the waves and lighting their wakes like earthbound vapour trails. Around him, the emerald greens of the trees and shrubs were so vivid as to appear unreal, like something from a painting by Hockney, and the flowers for which the road was named formed a train of flamboyant red, orange and yellow along the central reservation.

Unable to fathom the air conditioning without pulling over, he opened the window and let the warm air buffet his face and ruffle his hair, bringing with it the sappy smell of the pines and the fresh almost sharp scent of the sea. The road was smooth, its surface unbroken, a consequence, he supposed, of a lack of heavy frosts in the area. His compact car, a dark grey Cinquecento, felt powerless compared to the much bigger Ford he drove at home but it didn't frustrate him. He felt no pressure, no urgency.

Turning on the radio, he spun through the channels in search of something to sing along to, a bit of Springsteen perhaps, or something nonsensical from the eighties, like Spandau Ballet or Duran Duran. But he found only chatter, the hosts jabbering in Italian. And it made him smile, this barrage of speech, made him feel like he was on holiday, which, nominally at least, he supposed he was.

He stopped for lunch in Savona, zeroing in on a seafront restaurant with a pretty waitress and opting to sit outside under a blue parasol. Choosing at random from the extensive menu, he was served a meaty fish baked with olives and capers alongside a helping of tasty ratatouille. He washed it down with a cold Peroni then ordered a second bottle and sat staring towards the distant horizon, transfixed by the shimmering swell of the heaving, lumpy sea and the glinting spray flung from the whitecaps.

As he sat spellbound, he recalled the day he and Caroline first met, at the birthday party of a mutual friend – little more than an acquaintance in Ted's case. The gathering had been held in Brighton, at a hotel near the pier, and he'd spent a considerable amount of time that evening staring out onto an altogether different sea. Swollen and muddy and almost granular in appearance, it churned the pebbles on the wide beach in a manner both fearsome and mesmerising. Caroline had crept up on him and he'd no idea how long she'd stood at his side before he noticed her presence. They fell to chatting with an intimacy so immediate he was caught completely off guard. She had been single for years, drifting, she told him, from lover to lover. He'd recently come out of a long term relationship - a hellish five years, he confessed, which had left him mentally exhausted, financially straitened and suffering something close to clinical depression. Her smile alone had been enough to persuade him to consider the bright side, to regard his new singledom as a blessing. She had laughed easily and with abandon, she had dragged him onto the dance floor, she had ordered tequila shots and flaming sambucas. They had spent that first and several subsequent nights together. Within a few days colleagues had noticed and commented upon the change in his demeanour; within a few weeks he'd moved out of his digs and into her tiny flat. Suddenly life was worth living again. And it had remained so for two years, maybe even three. And then she had changed. Or perhaps the problem was that he had failed to change with her. Her tolerance of his long and unpredictable hours waned until exhausted and was replaced with a burgeoning impatience and exasperation. Tension replaced contentment, helplessness replaced happiness.

The waitress approached and asked if he'd like another beer. Startled, he nodded, and swigged greedily at the one in his hand, keen to finish it before she returned with his third.

After a time, he took out his map of Liguria, purchased the previous day from Stanfords on Long Acre. He spread it out on the table, weighting the far corners with oil and vinegar in chunky glass flasks. He traced his route with a finger, wondering at the region's place names as he did so, thinking them mysterious and somehow glamorous – Castelletto Soprano, San Bartolomeo del Bosco and his ultimate destination, Castelvecchio di Rocca Barbena.

He'd booked himself into a bed and breakfast in Loano and planned to drive up to Castelvecchio the following morning, getting an early start before the heat sapped his strength. He'd brought walking boots and a knapsack, also a compass, of all things, which he'd found in the loft while getting the boxes down for Caroline. He'd toyed with the idea of bringing a pup tent and a sleeping bag but decided against it in the end, using the excuse that neither would fit in his hand luggage. He didn't ever check in bags if he could possibly avoid it.

Before returning to his car, he strolled along Corso Vittorio Veneto, popping into a menswear shop to buy a pair of swimming shorts. If nothing else came of this trip, he told himself as he pushed his credit card into the slot, he would at least go home with a tan.

FORTY-SIX

A bell tinkled above Martelli's head as he entered the shop on Via Garibaldi, an establishment so small that the entrance, a door of regular size, spanned nearly half of the frontage. The whole place was painted a buttery yellow inside and out, perhaps to make up in brightness what it lacked in size. Inside, the floor space was tiny, barely wide enough for two customers to pass one another and only a couple of metres deep. To Martelli's right, a refrigerated glass cabinet held tubs and bowls of rich green pesto and nothing else. On the wall behind the cabinet, on narrow shelves, sat dozens of clear, crinkly plastic bags tied with scratchy raffia ribbon, each one stuffed with dried fungi in numerous unappetising shades of brown, waiting to be rehydrated and stirred into risotti. The aroma of basil, garlic and olive oil was heady and intoxicating, so delicious it made his stomach growl and his mouth water, and he wished he'd taken a few more spoonfuls of Michela Trigiani's surprise lasagne. He closed his eyes and pictured it emerging hot and steaming from the oven, the pungent sauces mingling as he cut himself a generous portion and slid it onto a plate.

At that moment, Signora di Natale, a notoriously acerbic character, lacking in mirth and rather wizened in appearance, forever fussing and rarely still, emerged from the kitchen through a clicking curtain of narrow steel chains. She was an outsider, Emanuella di Natale, who, according to the Loanese rumour exchange, had fled to the Riviera following a family scandal in her home town of Venice. Her perpetual sullenness seemed to bear this theory out, suggesting disappointment in all aspects of her life. Martelli had heard she was a churchgoer too and quite parsimonious with it, which must have brought her into constant conflict with her hard drinking, heavy smoking, card playing former boxer husband.

She recognised Martelli immediately and didn't smile. Instead she fixed him with a baleful stare, looked him up and down as though making a diagnosis and gradually let her features settle into an expression of fierce disapproval. The muscles around her eyes were tensed, trembling; ready to narrow at the slightest infraction on his part. He felt for a moment like a miscreant schoolboy dragged before the Mother Superior. He had a bad feeling she was a reader of the local newspaper.

"Is Salvo in?"

She paused for a moment then inclined her head towards the curtain of chains and shouted, with a voice like cutlery tumbling in a bucket, "Salvatore!"

After an uncomfortably long interval, during which she remained silent, her gaze never leaving his, her husband parted the chains and, to Martelli's great relief, smiled warmly.

Salvatore di Natale was one of those alarmingly hirsute men whose body hair begins on the knuckles of their toes and then makes its way, without interruption, across the feet and up the legs, merging at the genitals, rising up the belly, chest and neck, looping over the ears, pausing briefly to tuft the sides had the head, then scurrying down the back to nestle luxuriantly in the cleft of the buttocks. Though barely four o'clock, the shadow on his face said midnight. Perhaps because of his body hair, because she didn't want the customers to view their wares with suspicion, his wife kept him in the back room of what had always been his family's pesto shop and there he spent his days overseeing the maceration of countless tonnes of basil leaves, pine nuts, garlic, Parmiggiano Reggiano and Sardinian sheep's milk cheese in the town where, it was claimed, pesto – the word meaning something crushed or pounded - was invented.

Salvatore was a giant by Loanese standards and appeared rather menacing to those who'd never spoken to him. Standing a head taller than Martelli, he had a rough hewn face with a squashed nose and deep-set eyes devoid of sparkle. Well into his sixties, he retained an impressive physique by swimming great distances and making frequent treks into the mountains to hunt and to forage for the fungi. His voice however had a sing song lilt to it which sounded comical on such a big man and softened his rugged exterior. He wore a stained white coat and very crumpled linen trousers the colour of oatmeal from beneath the hems of which poked those ten very hairy toes, as though he was half beast. His toenails, Martelli noticed were blackened with dried blood. Perhaps he stubbed them frequently.

To Martelli's surprise, and before Salvatore had uttered a

word, from behind the refrigerated cabinet there appeared a young boy with large eyes and an inquisitive expression. To his further surprise, a moment later a little girl popped up next to the boy. She too had those large, round eyes and that same curious expression. They were unmistakably brother and sister. Martelli guessed they were around seven and ten years old.

"Ciao," he said, smiling at them, charmed by their silent, wide-eyed stares.

Signora di Natale spun round and, noticing the children for the first time, began shooing them out of the shop like an old woman who'd discovered hens in her kitchen. They took off like a couple of startled hares, disappearing in an instant through the swinging curtain of chains. She followed.

"Your grandchildren?" said Martelli.

"No, dottore. Pasqualino, my son, and Evangelina, my daughter," said Salvatore softly and a little sadly.

He was old to be parent to such young children, thought Martelli, as was his wife, although she was considerably younger than him, but an explanation was neither offered nor sought. Martelli simply nodded. "I had a visit from Ricardo Orso," he said. "He told me I should talk to you."

Salvatore inclined his head towards the door.

Outside the shop two wooden dining chairs stood side by side, facing into the street. They sat down and Salvatore took out a small leather tobacco pouch and began rolling a cigarette. After a few moments, he said, "I'm not sure there's much I can tell you about Mario Rossetti beyond the fact that he comes to the club." He licked the thin paper.

"How often do you see him there?"

"Oh, quite often. Maybe two or three times a week." Briefly, he examined the thin cylinder of tobacco then, satisfied, struck a match and applied it to the ragged end.

"How long since you last saw him?"

Salvatore shrugged. "Three weeks maybe." He offered the pouch but Martelli declined with a brief shake of his head.

"And do you speak to him? Do you know him?"

"Of course."

"What do you think of him?"

Salvatore wrinkled his nose. "A waste of space. He isn't serious about the training." He swung his arms wide, as though addressing a circle of onlookers. "He spends most of his time sitting on the benches, chatting to his friend, the Polish boy, and getting in people's way."

Martelli nodded encouragement. "And what about Tomasz? What's he like?"

"The same." With his free hand, Salvatore rubbed the shiny top of his head, which was liver spotted and patchy and peeling from over-exposure to the sun. "I tell you Mimmo, the pair of them are bone idle. We're short of lockers. Theirs would be better used by others." He rolled his eyes and took a drag on his cigarette.

Martelli looked up and down the street. The town was returning to life after a few hours spent sheltering indoors as the sun beat down on its pavements and paintwork. People had begun to emerge and already the first groups of late afternoon shoppers were strolling along, kids in tow, browsing at the windows of boutiques both open and closed, killing time before dinner.

From across the street came a pronounced screech

followed by cacophonous rattling as the owner of the general store rolled his metal security shutters upwards, using a boat hook to force the last half metre into its slot. The noise bounced back and forth between the buildings as the man shouted a cheery 'Ciao, bello!' which Salvatore acknowledged with a nod and a raised hand. The shopkeeper then began the painstaking process of attaching a selection of faded inflatable beach toys to the edge of the shop's awning, using the boat hook to lift them into place. He made slow progress.

"I'm sure Tomasz only joined the club to use the showers," said Salvatore with solemnity. He scratched at a green stain on the cuff of his white coat, reluctant to meet Martelli's gaze. "He always turned up filthy. I'm told he lives in a shed in Toirano."

"Do you know the address?"

The pesto maker shook his head. "I do know where he works, though."

Martelli raised an eyebrow. "I thought he worked for Mario. On the boat."

"Yes, but mostly he works at a garden centre in Albenga, on Via Aurelia. Always bragging about how much he can lift – bags of gravel, fertiliser, that sort of thing. He's a big guy." He shot Martelli a glance from beneath his heavy brows indicating that this last was meant as a warning.

"There are a lot of garden centres around there. Do you know which one it is?"

"Guzzi's. First on the right after the supermarket. Just past the junction." He eyed the remaining two centimetres of his cigarette. "Are you going to try to find him?"

"I'll call in today. Even if he's not there, they must have an address for him."

"Be careful, Mimmo. Mario is harmless, a feeble man, but this Polish boy is . . ." He searched for the right word. "Angry," he said finally. "He'll be dangerous if you back him into a corner."

Martelli examined Salvatore's face. Here was a man who knew a thing or two about violence, who understood exactly what it meant to back someone into a corner. "I'll tread carefully," he said.

Salvatore took a final drag and then, with a deftness born of practise, flicked the cigarette butt towards the middle of the street, where it disappeared down a drain. "I must get on, Mimmo. I'm bagging the fungi."

"Sure. Thanks for your help, Salvo."

They stood and shook hands, the big man's grip as firm as mahogany.

"I should be thanking you, Mimmo, for helping Aldo." Martelli felt the blood rushing to his face. "He is miserable these days," continued Salvatore, unaware of Martelli's discomfort. "Withdrawn. We've been very worried. It's not just the money it's the fact that the thief was Antonio." He shook his head; snorted angrily. "Believe me, Mimmo, when I get my hands on him . . ." He raised his fists and shook them. "He wanted to pay for a beautiful wedding for Valentina, you know, like Margherita would have wanted." He crossed himself at the mention of Aldo's dead wife. "It's great that you're sorting things out. Do you think you'll be able to cancel this debt?"

Martelli felt a tingling in his fingertips. In the few days since they'd spoken, he'd scarcely given Aldo any thought – too much had happened - and he felt embarrassment at having neglected his old friend. But his embarrassment was tempered by an immediate sense of pride. 'We've been very worried', Salvatore had said, that 'we' meaning the old boys of the caruggi. But now everything was going to be all right, they thought, because Mimmo Martelli was going to sort things out. To be held in such esteem by his peers was gratifying, to say the least. Of course, it also meant that he really would have to sort things out – a prospect so exhausting that when he thought about it, he felt like sitting down again.

"We'll see, Salvo. I've yet to speak to Aricò but . . . well . . . things are in motion." In an effort to manage Salvatore's expectations, he added, "The most important thing is to make sure he doesn't lose the house."

Salvatore nodded sagely. "Come," he said, gesturing for Martelli to follow him back into the shop.

Inside, he selected a bag of shrivelled morels, like a consignment of mummified testicles, and placed them carefully in a stiff paper carrier bag along with a tub of pesto; il meglio in Loano – the best in Loano - as the label proclaimed, and it was probably true. He passed the bag across the refrigerated counter.

Martelli reached for his wallet but this only prompted a flurry of hand waving and head shaking. His money, it was clear, was no good. For a moment it looked as though Signora di Natale, summoned by the tinkling bell, was going to protest but her husband silenced her with a stern look. Clearly furious, she turned and fled through the chains, where she launched into a spirited bout of remonstration with the kids.

Martelli stowed the fungi and pesto in the flight bag and, after promising to keep Salvatore up to date on progress with

Aldo's predicament, left the shop, a wry smile on his face at the thought that his approval rating with the Signora had sunk even lower.

FORTY-SEVEN

Gaetano Guzzi, a Neapolitan tanned the colour of a horse chestnut and known as Baffo for his bushy moustache, welcomed Martelli grudgingly into an office so untidy it might have been burgled. That said it took him less than a minute to locate an address for Tomasz so perhaps there was a system, Martelli thought, albeit unfathomable to all but Guzzi himself.

The office was a small glasshouse converted for its new purpose by the liberal and rather sloppy application of white paint to the outside of the panes. Inside, the walls and pitched roof, glowing like a lightbox in the late afternoon sun, were filmed with cataracts of dust and cobwebs. It was ridiculously hot inside, stifling, so much so that Martelli had to step back outside to take a breath.

Guzzi had the pickled eyes of someone perpetually deprived of sleep. They were small and unkind and rather too close together, and Martelli felt an immediate sense of distrust, along with pity for the man's employees. The office smelled faintly of liniment or bandages, as though Guzzi had just come from the hospital, which, for all Martelli knew, he had. In contrast to Salvatore, he possessed a suspiciously luxuriant head of hair, which Martelli felt sure had once belonged to someone else. Perhaps it was cancer.

Guzzi huffed and puffed as he dug out the paperwork, making a constant grumbling noise which Martelli found mildly disconcerting. Some people, he mused as he waited, can be described as glass half full types, others glass half empty. Gaetano Guzzi was a miserable sod who most definitely fell into the latter camp. And doubtless he suspected that what remained of the water was poisoned.

He'd recognised Martelli right away and was clearly under the impression that he was still a serving police officer, and Martelli, while not actually telling any lies, had done nothing to disabuse him of this erroneous belief. As a consequence, though grumpy and unfriendly, he'd answered Martelli's request for employee information without question.

Handing over the paperwork, Guzzi fixed him with a hard stare.

"Is this where you send his payslips?" said Martelli, frowning at the employment form.

Guzzi shook his head. "No – we pay cash. That's for our records."

"I'm pretty sure this is just a back alley," said a confused Martelli of the address. "No one actually lives there." As he spoke, he remembered what Salvatore had said about the Polish boy living in a shed. At the time he hadn't taken him literally.

Guzzi folded his arms and shrugged. "That's all we have."

"And this is his mobile phone number?"

A nod this time.

"Does he have friends here? Anyone he sees socially?"

Another shrug. "I've no idea."

"And does he work here full time or is he just casual?"

"We get deliveries once a week – usually on a Saturday morning. He unloads the truck and moves the stock; operates the forklift. That's it. One day a week, sometimes two. I call him the day before if I think he'll be needed."

"And when did you last see him?"

"Two or three weeks ago. This is our quiet period, Commissario. No one digs the garden in this heat."

Martelli nodded, sensing he'd almost exhausted Guzzi's reluctant hospitality.

"Okay. Can I take this?" Guzzi nodded again. Martelli picked up a pen and wrote his number on a pad next to the telephone. "Call me if you hear from him."

As Martelli turned to leave, Guzzi said, "If you see him, Commissario, do me a favour and tell him his wages are sitting here."

Martelli paused on the threshhold. "How long?"

"Hmm?"

"How long have they been sitting here?""

"Couple of weeks."

"Is that normal? For him to leave them a couple of weeks?"

Guzzi shook his head emphatically, his eyebrows gathered. "No. Usually he's knocking on my door first thing every payday. In fact, normally he's waiting outside when I get here."

* * *

Martelli's hopes of stealth were thwarted by the loud crunching of the crushed pumice gravel poured in over-zealous depth along the little-used lane on the outskirts of the village. His efforts to skirt around it were useless as there were no verges to speak of, and he had practically to wade towards the row of garages. As he took his fifth step, his phone rang shrilly, rendering useless any further pretence.

He answered.

"It's me," croaked Nardi. "You want coffee?"

"I'm in Toirano."

"Oh."

"I'm heading up to Castelvecchio," said Martelli. "To see a friend," he added hurriedly, and immediately wished he hadn't. "She's nothing to do with the case." This he *really* regretted. He clamped his mouth shut, hoping Nardi would leave it. He hoped in vain.

"She? A woman?"

"Si, a woman."

"Do I know her?"

"No." He lapsed into a silence. Nardi did too, waiting for some additional information. For a few moments all Martelli could hear from the handset was his old friend's wheezy breathing and a few faint gurgling noises from the depths of his windpipe. Eventually, Nardi cleared his throat and got to the point of the call. "So, I rang Firenze."

"And?"

"Estella Ramazotti is not at home and neither is her

mother. Neighbours saw them leave last night. They took bags with them, luggage. The local boys have been told of the situation. They're trying to find her but, Mimmo, she must come voluntarily. She can't be forced into protective custody."

"I know," said Martelli, sounding despondent.

"There's something else."

"What?"

"Cantoni called me," said Nardi, referring to the most harried of the local magistrates, the man directing the investigation into Steven Finch's death.

Martelli wrinkled his nose. Cantoni never called; had too much to be getting on with given his huge backlog of work. "What did he want?"

"He's thinking of taking Rubini off the case; thinks he's making a mess of things."

Martelli's frowned deeply. "I'm not sure even he can . . ." He tailed off. The only way Cantoni could affect who conducted the investigation was by taking it out of the hands of the Polizia di Stato altogether and handing it over to the Carabinieri. But at such an advanced stage? Martelli gasped.

"Exactly," said Nardi. "Rubini's not impressing anyone."

For a moment neither man spoke.

"Listen, I'll call you as soon as I hear anything about Signorina Ramazzotti."

"Thank you, Piero."

Nardi grunted. "So – have a nice time with your *friend*. You want coffee tomorrow? At Giacomo's"

"Thanks. Not sure about coffee. I . . . I'll call you first thing, tell you all about it."

He hung up and continued wading down the lane, looking as he did so for signs of life. Finding none in the neglected vineyard to his left, he turned his attention to the meadow on his right and saw, to his surprise a huge charolais bull sitting next to the fence, a sight rare enough in this part of Italy to momentarily stop him in his tracks. Perched on top of its head was a mop of golden curly hair like an ill-advised wig. Without warning it lurched to its feet then lumbered around in a tight circle before blowing ferociously through its nostrils and settling back down in exactly the same spot. It nodded at him and he felt strangely compelled to nod back.

Drawing closer, he saw that among the ramshackle collection of buildings there was nothing really that constituted a house, not even a farm worker's hut. Tomasz, it seemed, lived either in a garage or a shed. There were five garages in the block, the first four with metal up-and-over doors; the last with wooden double doors, each with six small panes of glass in the top half. Beyond and to the right of the garages was a graveyard of rusting machinery: a cement mixer, a band saw, two gutted motorbikes, half a dozen engine blocks and something like a giant mincer, with a hopper and a large rotating handle, which Martelli was unable to identify. Perhaps it actually was a mincer. Or used to be. Like the other items it gave no clue as to whether this small slum was home to a young Polish man.

He approached the last garage and pressed his face to one of the little windows but even with his nose touching the glass and his hands cupped around his eyes he was unable to see inside. The windows were just too dirty. He tried the doors but they were locked so he went round the side, where a series of increasingly dilapidated lean-to sheds tumbled into a stand of trees in the corner of the vineyard. They were constructed from old pallets and scraps of corrugated metal sheeting, the former bleached grey and shrinking, the latter half-devoured by rust. Windows were mostly glazed with translucent plastic sheeting, entrances filled with panelled doors taken from houses. One of the doors, bright red and relatively new, looked quite incongruous in such a setting. Feeling slightly foolish, Martelli rapped on it loudly, not expecting a reply.

He didn't get one.

He walked further, watching carefully where he put his feet, avoiding the machine parts lurking like animal traps in the long grass along with rubble and numerous old paint tins.

The last of the sheds was little more than a mess of broken timber. He circled around it and stepped through a gap in the fence. There he found a barbecue grill, two plastic chairs and a television perched on a packing case, all laid out beneath a canopy fashioned from an old mainsail pulled taught between three sturdy trees. So this place was occupied, he thought. The garages had rear doors which opened onto a rough concrete path barely the width of the doors themselves. A once sturdy wooden picket fence separated the path from the vineyard but this was now broken beyond repair, rotten and collapsing and missing completely at the spot where the sail created a broad triangle of shade. So the back door of this furthermost garage, which was held wide open with string, led onto what was essentially an outdoor living area. As he walked beneath the canopy, Martelli saw that the television was actually on, the sound muted, an old movie playing out silently. In the furthest corner of the shaded area sat a weightlifter's bench, its padding slashed and spewing perished yellow foam as though rabid, the bar bell balanced on top of it heavily loaded with rusting iron weights, too many for Martelli to lift. A length of blue plastic hose led from a standpipe in the corner of the field, snaking between the chairs and disappearing through the open garage door. A strong smell of burning marijuana hung in the air and Martelli fancied he could almost see the rich blue smoke drifting among the trees.

He walked cautiously towards the rear door of the garage. At a rustling behind him he turned but too late. The blow caught him in the small of the back, winding him and sending him stumbling into one of the chairs and sprawling on his hands and knees in front of the television. It was a moment before he registered that he'd been shoulder charged. Then a weight fell on him, so great he felt like he was being steamrollered into the arid earth, the pain lighting the nerve endings in his lower spine and down into the backs of his legs. The last of the air was expelled from his lungs in a loud grunt and he was flattened, the left side of his face pressed firmly into the prickly, gritty dirt until he felt his jawbone grinding painfully. His ribs were bowed, his left knee twisted, his right arm pinned beneath him. He tried to breathe but was unable to inflate his chest with that great weight pressing down on him. The pain in his jaw grew exponentially and a fear that it would be broken or dislocated added to his mounting panic. He opened his eyes to find the point of a screwdriver just a few centimetres away, the threat all too apparent: move and you will be blinded.

Straining, he kept waiting for the sound of air whistling in between his teeth, gurgling through the saliva collecting in his mouth and rushing into his throat. But it didn't come. Instead he lay there silently asphyxiating, staring at the glistening point of the screwdriver and the grubby fingers holding it. He felt the pressure building in the blood vessels of his face, heard a roaring in his ears and watched as his field of vision dwindled until all he could see was that sharp steel point viewed as though through a hole in a fence. He smelled burning marijuana again, then garlic and the fetid reek of halitosis. Hot breath, nauseating in its foulness, seemed to condense on his cheek and a quiet, girlish voice said in heavily accented Italian, "Who are you?"

He tried to answer, moving his lips, baring his teeth, but no sound came out.

"Who are you?" said the voice again. "What do you want?"

He moved his lips again, this time simply to signal his willingness to reply if only he was allowed to do so. The weight lifted slightly, allowing him to draw some air.

"Martelli," he gasped with what little wind he could muster. "I'm . . . trying to find Paul Finch." A lie but he hoped the right one.

The screwdriver wavered and withdrew. Much of the weight lifted from his back. The air rushed into his throat, cool and delicious. His attacker was straddling him now, knees either side of his hips.

"Paul?" said the voice.

"Yes," he gasped. "He hired me to track down whoever killed his brother. And then he went missing. I'm trying to find him."

His captor sighed heartily. The foul breath was enough to make Martelli wince.

"Steven's dead?"

"Yes. I'm working for Paul. I came here to speak to Tomasz." He lifted his head a little so his face wasn't pressed so hard into the rough ground. "Are you Tomasz? I just want to talk. I'm not with the police."

Silence then but for his own laboured breathing and the sound of his pulse thudding in his left ear. In the distance, a moped sounded like an angry wasp. The weight lifted from him altogether.

His face contorted with pain, Martelli rolled onto his back and pushed himself into a sitting position. Tomasz stood over him, screwdriver in hand, his nose wrinkled in disdain. He appeared poised to flee, or to attack.

"What makes you think Steven's dead?"

"His body was found in a barrel above the village of Carpe, a few miles from here." Martelli jerked his head to indicate the direction.

Though he remained ready, legs apart, arms raised from his sides, muscles tensed, Tomasz seemed to relax a little at this report of Steven's demise. He loosened his grip on the screwdriver, which Martelli now saw had been sharpened on a grinder.

"When did you see Paul?" said Tomasz.

"He came to see me a few days ago and asked me to find his brother's killer. He obviously doesn't trust the police."

"What do you want with me? Does he think I killed Steven?" At the thought of this, Tomasz gave a high-pitched giggle.

"No, but I thought you might be able to tell me if Steven

had upset any of his clients."

"Did you ask Mario?"

"Mario's missing as well. He hasn't been seen for a couple of weeks." Martelli arched his back, grimacing at the pain. "Listen, can I get up? I fell off a balcony yesterday and my back's killing me."

Tomasz stared blankly for a moment before waving the screwdriver at one of the white plastic chairs.

* * *

They sat opposite one another, either side of the television set, Martelli upright and rigid, gripping the arms of the plastic chair; Tomasz slumped absently, smoking an oily joint made using liquorice paper. A large black fly described figures of eight in the air between them.

"So," said Martelli, "they started off smuggling cigarettes, booze and caviar?" Tomasz nodded. "And then they moved into drugs and occasionally people." Again a nod. "And they carried on shifting drugs until a few months ago, when they were approached by . . ?"

The response was a lazy rolling of the shoulders. Getting information out of the young Pole was like pulling teeth. He seemed more interested in his own filthy training shoes than Martelli's questions. His obvious enthusiasm for Italian food had given him a rubicund complexion and a plumpness that belied his strength. His rosy cheeks lit a round face topped with dark hair cropped close to his scalp. A set of electric clippers lay on the ground in front of the television and Martelli presumed he gave himself a weekly trim. What remained of his teeth looked like he cleaned them with similar frequency. He wore ragged denim shorts and a black, sleeveless tee shirt with a picture on the front of a rock band, their faces faded beyond recognition. His grubby white trainers had no laces and the thick tongues drooped forward. The fingers of his right hand were yellowed and shiny with smoke. Moving slowly, he placed the joint between his lips, leaned forward, hands raised as though to make a catch, then suddenly he clapped, successfully killing the fly. He eyed the shattered airframe and smeared innards with distaste before twisting in his seat, flicking the corpse over the top of the television and wiping his hands on his shorts.

"And you went with Mario to collect the two heavy metal crates from a ship at anchor off the northwest coast of Corsica? Away from the ferry routes?" Tomasz gave a barely perceptible nod, leaning back in his chair and returning his gaze to his feet. Martelli sighed. "And you have no idea what was in them?" Tomasz shook his head. "And where were Steven and Paul when this was going on?"

"Paul?" Tomasz frowned. "He was already in France. Dunkirk, I think. Mario was supposed to drive there with the crates. Paul was going to transport them across the Channel using his flatmate's yacht."

"Whose flatmate?"

"Paul's. From London."

Eyes closed, Martelli smoothed his eyebrows with the tips of his fingers, exasperated. He shook his head and sighed again. "And Steven?"

"Steven was in London making arrangements for delivery."

"Delivery to whom?"

Again that languid shrug. "No idea."

"But they paid a lot of money up front."

"Yes. We collected the crates and also a parcel of money. A big parcel. Euros."

"Where's that money now?"

"Mario has it."

"And what happened to the crates?"

Tomasz shrugged again. "I don't know. Paul never turned up in London and Mario didn't come back."

"So Mario did drive to France?"

"He drove somewhere."

"And you've no idea where he's gone?"

Another shake of the head. The look in Tomasz's eyes wavered between mild curiosity and blankness, as though he was half-heartedly faking pleasant surprise. Martelli had seen this before, in the eyes of the software engineer from whom he'd bought, not confiscated as he'd told Nardi, his marijuana. He'd seen it in the eyes of other tokers, secret and otherwise: disengagement and their sometimes feeble attempts to disguise it.

"And Paul disappeared too?" asked Martelli offhandedly. Better not to reveal the truth about Paul to this man, he thought. "So Steven must have been furious. As far as he knew, his brother and his business partner had skipped with the money and the crates."

Tomasz nodded glumly. "Steven turned up in Loano ten days ago. He thought they'd ripped him off. The people in London were very angry - you know, the buyers."

"You spoke to him?"

"He came to the club looking for Mario. He kept ranting about killing him and Paul when he found them."

"And what about Estella?"

"What about her?"

"Well, she can't have been happy about Mario having a kid with Angela."

Tomasz looked up, surprised. "Does . . ?"

"Does what?"

"Does Estella think that? That Mario's the father of Angela's kid?"

"I think so. Why?"

"Mario's not the father." Tomasz snorted scornfully. "Have you met Mario?"

Martelli felt a rush of blood to his face. "Like I said, Mario's missing. But if he's not the father then who is?" He pictured the fair-haired tot, face crumpled with sleep. "You?"

Tomasz giggled shrilly. "Steven. Steven's the father. Or Paul. Jezus Chrystus!"

Martelli blinked three times. "You're sure of this?"

Tomasz nodded.

"Then why does Estella think it's Mario?"

"How would I know? I didn't even know she knew about the kid. Didn't you ask who told her?"

Martelli shook his head slowly, mournfully.

Tomasz jabbed a fat, filthy finger at him, animated now. "Listen, Estella's a cow. She doesn't give a shit about Mario. But she knew he was about to make big money and she wanted to get her hands on it." He took another hit off the joint, held it for a couple of beats then blew a smoke ring. "Her shop's in trouble and

345

she owes her aunt a fortune. And she has expensive tastes." He let the remaining smoke drift from his nostrils.

Martelli thought about this for a moment before steering the conversation back to the Englishman, wondering if the body in the barrel, what remained of it, really was that of Steven Finch. "So Steven might have been killed by his customers wanting their money back?"

"I guess."

"Or he might have been killed by Mario?"

Tomasz's spotty brows gathered at the bridge of his nose. He shook his head. "Mario's a total dopehead. He smiles for everyone. He's no killer."

"So where has he gone?"

"Fuck knows. It's a mystery."

Martelli stared. "Do you know where he might have hidden the money?"

Tomasz ignored the question. "I'm planning to go back to Poland soon."

"You know Mario has a house in the mountains, right? A farmhouse. Have you been there?"

"A few times. His family's place. He loves it there. Him and Paul go up there to get really off their heads."

"Angela was murdered." Tomasz jolted upright, eyes wide. Martelli held his gaze. "Whoever killed her, tortured her to death. Who would do that? Who would kill Angela?"

Tomasz thought for a moment, opened-mouthed. He shook his head. "If he wasn't already dead then I would say Steven."

Martelli's eyes narrowed. "When I spoke to Angela, she

was frightened. Estella's frightened too. Who are they frightened of?"

Tomasz scowled, holding the joint at arm's length to keep the smoke away from his eyes. "They were frightened of Steven."

"Just Steven?"

Tomasz nodded slowly.

Martelli let his eyes wander, taking in the mildewed canopy with its scattering of dried leaves, the red and white beer bottle caps trampled into the earth, the many strips of blue electrical tape used to attach a makeshift aerial to the top of the television set. He wondered if the owner of the garage even knew there was someone living there. "And you? Were you frightened of him?"

Tomasz closed his eyes. After a long pause he said, "Steven was a crazy man, a psychopath. You never knew what he was going to do next. Everybody was frightened of him."

A thought occurred to Martelli. "Did he have any tattoos?"

Tomasz leaned back, a mystified frown carving deep channels on his forehead.

Martelli hunched forward, his mouth dry.

FORTY-EIGHT

Martelli parked the Lancia in the communal car park and quickly changed from his sweat-soaked and grass stained shirt into the fresh one from his overnight bag. After some hesitation he decided to stick to his plan and leave the bag in the car but, as he crouched to look in the one remaining wing mirror, he found himself wishing he'd made more of an effort; perhaps made time to pop into Figaro's for a haircut. Still, he thought, with a sigh, it was too late now. He glanced around to make sure no one had seen him preening then descended into the dense huddle of houses, following a different route from the last time, on a path bulging and cambered as though swollen against some past seismic event, the shiny grey paving stones like a geometric lava flow snaking among the buildings. In one hand he carried the stiff paper bag containing Salvatore's pesto and fungi, in the other a sports jacket, brought to wear during dinner, and to place around Cristina's shoulders if she felt a chill – he'd thought through a few moves, had a plan of sorts, though he was still nervous.

As before, he found the door propped open with the smooth, black, octagonal stone. A candle flickered in the glass cylinder next to the bowl in which the water lily floated; the smell of cinnamon and cloves hung in the air. Expecting Cristina to walk in at any moment, he stood on the doorstep, waiting, chiding himself for his nerves. When, after a minute or so, she still hadn't appeared, he stepped across the threshold and stood there, taking in the forlorn stuffed elephant, the sleeping cat and the brooding and rather alarming dark wood phalluses.

After another couple of minutes his back began to ache from standing to attention so he bent over and looked at the cover of a magazine. As he did so, her feet hove into his field of vision. They were small and the toenails were painted a smoky grey to match her dress, which was similar to the one she'd been wearing when he turned up unannounced. The skirt billowed around her legs, the waist clung tightly and a halter neck revealed shoulders and collar bones which glittered faintly as she moved. Her freckles seemed, if anything, even more pronounced than he remembered, the effect, he supposed of spending time in that garden. Her hair was tied in a loose pony tail and kept at bay by the sunglasses perched on her head. As his gaze finally reached hers, her eyes sparkled with amusement and a raised eyebrow completed an expression of mild disapproval at his slow scrutiny. She put her fists on her hips and raised her chin, a gesture of mock outrage, then nodded brusquely towards the creaky stairs. He smiled, said nothing, and headed down to the kitchen, ducking as he did so, each tread creaking loudly under his weight. Behind him he heard the swishing of her bare feet on the polished floor as she moved around, shutting the door and extinguishing the candle; having a quick word with the cat before following him.

At the bottom of the stairs, a rich, meaty aroma filling his nostrils, he turned and watched her descent, admiring once more her delicate feet and graceful movements. When she stood before him, he closed his eyes, tilted his head back and breathed deeply, a broad smile of appreciation on his face.

"Scottiglia di cinghiale," she said. "From the local cacciatore."

Wild boar with onions and peppers stewed in wine. It was a favourite of his and he wondered if he'd mentioned this during his last visit or whether she'd simply made a brilliant guess. He realised he'd missed lunch.

"It smells delicious."

"And a few salads. I hope that's all right."

"Sounds lovely." They stared at one another for a moment. Handing her the bag from Salvatore's shop, he said, "I brought you these."

"Wonderful," she said, peering into the bag. "We can have the pesto with the salads." She examined the logo. "I've been to this shop."

"It's near where I live. Salvatore's an . . . acquaintance. It really is the best you can get," he added a little eagerly.

When she smiled broadly, dimples appeared on her cheeks. Is she laughing at me? he wondered. Seeing his discomfort, she reached out and stroked his arm. He looked down at her hand.

"Come on," she said, turning and opening the fridge. "I have an absolutely delicious wine." She extracted a bottle. "It was a gift."

"From an admirer?" he asked playfully, fishing a little.

She laughed. "Yes - from a very rich, very eligible admirer."

He hid his disappointment.

"But don't worry." The dimples again, followed by the briefest of giggles. "I'm not interested." She turned her back on him and stood on tiptoe to reach a high shelf. His gaze moved instantly to her backside, which he longed to reach out and touch. "Although he is a lovely guy," she said over her shoulder. From the shelf, she took a pair of wine glasses, holding them by the stems. Turning, she nodded towards the counter. "Can you grab the corkscrew?" And she wafted out through the open door and into the garden, where the table was already set for two.

The air was filled with the scents of summer, lavender and orange blossom the most prominent. Dozens of butterflies fluttered around them, bright yellow with black wingtips and dark patches like beady eyes, gulping the air with each flap of their papery wings. Occasionally one would land on Cosimo's snout, causing him to erupt into a bout of comic sneezing and snuffling. Now and again the cat, which had followed them into the garden in the hope of a morsel or two, leapt at one of the lower fliers without success. The odd hornet buzzed the table, circling a couple of times en route to somewhere else. Otherwise they were uninterrupted.

The wine was Finchimora - a rosé so dark it appeared red. Served chilled it was crisp and refreshing and they quickly finished the bottle, whereupon Martelli was sent inside to get another. As he passed by, Cosimo eyed him sleepily from a patch of shade beneath a bench. Martelli returned the dog's gaze with narrowed eyes.

The cinghiali was succulent, a second helping irresistible; the salads were simple and all the better for it. The meal was served with crusty bread and olive oil along with Salvatore's pesto in a blue glazed bowl. The wine flowed freely and he found Cristina topping up his glass as often as he refilled hers.

Surely, he thought, she doesn't expect me to drive home; and how humiliating to be so unsure, still, at my age. He pictured his overnight bag, sitting in the boot of the car and almost winced.

"What made you choose the police?" she asked. "Did you never think of following your father into the tannery?

"The tannery was a tough life - hard work and long hours." He reached for his left hand and fingered the broad, shiny scar. She glanced at it but quickly returned her gaze to his face. He smiled wistfully. "Sometimes, in the school holidays, I would go there to watch him work. Once, when I was . . ." He breathed deeply and exhaled a long whistling sigh. "I think I was eight or nine. I can't remember now. It was such a long time ago. Anyway, I suppose I was larking about, touching things I'd been warned not to touch, opening containers I shouldn't have been opening, and I got splashed with acid." He paused. "After that I never went back. I was too frightened. You cannot imagine the pain." With a finger, he traced the edges of the smooth patch of discoloured skin on the back of his clenched fist, thinking as he did so of the poor, unidentified soul lying ruined on Lelord's examination table. He suppressed a shudder.

"So how come you're still a Commissario?" she said, steering him away from melancholic memories. "Shouldn't someone your age be more . . ." She tilted her head to one side. Her eyes sparkled, amused. "Senior?"

"The higher you go," he said, releasing his hand and reaching for his wine, "the further you get from actual police work. And I was never any good at the politics or the meetings."

"So you turned down promotion?"

He frowned, feigning seriousness. "Well, mostly I just maintained a consistently high level of rudeness and insubordination. That way no one was put in an awkward position."

She laughed. "I like you, Domenico."

He grinned. "Mimmo. Everybody calls me Mimmo."

She tilted her head. "No - I think I'll stick to Domenico."

They held one another's gaze for a few seconds. Then she laughed again, throwing her head back and looking at the sky, and he stared at those white teeth and the hollows above her collarbones.

For dessert she'd made fruit salad – macedonia - which she served in the kind of heavy crystal glasses ordinarily reserved for scotch whisky. He didn't like banana, especially when it was wet and slimy among other fruit, but he ate it anyway.

Recalling that she lived in Amsterdam, he wiped his mouth on his napkin and said, "So, are you Dutch?"

She shook her head. "Swedish. I was born in Sundsvall, not too far short of the Arctic Circle."

He shrank back, almost shivering at the thought of it. "Snow," he said.

"Lots of snow." She chuckled. "Actually, I love snow."

"So what made you leave?"

She talked then of her life in The Netherlands, of the happiness she'd found there after years of wandering - first as a teenage nanny to the children of a US diplomat living in the UK; later as a waitress in Ibiza, a tennis coach in Santorini of all places and finally as a language teacher in Istanbul, where she'd met and married Cosimo, another diplomat, who worked at the Italian mission in Ankara. Soon after they wed he was posted to Leiden, near The Hague, where they lived together until his relentless philandering became too public a humiliation. She'd left him then and moved to Amsterdam, a city she loved for its vibrant social scene, and where she'd spent a few years of her itinerant childhood with a mother she described as 'kookie'. At first she'd lived on a boat, sharing with a friend, a fellow teacher, but eventually she'd saved enough to buy and renovate a tatty townhouse, renting out rooms to help pay for the work.

Her father had been absent for most of her life but had got in touch out of the blue six or seven years ago, prompted by a cancer diagnosis. She'd been reluctant to see him at first but had eventually relented and paid him a visit here in Castelvecchio. He had explained then that he wanted her to take over stewardship of the garden.

"That was the word he used," she said. "'Stewardship'. As though he didn't own the land but was merely maintaining it."

He'd died five years ago, since when she'd spent only a few weeks at the house. This, as she'd mentioned to him on his first visit, was her first full summer in Liguria. Her kookie Swedish mother now lived in Stockholm with Cristina's younger sister, Anna, and her family: a husband and three little girls.

"We don't talk much, my mother and I," she said. "She doesn't know about this place." After a pause she added, "Actually, neither does Anna."

"Was he Anna's father too?"

"No. Anna's father was a Dane who died in a car accident just after she was born. A matter of weeks, in fact. My mother cried for days. I thought it might never end, the crying." She gripped the stem of her wine glass and turned it on the spot, exhaling sadly. "Infuriatingly, I am like my mother, I'm afraid. I fall in love too easily, I think. Most of my life I've been in love. And yet here I am, alone." She swirled the wine in her glass, watching it. "What about you?" She raised her gaze to meet his, her expression a combination of amusement and regret.

"I've been in love." He shrugged. "A few times. I was in love with Aida." She raised an eyebrow. He shook his head. "At least, I think I was. It seems hard to believe now. It was years ago. But my job is . . . My job *was* a problem. The hours were long and irregular. I was always late home, always . . . missing things. Little things, really: dinners with friends, anniversaries, the odd evening out. We'd buy tickets for something and she'd end up going alone or calling a friend at the eleventh hour. I think . . . I think in the end she found it embarrassing more than anything else." He closed his eyes and said quietly. "Don't regret falling in love. Perduto è tutto il tempo -"

"Che in amor non si spende," she finished, slowly. "Lost is all the time not spent in love."

When he opened his eyes, she was smiling.

"Exactly," he said, surprised and delighted at her familiarity with Tasso. "And anyway," he added brightly, "you're not alone. I'm here."

She grinned and raised her glass. He did the same.

As twilight neared a high curtain of cloud was drawn slowly

across the sky but far from spoiling a beautiful sunset it provided a textured canvas for its colours, capturing bright pink and terracotta and all the shades between. There was something indefinable in the air, not mere heat and humidity but a tension like a rope stretched almost to breaking point. He felt a prickling of the skin and saw that the hairs on his arms were standing on end, and he fancied he could hear a high-pitched singing, as though a wine glass had been flicked with a fingernail.

Standing up, she said, "I'll be back in a moment." But instead of returning to the house, she headed down a wooden staircase to a lower terrace, from where there came a crackling noise and soon a twisting column of blue woodsmoke rose into the heavens, a scattering of sparks riding it.

On her return, he gave her a quizzical look, which she parried with a wagging finger. "A surprise," she said, a patent note of conspiracy in her voice. "But first . . ." She reached for his plate. He began to stand. She stopped him with a raised palm. "No. Wait. I'll clear up in the morning. First, let's watch."

She scraped his leftovers onto her own plate, which she carried to the northern boundary of the garden and placed on the ground before an explosion of lavender. She then ushered a reluctant Cosimo into the kitchen, closed the door on him, resumed her place at the table and sat silently watching. Intrigued, he did the same and before long a trio of scruffy grey fox cubs, stumbling about on paws too large, like toddlers wearing their parents' shoes, emerged from the bushes and began licking frantically at the plate, fighting over the juicier mouthfuls and tumbling about in the grass.

Martelli looked on in wonder. Turning to her, he raised an

eyebrow.

"Every evening," she whispered, nodding to herself.

The fox cubs made short work of the gravy and, after briefly casting about for more, returned to the undergrowth, barging one another and capering about as they did so.

"Can I ask you something?" he said, his tone serious. She gave the tiniest shrug. "Why do you keep the wine glasses on such a high shelf?" He grinned.

She looked down at the table top, a little tipsy now, shaking her head. "I don't," she said, her voice a little muffled. "I have other glasses in the cupboard. I just wanted you to see that I don't have a fat bum."

She looked up and they laughed together, loud enough for the whole village to hear them.

"It's perfect," he said. "Your bum, I mean." She closed her eyes and shook her head vigorously, raising her hands to signal that the subject was closed. "And I have a confession to make too," he continued, this time with genuine seriousness. "I spent the night in jail."

"When?"

"Last night. That's why I didn't make our rendezvous this morning."

"Really?" she said, uncertainty evident in her voice. He nodded. "But you're out . . . What? On bail?"

"No. No need for bail. I haven't been charged with anything."

And he told her about the investigation, about the unidentified acid victim and about Angela Vaccarezza, about his former client and about the discovery of the real Paul Finch, drowned and washed up on a beach in southern England. He spoke with a somewhat sheepish tone, frequently avoiding her gaze as though he were in some way responsible for the mess.

"I feel like I'm only now thinking straight again after . . . You know." He fiddled with his fork.

"Well, there's been . . . Upheaval." She reached out and put a hand on his.

He nodded.

"Anyway," he said with a sigh. "That's why I need to take a look at Mario's place up in the forest."

"Well," she said, matter-of-factly. "We'd better set off first thing. Tomorrow's going to be another ridiculously hot day."

They fell silent. A dog barked somewhere in the village, a coughing sound carried far on the still evening air.

"But now," she said, standing and this time taking his hand. "Come with me." And she led him down the wooden steps to the lower terrace.

The source of the fragrant smoke turned out to be a bundle of rosemary wood smouldering in a cylindrical wire basket which sat in the filament-like coil of stainless steel pipe protruding from the side of the large, water-filled and verdigris stained copper tub. The glowing embers heated the coil and the hot water inside it rose, spiralling around the fire, growing hotter as it did so, and eventually gurgling into the top of the tub. And as the heated water spilled out of the top of the coil, cold water was drawn in from the bottom of the tub, and thus the process perpetuated itself. And by this simple mechanism, in the few short minutes since Cristina had lit the fire, the water in the tub had already grown pleasantly warm. Martelli dipped his fingers in, dry-mouthed with nerves as he realised her intention. Behind him Cristina busied herself lighting candles. He turned to say something, trying to maintain an air of nonchalance, but his eyes betrayed his trepidation and she laughed lightly, girlishly, before unzipping her dress at the side and, with a lack of self-consciousness that he found at once arousing and unsettling, untied the straps of her dress and let it fall to the ground. She wore nothing beneath it. Without saying a word, she stepped towards him, leaned in close and kissed him lightly on the lips before starting to unbutton his shirt. Light-headed, he numbly took over unfastening the buttons, fumbling while she undid his belt.

When they were both naked, she kissed him again, more firmly this time, before turning, climbing quickly up the wooden steps and slipping gently into the black water, where she lay back, eyes closed, and luxuriated in the warmth.

Holding in his stomach, he followed.

* * *

Silence but for the gentle trickle of the water and the almost indiscernible hiss of the embers. On the far side of the valley, a set of headlights made its way noiselessly along a narrow road through the trees. Pipistrelle bats flitted across the moon, wheeling and diving, visible for only an instant; an owl hooted twice and received a single note in reply; unseen creatures scurried in the undergrowth. The clouds had moved on and stars filled a sky still pale in the dying twilight. The heady scent of the fragrant smoke, the wine, the touch of Cristina's skin, soft and slippery in the warm water, and the heat soaking into his aching vertebrae had all served to untie the knots inside him.

Laughing quietly, they plucked figs from a tree trained against the wall behind the tub, tearing them open with their fingers and sucking at the flesh.

Later, they lay in her bed in a room accessed across a broad roof terrace from which, by day, the view must have been astonishing.

"It's midnight," she whispered presently, sliding an arm across his chest. "The witching hour."

"Inclinatio the Romans called it," he said sleepily, pulling her close to him. "And it looks like tomorrow the moon will be full."

In Loano, in his house with no air-conditioning, he was accustomed to lying sweating into the sheets; changing the bedclothes frequently, perhaps every other day. But here, high in the mountains, the night was pleasantly cool, and sleep promised to be a refreshing sojourn rather than a series of feverish interludes. Consciousness soon melted away and he slept with a profound feeling of contentment at the thought, at the real sensation, of another heartbeat so close.

FORTY-NINE

Unable to find a hotelier willing to take a booking of fewer than ten nights during the peak holiday period, Ted had checked into an albergo on Loano's Via Sant'Erasmo, next to the railway line which followed the coast. His ground floor room had double doors onto a small garden in which there grew an orange tree, its fruit blackened with rot and crawling with ants. There was no air conditioning so his only option was to lie naked beneath the gaze of a rattling fan which swept the room, stalled, ground its gears and wobbled precariously on its stand before changing direction. He'd expected to be fresh meat for a thousand mosquitoes but in the end received no bites at all – none that itched at any rate.

Breakfast was a generous buffet of cakes and pastries supplemented with yoghurt and a cup of deliciously treacly coffee, none of which he would ordinarily have chosen at home. He helped himself to several jam-filled brioches, uncertain when or where he would have a chance to grab lunch. The other patrons in the gloomy dining room, all Italians, smiled but said nothing other than muted 'Buongiorno's, each of which he acknowledged with a self-conscious nod. He was the only person eating alone.

As he ate, he thought of DC Burns - Graham Burns - with his fastidious note-taking and his organised life, whose smartly dressed kids and neat, petite wife smiled unstintingly from a series of photographs on his desk, the pictures taken at family barbecues and school fêtes - events which felt further than ever from his own reach now that Caroline was gone. He fixed his gaze on a woman at a nearby table, watching as she shovelled sugar into her coffee. She was fifty-ish, jowly and heavily tanned. The flesh of her upper arm wobbled as she began to stir. Did Burns know that colleagues thought him dull? That they mocked him? Mocked his wife too – those who'd met her. He pondered these questions, relishing for a moment the descent into bitterness. The jowly woman nudged her companion – a man of similar age and complexion - who leaned in to hear her whisper before turning to look quizzically in Ted's direction. Realising he was scowling Ted forced a brief smile and lowered his eyes. He shook his head, chiding himself. Burns was a thoughtful person and a conscientious police officer not deserving of his scorn.

Taking a bite of brioche, he made a conscious effort and turned his thoughts to work. He wondered if the night watchman had emerged from his coma to shed any light on the burglary at the wholesalers; wondered too whether any progress had been made towards finding the intruder who broke into the old folks' home. But mostly he wondered what lay behind the attempt to smuggle radioactive material into the UK. The officers from CTC had given little away during the rigorous debrief but, though they were highly skilled questioners, he'd got the overwhelming impression that they'd been caught, not on the hop - that would be an unfair assessment – and not off guard either, but unawares. The shipment had been unexpected and from a quarter not known to them and the intended recipients, the buyers, had yet to be identified. Doubtless Warren Devlin's caravan, 11 Meadow View, had already been quarantined; his flat too. And doubtless also someone would soon be despatched to Liguria.

Ted was supposed to have informed them of his whereabouts, had promised to contact them if for any reason he left London, but he had yet to make the call. Sipping his coffee, he told himself he'd take a look, just a look, at whatever lay in the mountains above the village of Castelvecchio di Rocca Barbena. After that he'd check out of the albergo, drive an hour west across the border into France and perhaps on into Monaco, from where he would get in touch, giving no indication that he'd even been to Italy. If asked for his itinerary, he'd fudge things a little; say he was just going wherever the wind took him. Whether or not he was believed . . . well, at that moment he didn't care. All he had left was his job and he was damned if he was going to be denied the satisfaction of making further discoveries for himself.

* * *

The journey towards Castelvecchio took him through the centre of Loano of which he'd seen very little the previous evening, having limited his sight-seeing to the marina and a little restaurant on the waterfront. He'd expected a quaint little fishing town and was surprised to find himself in a mostly modern, if a little shabby, beach resort.

Thirty minutes later, barrelling along the A10, he'd passed Ceriale, Albenga and Alassio and had travelled as far as San Bartolomeo al Mare before he realised he'd missed the turn-off for the 582. At first he swore aloud but then he reminded himself he was in no hurry. So he took the exit for Via Pairola and drove down to the waterfront, where he parked and went in search of a cold drink and some snacks. It was still early, he mused. He had all the time in the world.

*　*　*

Consciousness returned to Martelli in stages, the first being an awareness of daylight, an experience alien to him as his bedroom shutters were perpetually closed. The second was a feeling of warmth on his bare legs as sunlight slanted through a small window in the back wall of the house, its low angle a measure of the hour. Next there came birdsong and an irregular, sharp tapping noise. And it was the latter, along with the smell of freshly ground coffee percolating, which served finally to draw him out of his deep and blissful sleep.

In the kitchen, Cristina stood at the counter wearing only a pale blue shirt, and he couldn't help but pause and admire her legs awhile. From a fresh pineapple she was cutting thick slices, which she laid on a plate and dusted with peppermint sugar. Her knife swished through the flesh of the upright fruit and banged loudly against the hardwood chopping board - the source of the tapping noise.

"What time is it?" he said presently, blinking, hoping he didn't look too . . . What? he wondered. Old?

Looking up, she gave him the dimples. "Seven. I'm sorry if I woke you but I can't resist the sunrise. It's the very best part of the day, full of hope." Martelli chuckled, thinking of Bracco. "My grandmother used to say that every sunrise was an opportunity to start again," she said. "To start anything again; your whole life even."

He walked to the open door, took in the spectacular view and breathed deep of the cool, fresh mountain air. Trying to work out how he felt, he settled on a blend of delight and disbelief. He'd had the best night's sleep he could remember, alongside a woman from a dream. The smile on his face was irrepressible.

"Do you have anything planned for this evening?"

He turned, frowning. "Well, actually . . ." He flashed a lopsided smile. "I had a vague notion I might clean and tidy my house. It's long overdue."

She laughed. "Stay another night. I'll cook. Tomorrow I'll help you clean your house." She paused before adding, "I'd like to see where you live."

He thought of his house with its dark, moody paintings, dusty books and dated fixtures, and of his bedroom with its mismatched linen and its creaking bed frame. It was hardly a place conducive to romance, particularly now that it had been subject to a little light ransacking. But he liked her suggestion of another night in Castelvecchio, and perhaps he could contrive to have her give him a head start; time to change the bedclothes at least.

"I'd like that," he said. "But you don't have to help with the cleaning."

She carried a tray out onto the terrace, pausing to lean over and kiss him fleetingly on the lips as she went past. "I don't mind," she said as she stepped outside.

"Okay," he said.

"That's settled then. We're having pesce all'acqua pazza."

Fish in crazy water. It was another of his favourites. He shook his head, grinning again. "Don't go to any trouble."

"It's no trouble. It's nice to have someone to cook for."

They ate breakfast sitting side by side at the table with the sun at their backs, gazing out at the mountains as the morning haze melted away. Cosimo sat with his nose close to Martelli's thigh, muzzle raised, eyes following each mouthful. As Martelli chewed, the look in the old dog's milky eye might have been interpreted as disapproval. After Martelli fed him a sliver of ham it became one of expectation.

Over to their right, the village was coming to life. An unseen motorino rattled and pop-pop-popped as it bounced through the narrow, uneven streets; a woman unfurled pink sheets, hanging them out to dry on her terrace; a dog yapped for its breakfast; greetings were shouted from windows, over fences and across rooftops.

A few metres away, a little bird hopped about, its face a blood red mask. It pecked at the ground where Cristina had scattered a handful of seeds. Martelli touched her arm and pointed as the sleepy cat emerged from the shadow of the brilliant lavender bushes, ears flattened, belly close to the ground, its stance all elbows. They watched in silence, ready to startle the bird before the cat had a chance to pounce. But the many bees attracted to the lavender proved a distraction and, during a lapse in the cat's concentration, the little bird spotted it and took to the air.

"Oh, he'll find another one," said Cristina. "They're all the same to him, the sparrows and finches."

Martelli fell still, staring into the middle distance, a glass of orange juice halfway to his mouth, his cheeks suddenly pale.

"What is it?" she said, after a few seconds of silence.

He twitched. "Sorry. It's . . . I need to make an urgent call," he said.

"Go ahead, she said, concerned. "Is everything okay?"

"I'm not sure," he said, putting down his glass and standing, staring intently at his mobile phone. "It's just something I . . ." He shook his head. "Something I forgot to do. I won't be a second." He held the phone to his ear, striding towards the far end of the terrace. The cat took fright and high-tailed it into the house.

Nardi answered after just one ring. "You want coffee? I'm nearly at Giacomo's"

"I'm still in Castelvecchio."

A short pause signalled his old friend's disappointment. "Okay."

"Did they find Estella Ramazzotti?"

Nardi exhaled deeply, a bubbling, gale force roar in Martelli's earpiece. "They found her mother," he said, sounding gruffer than ever.

"And?"

"She's been badly beaten. Estella is missing. A priest, a Fra Benedetto, was shot. He's old. He might not survive. The bullet cracked his pelvis and he lost a lot of blood. He's in terrible pain."

"Did they give a description of the attacker?"

"No. The priest was shot from behind so, even if he was conscious, he probably couldn't tell us anything. The mother's hysterical; keeps shrieking and wailing and shouting for her daughter. She's well known at the hospital. Apparently she's not the full ticket."

"Gesù Cristo."

"It seems they sought sanctuary at the canonica after hearing about Angela Vaccarezza's death from a friend back home in Loano. But someone found them." Nardi lapsed into silence.

"Have you spoken to Bracco?"

"Today? No." He was irritable now.

"Pippo?"

A snort. "No. What's going on?"

"I think I . . . Never mind. I'll call you later."

"W -"

Martelli hung up and marched back to the table, dismissing images of a furious Carabiniero doubtless stamping his feet and cursing aloud in the street. "How quickly can we get going?" he said urgently.

* * *

The gully wound its sinuous way up the mountainside, twisting around the largest of the boulders and the oldest and most deep-rooted of the trees. Its steep walls and dry bed were strewn with withered sticks and branches brittle as glass, all of which crunched loudly underfoot. In places the mass of dead vegetation was so thick they had to scramble up the bank to get around it. The rocks were flinty and sharp and more than once Martelli stumbled and barked his shin. A fug of dust hung in the air, raised by their footfalls and the constant cool breeze funnelled up the gully from the valley below, visible only in the shafts of bright sunlight which here and there penetrated the dense forest. Above their heads, flying insects chased and circled one another in aerial dogfights. Occasionally birds were startled into an eruption of flapping and squawking, shooting into the air with an excited Cosimo in vain pursuit.

At several points along their route, tall trees, their roots undermined by the shrinking of the parched ground, had fallen to bridge this channel but the gully sides were mostly high enough that they didn't have to duck to pass beneath them. Now and again the walls rose higher and drew closer together until they could touch both sides simultaneously and it seemed as though they were becoming wedged in a crack in the Earth. At other times the walls sagged outward, flattened, and they found themselves struggling over a shifting surface of pebbles, as though they were following a river, which, had they been hiking the same route during the first weeks of spring, when the snows melted, would have been the case.

Martelli stopped for a moment; blinked to clear his eyes of sweat and wiped his forehead on his folded cuff. Smiling, he stared intently at Cristina's taut buttocks and sinewy legs as she walked ahead, taking long, loping strides. Funny, he thought, how things can appear so different depending on one's mood. Only yesterday, he had been a washed up detective, newly freed from jail, his reputation in tatters, his name mud, a laughing stock in his own neighbourhood and no doubt the object of derision among former colleagues. Yet now, just a few hours later, in the company of this charming woman, and, yes, after spending the night in her bed, he was able to shrug off his humiliation and think simply: let them scoff, let them deride him, and let them waste time and precious manpower in their fruitless search of the wrong property. Before long he would be proved right. He was certain of that. He was close. He knew it.

They struggled on like this for an hour and a half, making slow progress, the journey taking more of a toll on him than on Cristina. And Cosimo seemed unaffected, tireless despite his age. By now the heat was feverish, the sky a shimmering pale stream growing wider overhead as the forest grew thinner. They stopped in a patch of dappled shade and sat on a smooth, flat rock which protruded from the side of the gully like a shelf. The previous occupants, a pair of wall lizards, their backs streaked with iridescent green, darted into the undergrowth. Cristina unzipped his backpack and took out a bottle of water. He shook his head as she offered it to him first.

"I can't help thinking it might have been easier to follow Mario's track," he said, watching her tilt her head back and drink.

She shook her head and handed him the bottle. "I've no idea where the entrance is. It might join the road five kilometres from here, maybe ten. Who knows?" She shrugged. "It might not join the road at all, might be a branch of another track. And most of them aren't on any maps."

She unslung her own backpack and took out a white bone-shaped treat which she fed to Cosimo before giving him some water from another bottle.

"Do you think he'll be there?" she asked. "Mario, I mean."

"Listen," he said soberly. "When we get close, let me know

and I'll go on ahead."

She shrank back but laughed. "Are you expecting trouble? From Mario?"

"No. I'm expecting trouble from the killer."

"Seriously?"

He nodded slowly, emphatically, but he didn't tell her what he suspected, that the killer had kidnapped Estella and forced her to reveal the location of Mario's mountain hideaway; that even now she might be lying dead, up ahead, while her murderer rifled the place in search of . . . Money? The mysterious cargo?

"So where do you think Mario's got to?"

Martelli puffed out his cheeks and blew. "I have a feeling . . . I mean, I'm not picking up some resonance in the cosmos or anything, but I have a feeling he's gone."

"Dead?"

He pursed his lips and nodded again. "There's something about this bunch. They seem . . ." He tailed off once more.

"What?"

"Doomed."

"Okay." She sprang to her feet. "You're making me nervous. Come on, let's go. Let's get it over with."

He followed, head down, slightly disappointed that they hadn't rested for longer.

Ten minutes later, as they approached a tight bend in the gully, the landscape reared up abruptly so that the walls loomed over them. It rose still higher at the point where the gully turned to the right, forming not quite a cliff face but a very steep, rocky bank perhaps ten metres high, topped with thick vegetation and teetering trees. A few valiant oaks had managed to find purchase on this vertical garden. They stuck out sideways, their trunks like crooked elbows, their boughs contorted in frozen agony.

Cristina stopped and turned around, glancing up at the lip of the gully on either side. "Where's la belva?" she said, meaning Cosimo.

Martelli gave a ragged shrug and a swift shake of his head, flicking droplets of sweat from his hair. "He ran on ahead, I think," he said, pointing and panting.

"Cosimo!" she called.

He winced, ducking his head. He wanted to tell her to be quiet but how could he encourage stealth without making her anxious?

"Cosimo!" she shouted, more sharply this time.

He placed a hand on her shoulder and she spun round, eyes flaring briefly at this proprietorial gesture. But her anger quickly abated as she searched his expression. "He'll find us," she said resignedly.

The ground beneath their feet grew more uneven as they rounded the bend, the going more treacherous. To avoid turning an ankle, he had to watch very carefully where he was putting his feet, so he didn't notice Cristina stop again until he very nearly walked into her.

She twisted at the hips, looking over her shoulder at him, her feet planted firmly but her face ashen.

"What's wrong?" he said, but, looking past her, he saw it for himself before he finished the second word.

A few metres ahead, its rear bumper resting against the trunk of one of the crooked oaks, its windscreen aimed at the sky, was an elderly green Land Rover. It sat there as though attached to the gully wall, like the space shuttle prepared for lift off, upended, out of reach, suspended about three metres above the ground. A dense cloud of flies hung around it like a dark smudge in the air. Beneath it stood Cosimo, agitated, whimpering. As Martelli and Cristina approached, the old dog looked their way and yelped fretfully. Slowly they drew closer, taking small, cautious steps, unable to take their eyes off the vehicle. Apart from a long, ragged tear in the canvas side panel, it appeared undamaged, as though installed there for some legitimate purpose. But its condition and even its incongruity was not what held their attention, for lolling out of the driver's side window, opened as though in greeting or goodbye, was what appeared to be a hand.

FIFTY-ONE

At one of the numerous hairpin bends of which the looping, ill-maintained forest track consisted, the shrubs thinned out and the corner widened to form a roomy, flat verge in the shade of a broad conifer, its low hanging boughs laden with long, thin needles of an almost iridescent silvery blue. Ted pulled over, concerned at an unhealthy clunking noise emanating from the nearside front wheel, most pronounced when he negotiated the tight bends. Though narrow enough to avoid a thrashing along its flanks from the wall of unyielding vegetation on each side of the track, his rented Fiat Cinquecento was not built for such rough treatment and he was beginning to regret ever attempting the drive. On the way up he'd winced each time the car bottomed out, had watched the temperature gauge nervously and had frowned at the constant scraping on the underside of the body.

Yanking on the handbrake, he cut the engine and climbed out, glad to be giving the car some respite; glad too of a little relief from the constant lurching and tilting.

A city boy, he couldn't remember ever having stood in a forest. Woodland, yes, during shambolic forays into the Kent countryside with his classmates three decades ago, but nothing like this, nothing on this scale and on such mountainous terrain. He bounced up and down a few times on the springy bed of dried needles, which gave like a pillow and crackled underfoot. He took a deep, heady lungful of the scented air and surveyed what to him looked like a primaeval landscape, bountiful and unsullied. He stood marvelling at the sheer immeasurable power of this force called nature, the gentle pinging of the cooling car the only sound.

A dog yelped, making him jump. Every muscle in his body tensed and he felt pin pricks on the back of his neck. Shaking, he cast nervous glances into the dense mass of trees, head cocked to one side.

Nothing.

Had he imagined it?

No. He didn't think so.

Still trembling, he climbed back into the car and sat pondering his next move. According to the last line of the directions found in Warren Devlin's sports bag, his destination was no more than half a kilometre further along the track – a five or ten minute walk on the level pavements of central London, perhaps half an hour on this uneven mountain road. He quickly resolved to complete the journey on foot. It would be good for him, he thought, fresh air and a little healthy exertion to blow away the cobwebs.

He started the engine, executed a five-point turn and reversed the car as far as was possible into the darkest patch of shade beneath the broad conifer. He then put on his hiking boots, stowed his map and compass, a bottle of water and several bags of potato chips in his rucksack and set off.

* * *

Martelli's greatest fear about retirement had been that it would consist of a prolonged period of torpidity followed by an ignoble fizzling out, probably with a tube up his nose and a cannula in the back of his hand, the sickly smell of disinfectant and the buzzing of a flickering fluorescent light his last sensations on this Earth. Life would come to a premature end, like a stream diverted, dammed and left to become stagnant, mosquito-ridden acqua morta. But, he thought, as he peered down at Mario's stricken vehicle, pondering the events of the past few days, so far retirement hadn't been nearly as dull as he'd anticipated and, while he hoped he wasn't about to go down in a blizzard of gunfire, clearly the Frenchman had been right - the potential was there for things to remain interesting.

Up close the smell emanating from the Land Rover was quite nauseating and the flies were pestilential, their droning incessant.

"British plates," he said, thinking aloud.

"Mmm?"

"The licence plates," he said. "They're British."

"I didn't know," said Cristina, matching his low tone.

"And he's sitting on the right – the driver."

They'd retraced their steps to the flat rock shelf, from where they'd scrambled out of the gully and made their way through the dense woodland until they encountered the track, little more than a pair of deeply rutted furrows with thick undergrowth encroaching on either side and sprouting along the centre. They then followed it to the hairpin bend at which Mario, or whoever was behind the wheel, had met his end.

From where they sat, several metres above the stricken vehicle, reflected light made it impossible to see through the windscreen, but the smell more than made up for what they were missing, and of course there was the hand, blackened and outstretched.

By this time the sun was high in the sky and the heavy foliage was speared by bright shafts of light in which insects glittered and cobwebs glowed. Overhead the backlit leaves shone emerald, their veins visible like bones in an x-ray.

"Something's very odd about this," said Martelli, scrambling to his feet and leaning out over the drop, bent at the waist, hands on his knees.

Cristina sat comforting Cosimo; gently stroking his neck. "What do you mean?"

"Well, for a start, he left the road backwards, at a hairpin bend, heading up a steep hill." He turned to catch her eye and pointed. "Up."

She held out her free hand, palm upwards. "It's a very tight bend." She fended off a fly with a lazy backhand.

"Yes, but backwards? He was past the dangerous section." Returning his attention to the upended jeep, he continued, "It looks like he made it around the bend then stopped and reversed over the edge. Either that or he simply rolled over. There's no sign he hit the brakes and skidded. How fast would he have been going?" She shrugged. "Not even walking pace," he said. "It would have been easy for him to stop with the footbrake or the handbrake or both."

"Maybe they failed."

He shook his head. "Maybe. But then why not simply turn the wheel. The bushes would have stopped him. They overhang the track on both sides."

"Maybe he panicked," she said.

"At two kilometres per hour? I don't think that's it."

"Could he have fallen asleep?"

He wrinkled his nose. "I suppose that's possible but . . ." He tutted. "People fall asleep at the wheel on the autostrada, not on a twisting, bumpy track through a forest, halfway up a mountain. Some of those potholes would practically throw you out of your seat." Standing upright, he stepped back and wiped a sleeve across his forehead.

"Here." She handed him the water and he took a few gulps. "So," she said. "Do you think he did it deliberately?"

"Well, no. But, even if he did, it's not exactly a very long drop, is it? He hasn't plummeted into a chasm. The bushes would probably have slowed him down." He indicated the ground around him. "And the grass at the edge is a metre high. He basically travelled backwards eight metres or so then dropped a further . . ." He shrugged. "What do you reckon? Six metres? And he ended up jammed against a tree. There's hardly any damage to the jeep."

"So?"

He furrowed his brow. "So would that be enough to kill him? The headrest would stop his neck from snapping."

"Maybe he had a heart attack."

He shook his head. "I suppose so."

"There are plenty of possible explanations." She nuzzled Cosimo's snout.

"You're right but . . ." He tailed off, shaking his head again. He sighed a deep sigh of resignation. "I need to take a closer look."

* * *

It took him just five minutes to climb down to the stranded Land Rover, the undergrowth providing ample hand holds, a pair of oak saplings anchored firmly enough to hold his weight. He wanted to take a look at the body and perhaps get a better idea of what had happened to Mario Rossetti, the missing man around whom the whole sorry business appeared to orbit, if indeed that was his corpse waving at them from the driver's seat.

Up close the smell was more bearable, though perhaps he had simply grown accustomed to it. The blackness of the hand was due not only to decay but also to a seething mass of insects and their larvae: glistening flies; ants roaming ceaselessly; maggots dark with human blood. Having pushed and kicked at the Land Rover until he was satisfied it wasn't about to go crashing into the gully, he clambered onto the radiator grille and over the bonnet, gripping the spare wheel, and squatted awkwardly with one foot on the lower part of the windscreen frame and one on the upper, squinting through the glass between his feet, trying to get more than merely a glimpse of the grotesquely decomposed corpse in the driver's seat. But the sunlight was too bright and the interior too dark so, gingerly, he knelt down, gripped the A pillar with both hands and lowered himself until he was lying flat across the windscreen, head and feet protruding at either end.

The putrescent hand was now sickeningly close to his face, barely half a metre away. He lay quiet for a few seconds, eyes closed, gulping air through his mouth as he steeled himself for what was to come.

Concerned by this apparent inactivity, Cristina called down to him. "Are you okay?"

He opened his eyes and winced. "I'm fine," he said. "I'm just taking a closer look at his hand. He was injured - probably in the crash. There's a gash on his arm."

Maggots writhed in the wound. A bead of sweat dripped from the tip of Martelli's nose. He watched it fall and thought he saw the dark spot it formed on a dusty rock several metres below.

He called up to her, "Have you ever seen anyone else use this track?"

"No. It only leads to Mario's place, another kilometre or so further on. I guess hunters might use it."

Gritting his teeth, he shuffled a little further out and hung his head so that he was looking directly into the cab.

The festering horror in the driver's seat seemed to mock him. The eyes were closed and the lips puckered in a ghastly engorged kiss. Bloated and blackened like a cannonball, the face, like the hand, was alive with insects: maggots spewed like liquid from the nostrils and eye sockets; ants marched like clockwork. Dozens of flies took to the air at Martelli's intrusion and he closed his mouth and eyes as they collided with his face. Blinking, he noted that the driver's long, black hair hung behind him, oddly glossy and healthy looking. Mario's t-shirt – and it was definitely Mario, fit precisely the description given by Cristina - had ridden up to reveal twenty centimetres of belly, distended with the gases of putrefaction, discoloured but not nearly as dark as the head, into which the blood had drained after death. The knees were jammed under the steering wheel and were all that prevented the corpse from sliding off the upended seat and falling into the rear of the vehicle, for Mario was not wearing his seatbelt. The decomposition, under glass and only partly shaded by the trees, generated a noticeable heat and a putrid humidity, which Martelli felt on his cheeks and, though he'd grown used to the stench, he could taste both the sweetness and the acidity of the rotting flesh. He shuffled even further out over the edge of the windscreen and tentatively extended an arm, grasping, feeling a little light-headed. As the blood rushed to his own head, he wondered if Mario had noticed a similar wooziness as he lay gasping his last, or whether he was already beyond caring, beyond feeling, in the minutes before his heart finally shut down.

Like a kid operating the mechanical claw at an amusement arcade, head swimming, Martelli had to concentrate hard to send his hand to the right place on the metal dashboard fascia. A noise escaped his lips like someone heaving at a heavy load. His fingers drummed the air as he strained to reach the bunch of keys hanging from the ignition; the pressure in his face increased. He blinked away sweat and blew at a particularly persistent fly. Finally, he grasped the keys, turning them and pulling them free with one fluid motion. He raised his head and gasped for air, pushed himself into a safer position then rolled onto his side and examined the bunch. There were seven keys besides the one from the ignition, of which two were clearly house keys. The others he couldn't identify although one he guessed might be for a post box.

Working carefully for fear of dropping them into the gully, he removed the ignition key from the ring and pocketed the rest.

"Should you be doing that?" said Cristina, watching from above.

"No, but it'll save me from having to do something that I really shouldn't."

"What's that?"

"Breaking in to Mario's farmhouse."

He then repeated his acrobatics, replacing the Land Rover key in the ignition.

Other than the gash on his arm, Mario bore no obvious signs of injury but Cristina was absolutely right, he might well have suffered a heart attack or succumbed to some other ailment. The mystery would doubtless be solved by Lelord in the undisturbed peace of his chilled laboratory rather than here among the trees, in the sweltering heat.

Instead of attempting to climb back up, he lowered himself gingerly along the side of the vehicle, discovering as he did so that the rear compartment was empty but for the usual junk: jump leads, a length of rope, a jerrycan and some folded plastic sheeting, along with countless discarded chocolate bar wrappers, drinks cans and crisp packets. He then dangled from the rear bumper and dropped the last metre or so into the gully, tumbling over as he landed and gaining a liberal coating of pale dust. He didn't care. He was just glad that he'd managed it without bringing the Land Rover down on his head.

"Are you okay?" shouted Cristina, having heard but not seen him land.

"Fine," he called up to her. "Make your way back down.

I'll meet you on the track."

She paused, thinking, before shouting down, "I thought we were going up to the farmhouse."

"No," he replied. "We need to report this right away. I need to call my friend, Gianpiero."

FIFTY-TWO

Ted had no expectations about his destination other than that, if it were a dwelling of some sort, it would be small, so he was surprised when the path emerged into a wide, roughly diamond-shaped clearing at the centre of which stood a substantial and ancient farmhouse with adjoining barn. The buildings were constructed of pale, honey coloured stone, all of which, he mused, must surely have been quarried nearby, otherwise they would have had to have been carted up the mountainside by donkey, including the massive lintels above each of the doors and windows of the house, and the huge keystone which surmounted the centre of the arched entrance to the barn. That said, the sagging roof was formed of heavy, curved clay tiles and construction must have required tonnes of sand and cement, so the whole enterprise would surely have involved days, if not weeks of transportation. He noticed too that the track approaching the house and the clearing surrounding it had been recently and crudely repaired with crushed brickwork and broken masonry.

Breathless from his hike, Ted stood for a minute at the edge of the clearing, panting, fists on hips, before remembering that he should probably approach the place with caution. People were dead, he reminded himself, Warren Devlin was missing, danger might well lie behind the flaking blue paintwork of the heavy double doors.

The sun was several degrees past its zenith and he could feel the powerful rays reddening his scalp as he picked his way cautiously, as quietly as the uneven, rubble strewn ground would allow, towards the front doors. As he drew near he saw that the date – 1656 – had been crudely carved into a rectangular stone set into the wall below the central window of the upper floor. Many of the smaller windowpanes were broken and, although the house was secured with a relatively new pin tumbler lock, the doors to the barn were simply tied with orange, plastic twine. On the far side of the clearing, peeking out from behind the house, sat the cannibalised carcass of an old Citroën van, its wheels removed and not in evidence, a spider's web of cracks obscuring the windscreen, the body panels all but consumed by rust. Beyond it, dozens of blue and black plastic barrels, of the type used to transport chemicals, formed a jumbled heap. They were dusty and paint-spattered and those without lids had doubtless filled up with water and dead leaves.

Cupping his hands around his eyes, he leaned close to look through a small window next to the front door, the pane no bigger than a paperback book. Inside he saw a dusty flagstone floor. A hallway led off into the darkness, a door on either side giving access to the ground floor rooms. A crude wooden staircase led to the upper floor. A battered steamer trunk sat at the bottom of the steps. Next to it, on the floor, stood a pair of rubber boots and a collection of battered torches. On the wall, a row of coat hooks held a waxed raincoat, a moth-eaten knitted cardigan and striped woolly hat with a pom-pom. A man strode out of the doorway to the left, crossed the hall and disappeared through the doorway on the right. Ted's heart jolted. He dropped to all fours and scuttled to his left, towards the barn. His breath came in panicked gasps, his rucksack bounced against the back of his head; something sharp pierced the heel of his hand and became lodged in the flesh. Gone were any notions he'd had of pretending to be a lost hiker. Gone too were any doubts he'd had about the directions, and any lingering thoughts that he was on some sort of wild goose chase.

He didn't rise to his feet again until he was around the corner with his back to the barn doors, his pulse and mind racing. Fighting to breathe quietly, he extricated himself from the straps of his rucksack, unzipped the main compartment with a trembling hand and retrieved his mobile phone. To his great relief, there was a signal. But who should he call? The Italian police? And what would he tell them? That a smuggler of radioactive materials was at large in the Ligurian mountains? He'd raise a laugh perhaps but little else. And anyway, he spoke no Italian. The only sensible course of action was to call Nichols back in Plumstead, to come clean to him about the trip to Italy, to have him call Counter Terrorism Command and then leave it to them, CTC, to contact their Italian counterparts, who would then mobilise the local force . . . But how long would that take?

He hung his head, inwardly cursing himself.

Keeping the barn between him and house, he ran, crouching, into the forest, weaving between the trees and leaping over fallen boughs until he tripped and fell into a mossy hollow. Unhurt, he rolled onto his back and lay there, breathless, listening.

He put a hand over his eyes and recalled details. The man inside the farmhouse was wearing a white linen shirt and loose fitting khaki trousers. A pair of black sunglasses was perched on top of his head, flattening a strip of his dark curly hair. He was deeply tanned and looked like he kept himself in good shape. In his right hand he held a large calibre revolver, an elderly Webley by the look of it but no less dangerous for its age. Ted fought to control his breathing. Should he simply knock on the door? Wing it, somehow? Gain entry and then hope to overpower the man? His train of thought was interrupted by raised voices, speaking in English, one deep, masculine and sonorous, the other shrill, feminine and filled with fear. A door banged. Heavy footsteps scratched on the hard, dusty ground and swished into the undergrowth. He heard the double click of a ratchet, like a clock preparing to strike . . . Or someone cocking the hammer of an antique revolver.

FIFTY-THREE

"So, to be absolutely clear about this, you just happened to find Rossetti's body? By chance? While hiking?" Nardi's rising tone signalled disbelief bordering on mockery. He raised one sprouting eyebrow but the other remained locked in a deep scowl of scepticism. He was glazed with sweat, his shirt sodden to near transparency, his irascibility apparent not only in his face but in his every move. He'd yanked his tie until the knot was no bigger than a throat lozenge and, in the process of unfastening his collar, had lost a shirt button. He'd nonetheless managed a courteous smile and friendly handshake for Cristina. Lelord on the other hand, though calm, had greeted her with rather cold formality. Cosimo he eyed with considerable unease.

"He won't bite," Cristina said, noticing his discomfort.

Lelord smiled weakly and gave a swift double nod before turning and shuffling even further away from the panting dog's bared fangs and lolling, meaty tongue.

They were gathered on the verge, next to Nardi's

Carabinieri Land Rover, at the point where the meandering track
to Mario Rossetti's farmhouse emerged from the forest. Fifty
metres distant, the metalled surface of the road shimmered in the
heat.

Nardi was shaking his head. "Do you really expect Rubini
to believe that you simply stumbled across his prime suspect's
corpse? You of all people?"

"Right now I don't care what Rubini believes. And when
you see the body, when you see where it is, you'll understand that
it can only have been by chance." Martelli opened the vehicle's
rear door. "Come on. Andiamo."

Nardi pursed his lips and exhaled, the air whistling
through his nostrils. "Okay, but you're going to have to help me
out. We've got to think of a better story."

"All right. We'll think of something on the way. Let's get
going."

"Wait." Lelord spoke with quiet authority. Martelli gave
him a curious look. In one hand, the Frenchman held a yellow
metal box the size of brick. An electronic device of some sort, it
had a large glass dial at its centre. In the other hand he gripped a
stubby metal cylinder like a microphone, connected to the yellow
box by a long, drooping spiral of black cable. Still clearly shy of
Cosimo, he took a step towards Cristina and held the cylinder close
to her midriff and chest. "Stand still, please."

"Che è ciò? What is that?" said Martelli making no effort to
disguise his impatience.

"Quiet," snapped Lelord. "Stand together." He gestured
for them to move closer to one another. "Hold your hands out,
both of you, please."

Exchanging glances, they complied and watched as Lelord passed his electronic snout over their palms, staring intently at the dial.

"Nothing," he concluded, visibly relieved. "Have you noticed any ill effects? Any nausea? Headaches?"

They shook their heads, perplexed. Martelli glanced down at the device and then back at Lelord.

"It's a Geiger Counter," said the Frenchman soberly. "A radiation meter."

Once more Martelli and Cristina exchanged glances then together they looked at Lelord, who turned to Nardi. Nardi nodded. "Remember I told you the brother had radiation sickness? Well, it may be that Rossetti transported radioactive material." He opened the driver's door and put a foot on the jamb. "No air con in this old thing, I'm afraid." He snorted. "No seats in the back either." Smiling grimly, he removed his tunic jacket, revealing the ample dome of his dirigible belly, and climbed in behind the wheel.

* * *

It had taken Martelli and Cristina more than two hours to hike down to the point where the track met the road. They'd then waited nearly an hour for Nardi and Lelord to arrive. The journey back up the track, Martelli, Cosimo and an apprehensive Lelord sliding about in the back while Cristina sat up front with Nardi, took a further hour and a quarter, so the sun was already setting light to the hills when Cristina finally pointed and said, "This is it".

A further two hours later, crouching behind a dense thicket,

Martelli watched as another vehicle, a patrol car of the Polizia di Stato, swayed into view, its headlights serving only to deepen the gloaming. The car came to a standstill behind Nardi's Land Rover and Martelli held his breath as the passenger door opened. He sighed with relief as the familiar figure of Bracco appeared.

Unable to fully open the door, the young detective had to squeeze out as though freeing himself from the grip of a giant beast. Moments later, a uniformed officer struggled out of the same door; the leather pouches on his belt, for handcuffs, torch, pistol and pepper spray, impeding his progress.

Martelli smiled. Rubini had, at least for the time being, been excluded from this jaunt into the forest.

In the end, they'd kept it simple. Nardi had informed Squadra Mobile of the discovery but told them only that a woman tourist, Cristina Källström, had found Mario Rossetti's body. Bracco was kept in the dark too, to save him from having to lie to his new boss, or reveal the truth about his old one. Martelli wished he could talk to his trusted former colleague, wished he could ask him if Rubini had paid any heed to what they had discussed in the jail cell. Were steps being taken to correctly identify the first body? Had DNA samples been sent for analysis? Was at least one officer from the team looking at missing persons reports? But that was going to have to wait.

As the new arrivals joined his friends at the apex of the hairpin bend, peering down into the gully, playing the beams of their torches on the distorted face of the late Mario Rossetti, Martelli, satisfied that Cristina and Cosimo were in good hands, turned and headed further up the mountain.

Nardi had at first raised objections to Martelli's heading off alone but he'd soon given up, recognising the look in his old friend's eyes and realising that argument was futile. Besides, he had a decaying corpse to deal with, not to mention the logistical difficulties of hauling Mario Rossetti's Land Rover out of the gully. And Bracco was still unaware of the farmhouse further up the mountain; would find out in the morning, after the identity of the corpse had been confirmed and it was deemed necessary to investigate Rossetti's likely destination. 'Do you at least have a torch, Mimmo?' he'd said finally and with the weariest of exhalations. Martelli had assured him that he did and that he would call him at the first sign of trouble. The late night hike would be for reconnaissance, he'd promised, and nothing more. And by the time Nardi turned up, at first light and doubtless mob-handed, he would be back in Loano, or at Cristina's, sleeping contentedly.

Rejoining the track, he found that his eyes quickly grew accustomed to the semi-darkness and soon he was able to see every detail of the ground beneath his feet and the forest floor around him. A gentle breeze began tickling the long grasses and flipping the leaves but it remained warm and before long he was once again slippery with sweat.

After twenty minutes, he stopped for a breather, tilting back his head to look up between the treetops at the last faint streaks of crimson dissolving in the west and the first scattering of stars in a sky of immeasurable depth. It was a beautiful night and, though warm, it was considerably cooler than in Loano, where the ancient stone buildings of the caruggi gathered heat during the day and radiated it throughout the night. The ground felt soft and springy despite weeks with scarcely any rain and he wanted to flop down right there, to recline against a tree and close his eyes. He wanted to forget the turmoil of the past few days and simply sleep. He thought of Cristina, of the smoothness of her skin and the easy grace with which she moved. Checking his phone, he saw that the signal strength indicator showed just one bar but it was enough for a text message. He could make his way to the road and have her meet him. He could forget all this; leave it all to Commissario Fabrizio Rubini or whoever was to replace him from the ranks of the Carabinieri. He inhaled deeply, savouring the spicy scent of the forest, and recalled his conversation with Nardi. If Paul Finch had drowned only after succumbing to radiation poisoning, it might be that Mario Rossetti had suffered the same fate, collapsing behind the wheel of his car, which then rolled backwards and unchecked into the ravine. Perturbed, he bit the inside of his cheek and began walking again.

Around the bend, a dark coloured Fiat Cinquecento sat beneath a magnificent conifer, whose laden branches drooped as though mirroring his weariness. He approached cautiously, his breathing shallow, alert for the slightest noise or movement. The bonnet felt cool beneath the flat of his hand. Peering in through the window, he saw a rental agreement in a brightly coloured cardboard wallet on the passenger seat. Next to it was a map of Liguria, its title in English.

He slid his backpack from his shoulders and delved inside. When they'd parted company, Cristina had left him with two surprises. The first, the smaller of the two, was a lingering kiss, wordlessly urging him to be cautious. The second had left him speechless. It was a Beretta pistol of World War Two vintage. 'My father's,' she had said as he stared at it, weighing it in his hand. 'It came with the house. Be careful, it's loaded.' And then she'd headed off at a trot, back to the safety of Nardi's Land Rover, Cosimo panting at her heels. Now, standing by the car, hemmed in on all sides by ominous shadows, he curled his fingers around the handgrip and closed his eyes.

By the time he reached the clearing, the moon had risen and the galaxy had emerged from the depths of the sky as a river of stars which appeared to fizz and crackle with electricity. He stood still for a few moments, staring at it, listening to a silence that felt vast. Directly in front of him was a substantial farmhouse. Old but considerably more recent than his own home, it was built in the traditional local style: stone walls and a shallow sloping roof typical of a region with little snow, layered with heavy cap and barrel tiles. Squat chimneys at either end of the building were each surmounted with a pair of flat stones, arranged like the first element of a house of cards, there to prevent the rain from getting into the walls. Adjoining the house was a small barn the width of the house itself and half as long, accessed at the end of the building via tall double doors. Honey-coloured light leaked out through the gaps between their shrunken boards. The smell of an overflowing cesspit floated from somewhere nearby.

Without warning, an explosion of squawking detonated a few metres behind him, causing him to drop into a crouch, wide-eyed with panic, arms raised about his head. A startled bird shot out of the forest, beating its wings with frantic rapidity, passing overhead, momentarily silhouetted against the sky. As it merged with the night, Martelli grasped his chest and felt his heart knocking like an insistent fist. His mouth was dry and his fingertips tingled. He glanced nervously at the farmhouse, half expecting the front door to burst open as someone came outside to investigate the disturbance. He wondered what it was that had frightened the creature and whether he should be worried about it too.

As though at the bird's signal, a gust of wind marked the graduation of the breeze. Another followed, and another, and soon the forest was sizzling like bacon in a pan and the air was loaded with dust, pollen, floating seeds and spinning fragments of dried vegetation. Pregnant clouds began to unfurl across the heavens, colliding and dividing, snuffing the stars and obscuring the full moon, plunging the landscape into a sooty darkness.

Steeling himself, taking a deep breath, he hurriedly crossed the open space to the barn doors. One of them stood slightly ajar and he risked looking inside. The source of the honey coloured light was an old paraffin lamp sitting on a workbench in the far left hand corner, its shimmying flame licking the inside of a cracked glass enclosure. He could smell it, could feel its particles inking his lungs. It might have been burning for hours. A car was parked to the left, near the doors, a boxy, black Alfa Romeo saloon, like his Lancia Gamma a survivor from the 1980s. On the far wall, barely visible in the gloom, was a doorway into the house.

Seeing no one, he withdrew and made his way around the building to the front doors. There, his heart in his mouth, he selected a key from Mario's bunch, inserted it into the shiny, new lock and let himself in.

Pulling the door closed behind him, he paused, willing his eyes to grow accustomed to the darkness, before taking slow, cautious steps. Through an open door to his right was a large room, six metres by six, empty. To his left was a room of similar size. A stone sink under the window suggested it was once a kitchen. Straight ahead was a roughly hewn wooden staircase at the bottom of which sat a pair of mud-caked rubber boots next to a wood-ribbed steamer trunk. The lowest tread creaked loudly as he put his weight on it. He waited, listening, but heard nothing. The stair creaked again as he applied his foot once more. A scuffing noise from the upper floor sent his pulse into overdrive. He froze. There it was again. On tiptoe he took three strides and entered the kitchen, his breath coming in short gasps. He stepped to one side and pressed himself against the wall. The stairs creaked once, twice. He held his breath. They creaked again.

Momentarily uncloaked, la luna di cacciatore's silvery light penetrated the cobweb-frosted windows allowing him a snapshot of his surroundings. A rusty bed frame, robbed of its mattress, cast parallel shadows on the pocked and scarred plaster. In the corner beyond was a scrum of tatty farm implements from another age. Next to them, a dozen squat, heavy glass bottles nestled in wicker baskets, each one half a metre in diameter. A pair of white trainers, the only modern items, peeked from behind the open door. An ancient terracotta pot was set into the wall to the left of the sink, its rim at waist height, its base almost on the floor. It was a washing machine from a bygone age when the laundry would have been cleaned with ash, swirled around in the pot using a wooden paddle. Directly opposite where he stood was a fireplace and next to it the door to the barn, fastened shut with heavy iron bolts at top and bottom. The clouds closed around the hunter's moon, plunging the room once more into an impenetrable darkness. He shivered. The stairs creaked again, closer this time, a lower step. It was just six or seven paces to the opposite side of the room. Maybe he could slide back the bolts and make it into the barn before being seen. If he held his right hand out as he walked, he should encounter the end of the bed frame with his palm. He took a suspended step, then another, walking on the balls of his feet, treading as lightly as he could, listening intently.

He was halfway across the room when he sensed that he wasn't alone in the dark. Grit and dust scratched beneath the sole of a twisting shoe. He half turned, cocking an ear. A movement caught his eye – the white trainers. The blow caught him at the base of the skull, sounding a klaxon inside his head. Time unwound, its microscopic mechanisms meshing, turning; levers clicking into place. His eyes closed of their own volition and his last thought before he lost consciousness was to wonder if he would hit his face on the bed frame as he fell.

FIFTY-FOUR

Agony woke him. His hands throbbed from a lack of circulation
and were flushed with excruciating pins and needles. A
considerable weight crushed his fingers and it was a few moments
before he worked out that he was sitting on them. There was a
sharp pain in his wrists too, and he quickly realised they were
bound tightly with thin wire. His left shoulder was badly bruised
and swollen and he wondered if it might have been dislocated and
then forced back into place. His trousers were hoisted up painfully
in the crotch and the keys in his pocket – Mario's keys – gouged
his hip. His shirt was twisted and pulled tight around his body,
digging into the flesh under his arms and constricting his
breathing. Opening his eyes, he saw nothing, a darkness just a few
degrees shy of absolute, and he wondered how long he had been
unconscious. There was a strong smell of petrochemicals, like the
whiff of a new magazine only stronger, overwhelming all else. He
was leaning hard against something solid and curved. His feet
were cramped and his toes were pressed against something heavy

and immovable. He blinked again but found his eyes were not getting used to the darkness. Had he gone blind? Panic set his heart beating like hooves at a gallop, increasing the pain in his hands and shoulder. No, he told himself, no, he had not lost his sight. It was simply very dark and he was shut inside a well sealed room or perhaps a cupboard. The stifling heat and humidity confirmed this. He tried to lift himself up a little, to take the pressure off his hands. Gritting his teeth and holding his breath, he heaved himself over to his left, igniting the nerves in his damaged shoulder. Immediately he collided with something which didn't give; something with a smooth, concave surface; something close.

Realisation sent adrenaline coursing through his arteries. He felt the rush of it in his chest and writhed as the pain in his hands became electrifying agony. His own panic breaths blew back in his face - stale garlic mingling with the chemical smell. He pulled hard at the wire binding his wrists, feeling it tear into his flesh, driving the throbbing in his fingers and thumbs to even greater heights of pain. He imagined them swollen and discoloured, a bright, livid red. The scar on the back of his hand felt like it was on fire and he was transported to that day, half a century ago, at the tannery: the reeking pelts, the steaming vats, the filthy workbenches, his eyes smarting in the fug of noxious vapours, his father sharing a joke with his colleagues, a cigarette twitching between his lips. Outside, bright sunshine bleached another glorious summer day. Inside, his stinging eyes had struggled to adjust to the gloom. The ferocity of the pain had shocked him to the core. He'd screamed and fainted and wet his pants. When he came to, the look on his father's face hovered between concern and shame. Martelli extinguished this mental picture only when he thought he might pass out.

He took a couple of hot breaths, fighting to control the crazed staccato in his chest, but was gripped again almost immediately by an uncontrollable panic. He threw himself this way and that, moaning and wailing at the pain in his left side as he battered it repeatedly against the broad ridge on the inside of the plastic barrel. His hands grew numb, though he still felt the immense pain in his wrists. Tears rolled down his face, tears of frustration, anger, self pity and sheer terror. He tried desperately to banish all thoughts of what might await him but, of course, it was impossible. He couldn't help but picture the partially dissolved horror that had lain on the Frenchman's metal table; couldn't help but remember the vile smell from the exposed internal organs and the thick lumpy broth of liquefied human tissue mixed with faecal matter. He gagged and heaved and vomited into his mouth, spitting it out and feeling it slide down the front of his shirt. Stomach acid burned his throat and the smell of his puke was rancid. He was suddenly and acutely aware of the rhythm of his breathing, of the pulse firing in his blood vessels. He hung his head, momentarily despondent, then once more launched into a frenzy of thrashing and writhing; an expression of anger and frustration rather than a serious effort to free himself. Once more the pain in his hands and shoulder brought him up short. He collapsed against the inside of the barrel, utterly dejected, lost, defeated. His mind racing, he thought of his friends. They knew where to find him but would they come looking? Yes, but probably too late. And now he was to pay the price for his foolishness, for his inability to let go, for his egotism.

Nardi's words rang in his head and seemed to echo inside the barrel: 'You are an idiot, Mimmo'. How right his old friend had been. He squeezed his eyes tight shut and felt more tears toll down his cheeks. He tried to imagine a place of tranquillity: the silent monastery of Monte Carmelo in Loano, the royal palace in Seville, Cristina's plentiful garden, but his pounding heart and the sound of his own panic breaths echoing back at him in the confined space prevented him from conjuring up any but the most fleeting of images.

In an effort to soothe his burning throat he attempted to swallow a little of his own saliva, then pushed down hard with his feet, lifting his weight, bringing blessed relief to his hands and wrists, though transferring the pain to his toes and calves. He held this position for as long as he could, his head forced against the inside of the barrel's lid, his back pressed painfully against the thick circular ridge, all his weight bearing down on his toes, and he cried out as he sagged back down and his hands were crushed once more.

"Think," he said aloud, gasping the word. "Think, you old fool."

He rewound recent events to his arrival at Bar Reale in Carpe. What had he seen then that might help him now? What had he learned? He closed his eyes and tried to picture every aspect of the scene, every tiny detail, and what he realised very quickly was that the true horror of the crime stemmed from the meticulous planning, the careful attention to detail and the resulting absolute impossibility of escape.

On the brink of tears again, he shook himself mentally, and tried to visualise his circumstances from the outside of the barrel.

The good news was that no acid had yet begun to trickle over his face so presumably his captor had either changed his mind - unlikely - or had gone to fetch the reservoir, as the Frenchman had called it. Of course, he might return at any moment, so if Martelli was going to do anything he had to do it quickly.

Voices penetrated his container, a man and a woman, speaking English in tones he thought he recognised. He held still, not daring to breath, trying to work out if they were drawing closer. The screech of corroded metal preceded a hollow boom and reverberating rattle. The barn door, he thought, thrust by a human hand or swinging in the wind; colliding with its twin and rebounding. So I'm still here at the farm, he concluded, a long hike from hope, idle retirement a dream.

The voices grew distant, faded to nothing. He took a deep breath through his nose, straining to fully inflate his lungs, counting steadily to four as he did so. He held it for another count of four before puckering up and blowing, trying to maintain a consistent stream.

The lids at Carpe had been fastened down with steel bands, narrow collars fed through small buckles and cranked tight around the necks of the barrels; the result much like the sealing of jam jars with elastic bands and cloth caps. But how much effort had been put into the closure of his own tiny cell? Did Mario retain the means, here, in the middle of nowhere, to reseal the containers? Or had the lid simply been forced into place with the heels of hands, snapped over the neck but left unsealed? He pictured the barrel, sitting on the lowest terrace at Bar Reale, afloat on a pool of reeking sludge.

Holes, he thought. Yes! A ring of holes had been drilled

through the plastic around the circumference of the barrel. Those holes were the source of that crusty puddle of liquefied flesh and ordure. Concentrating, he strained his eyes, searching straight ahead for any interruption in the dark, a small, circular patch of night in the blackness. He saw nothing, which meant either that his eyes were failing him or the lid remained unsealed, otherwise, he reasoned, how would he breathe? He steeled himself, gritted his teeth, directed his waning resources to the muscles of his legs and thrust himself upwards, forcing the top of his head against the inside of the lid. The agony in his hands receded at the same rate that the pain in his feet and inflamed shoulder increased, his losses cancelling his gains. He pushed with all the force he could muster, his breath escaping between gritted teeth in a throttled hiss. And it flexed. He was able to force the stiff plastic lid into a shallow dome. And just before his strength gave out, he was sure he felt it move too, just a little. He collapsed, his weigh dropping onto his hands, his wrists pulling hard, the thin wire slicing into the flesh until it felt as though it was sawing into the bones of his arms. He cried out, a plaintive wail stifled by his lips, which he strove to clamp shut.

Panting, eyes roving, throttled by his own clothes, he prepared himself for another try, fighting the temptation to give up and resign himself to death. The barn door shrieked, banged and rattled again, this time accompanied by the howl of an escalating gale. He fought to focus, to bring to bear every remaining scrap of his energy, mental and physical. He took deep breaths, counting again, straining hard to extract what oxygen he could in the stifling conditions. As he did so, he tried to relax his burning muscles, to rest them, if only for a moment.

Taking as his signal another shriek of rusted hinges, he thrust upwards again, eyes squeezed shut, lips pulled back. The pain electrified his every nerve ending as he pushed against the inside of the barely yielding lid. Images of ruined flesh and ragged clothes, of bleached bones and exposed entrails flashed through his mind. The pain he was feeling would, he knew, be as nothing compared to what awaited him if he failed to free himself. The lid bowed outwards and moved a little but not enough and he felt his strength ebbing away far too soon. He pictured the exposed teeth in that ruined face grinning at him, taunting him, mocking his vanity and blundering stupidity, and a furious anger rose within him, driving him to fight back, to free himself, to tear through his own wrists if that was what he had to do to survive. Forgetting the lid, he threw himself against the right side of the barrel, snarling with rage as he did so. Then he threw himself to the left, wincing, and then the right again, then left and right, until he felt the base lift beneath him. And left, right, left, right, tears rolling down his cheeks as the pain in his injured shoulder and swollen hands radiated throughout his entire body. And just as he thought it futile, he felt the barrel pass the point of no return and topple. And as it did so he drove his head upwards, forcing it against the inside of the lid, riding the barrel as it fell, using the momentum, guiding his own weight to crash against it as the barrel hit the ground with what he feared but also hoped would be a bone jarring collision.

The impact hit him like a bolt of lightning and he passed out instantly, like a television switched to stand by.

He came to with his face pressing down hard on the dirt floor, his tongue covered in grit and fragments of ancient dung, his nose squashed and his forehead cool. He opened his eyes and swivelled them sideways towards a source of yellow light, which turned out to be the dancing, horned flame of the cracked paraffin lamp, still perched on a workbench in the corner of the barn. He rolled onto his side, gulped cool air and wriggled out of the barrel like una lumacha – a snail - emerging from its shell.

He saw no one.

He rolled over, arching his back so as not to put any weight on his bound wrists.

Again he saw no one.

He was alone.

He felt weak from hunger and fatigue. Cristina had brought food for their hike but they'd barely touched it. He'd eaten an apple while they waited for Nardi and Lelord to show up. His last full meal had been breakfast. He wondered where Cristina was and what she was doing, if she was lying in bed, wide awake, worrying about him, waiting for him to return, or if she was sleeping soundly. He hoped it was the latter.

Outside it was still dark. The trees creaked in the rising wind and the forest's crackle had risen to riotous applause. The air had cooled since the setting of the sun but there was a closeness in the atmosphere and a palpable voltage. On the workbench near the lamp sat his backpack, next to another of similar size. For a few moments he could do nothing but lie there staring at it, motionless but for his heaving chest, listening to the storm grow and allowing the searing pain of confinement to ebb and flow, and gradually, but for his wrists, hands and shoulder, dissipate and fade to a bearable ache.

The barn smelled stale and faintly mildewed, like the inside of an old work boot. It evoked memories of his grandfather's coat, which had hung, untouched, in the hallway of their apartment long after he had died, and which Martelli used to explore every morning, burying his face in it before leaving for school. He flinched as the door banged behind him, sounding so much louder now that he was out of the barrel.

Struggling to his feet, he considered simply walking out into the darkness but the prickling pain in his hands was hard to bear and the thought of negotiating the track, at night, in a gale, with them tied behind his back, was terrifying. Unsteadily he walked towards the source of the light. On the workbench sat a rusty pair of pliers with a sharpened notch for cutting wire recessed into the blades. Using his forehead, he dragged them to the edge of the bench then turned, twisting to see behind him, feeling for them with his aching, swollen fingers. The barn door shrieked as it was flung open again. The pliers clattered to the dirt floor. Martelli's chin sagged to his chest and he mouthed a curse. Crouching, he retrieved them and took five excruciating attempts to locate the strands of wire in the notch. He used his body weight to bring the handles of the pliers together, sitting down hard to bite through the wire and finally free his hands. The relief was so great he felt like whooping with joy.

Standing again, he removed the curls of wire from his bloodied wrists and flexed his fingers in an effort to restore normality. As he did so, he walked to the swinging door and peered cautiously out into the night. Though only a few metres from the relative safety of the forest, he was in no condition to run so he needed to be sure the coast was clear before breaking cover. The dense mantle of low cloud had brought a darkness that worked in his favour but the chatter of swirling leaves and the gusting gale made it all but impossible to hear if anyone was nearby. He would just have to take a chance, moving as fast as he could.

He returned to the workbench, retrieved his backpack and was about to extinguish the lamp's guttering flame when his jumbled thoughts suddenly crystallised and he paused, rigid, looking directly at the second backpack. A few seconds ticked by. He blinked, turned around and stared at what he had already seen but failed to register. In the corner of the barn there stood another barrel.

FIFTY-FIVE

It beckoned him like an addiction, at once irresistible and horrifying, standing in the gloomiest corner of the barn, in the shadow of a tower of firewood arranged neatly to the right of the kitchen door. Bundles of dried sticks, white as bones, had been tied into faggots and stacked against the wood and the ground around them was liberally scattered with crisp, curling flakes of dried bark which crunched under his feet as he approached. Beyond all this, a large, plastic jerrycan, reeking of petrol, sat on a pile of stained, threadbare sacking, a dribbling spigot attached to it via an oozing hand cranked pump.

And then there was the barrel.

He walked slowly, feeling its menace as he drew nearer. Glancing over his shoulder at the second backpack, he wondered for a moment if it might be better to examine its contents before proceeding. Then the door banged and he heard something, a shuffling or rustling, above the roaring of the wind, and the buttery flame, despite its glass flute, danced in the gust, bringing leaping monsters to life on the walls and ceiling. He tilted his head and, though he didn't hear the rustling noise again, it served as a reminder that his captor might return at any moment. He didn't have time to waste.

As he reached out to touch the barrel's lid, a series of tremors took hold of his upper vertebrae, starting between his shoulder blades and rising to his skull, causing his shoulders to judder, his arms to tremble and his head to shake; raising the hairs on his neck. He wanted but didn't want to know what was inside, or who. Logic told him that the barrel had not been altered, that there was no hole in the lid and no reservoir, but he was unable to suppress the fear that the backpack belonged to Estella, and that he would find her inside.

He curled his fingers over the rounded circumference of the lid, gripped it firmly and pulled.

The man gulped air like a landed fish, emitting a deep lowing noise with each hungry gasp. Martelli leapt back in shock, stumbling and almost falling over. Regaining his equilibrium, he looked down at the occupant of the barrel and said sharply, "Chi sei?"

Ted blinked rapidly, bewildered and frightened, shaking his head fitfully. "English," he said, his voice sounding strangled, the desperation immediately evident. "Inglese, I mean. Non parlo l'Italiano."

Martelli winced at the loudness of Ted's voice. He put a finger to his lips. "Who are you?" he said quietly before casting a nervous glance at the kitchen door.

"Edward Logan," said Ted.

Martelli frowned and shook his head. He looked down at

the pale, filthy, sweat-soaked man and mouthed, 'Who?'

"I'm a police officer. From London," said Ted, gasping and breathless. He choked and began to cough. The wind howled down the chimneys of the neighbouring house. It whistled through the gaps between the heavy roof tiles.

Martelli pressed his fingertips to his forehead and exhaled sharply. "Brace yourself," he said quietly. "This is going to hurt." And he heaved at the lip of the barrel until it tipped over.

* * *

"Is that your car parked under a tree? The Fiat?" said Martelli.

Ted sat on the dirt floor, legs wide apart, hands still bound behind him. Martelli kneeled and brought the pliers to the wires wound around his wrists.

"Yes," said Ted, wincing.

"Do you still have the key?"

"In my rucksack," he said, his voice strained. "If it's still there."

The wires parted with a pronounced click. Ted sagged a little and sighed deeply. He laid his hands in his lap and Martelli helped him remove the twisted loops of filament from around his bloodied wrists.

"So you're a *copper*?" said Martelli, snorting and managing the briefest smile at his use of the vernacular. "How did you wind up here?"

Ted hung his head. "Stupidity." A tear splashed onto the leg of his shorts.

"Yours or someone else's?"

Ted puffed out his cheeks as though nauseous and closed his eyes for a moment. "Oh, definitely mine." Gingerly, he pressed his swollen hands to his temples. "God, my head is killing me. The fumes in there . . ." He sucked air between bared teeth in the manner of someone witnessing an accident.

"And did . . . I mean, who told you how to get here?"

"No one," said Ted. "I followed directions."

"What? You -"

Ted brought him up short. "You haven't told me who you are." He spoke brusquely now that his hands were free.

Martelli pondered this for a moment. "I'm the former head of this investigation."

"Former?"

Martelli shook his head absently. "Retired." Ted gave him a quizzical look. "Not my choice. I'll explain when we're out of here. My name is Domenico Martelli."

Ted nodded. "Well, Domenico, it started with a raid at my local boxing club and -"

Martelli stopped him with a raised hand. Ted spoke quickly and with an accent Martelli found a little difficult to follow. "A boxing club?"

Nodding, Ted flexed his fingers and prodded gently at his bruised wrists. "We found a large amount of money stashed in a locker at the club, along with passports and -"

"When?" Martelli hissed urgently. "When did you find the money? And how much?"

Ted narrowed his eyes. "About a week ago. No - more."

"Ah," said Martelli, disappointed. "I see."

Ted shuddered and looked down at his hands. "I can't

remember how much exactly - about a-hundred and ninety thousand."

"Euros?"

"Euros. In an old sports bag. And along with the money and the passports there was a set of directions to this house."

Martelli considered this for a moment before asking, "Whose locker?"

"A guy called Warren Devlin."

"And who is he, this Warren . . ?"

"Devlin? He's one of the guys behind all this, I think. But he came to Italy, to Loano, and hasn't been seen since."

"When did he come here?"

"Two weeks ago."

For a few seconds Martelli was silent, staring into the shadows, then slowly he raised a hand and lightly tapped the tender flesh of his damaged shoulder. "Does he have a tattoo?" he said quietly. "Here, on his arm?"

Ted, watching with rapt attention, nodded. "Yes," he said. "A blue seahorse." He indicated the workbench. "I have a photograph in my bag."

"Then he's dead," said Martelli solemnly. "Murdered. Not far from here. He was dissolved with acid in a barrel just like this."

Ted sat quietly for a moment, wide eyed and blinking. "I guessed as much," he said at last. "His flatmate turned up dead too. Paul Finch. He drowned."

Martelli nodded assent. "So I heard. And he had radiation poisoning?"

Ted raised his eyebrows. He was about to speak but

Martelli cut him off, looking troubled.

"So this Warren Devlin ran the British end of things," he said flatly, shaking his head. "Perhaps Steven Finch just organised things in Italy." He chewed the inside of his cheek.

"Related to Paul Finch, I suppose," said Ted.

Martelli nodded. "Brothers. What do you know about Paul?"

Ted looked pained. "Very little, I'm afraid. He's Warren's flatmate. I have a picture of them on a beach together. Like I say, it's in my pack."

"Okay," said Martelli with a sigh. "I'd like you to tell me everything, starting at the beginning and leaving nothing out, but right now we've got to get going."

He stood and offered his hand and for the first time Ted noticed the bloody welts around the Italian detective's own wrists. He turned and squinted at the other upended barrel then levelled his gaze at Martelli, who shrugged and said, "You're not the only one guilty of stupidity. Come on. There are Carabinieri and officers from my old squad a little further down the track." He braced himself and helped the younger man to his feet.

Instead of making for the door, Ted limped unsteadily to the workbench and paused for a spell, eyes unfocused, gripping the edge of the bench as though it was the only thing keeping him anchored to the spinning globe.

"Come on," said Martelli impatiently, thinking the Englishman delirious. "We need to go."

Shakily Ted reached for his backpack and began fishing around in it.

By now the barn door was banging incessantly and the

howling of the wind had risen to a high pitch. There's no way, thought Martelli grimly, that the occupants of the house are sleeping through this.

Ted turned around and, with the closest he could manage to a smile, held up the key to his little car. He looked Martelli up and down then. It was the first chance he'd had to give his rescuer any sort of appraisal, and Martelli got the feeling that he was not especially impressed by what he saw. Without thinking, he placed a hand over the smear of vomit on the front of his shirt.

"Okay," he said to Ted. "Let's go."

But at that moment the door to the kitchen opened and they froze, each man holding his breath and watching as the pistol, the compact Beretta semi-automatic left to Cristina by the old Lothario, emerged from the shadows. They sighed in unison when they saw the slender fist in which the gun was tightly clenched.

FIFTY-SIX

Slowly Estella crossed the threshold into the barn, one eye wide with terror, the iris dark and glistening, the other hidden behind two livid hemispheres of bruised flesh. In her left hand she cupped a spherical bulb of paraffin, like a glass grenade from another age. A feeble, naked flame swayed like a belly dancer on its stubby wick, lighting her face from beneath; painting it with deathly shadows. She looked startled as though caught in the headlights of a phantom juggernaut. Ignoring Ted, she advanced slowly towards Martelli. "Did you find it?" she said in English, in a voice as soft as talcum powder.

Martelli, every muscle tensed, glanced over at Ted before asking, "Find what?"

"His money," she breathed. "The money Mario stole. That's all he wants."

Martelli shook his head minutely, thinking, He? He stared at her warily from beneath deeply furrowed brows. "Are you alone?" he said.

She nodded. Again in that tiny voice, she said, "He's asleep. Did you tell him where to find us? Did you lead him to my mother's house?"

Centuries of cobwebs, drooling from the rafters in great flaccid ropes, were stirred by the gale. Martelli, straining to hear above its tuneless song, shook his head but didn't ask, Who?

She stopped in front of him and touched the muzzle of the pistol to his chest. "Did you search Mario's place? The cantinas? The outhouses? Did you search his boat?"

"No," he said simply. "The police took care of all that."

"Why are you here?" she said.

Out of the corner of his eye, Martelli could see Ted making a furtive examination of Estella, assessing his chances of tackling her before she was able to take aim and fire. He willed him to be still. "I came to get you," he answered, not entirely truthfully. He looked down at the pistol and then back at her. "But it turns out you don't need my help."

She smiled wanly, lowering the gun, turning it over and offering it to him. "Here, this is yours."

Martelli took it and weighed it in his hand. It felt . . . different . . . but his mind was racing and his main concern was to steer the Englishman, and now Estella, towards the swinging door and the darkness.

"Estella," he said. "We need to leave. There are police further down the track."

She gasped. "Really? Police?"

He nodded.

To his dismay, Estella turned and crossed to the workbench. Putting down the glass lamp, she faced Ted, put a bony finger to her lips and said quietly, "He's asleep."

Ted nodded, uncomprehending. He swallowed, his Adam's Apple bobbing, and it triggered another bout of coughing, a noisome, wheezy outburst which caught in the back of his throat. Estella stiffened. Her fear electrified the barn with a palpable, contagious tension and Martelli found himself exchanging glances with Ted, urging him to be quiet with an upraised index finger. For a moment, they all stood silent and still, listening keenly but hearing nothing above the storm.

"Estella . . ." began Martelli at last. But he tailed off, exasperated, hating his own imploring tone. He sighed and glanced down at the gun before continuing. "Tell me," he said, more firmly this time. "Did you know all along? Did you know when we talked?"

She stared at him blankly with her one functioning eye.

"Know what?" boomed a deep, resonant voice from the impenetrable shadows of the kitchen.

Estella cringed, hugging herself. Ted grabbed the edge of the workbench, his face ashen. Only Martelli remained calm. "Did she know that you were alive," he said. "Steven."

Steven Finch stepped into the flickering light and stood glaring at Martelli. His eyes were red-rimmed and the skin beneath them was bruised and puckered from a lack of sleep. There was a look of dazed fascination on his face, and Martelli suspected he was high. He wore the same thin, white, short-sleeved shirt and khaki trousers but on his feet, instead of sandals, he had a pair of heavy boots. The baseball cap and sunglasses were gone and his dark brown hair was greasy and unkempt. In his right hand he held Aldo's heavy pistol.

He smiled and said, "When did you work it out?"

Martelli paused. He looked down at his hands, at the Beretta, then back up at his former client. "To be honest just yesterday when I spoke to Tomasz. I mean . . ." He faltered, sighing and shaking his head. "I suppose I knew already but didn't want to accept that I'd been fooled. Even then I . . . well, it was really only this morning that I was prepared to admit it." He couldn't help but look sheepish.

Slowly Finch knitted his brow in mock concern. His eyes twinkled with amusement. "Oh, don't be so hard on yourself, Commissario. You had no way of knowing. And your former colleagues didn't even come close to catching on." He shrugged and made an expansive gesture with his outstretched hands, waving the heavy pistol in a rather disconcerting fashion.

Ted remained still, Estella twisted left and right, left and right, her eyes closed. Martelli tightened his grip on the Beretta and slid a surreptitious finger over the trigger. "So why all this?" he said. "Why kill that poor soul in the barrel? Was it just to make people believe you were dead? And why murder Angela?" He shook his head sadly. "Surely that was unnecessary."

Finch spoke slowly, spitting each word. "Yes. So people thought I was dead. And that 'poor soul' as you so charitably put it was a lying little weasel called -"

"Warren Devlin," said Ted balefully. "We know."

Martelli and Steven turned to look at him.

"I'm guessing those are size elevens," continued Ted, nodding at Finch's feet. "And it's your boot print on Devlin's front door."

Finch raised an eyebrow. "You be quiet." Turning his

attention back to Martelli, he said, "So you didn't find it? My money?"

Martelli gave an exaggerated shake of his head. "I'm afraid not, Steven." He raised his arms from his sides and let them flop back down. "So . . ." He forced a smile. "What a situation. Mario has all the money, stashed away somewhere, but his health is not what it was. Whereas you, Steven, are alive and well but have nothing. In Italy, we say, 'Chi ha denti non ha pane, e chi ha pane non ha denti.'" He chuckled. "He who has teeth has no bread, and he who has bread has no teeth."

For a moment Finch looked as though he was about to snarl but he reined himself in and simply glowered. "Very clever, Commissario." He raised Aldo's pistol and took aim.

Martelli stared at the gaping muzzle and then beyond it, into the eye of his former client. He arched an eyebrow.

"What?" said Finch. "This?" He tilted the old handgun and glanced at it admiringly. "Oh I planned to return it, Commissario. Still smoking perhaps. For that young and so very keen detective to discover." He smiled. "But here you are. You've saved me the trouble." He took aim again.

Something registered with Estella. She opened her eyes and said, "What did you mean about Mario? About his health?"

"Mario's dead," said Martelli abruptly, turning and addressing her directly. "And so is Paul. Mario's old Land Rover went off the road and into a gully back that way." He gestured over his shoulder with his thumb. "He collapsed and died behind the wheel. He's been dead about a fortnight." Estella clasped her hands to her mouth. "Paul Finch was found dead on a beach in southern England. They both died of radiation poisoning."

Turning back to Finch, Martelli said, "They didn't rip you off, Steven. They didn't run off with your money. They died smuggling that poison." He raised an eyebrow. "But my guess is that you knew the dangers and that's why you chose not to handle the stuff yourself. Am I right?"

"Fuck you!" said Finch, ignoring the question. He brandished the gun. "Who told you Paul was dead?"

"It's true," said Ted, matter-of-factly, stepping away from the workbench as he spoke. Martelli caught his breath but remained rooted to the spot. "He ran aground on the Hook Sands near Margate," continued Ted. "Devlin's boat was wrecked and Paul's body washed up at Birchington. He'd suffered severe radiation poisoning. That's probably what caused him to lose control of the boat."

"You fucking liar!" Finch swung Aldo's pistol and fired, hitting Ted in the chest. The Englishman performed a puppet pirouette, teetered on tiptoes, reeled spasmodically, and then collapsed, folding like a kicked deckchair.

Estella screamed. Ignoring a barked command from Finch, Martelli dashed to Ted's side. Kneeling down, he felt for a pulse but his fingers trembled too much. Blood - black as treacle in the soft yellow light - crept silently away, spreading outwards from Ted's lifeless shoulders like the wings of an angel, its lustre diminishing as it soaked into the dirt. Martelli slid a hand beneath the body and found an exit wound the size of a fist.

He stood, tears of fury misting his vision. Turning, he levelled his pistol at Finch and issued a warning. "Put down your weapon or I will shoot."

Finch laughed and raised Aldo's pistol again, quickly and

with murderous intent. Martelli took no chances. He squeezed the trigger and fired.

But the hammer drove the steel pin into an empty breech and the gun emitted nothing more than a clicking noise. He pulled the trigger again with the same result. Finch laughed, swaying slightly as he held Martelli in his sights. Fumbling, his hands slippery with Ted's blood, Martelli worked the slide of the compact semi-automatic. Had Cristina made a mistake? he wondered. But no, of course she hadn't. The gun felt different because it was empty. His shoulders sagged and he levelled his gaze at Estella. She turned away, unable to face him, ashamed of her collaboration despite the bruises of coercion. He let his arms hang loosely by his sides. The storm was by now a mighty interference, an all-consuming white noise, and he realised with dismay that the sound of the shot which killed Edward Logan would have been lost in the maelstrom. Nardi, Bracco and the Frenchman, if by chance they were still at the crash site at such a late hour, would not have heard it. Looking down at his feet, he slid Cristina's pistol into the back pocket of his trousers. And woefully he wondered if he would have the opportunity to return it, or if his life was to end here, in a barn in the forest, in circumstances that even his friends would be forced to concede were tragically ignoble. He stared at Finch, and at the metal snout of Aldo's pistol, which described uneven elipses in the air.

"What about the boy?" he said. "Angela's son? Are you the father? Or is he Paul's?"

Finch started to speak but changed his mind. Instead he pursed his lips, blinking repeatedly.

"What?" said Estella, addressing Finch. "You said -"

421

"That the baby was Mario's? That he was cheating on you?" said Martelli with an undisguised note of angry triumph. "A little blue-eyed boy? I don't think so." He snorted with derision.

Estella gasped and turned to lean on the workbench, head down.

"I think we've heard enough from you now," said Finch to Martelli.

He steadied the gun and took a step forward. Instinctively, Martelli ducked. Estella grunted with exertion and something flashed in the lamp light. The glass grenade caught Finch on the side of the head, shattering against his temple. He staggered, arms flailing, eyes squeezed tight shut against the sting of the paraffin. Aldo's revolver spat flame with a sharp crack. The bullet shattered the driver's side window of the Alfa Romeo and drilled into the dashboard. Martelli charged. Blindly, Finch fired again and the report filled Martelli's ears with a deafening roar. He drove his injured shoulder into Finch's midriff, lifting him off the ground and propelling him backwards. They fell, Finch sprawling, Martelli rolling to one side. The spilled paraffin caught with a muffled thump and Finch was instantly engulfed in pale yellow flame.

Martelli scrambled to his feet. His left arm hung limply and the pain in his shoulder ignited sparkling pinpricks of light in front of his eyes. The roaring in his ears shrank to a mosquito whine. "Come on!" he shouted at Estella, who stood rooted to the spot, staring at Finch with a malicious fascination. He gripped her arm, digging with his fingertips into her insubstantial flesh, and dragging her away.

Behind them, Finch rolled around in an expanding pool of

fire, his hands clamped to his face, muffling a plaintive screeching, his shirt and trousers ablaze. The flames toasted the corners and ragged seams of the fuel-soaked sacks, which caught fire with a mighty crackle, instantly obscuring the plastic canister of petrol within a broad column of dense, black smoke.

Martelli and Estella stumbled out into the chill night air and ran, leaving the swinging doors to fan the blaze like a giant bellows. As they reached the edge of the clearing they heard another gunshot and Estella cried out in pain, pitching forward on the uneven ground. Crouching at her side, Martelli turned and saw Finch, incandescent in the open doorway, his tattered clothing still burning. He levelled Aldo's pistol, ready to take another shot. Martelli simply stared, too exhausted to sprint for cover. Finch met his gaze, lip curled, face trembling in a furious snarl. The two men remained like this for the briefest of moments before the petrol canister exploded. Finch was momentarily silhouetted against the expanding fireball before being swallowed by the inferno. Martelli collapsed backwards as the wave of hellish heat washed over them then he hauled Estella to her feet, heaved his good shoulder under her armpit and together they hobbled down the track.

Fires sprang to life on all sides, crackling like Christmas paper, as burning debris fell onto the tinder dry forest floor. Martelli picked up the pace, growling with pain and grunting rhythmically, his breathing laboured. Estella seemed delirious, moaning and gasping, head rolling on her shoulders.

Clinker rained down, singeing his hair and stinging his scalp and the air quickly became thick with floating flakes of ash. His clammy skin was soon dark with soot and streaked with rivulets of sweat. Behind them the fire inhaled deeply of the night air and the crackling became a roar that drowned out the gale. Martelli stopped, turned and watched as a writhing serpent of smoke switched and twisted and corkscrewed towards them. He knew then that they couldn't outrun it, that the entire mountain could be consumed, him and Estella with it.

Then all at once the heavens bellowed, the wind subsided and the rain came, as though at the turning of a tap - a thunderous, drenching downpour of glinting crystal droplets as big as your eye. Sheet after sheet marched diagonally across the mountainside, leaving everything lacquered and gleaming. And almost instantly the ash was gone, obliterated, and the fires began to fizzle and die. And Martelli could have wept when he heard the unmistakable sound of a dog barking.

FIFTY-SEVEN

The consumptive rattle of the little three-wheeled delivery van, returning for its second or third load, roused him from a deep sleep long before his alarm clock buzzed. The caruggi were still deserted, only the bakery staff having ventured forth at such an early hour, but the sun had already risen and the dome of San Giovanni Battista was already outlined in burnished gold.

After a quick shower, he decided to pop round to the bakery for some fresh croissants, and it was on the way back, steam-filled paper bag in hand, that he spotted Eduardo, asleep among his wines, jack-knifed on the cold, stone floor and yet snoring with gusto - if not content then contentedly unconscious. On hearing Martelli tap the window, the young vinaio opened his eyes and perked up in an instant, swaying to his feet, unlocking the door and greeting his landlord with a lopsided smile and a loose, clammy handshake.

They drank espresso on the roof, two apiece, then wolfed down the croissants, admiring the view as they listened for the first of the competing clocks to chime the hour. They were due to meet Salvatore di Natale at five on the dot and, like all Loanese, regarded the first off-key volley as a six-minute warning.

As arranged, Salvatore was waiting next to the garbage chutes arrayed beneath the trompe l'oeil woman and her grumpy cat at the bottom of Via Stella. The big man greeted Martelli with a kiss on both cheeks and a handshake that could have crushed billiard balls. Eduardo received a raised eyebrow and a paternal pat on the shoulder, which said, 'I am the accomplice here, the contemporary of Commissario Domenico Martelli. I am also the senior shopkeeper. You are merely the help.'

"Eduardo has kindly agreed to be our lookout and getaway driver," said Martelli cheerfully in an effort to mollify the young wine merchant, who was clearly miffed by the pesto man's condescension.

Their journey, a mercifully short walk to Martelli's car followed by a ten-minute drive, passed in uncomfortable silence.

Gaining entry to Spinetti's Boxing Club was easy as Salvatore practically ran the place. But gaining entry to Mario Rossetti's locker proved more difficult as the hefty padlock accepted none of the seven keys pilfered from the crashed Land Rover. In the end Salvatore broke the shackle of the lock using the jack handle from the boot of Martelli's car.

"Happens all the time," he said with a wink and a sly smile.

Inside the locker nestled a tatty grey sports bag. And inside the sports bag they found what Martelli guessed to be about a million euros, along with a passport featuring a much younger Mario beside the pseudonym Giulio Morfeo, described, rather ambitiously in Martelli's view, as a doctor of medicine. There was also a loaded revolver, a dog-eared road map and a pocket-sized bag of pungent marijuana.

Salvatore, to his eternal credit, scarcely batted an eyelid when Martelli unzipped the bag to reveal this fortune. He didn't plunge in with both hands and delve among the loosely bound notes, nor did he utter a single word other than to ask, after a short, stunned interval, if Martelli was done. In fact, thought Martelli later, Salvatore had acted throughout like a man engaged in commonplace business, the ordinary duties of a boxing club coach.

Afterwards, keen to bring matters to a swift conclusion, Martelli called Estella from the car as they drove back to Loano.

"Aricò is the girl's aunt," he explained after making the call.

Salvatore laughed wheezily. "In Loano, everybody's related to somebody," he said, shaking his head. He resumed his laughter but it quickly disintegrated into a hacking cough.

Eduardo dropped Martelli, the money and an attendant Salvatore outside Vittorino's on Corsa Roma before heading off to park the Lancia. At Via Garibaldi, Salvatore and Martelli parted company. No banter was exchanged - the pesto man simply nodded and walked away, happily leaving Martelli to allocate the cash, however much was there, as he saw fit. The streets by now were bustling and Martelli, though his gaze was fixed straight ahead, encountered two acquaintances as he walked the dozen or so metres to his front door. He greeted each with a half smile and a muted 'Buongiorno', maintaining a steady pace with, he hoped, the air of a man who had urgent business to attend to.

Back at his apartment, it took him an hour and a half just to count the money. His earlier guess hadn't been far wrong.

There were nine hundred and forty-two thousand euros.

Estella kept her promise to orchestrate a meeting with her notorious aunt, and called him back just as he'd finished totting up, having made the arrangements by phone from her hospital bed. The meeting was set for nine that same morning, barely thirty hours since she and Martelli had emerged from the darkness into the bright cones of Nardi's headlights, circled excitedly by a blue merle border collie with one pale brown eye and one milky grey one.

* * *

A Gran Fondo - that most Italian of spectacles - was making its weary way up the punishing mountain roads, climbing ever higher in the fierce heat, the stragglers some two kilometres behind la maglia rosa – the pink jersey. The competitors were soaked in sweat, heaving on handlebars and forcing down pedals, baring their teeth in silent agony, the ropes and cables of their ham-like thighs stretched taut and shifting beneath mahogany skin, their backsides swaying above unforgiving saddles, their eyes mere slits or else protected from the sun's fierce glare behind gold lenses. They skirted every precipice, passing carelessly close to the steepest of drops; they whirred through villages, where shrieking kids and yelping dogs ran alongside the peloton.

Martelli drummed on the steering wheel with his fingertips, exasperated by delay after infuriating delay as marshals stopped traffic to allow knots of riders to negotiate the narrower sections and tightest bends.

He did not want to be late.

He did not want to be there at all.

But what choice did he have?

When he finally arrived at Bar Reale, he found the wide shoulder busy with marshals, medics and mechanics; dozens of spectators too, some of them fans but most of them family members. Their vehicles took up much of the space and Martelli was forced to cruise past them and head downhill more than a hundred metres before finding a spot for the Lancia. Opening the door he very nearly took out a rider, who, after swerving with lightning reflexes, shouted a heartfelt 'Vafanculo!' as he sped down the increasingly steep incline, his head so low that his chin was touching the handlebar stem, his haunches high in the air. Tutting and making a mental note to replace his missing mirror, Martelli closed the door, clambered awkwardly over the centre console and climbed out on the passenger side. Squinting in the bright sunlight, he opened the boot and stared at the tatty grey sports bag with its dark stains and bitten corners. He wrinkled his nose. It smelled of vomit and cigarettes. Next to it sat an old sports bag of Eduardo's; blue and red with a broken zip and an L-shaped tear patched with duct tape. Into it Martelli had decanted the amount owed – a quarter of a million euros. Sighing deeply, feeling weary to his core, he grabbed its worn handles and grimaced as he heaved it onto his injured shoulder.

Outside the bar, ragged ribbons of blue and white plastic crime scene tape flickered in the breeze and Martelli paused, staring at it, catching his breath as he tried to remember how long it had been since the discovery of the barrel containing Warren Devlin's remains. Was it really only a matter of days?

Aricò was waiting for him, standing on the upper terrace,

gazing out admiringly at the magnificent view. A few metres away, arms hanging loosely at his sides, eyes hidden behind the blackest sunglasses, stood her driver.

Loano was a town in which some of the most influential people looked like they'd slept in their clothes, on the beach. But not Mariacarmela Aricò. She was stylishly dressed in a figure-hugging grey skirt and pristine white blouse. Her shoes were high and doubtless expensive, her shoulder-length hair bleached and neat, her tan deep and even.

As Martelli slung Eduardo's old bag on the ground at her feet, she turned, unruffled, and eyed with amused interest his unpressed clothes, scuffed shoes, scratched face and forehead beaded with moisture. He met her gaze, wondering how it must feel to lead a life of callous disregard.

Her driver approached and lifted the bag onto the concrete balustrade, where he held it open to reveal the contents.

"Do I need to count this?" she said, smiling to reveal unnaturally white teeth.

"No," said Martelli quietly, shaking his head.

She turned and gazed once more at the magnificent view.

After an interval so long that he thought their business must have reached its conclusion, she said, "Aldo Bonetti – what is he to you?"

"An old friend," he replied.

"That's it?" she said scornfully.

"Yes," he said, raising his chin defiantly. "Is that not enough?"

FIFTY-EIGHT

In stages, he was plucked from the arms of Morpheus.

The first stage was a dull ache in the small of his back, growing increasingly sharp the longer he lay still. Second came the sounds of the caruggi: the squeak, clunk, squeak, clunk of a badly maintained bicycle as Marco the florist made his way to his shop on Via Garibaldi, hurried 'Buongiorno's and cheery 'Va bene?'s, flushing toilets and gushing showers, toothpaste spat and mouthwash gargled, bursts of radio and banging doors, the tinkle of spoons in coffee cups and the screech of knives on plates. He heard the Trigiani boys bickering, up to no good, and he heard their mother - Michela, as he had learned - end negotiations and begin yelling. They're up early, he thought, his eyes still closed. But then he realised that August had become September, and the boys were being readied for their first day back at school. Naturally they were resistant.

He smiled, remembering his own schooldays and the irresponsibility of childhood. As he did so he swept a hand across the sheet, under the duvet, and felt the cool empty space on the other half of the bed. It was only three days since Cristina had returned to Amsterdam and yet already he missed her. She'd left with a promise that she would return at half term and also an invitation to visit, if he found the time, she'd said, grinning and squeezing his arm. In the two weeks since the death of Edward Logan and Steven Finch, they'd spent most evenings and every night together, and he'd grown so quickly accustomed to sharing his bed with her that now he felt her absence like the prickle of a lost limb or the yearning for a missing child. She'd entered his life from nowhere and had left it equally abruptly. Apart from everything else, he thought with a sigh, eyes beginning to flicker, he would miss her wonderful cooking. Which reminded him: that night he was due at the Braccos' apartment for dinner. And he'd been warned that Bernardo's mother-in-law - a randy widow of some renown - was eagerly anticipating his presence at their table. He almost chuckled at the thought of fending her off.

He'd relayed to Bracco what Edward Logan had told him about the raid on the boxing club in London. A subsequent raid at Spinetti's had netted Bracco, among other things, a shabby holdall containing six hundred and ninety-two thousand euros, a passport in the name of Giulio Morfeo, a loaded revolver, a dog-eared road map, the admiration of his colleagues and the grudging approval of his boss.

Bracco had also paid a visit to Tomasz's garage home but had found it abandoned, water trickling into a filthy sink from the blue plastic pipe, the television playing soundless soaps in the shade of the fraying canopy. A description was circulated, an alert transmitted to ports, airports and border crossings but in the end it was assumed that Tomasz was gone and would not be seen again.

The final stage of Martelli's return to consciousness was the rude and insistent buzz of his mobile phone, turning in desperate circles on the bedside table.

Blindly, he groped for it. "Pronto."

"You want coffee?" said Nardi.

Martelli yawned and dug at the flesh of his forehead. "What time is it?"

Nardi sniffed freely, the noise like a waterfall in Martelli's ear. "Six forty-five," he croaked.

"In that case, yes, I do want coffee."

At Nardi's end there was silence, but Martelli detected satisfaction in it. Groaning but unable to stop himself from smiling too, he said, "I'll see you in fifteen minutes.

Printed in Great Britain
by Amazon